CASUAL KISSES

The light knock on her bedroom door didn't surprise her. She half suspected Isaac wouldn't be able to sleep with things as unresolved as they'd left them.

"Come on, Amanda," Isaac said in a loud whisper.

She reached for her robe, then changed her mind. She wanted Isaac to see what little her modest nightgown revealed. Opening the door, she silently appraised him. Barefoot and shirtless, the hair on his chest still had a damp look from his bath.

"Maybe I should come in."

Maybe so, thought Amanda. How could she be so furious with him and yet still want him near? She quietly closed her bedroom door behind him.

Feeling self-conscious, Amanda stood in front of the mirror and let Isaac pull out the pins holding her hair. He brushed through her locks in smooth, steady strokes. "Your hair's so soft, and it smells just like flowers."

Isaac smoothed back a lock of hair and leaned toward her. Gently he kissed her. She kissed him in return. He rubbed his cheek against hers, and Amanda heard him sigh. Three more quick kisses, placed here and there on her lips. "I guess I better let you get some sleep," he said at last.

At her bedroom door, he raked through his hair with one hand before speaking. "Amanda, don't misinterpret what I just did. You might tempt me, but your kisses don't change what I expect. Those kids better be in their beds at night or you're gone."

He might as well have thrown a bucket of cold water on her.

BOOK YOUR PLACE ON OUR WEBSITE AND MAKE THE READING CONNECTION!

We've created a customized website just for our very special readers, where you can get the inside scoop on everything that's going on with Zebra, Pinnacle and Kensington books.

When you come online, you'll have the exciting opportunity to:

- View covers of upcoming books
- Read sample chapters
- Learn about our future publishing schedule (listed by publication month *and author*)
- Find out when your favorite authors will be visiting a city near you
- Search for and order backlist books from our online catalog
- Check out author bios and background information
- Send e-mail to your favorite authors
- Meet the Kensington staff online
- Join us in weekly chats with authors, readers and other guests
- Get writing guidelines
- AND MUCH MORE!

Visit our website at
http://www.zebrabooks.com

TIES OF
LOVE

ANITA WALL

Zebra Books
Kensington Publishing Corp.

http://www.zebrabooks.com

ZEBRA BOOKS are published by

Kensington Publishing Corp.
850 Third Avenue
New York, NY 10022

First Printing: February, 2000
10 9 8 7 6 5 4 3 2 1

Printed in the United States of America

For my mother Joan:
Thanks for a lifetime of encouragement and acceptance.

And for my husband Ray:
Thanks for many happy years of love and inspiration.

CHAPTER ONE

Lariat, Wyoming
April, 1893

"Gosh-darn stinkin' animals!" snarled one of the railroad workers as he jerked on the door of the stock car. "Goats and a damned half-breed kid! What they gonna let ride these trains next?"

Though Amanda Erikson realized the loud comment had been made for her benefit, she calmly repositioned her black veiled hat and picked up her large traveling bag. "This must be Lariat, Joe Pete," she said to comfort the trembling boy beside her. "Otherwise, they wouldn't be opening the door. Once these men finish unloading my things, we won't ever have to tolerate their ugly remarks again. Let's go." Squaring her shoulders, she walked toward the door of the stock car.

It took a moment for her eyes to adjust to the bright sunlight; then she stared at the ground. *It must be nearly five feet down.* She considered the sensible, but cowardly, method of sitting down and scooting off until she realized the men who had made her last twenty-four hours so miserable were grinning up at her, gloating. Of course, not one of them stepped forward to give her a hand. Gathering her nerve, she jumped, one hand holding onto her hat, her bag clutched tightly in the other.

The three burly railroad workers laughed uproariously when her foot became tangled in her long skirts and she fell on her backside into the swirling dust. One of the men sent her a scathing look when young Joe Pete appeared in the doorway of the stock car. Ignoring the crew, Amanda rose, intending to help Joe Pete to the ground, but the boy scrambled down unaided and hurried to stand close to her.

After giving him a reassuring look, she brushed the dust from the back of her voluminous woolen coat. Finally, she allowed herself a surreptitious glance toward the tiny ram-shackle depot, praying that no one besides the workers had seen her unfortunate landing. No such luck. Standing smack dab in front of the depot steps was a long, lean cowboy, com-plete with bandanna and six-shooter. Her cheeks grew warm.

Oh, well. Nothing like making a grand entrance.

She took a fortifying breath of sage-scented air before turning fully toward the rangy cowboy. She'd just walk right up to him and ask directions to the livery.

The workers behind her let the cage holding Nanny drop to the ground with a resounding thud. Amanda whirled to face them.

The nearest man gave a smirk, then spat a disgusting wad of chaw close to her feet.

When Amanda had first boarded the train in Denver, the crew had merely acted annoyed at having to transport a female and her animals. They'd become openly hostile after a refueling stop when she'd returned to the train with Joe Pete.

Poor child. Although she'd purchased a ticket for him, the crew had refused to let a ''half-breed'' sit in the passenger car with her. Not wanting to leave the frightened boy alone, she'd moved into the stock car with him and her animals. The ride to her destination in northeastern Wyoming had been smelly and uncomfortable. Amanda hated dirt in general and dirt on her person in particular. Now, thanks to the train crew's unchari-table attitude, she was hungry, tired, and filthy.

She'd taken all she intended to take from this surly bunch.

If these men dropped one more of her crates, she'd get their attention and then discuss how she expected to have her things unloaded. Casually, she slipped one hand inside her coat.

From his vantage point in front of the depot, Isaac Wright had an unobstructed view of the tall woman, the skinny kid, and the unloading proceedings. Just what this cattle country needed, he thought when he saw their possessions. Another fence-building farmer. For a moment there, after the woman fell, he'd moved a step toward the stock car. When it appeared she wasn't hurt, he'd turned his attention back to the door of the Pullman car. Let her husband deal with the unloading. Isaac had enough problems of his own.

Problems. Like what to do with his nieces and nephew for the next month or two. He couldn't leave little Nellie and the twins very long at one time with his younger brother, Luke. No better than Luke cooked, they'd starve. And he couldn't haul around a toddler and two five-year-olds while he checked the cows he'd left on the winter range.

Used to be that Joshua and Mary watched over their own kids and took care of the animals kept near the main ranch house while he and Luke took care of the calving range cows. No more.

Isaac's eyes burned. Damn. It'd been almost three months since Joshua and Mary had died of influenza, and he still had to fight tears when he thought about them.

And if missing them weren't bad enough, it looked as though he'd gone and made a mistake with Mary's family concerning the kids.

Three weeks ago, the snow finally had melted enough for him to get into Lariat and wire Mary's family with the sad news about Josh and Mary. He'd asked if someone in the family could come and help him temporarily with their kids.

It'd seemed like the thing to do. He just needed help until he could find a housekeeper.

But he'd returned to town yesterday for supplies, and there'd been an answering telegram waiting for him. It said one of

Mary's unmarried sisters would be coming to take custody of the children as soon as arrangements could be made.

Like hell some stranger was taking "custody" of the kids!

He'd waited in town to meet the weekly train. If Mary's sister arrived today, it'd save him a trip next week. What he had to say to her would be to the point. Those kids were staying with him, not traipsing off with an old-maid aunt.

She didn't know the first thing about these kids; she'd never even laid eyes on them. And she damn sure didn't love them the way he did. He'd helped bring them into the world, walked his share of floor with them when they had tummyaches, and worried right along with their ma and pa about their safety. No one was taking them away from him now—or ever.

As he watched the door of the passenger car, it became obvious that he'd wasted his time staying in town overnight. No one alighted. Hang it. Now he'd have to come into town again next week to meet the train. He didn't have time for this.

He started to walk toward the general store when the racket from the unloading crew increased. The woman and the boy stood beside a crate, trying to calm some wildly barking dogs inside. Isaac looked around. Where the devil was her man?

Just then a crew member threw a large crate of chickens out of the stock car. The crate landed with a crunch, and a cackling uproar arose from the hens.

He'd seen enough. Putting a farmer's woman in her place was one thing. Homesteading in ranching country, she'd have to develop a thick skin and learn to ignore a lot. But abuse of helpless animals riled him. He turned back to intervene.

Before he'd covered ten of the thirty feet to her, the woman produced a handgun from somewhere inside her big, black coat and aimed it at the worker standing in the door of the stock car.

She spoke loudly and emphatically. "If you ever plan to father a child, you better lower my animals and the rest of my belongings with the utmost care."

The husky railroad man roared with laughter and brought his arms up to fling out a small cage.

Isaac dang near ducked himself when bullets whizzed by the man's head, sending chunks of the wooden railcar flying.

"The next one is between your legs," the woman promised the gaping man. "Now lower my things. Gently!"

Isaac concealed a smile. The old gal had grit. He'd just decided she didn't need his help when the rest of the train's crew came running. He stepped out in front of them.

"What's the problem here?" the engineer asked.

"It appears some of your men forgot how to do their work. The lady reminded them."

Isaac watched the engineer make a quick survey of the situation. By now, most of the twenty-two permanent residents of Lariat had gathered between the general store and the depot.

"You need any help, Isaac?" a man called.

Isaac? Amanda winced when she heard the name spoken behind her. *Please, God,* she prayed. *Please let it be Isaac Smith or Isaac Jones. Please don't let it be Isaac Wright.*

"Everything's fine," the cowboy named Isaac answered. Behind her, he spoke to the train's crew. "Get back on the train and get ready to move."

"Yes, sir, Mr. Wright," the engineer answered.

Oh, no! The cowboy was Isaac Wright. She'd probably made a wonderful impression on him, what with her fancy landing on her bottom and losing her temper and shooting at people. Drat! Double drat! She kept her eyes and her gun on the surly workers.

Silently and quickly, the crew finished unloading. The worker in the stock car prepared to jump to the ground to join his friends for the walk back to the caboose.

"Stay where you are." Amanda waved the gun in the direction of the two railroad men on the ground. "Get up there with him."

One man turned and snarled, "Who the—" He stopped in mid-sentence when a shot rang out and dust boiled at his feet.

"I told you to get in there. Now move!" She tipped her head toward the door of the stock car. "If it's good enough for paying customers like Joe Pete and me, it'll do for you."

After the men climbed into the car, Amanda spoke to Joe Pete. "Can you shut that door?"

He nodded and scurried to do as she asked.

Isaac stepped up to help the boy. Obviously, the woman had no idea how heavy the door was or she wouldn't have asked the kid to do a man's chore. After securing the door, Isaac stepped clear and signaled the engineer.

After the train began to pull away, the woman tucked her revolver back inside her coat and turned to Isaac. "Thank you. I never thought about the rest of the crew coming when I fired my gun." As she talked, she glanced at the small crowd of people who had come out to see the ruckus. "Are those your friends? Goodness, I must look a fright."

It did look as if she'd been ridden hard and put away wet. Her dusty black coat had straw sticking to the hem in several places. The black hat and veil that concealed most of her face might have been stylish at the beginning of the trip, but now it appeared for all the world as if someone had sat on it. Amused, he watched her brush ineffectually at the front of her coat.

"Well," she said, "nothing can be done about it now. You may as well introduce me."

Introduce her? What the devil did he look like? The official homesteaders' greeting committee? Not likely. He watched as she strode matter-of-factly toward the waiting people. The bossy old gal must have gone twenty feet before she realized he wasn't following.

She turned around and snapped, "For heaven's sake, Isaac. You don't expect me to introduce myself, do you?"

What the devil? How did she know his name? "I'd be plumb tickled to introduce you, ma'am." He used a sarcastic, put-on Western drawl. "But just for the record, who are you?"

She hesitated, then laughed. "I'm sorry. I knew who you were because I heard someone call to you. I forgot you wouldn't know me. I'm Amanda Erikson." She reached out to shake his hand. "I've come to take my sister's children off your hands."

Isaac had smiled when he first heard her bubbly laugh. Now he felt as if someone had clubbed him. "Amanda?" How could this gun-toting female be gentle Mary's sister? Hell, the woman must be eight or nine inches taller than his late sister-in-law. Mary was tiny and neat, a real lady. This woman didn't appear to have a ladylike bone in her entire body. "Amanda?" he repeated.

"Good heavens. Surely my sister told you sometime during the past six years that she had a sister named Amanda. Didn't you get my family's telegram?"

He managed to nod, but he couldn't quit staring. *Good Lord! This woman with a half-breed boy and enough gear to start a homestead was here to get Josh and Mary's kids. This was the Amanda Mary had talked about all the time?*

In spite of his surprise, her black attire reminded Isaac that she was in mourning for her sister, and he hadn't offered his condolences. He removed his hat. "I'm real sorry about Mary. I think it was influenza. We all got sick, but Mary and Josh didn't get better." Isaac swallowed the lump that seemed forever in his throat these days. "I did everything I could."

"I know that without your telling me, Isaac. When my sister wrote home, she always spoke highly of you."

Her voice had become soft and warm, like Mary's. She reached beneath the veil and brushed at her eyes. "I'm sorry about Joshua, too." She sniffed, then squared her shoulders and turned toward the waiting people. The softness was gone. "We'll talk about it later. Right now I'm going to smile and meet these fine folks."

Might as well save her the trouble. She wouldn't be here long enough to bother meeting anyone. "I have something to say to you first, Miss Erikson." Isaac dug in his shirt pocket. "I'm sorry I didn't know you were coming until I got to town yesterday. If I had, I'd have brought the kids to meet you, at least. But maybe this is best. They don't need any more turmoil than they got right now." He handed her an envelope. "Here's money for a ticket back to Denver. My nieces and nephew aren't leaving Lariat with you or anyone else."

Amanda warned herself to hold her temper. For the first time in three weeks, she was glad to be engaged to an over-cautious doctor. It had been her fiancé, Tom, who had suggested that Isaac might not be willing to part with the children.

Tom's suggestion had led Amanda to seek advice from a lawyer, who'd assured her that she would be in an excellent position to obtain custody of her late sister's children. Even if Isaac Wright chose to dispute her right to them, it would be obvious to any judge that Amanda would be the better choice as guardian. After all, she was engaged to a doctor—and she was a woman. What could a bachelor possibly know about child rearing?

Armed with that knowledge, Amanda looked up into Isaac's stormy gray eyes. "Let's get something straight, Mr. Wright. I take my orders from God and no one else. And I *am* going to raise my sister's children."

Judging from the fury in Isaac's eyes, she wouldn't have been surprised if he'd grabbed her by the scruff of the neck and heaved her onto the next train through town. She rushed on. "However, I agree with you about the children not needing any more changes right now. So I've come prepared to stay a while. That way they can get used to me gradually." A partial truth. But in her letters home, Mary had warned her how Isaac felt about farmers. No sense fanning a flame by mentioning her intent to homestead—not yet, at least.

"It doesn't matter how long you stay or how used to you they get, the kids aren't leaving the Lazy W. I promised my brother on his deathbed that I'd see to his kids."

"Then you've made a promise you can't keep. Years ago, Mary and I agreed to care for each other's children if the situation ever arose."

"The kids stay right here in Lariat with me!"

The way he bellowed, everyone in town must be able to hear. She faced him with her hands on her hips. "Will you lower your voice? You'll have the whole country knowing our private business. That would be *really* good for the children."

Isaac glanced around, then stepped in front of her and positioned his back to the waiting crowd. "The kids stay right here in Lariat with me." He punctuated every word with a jab of his forefinger, stopping just short of Amanda's shoulder.

She forced herself not to flinch. In like manner, she punched at his shoulder and imitated his one-jab-per-word style. "Then I stay right here in Lariat with them!"

He tried to stare her down, but Amanda had the advantage. Though she could see out through her hat's black veil, he couldn't see in, and she knew it. "I'm not budging without the children, so you better get used to having me around." She turned to walk the remaining half block to the general store.

This woman is a pain in the patoot! Isaac thought, striding along beside her. She wasn't at all like Mary. Josh's Mary had been kind and sweet, soft and pliable, the way a woman should be. You wouldn't catch Mary jumping off a train, shooting at people, or refusing to listen to reason.

Another thing. Who was this dirty, scrawny, half-breed boy hovering in her shadow? "Joe Pete's your boy?" he asked.

"Joe Pete's an orphan. I found him in Cheyenne."

"You *found* him?" This he didn't believe. She found him. If that boy were part Sioux, his being here wouldn't sit right with the army, the Sioux, or a good many white civilians in the area. The bloody feuding over the nearby Black Hills had left too many permanent scars.

Amanda interrupted his worried thoughts. "I think I'll buy Joe Pete some clean clothes. Do you suppose the store will have pants and shirts to fit him?"

"Hold up, Miss Erikson. You can't go around keeping kids you *find*. I bet he's got family somewhere."

"He says not. He told me his father died two years ago and his mother died this winter."

"Maybe he'll tell me something more." He hated the way the boy cringed when he turned to talk to him. Hell, he wouldn't hurt a kid. But he needed some information. In a tone geared to let the child know he wanted straight answers, he asked, "What about it, boy? Do you have kin who'll be worrying about you?"

Amanda stepped between him and the trembling boy. "I'll thank you to mind your own business. Joe Pete's not your responsibility. I won't have you scaring him to death."

"I'm not scaring him. I'm talking to him."

"Then lower your voice and talk like a normal human being."

"I'll talk any way I want to talk, lady."

"Then you'll talk to yourself!"

She grabbed Joe Pete's hand. She'd about had it with men and their know-it-all attitude! Her skirts snapped around her ankles as she whipped along the track toward the store and the waiting people. She noted with wry satisfaction that Isaac had to hustle to catch up to her.

When they reached the crowd, the tallest, widest man she'd ever seen broke from the group.

Isaac stepped forward and made the introduction. "Jim Callahan, this is Amanda Erikson, Mary's sister. She's come for a short *visit* with the kids."

Amanda glanced at Isaac when he emphasized the word visit, but she held her tongue.

"Miss Erikson," he continued, "I want you to meet Jim Callahan. Jim runs the post office, livery, and mercantile here in Lariat. Jim's wife, Martha, was Mary's close friend."

Jim reached out a massive hand. "I'm sure sorry about Mary and Josh. Martha will be glad you're here. She's been worried sick about how Isaac and Luke will take care of three kids and run a ranch the size of the Lazy W. Luke's not much more than a kid himself."

Amanda allowed herself a smug glance at Isaac, but he didn't make eye contact and continued with the introductions.

After the third or fourth "so sorry about Mary and Josh," she quit trying to remember names. Instead, she concentrated on not losing her composure in front of everyone. She refused to cry in front of strangers. It took forever before Joe Pete and she were left with only Isaac and the Callahan couple.

Martha Callahan had stood aside as the others offered their condolences. After the last of the townspeople left, the middle-aged woman simply stepped close, folded her arms around Amanda, and patted her on the back. "Mary often told me how much she loved and missed you. I'm so glad you're here for her children."

Unexpectedly, the tears Amanda had been holding at bay

came up by the bucket. She cried because she was hot and dirty, because she'd fallen on her bottom when she jumped out of the stock car, and because she had been shooting at men when she'd never before shot at anything other than empty bottles. She cried because Isaac Wright was an overbearing, pigheaded bully. And she cried because the person she loved most in the world had died, leaving behind three little children who would never remember what a wonderful, loving woman their mother had been.

Jim Callahan made a hasty excuse about needing to hitch the horses to Isaac's wagon. Seconds later, mumbling something about helping Jim, Isaac headed toward the livery after him.

Shifting from one foot to the other, Joe Pete stood beside her perhaps a minute more before sputtering, "Maybe I better go help, too." He bolted down the street, obviously more willing to take his chances with Isaac's gruffness than with her tears.

"That's one way to get rid of men." Amanda dried her eyes.

"Never mind about them. Come on to the kitchen and let me make you some tea," offered Martha.

"I really should go take care of my animals first."

"Why don't you let the menfolk take care of your livestock and rest yourself?"

"I always take care of my responsibilities." She dug out her handkerchief, wiped her nose, and straightened her hat before walking back to the depot.

Isaac, Jim, and Joe Pete drove up in an empty supply wagon as Amanda poured a bucket of water into the chickens' watering can.

Jim grimaced. "What in tarnation is that smell?" He peeked inside the largest cage. "Goats!" He stared at Amanda in amazement. "You're taking goats out to the Lazy W?" He snorted in an obvious effort to stifle a laugh.

"She sure as hell isn't," Isaac snapped. "What the devil did you bring all this livestock for anyway?"

Amanda started to answer that she'd need them on her home-stead, but then she looked at Isaac's forbidding expression. Again deciding she'd be better off not telling Isaac of her intention to homestead until a more opportune moment, she turned to the cages and spoke to the largest of her goats. "Pay no mind to him, Nanny. You'll get along fine on that ranch."

"You didn't hear me, lady! You aren't taking goats onto my ranch!"

That did it! She'd put up with her fiancé's ultimatums for over two weeks before she left Denver. *One year, Amanda!* Tom had warned in his smooth, cultivated way. *If you haven't come to your senses and returned in one year, I'll consider our engagement at an end.* Now Isaac Wright was trying to tell her what to do and she wasn't even engaged to him.

Infuriated, Amanda turned to Isaac. Though she hated to air the family laundry in front of Jim Callahan, she had to set this overblown tyrant straight. "Mr. Wright, I assume there's a wagon for rent up at the livery. Either I load these animals into your wagon and ride with you to your ranch, or I load these animals in a rented wagon and follow you to your ranch. You make the choice. But rest assured, I'm going to put my arms around my sister's children *tonight.*"

Glancing at Jim, she saw him run his hand down his face as if trying to wipe away the smile tugging at his mouth.

She studied one man, then the other. It had been three weeks since she'd heard about Mary's death, and her life had been one unpleasant scene after another. Her fiancé had been fit to be tied when she told him her plans. Her friends and family had acted as if she'd lost her mind. Emotionally drained, she would have liked nothing more than to sit in this dusty street and cry until some sympathetic person came along and solved all her problems.

Unfortunately, ladies in distress got rescued in fairy tales, not in Wyoming. If she backed down now, Isaac Wright would probably drive off chuckling, leaving her and her animals behind. Surely Isaac and his younger brother, Luke, could use *some* help. Little children took so much time.

She decided to try a different tactic. "Once we get to your

ranch, I'll take care of my own animals. I'll tend the children and keep out of your way. You'll hardly notice I'm around."

Isaac shifted. He and Luke had ranch work begging to be done and no time to do it with three little kids underfoot. Things were going to hell on the Lazy W. And he sure wasn't getting anything done standing in Lariat arguing with this stubborn female. Maybe it would be best to take her out to the ranch so she could see that the kids were fine, that there was no need to go hauling them off. "I suppose Luke and I could use a little *temporary* help. I'll take you and the boy," he agreed. "The goats stay in town. I won't have goats on the Lazy W."

"Are you going out to the ranch today?"

"As soon as I can get loaded."

"Then starting today, you *will* have goats on the Lazy W!"

Before he could say another word, the danged woman actually turned her back on him and spoke to Jim. "Mr. Callahan, will you give me a hand loading these cages? I wouldn't want to trouble Mr. Wright with such trivial animals."

"Sure will." Jim cast a big grin in Isaac's direction. "Where do you want them? Up close to the seat so the driver can get full benefit of the aroma?"

"I think that's an excellent idea."

Jim chuckled.

Isaac glared at him. If Amanda's stubbornness entertained him so much, he *could* just help her load alone. Though Isaac usually wasn't much of a drinking man, today seemed like a good day to take it up. "I'll be at the saloon."

After Isaac stomped off, Amanda wasted no time brooding over him. Let him sit in the saloon and pout. It'd be easier to load her things without him bucking her at every turn anyway. Turning her mind back to the problem of getting her things to the ranch, she said to Jim, "All I'm really worried about now are the animals. Do you have room to store the rest of my things in the livery until I get settled on my homestead?"

"You're planning to homestead?" Jim stopped working and stared at her. "Isaac said you were here to visit."

"Isaac and I haven't exactly discussed all the details. I filed on an abandoned homestead next to the Wright ranch."

"Next to Isaac's ranch? That must be the old Anderson place."

"That's what Mary called it."

"Anderson was a farmer. You planning to farm?"

She nodded.

"If you don't mind some friendly advice, you might wait to tell Isaac until he's in a better mood."

Amanda glanced down the street toward the saloon. "Perhaps you're right."

They loaded the goat cages; then Jim pushed his wide-brimmed hat back on his head and cleared his throat. "Personally, I don't care. Farmers buy goods at my store just like ranchers. But I wonder if Mary told you that Isaac and most of the other ranchers in the area don't cotton to farming homesteaders?"

"She mentioned something about that in her letters." Actually, Mary had mentioned a lot about how Isaac disliked farmers' fences blocking his access to water holes and good range. Still, Amanda had always wanted land of her own. Even when they were children, she'd often insisted they play "homesteaders" instead of "house."

At her request, Mary had sent her the legal description of the abandoned homestead near Isaac's ranch, again warning Amanda that Isaac didn't like farmers. But Mary had felt sure that Isaac wouldn't object to her *sister* being nearby. According to Mary, Isaac was a kind man and would understand how much Mary and Amanda wanted to live close to each other. Surely, Amanda's little homestead wouldn't bother him. He had thousands of acres of his own to worry about.

Over the past few years, one thing had come up, then another. Amanda kept having to postpone coming to Wyoming. Then last year, she'd reluctantly put her homesteading dream to rest altogether. She given in to the pressures of Denver society and agreed to marry Tom. After all, no young woman wanted to be a spinster, and Dr. Tom Johnson was considered an excellent catch. Mary had understood when Amanda wrote of her decision to stay in Denver.

Now, by a tragic turn of fate, Amanda was finally in Wyoming. Unfortunately, there would be no Mary close by to help her as she learned to homestead. Judging from what she'd seen of Isaac Wright's temperament, there'd be no help at all. Not that she needed help. She could take care of herself, Mary's children, *and* her homestead.

Keeping that in mind, she continued to load the wagon. Less than an hour later, she stopped the team in front of the saloon. Before she could get down, Isaac stomped out.

"What a lash-up," he snarled, examining his heavily laden wagon. When he stepped up into the wagon, Amanda scooted to the middle of the seat between Joe Pete and Isaac. She handed Isaac the reins. They started down the street with her two dogs following, romping and barking. Joe Pete sat rigidly staring straight ahead of him with her cat clutched tightly in his arms.

Amanda studied the seven buildings comprising Lariat. There was Callahan's store, the ramshackle depot, the livery, the saloon, and three residences. They passed a little frame house with a yard full of playing children. "Who lives there?"

"The preacher's family. He rides a circuit and comes back here the first week of each month. His wife is our schoolmarm." Amanda could hear the pride in his voice as he added, "Not many towns our size have a preacher *and* a schoolteacher."

"Where do the children go to school?"

"Upstairs in the rear room of the saloon."

"The saloon?"

"It's the biggest place in town. The saloon keeper and his little girl live in the front two rooms. He lets us use the downstairs for church on the first Sunday of every month."

"Do we come in to church?"

Where did she get this "we"? Isaac wondered. Still, her question caused Isaac to recall how much Mary and the kids had loved to come to town. Now he wished he'd insisted Joshua take a day off more often and bring his family to town. Instead, Isaac had come without them because it made it more convenient to visit Tess. He'd been downright selfish.

Of course, Josh wouldn't have wanted to come in anyway. Joshua had worked hard every day of his married life, trying to make a good life for his family, trying to be sure he did his share of the ranch work and more. He'd have had no time for lollygagging in town on Sundays.

Still, Isaac wondered if his sister-in-law wouldn't have been so tired out if she'd rested some Sundays. Maybe she would have been strong enough not to die. If her life had been less difficult, perhaps she'd be here to watch over her own kids.

When he'd buried Mary, Isaac had promised himself that never again would any woman close to him be so neglected. He hadn't even noticed how thin and fragile Mary had gotten over the past six years—not that she was ever the real hearty type. He blamed himself for not noticing Mary's condition, for not helping Josh make things easier for her. Just like his mother, Mary never had complained and had worked too hard. Life in this country wasn't kind to women, not kind at all.

It wouldn't kill him to bring Amanda and the kids in to church. After all, she wouldn't be staying long. He wouldn't have to bring her to town but once—possibly twice. He finally answered. "We'll try to come in for church some Sundays, if you like. It'd be good for the kids."

Before she could agree with him about the children and church services, Amanda's attention was drawn to the yard of the biggest house on the street. A woman stood at the fence waving her handkerchief to catch their attention.

"Damnation," uttered Isaac under his breath.

In spite of his cursing, he stopped and politely introduced Amanda and Joe Pete to Mrs. Teresa Brown, proprietor of the town's only boarding establishment.

"I washed and mended the shirt you left here last night." Mrs. Brown tittered as she handed Isaac the package.

"Thanks, Tess." Isaac stuffed the shirt under his seat.

"I was glad to do it. One likes to help when one sees such a *good* friend in need."

Amused, Amanda watched as Teresa Brown postured fussily in her silly, ruffled dress.

"I'm so sorry about your sister, Miss Erikson. Isaac told me all about it when he came to town, didn't you, dear?" Mrs. Brown reached up and patted Isaac's thigh. "Of course, I offered to leave my business and put his house in order, but he insisted that my hands were far too lovely to ruin doing common ranch work. He does admire my hands so,'' she gushed.

La-di-da, thought Amanda.

''He told me Mary had an old-maid sister coming to help out.'' Mrs. Brown again patted Isaac familiarly on the thigh.

Old-maid sister indeed! Amanda glared at the side of Isaac's head. *Mr. Isaac Wright would suffer for that remark.*

Isaac shifted his legs toward Amanda. ''If you'll excuse us, Tess, we need to get on to the ranch. Miss Erikson is anxious to see the kids.''

''Before I get any older,'' Amanda muttered in a whisper that reached only Isaac's reddening ears.

Teresa Brown flounced back inside her white picket fence and waved daintily to them with her lace handkerchief.

Amanda turned around once to verify that her eyes hadn't deceived her. Imagine, this rugged, lanky rancher with that ridiculous, flat-chested old biddy. The woman had to be at least forty years old. That would make her fully ten years older than Isaac. And sixteen years older than herself. Amanda choked as she tried not to laugh. Pickings must be mighty slim in Lariat, Wyoming.

CHAPTER TWO

The mid-morning sun beat down on the wagon as Isaac, Joe Pete, and Amanda rode toward the ranch. Amanda felt sweaty in her woolen coat and black hat. She would never admit it to Isaac, but the stench from the caged goats made her eyes water.

After several days in the same clothes, she feared she smelled a lot like her goats. Of course, who could tell? Isaac smelled like whiskey, and Joe Pete just plain smelled.

Three miles out of town, the road curved to meet the Powder River. Isaac halted the wagon in a stand of quaking aspen. "Get down and stretch if you like. This is the last shade and water for a bit. We usually stop and clean up here on our way to town. That way the kids only have to stay clean until we get to Lariat. Those kids get dirty faster than any hogs I ever saw," he added with a small smile.

Why, he's handsome when he isn't scowling, Amanda thought. Obviously, her arrival hadn't been a pleasant surprise to him. She hated to irritate him further over empty stomachs. But she could hear Joe Pete's growling, and her belly button felt as if it were glued to her backbone. "Martha made us a lunch," she said hesitantly. "It's under the wagon seat."

Isaac looked at Joe Pete. "It's early for lunch. How about it, boy? Is your belly talking to you?"

Joe Pete lowered his head and nodded.

"Then this is as good a time as any to eat."

Amanda gazed at the river. "Isaac, I rode the last thirty hours in a stock car, and I feel filthy. If I hurry, do I have time to bathe?"

"That river's ice-cold this early in April. Why don't you heat water and take a bath when we get to the ranch?"

"I hate to meet the children looking like this."

"The kids won't care."

"I will."

He shrugged. "Don't say I didn't warn you about the water. While you're cleaning up, I'll water the animals and build a fire. I don't know about you, but I could use some coffee."

Judging from the whiskey smell, a pot of coffee would do him good. Amanda congratulated herself on her restraint when all she said aloud was, "I'd love a cup of coffee."

Isaac untied the coffee pot from the side of the wagon and handed it to Joe Pete to fill.

Amanda gathered a quick armload of firewood before she walked to the far side of the wagon to remove her coat and hat. "Joe Pete, would you get the package I put under the wagon seat?" she asked when he returned with the coffee pot. "I bought some soap and things at Callahan's store."

The boy hurried to do her bidding.

"While you're up there, reach into that front valise. Hand me the brown-and-white checkered dress right on top, please."

When Joe Pete pulled the dress from her luggage, some white unmentionables fell out of the folded dress.

Isaac smiled when the beet-red boy handed the jumbled pile of clothing down to Amanda, then rushed to stand by him.

Moments later, Amanda walked around to their side of the wagon without her hat and coat. He stopped smiling. *Mercy on a poor man.* She was beautiful.

"Where's a good place to bathe?"

She had the biggest, greenest eyes he'd ever seen.

"Isaac?" Pulling at the pins in her hair, she looked at him quizzically. "Isaac? Are you all right?"

"All right?"

"I asked about a place to bathe?"

"Th . . . there's a little sandy beach on the other side of the willows." He couldn't even remember the last time a pretty woman had him so flustered. He watched while she walked toward the river in her quick, no-nonsense style. As she moved, she shook loose her dark-brown hair, letting it tumble down in waves well past her waist. He'd bet big money that hair was as soft as silk.

Down at the river, Amanda took a minute to verify that no one could see her bathing spot before stepping into the frigid water. Clenching her teeth, she submerged her entire body, then quickly washed and rinsed her hair.

She'd pulled on her clean pantaloons and chemise, and was reaching for her fresh dress when she glimpsed a gray body slither under it. Shrieking, she charged toward the clearing.

Isaac, carrying his rifle and running, met her as she came out of the willows. He shoved her behind him and aimed the rifle down the path. "What is it?"

"A snake!"

He moved back a couple of steps and lowered his gaze, scanning the path from side to side. "Where?"

"On the riverbank under my clothes."

"On the bank?" Isaac lowered his rifle and turned to face her. "Damn, woman! You ran this far to get away? Did you think it was chasing you?"

"There's no need to curse." She couldn't quit shivering.

Isaac glared at her with stormy gray eyes.

As she calmed down, she realized how ridiculous she must have appeared, running clear up the path to get away from a snake. Drat. She hated to look like a hysterical female. Especially in front of Isaac. He obviously had little tolerance for female frailties. She did so want to get along with him. "I'm sorry, Isaac. I don't think too well around snakes."

But it appeared he'd forgotten about the snake. He was still staring, but he'd lowered his gaze to her . . . bosom.

Isaac Wright was quite openly staring at her bosom.

Fighting the reflex to cover her chest with her hands, she left her arms by her sides. She'd be living in the same house with this man until she moved to her homestead. No sense acting like a priss. Besides, she chortled inside as she thought about the Widow Brown, apparently his tastes ran to older, scrawny, flat-chested, handkerchief-waving women.

Shaking his head, Isaac tore his gaze from Amanda's shapely body and started back toward the fire. Didn't it just figure that a woman with a penchant for goats and half-breed kids would be built too fancy for words.

Still, she was a sight to soothe a lonely man's soul. Those huge green eyes surrounded by long, dark eyelashes could tempt any male to forget all he ever learned in Sunday School. As if her eyes weren't enough, the full, gorgeous breasts peeking over the top of that chemise almost begged for a man's loving touch.

"Wait!" she called from behind him. "Aren't you going to go get my clothes for me?"

"They're your clothes. If you want them, get them." He'd wrestle a grizzly bear before he'd deliberately search for a snake. Besides, it was probably nothing but a water snake and long gone by now.

"Jackass!" she sputtered loud enough for him to hear.

He'd been called worse. But for a lady, she had quite a mouth on her.

Joe Pete spoke up. "I ain't scared of snakes, Amanda. I'll get your clothes."

Groaning internally, Isaac turned around. He couldn't let a kid face something he feared. "Ah, hell." He stormed back toward the river. "I'll get your dag-blasted clothes!"

"Never mind." Amanda moved into his way and stood there in her underwear, her tall, curvy body blocking the path. "Joe Pete and I will take care of ourselves."

This he wanted to see. Isaac flat enjoyed the walk behind her to the river. The cheeks of her pleasantly rounded bottom seemed to have separate lives inside her pantaloons. One moved, then the other. They reached the river bank too dang soon.

Joe Pete used a willow branch to lift Amanda's dress. A movement in the grass was all the boy needed. He dropped the stick and made a lunge. When he triumphantly held up a two-foot-long water snake, Amanda backed into Isaac.

He held his ground. If she hadn't been trembling so badly, he'd have enjoyed the luxury of having a curvy, sweet-smelling woman pressed against him.

After the boy chucked the snake out into the river, Isaac touched Amanda's shoulder. "You're shaking. Are you all right?"

She practically jumped away from him, and her cheeks turned all pink. "I'm a little cold, is all."

Isaac picked up the checkered dress and shook it good. "Look, no crawling things." He tossed it to her.

She jerked the dress from her head where it had landed. "Thank you. I don't know what I'd have done without *your* assistance."

Isaac grinned at her and put a hand on Joe Pete's shoulder. "Come on, boy, let's go see to the fire while Miss Erikson puts on the rest of her clothes."

After she dressed, Amanda left the soap on a rock at the edge of the river. "Ah, that was so refreshing," she declared as she walked into camp. "Some cowardly people might be hesitant to get into a little cold water, but not the people I admire."

She felt slightly guilty about entrapping Joe Pete, but he desperately needed a bath. "If there's one thing I hold to, it's that cleanliness is next to godliness. Don't you agree, Joe Pete?"

The perplexed-looking child glanced at Isaac.

Isaac fed another stick into the fire under the coffee pot. He appeared as confused as the boy.

Catching Isaac's eye, Amanda raised an eyebrow and nodded slightly toward Joe Pete, then toward the river. "It feels wonderful to be clean," she gushed, hoping Isaac would understand what she meant.

"Oh," he said—finally. "You know, I was going to clean up later, but you're right. Cleanliness is next to godliness. I think I'll go down and take a bath right now." He made a great show of taking off his hat and laying it aside. "How about you, boy? Wouldn't you like a bath, too?"

Amanda almost could see Joe Pete's mind racing, trying to think of a way out. Sudden relief showed on his face. "No use in me getting all washed up. I don't have any clean clothes, and I'll just get dirty putting these things back on." She nearly laughed aloud at his attempt to look properly disappointed.

Fast thinking, Joe Pete. She hated to spoil his victory, but he had to have a bath. "The package you handed to me earlier has new clothes I bought for you at the store. Aren't you the luckiest boy to have soap, water, *and* clean clothes?"

Joe Pete looked for all the world as though he was being dragged to slaughter when he and Isaac started down to the river.

The painfully skinny boy seemed like a different child when he returned to the clearing a short time later. With his long, raven-black hair slicked back, Joe Pete appeared older than Amanda had originally assumed him to be. He was at least eleven or twelve, maybe more.

While Isaac cut the bread and cheese for their lunch, she stood in the sun and pinned up her hair. Joe Pete would barely finish a thick slice of bread or cheese before Isaac handed him another. Each time Joe Pete looked surprised to find more food being offered, but he wasted no time eating it.

Isaac had left off his shirt, letting the sun beat down on his wide shoulders. His curly chest hair was a little darker than the very fair, wavy hair he'd combed away from his face. The rippling muscles in his back were long and lean, like the rest of his body. Amanda's gaze followed the thin line of hair leading from his navel downward.

An unfamiliar warmth, most pleasant, spread through her. When she realized what her body's reaction meant, she glanced at Isaac's face. Busy pouring coffee, he hadn't noticed her practically lusting after him.

Thank goodness.

She had no business noticing Isaac's body. Obviously, he had something going on with the Widow Brown back in town.

Besides, there was Tom.

Strange. Looking at Tom had never made her warm inside the way she'd felt when looking at Isaac. Of course, she'd never seen Tom without his shirt. She couldn't even picture proper Dr. Tom Johnson baring his back to the heat of the spring sun. She couldn't picture him slicing bread and cheese, or sitting on a log next to a part-Indian child, either. Most of all, she couldn't picture him on a homestead in Wyoming. But surely he'd change his mind and join her instead of continuing to insist she return to Denver. Surely he would. Wyoming needed doctors, too.

At any rate, she couldn't worry about it now. Right now, she had Mary's children and their welfare to worry about.

After lunch, during their continued wagon ride toward the Lazy W, Isaac nodded at the revolver in her lap. "I like the way you handled that gun today. The time might come when you're alone with the kids on the ranch and need all the shooting skill you have."

"That sounds ominous. What might I need to shoot?"

"Oh, varmints and such."

Varmints? Well, she'd figured on things like that in an unsettled area like Wyoming. She wasn't concerned about being left alone with the children. After all, that would be the natural state of affairs on her homestead. But she was curious about the habits of the Wright family. "Did Mary and the children stay alone often?"

"The Lazy W is a big spread with more work than three men can rightfully handle. We had to leave Mary and the kids alone more than any of us liked. But we never all left at the same time unless she was safe on the homeplace."

"Homeplace?"

"The homeplace is our dad's original homestead. It's got a

good water supply and we store most of our supplies there. That's where we winter."

"Winter? Where do you live in the summer?"

"Josh and Mary lived on the homeplace year round after they proved up on their homestead. The cabin's big enough for their family. Luke and I spend most of our time riding the range checking on cattle. We stay in the shack on my homestead or in Josh and Mary's little homestead cabin. In the winter, we all crowded in together. It was safer for everyone that way."

Amanda knew Josh had staked out his homestead when he turned twenty-one, the month after he married her sister. They'd had to live on the homestead for five years to "prove up." She hadn't realized Josh and Mary had moved to the main ranch in the winter. "Is it legal to live on the homestead only in the summer when you're trying to prove up?"

"In this country, it takes a lot of land to run cattle." He shook the reins to hurry the horses. "We don't see two people a year out here. If we have a cabin, a little barn, and a water source, who's to say we don't stay on the land year-round?"

"You cheat?" She didn't even try to keep the disdain from her voice.

Isaac shrugged. "We keep to the letter of the law as much as possible, but we do what's necessary to survive and thrive. Luke's staked out his homestead along the west border of the ranch. Next month, after his twenty-first birthday, he'll put up a cabin and live there the next five summers. He'll move to the homeplace in the winter."

"You sound pretty sure of yourself. What if Luke wants to stay on his homestead next winter and start a ranch of his own?"

"He won't. Our family intends to have the largest cattle ranch in this part of the country. We've been homesteading and buying land in this area for eighteen years now. Luke will file for his homestead, six-hundred-and-forty acres of desert land and a hundred-and-sixty acres under the timber-culture entry. That's what my pa, Josh, and I have all done. Even with public grazing, it's hard going to make a ranch pay for itself in Wyoming. We work as a family."

"I still find it curious that he doesn't want land that belongs only to him. I certainly do."

"Like I said, we work as a family. Except for legal purposes, we don't keep tabs on who owns what. We all own everything."

Trying to total the number of acres they might have, she sat silently, thinking. Maybe she could file a timber-culture claim and a desert-land claim, too. She'd ask Isaac to explain it all more carefully soon. However, as Jim had mentioned earlier, today didn't seem the best time to ask Isaac for homesteading advice.

She slid forward and had to catch herself when Isaac eased the horses down an embankment and across a shallow stream.

"We're almost home," he said. "This creek is the southern boundary of the Lazy W."

Amanda noticed a tiny, fenced-in graveyard when they had traveled about a mile and a half farther. *Oh, no. Please, God, no. Don't let it be true.* She touched Isaac's sleeve.

Isaac glanced her way, briefly covered her hand, then drew the wagon to a stop.

Simple crosses marked two new graves. She suddenly realized she'd clung to some wild, irrational hope that it was all a mistake, a nightmare from which she'd awaken.

With her hand on Isaac's offered arm, she put one foot ahead of the other and somehow made the walk to the wooden gate. It was so hard to breathe. For a moment, she supported herself on the gatepost; then she walked inside the fence, leaving Isaac waiting outside.

Kneeling, she rubbed her finger along the engraving on the wooden cross marking Mary's grave. *Dead. They really are dead.* She wanted to throw herself on the ground and scream and cry. But then, she'd couldn't do that. Not even if she were alone. For the sake of Mary's children, she had to be strong.

Bowing her head, she whispered, "I'll take good care of your babies, Mary. They'll never want for love or anything else I can give them. No matter what I have to do, I'll take care of them."

Bending forward, she straightened the wilted wildflowers

she found in cans at the foot of the graves. "I have to leave now, Mary. I'll come back soon."

She stumbled on her hem as she rose, and Isaac instantly was at her side. Silently, he latched the gate; then he walked close beside her, guiding her to the wagon with a tender touch upon her waist.

"Who else is buried back there?" she asked after they'd been moving a few minutes and she trusted her voice.

"The two big crosses mark my folks' resting places, and the little cross is for Josh and Mary's second set of twin babies. Mary wanted them buried together so they wouldn't be lonesome in God's hands." He shook the horses' reins.

"I didn't know Mary and Joshua had a set of twins who died," she confessed. She looked back at the small cemetery, and her eyes filled with tears.

"There was nothing any of you could do. Mary didn't want to worry your family. You know how she was, always looking out for the welfare of others."

That was Mary. Forever taking the smallest piece of cake, giving up the prettiest ribbon to one of the other sisters, or keeping her deepest sorrows to herself so the rest of the family wouldn't hurt. Sweet, caring Mary. Death was not fair!

Amanda folded her hands tightly in her lap to keep them from shaking and took a ragged breath. She should have come to Wyoming sooner. Mary had needed her.

Reaching out, Isaac covered Amanda's clasped hands with one of his. He supposed he needed to tell her what he'd discovered when he had buried Mary. But it could wait. She wouldn't be leaving right away. He'd finish telling her about the babies. "Mary had those twin girls between the older twins and little Nellie. One winter morning, she slipped on the ice on the porch and fell hard."

Isaac cleared his throat. "The babies were born that afternoon. So tiny, so perfect, but they came into the world way too early. They didn't live the night. Josh was half crazed for a while. He dug the grave himself. Had to use a pick to break the frozen ground. He wouldn't even let me help. He and Mary carried the babies up the hill in a snowstorm."

It had been painfully lonesome, waiting inside the cabin, tending the older twins. Through the frosted window, Isaac had watched Mary and Josh fill the tiny grave, then kneel in the icy wind on the hill. He'd grieved with them, imagining how he would feel if he were burying his own babies. That was one of life's heartaches he intended to do without. With God's help, he'd raise Josh and Mary's kids up safe. But he wouldn't inflict his ranching life on a woman. No wife. No kids of his own.

"I wish I had known about the babies," Amanda said. "Mary's heart must have broken into a million pieces."

"I guess so. She was never the same after they died. She put on a brave front, but I think she was terribly sad deep inside. I came up on her once while she was sitting by the babies' grave. She was humming a lullaby to those poor dead babies. She hummed the same line, over and over. Didn't even answer me when I spoke to her."

Damned ice!

Josh and he had spent every spare minute the next spring putting a roof over the porch so the melting snow could never make a sheet of ice on the porch again, but it'd been too late for those baby girls. And too late for Mary, he guessed.

Devil take it. He swiped at his nose. "This country's not kind to women, Amanda. It takes their strength, their spirit, and then it takes their children."

CHAPTER THREE

Amanda could see the five-year-old twins, Will and Susie, holding hands and waiting on the stoop of the log cabin. Willie stood half a head taller than his sister. They looked so young and defenseless. *Please God, help me say and do the right things,* Amanda prayed. *Help me to be a good parent.*

A tall, heavily muscled young man stopped working on the corral fence. In the time it took him to pull on his shirt and greet her over-friendly dogs, their wagon had reached the ranch yard.

Isaac jumped from the seat, then grasped her around the waist and lowered her to the hard-packed dirt. "Luke, this here is Mary's sister, Amanda. She came on the morning train."

Luke grinned. After wiping his palms on his pants, he reached out to shake her hand.

Returning his smile, Amanda noted that Mary's letters depicted Luke accurately. He *did* look like a Norse God with that blond hair curling all helter-skelter and those gorgeous blue eyes. Too bad her little sister, Anne, couldn't be here. Unless Amanda missed her guess, Anne would be instantly smitten.

Luke glanced up at Joe Pete, who was still sitting on the

wagon seat clutching her cat. Amanda introduced Luke and Joe Pete, then took the cat and put it on the ground.

As Joe Pete climbed from the wagon, she turned to the twins standing shyly on the porch. "Will and Susie, I'm Aunt Mandy." She held out her arms. "Come here and give me a hug."

As she pulled them close, she felt a renewed sense of purpose. She'd always wanted children. Now she had them. Not the way she'd dreamed, but she would raise these beautiful children with love.

"Where's Baby Nellie?" she asked when she could let go.

"She's sleeping in the old wagon out by the barn," Luke answered. "And she's not much of a baby anymore."

"I sometimes forget she's over a year old. Does she walk well?"

"We've never seen her slow down enough to walk." Luke sighed in exasperation. "She gallops from one piece of mischief to another. I had work to do, so I put her in the wagon and wired up the back. So far, she hasn't figured how to get out."

"If I don't wake her, may I take a peek? I can't imagine what she looks like."

"See Susie there? Picture red hair like Mary's, and you have Nellie. Come on, I'll show you," Luke said.

Nellie woke when they crowded around the end of the wagon. She stuck one thumb in her mouth and reached the free hand out to her Uncle Isaac. He kissed her brow and brushed the curly wisps of red hair off her forehead before turning her over to Amanda.

Cuddling the bedraggled angel, Amanda couldn't help but notice that the poor darling smelled. Men! The child needed a bath and a change of clothes. It was time to go to work!

Setting Nellie on the porch, she proceeded to direct the unloading of the wagon. "Turn the chickens out; they'll fend for themselves. We better stake the goats for a few days."

Luke stopped working. "Goats?" He peered through the slats of a cage. "Whew!" Fanning his nose, he backed away. "I'm not messing with goats." He looked to Isaac for support.

Amanda expected Isaac to side with Luke. Instead, he stood

beside her, an unreadable expression on his face. Waiting for her to make a move, she guessed.

"I didn't realize you'd be afraid of goats," she said. "Sometime when you are feeling brave, I'll introduce you to these man-threatening animals."

Luke started to bristle, and Isaac burst out laughing.

"What the hell's so funny? You going to tell me it's all right with you that we keep goats on the Lazy W?"

"She assures me it's only temporary."

"Temporary?"

"That's what the lady says. It seems she came to take the kids off our hands."

Amanda chased across the yard after Nellie. She wasn't out of earshot when Luke spoke to Isaac. "You ain't gonna let her take the kids, are you?"

Isaac started unloading and raised his voice, obviously for Amanda's benefit. "No one's taking these kids anywhere. Now give me a hand here with these damned goat cages."

They struggled a minute before Isaac slammed his corner down. "I have too much to do to play guessing games, Amanda. How the hell did you fit this in here anyway?"

"You'd know if you hadn't stormed off to the tavern. And I'll thank you not to cuss in front of the children!"

He pushed back his old gray cowboy hat and took a deep breath. "Listen, lady, if you want me to unload this crate, you better stop the sass and give me some direction."

"Yes, Master!" She curtsied deeply, causing Luke to snort back a laugh.

Isaac shot him a quelling look.

Luke continued to grin.

"Lift the cage straight up until it clears the sides of the wagon," she told them. Then she turned to Joe Pete. "When these big, tough, tolerant men manage to unload the animals, please stake the goats where they can reach that water." She pointed to a narrow stream flowing across the far side of the yard and through the corral. "With any kind of luck, we'll have fresh goat's milk for supper."

"Regular milk?" Will asked, speaking and moving away

from Susie's side for the first time since Amanda's arrival. "Not from a can?"

"Don't you have a milk cow on this big place?"

Isaac stomped past Amanda, carrying her small trunk inside the cabin. The screen door slammed behind him.

Luke stopped unwiring a cage. "We had two milk cows, but one dried up and a mountain lion got the other." He studied the nanny. "It'll be good to have fresh milk for the kids."

Isaac had returned to the porch and glanced at the twins' anxious faces before speaking to Luke. "You better rig up a couple stalls in the barn before nightfall. We don't want to lose these da—" Isaac caught his slip of tongue in time. "We don't want to lose these *darn* goats the same way we lost that milk cow."

Amanda waited until the twins had followed Luke into the house, carrying the last of the things from the wagon. Then she moved to stand beside Isaac. "Is that mountain lion still around?"

"It appears so. We see signs now and then."

"I know you don't like my goats, Isaac. I appreciate your having Luke fix a place for them in the barn." She brushed a deer fly from his shoulder. "Nanny's a special pet of mine, and she's a fine, heavy-producing milk goat."

Instantly, much of Isaac's earlier irritation with Amanda disappeared. Without his mind's permission, his body responded to her nearness. He wanted nothing more than to pull her to him, let down all that beautiful brown hair, and kiss her.

"What about my chickens? Are they safe?"

"What?" Isaac tried to remember what they'd been talking about before she came and stood so close to him.

"The chickens? Will they be okay?"

"There's a coop behind the barn. The door blew open during the first blizzard this winter and the hens froze. We do have one ornery old rooster left. He'll be tickled to see your hens."

"I brought a rooster, too. I guess they'll have to decide who's ruling the roost."

Isaac looked down into Amanda's eyes. It wasn't just the chickens who needed to decide who ruled the roost. This sassy green-eyed hen needed a lesson, too. A month's hard work ought to bring her around to where she could see sense when he talked to her.

Meanwhile, he'd better not give in to his manly urges. Amanda wasn't like good old obliging Tessie back in town. Tess didn't expect anything of a man but a night's companionship. Amanda was Mary's sister, and a spinster lady. Wouldn't surprise him if she'd never been with a man. If he didn't watch himself, this could turn into a hell of a mess!

Even so, he couldn't help smiling as she again chased down Nellie. Amanda had a quick way of moving that set her backside in motion—and got him to thinking things he'd be better off not thinking. Still, thinking wasn't acting. No harm in enjoying the view while he could.

Over Nellie's loud protests, Amanda carried her back to where he stood. "This one must have kept you two mighty busy."

"Miss Contrary doesn't hold still a minute."

Amanda laughed.

When Isaac heard her easy, bubbly laugh, he relaxed a little. Maybe things would work out.

Amanda got acquainted with the children while Joe Pete helped Luke and him unload. Joe Pete seemed like a good enough kid. Isaac wondered about the whole story. Amanda must have had a good reason not to leave him in Cheyenne. At least, he hoped so. He'd have to nail her down about the details soon.

After the animals were freed from the cages, Isaac glanced at the sun. He hated to leave Amanda on her first day; it didn't seem mannerly. On the other hand, he had plenty of daylight and weeks of work to catch up on. "If you're okay," he said to her, "I need to search for some heifers that got away last week. They should be calving any time."

"Don't worry about me. I came to help. I'll settle in while you're gone."

That was what he was afraid of.

While he saddled his horse, Amanda came into the barn with the cheese and bread left from lunch. "I thought you might want this. Luke says there's nothing else cooked to send with you.''

''Thanks.'' Selfish as it was, it felt good to have someone tending to *his* needs for a change. Slipping the food into his saddlebags, he wondered if Amanda liked to cook. He hated the chore; it took too damn much time. And Luke was plumb incompetent at the stove.

Instead of going back outside, Amanda rubbed the nose of his horse and watched him saddle up. Somehow it felt right to have her standing around the barn while he worked. Though she was a tad bossy and over-confident, if she'd let go of her notion of taking the kids away, he might enjoy having her around—for a month or two.

He had a vision of Ma following Pa to his horse and watching as he rode away. Come to think of it, Mary used to see Joshua off. But as good as it was to have a pretty woman standing close, he didn't plan to get used to it. The West was too hard on women. The weather, worry, and work wore them down. He had to take advantage of Amanda's presence right now because he was backed into a corner. But he wouldn't be responsible for making any woman end up like his mother and Mary, worn out and old beyond their years. He reached to get his blanket from where he'd thrown it over the top rung of a stall.

''Are you going to be gone all night?''

''I don't plan to, but cows tend to wander.'' It came as a surprise to realize he *wanted* to be home tonight. Lately, he'd been relieved in a way to have excuses to get away from the house.

The unfamiliar responsibilities forced upon him by the deaths of Josh and Mary weighed heavy on his mind. Not that he begrudged the kids. He loved them as dearly as if they were his own. But so many things could happen to a kid if a person weren't watchful. And they were always hungry or needing something. He didn't understand how Mary ever got any work done.

And thinking about work, he had a passel to do. ''Can you handle being left alone with the kids tomorrow, Amanda? Luke and I should both start riding the range. We're so far behind, it'll take at least a hard month's work to catch up."

"The children and I will be fine."

She followed him to the yard, where he ruffled the twins' hair, kissed Nellie good-bye, and found himself apologizing to Amanda again. "I'm sorry to have to leave you on your own so soon."

Luke spoke right up. "I'll keep an eye on her."

That was another thing that had him worried.

Amanda smiled as Rasty, one of her dogs, nonchalantly followed Isaac's horse. At the yard's edge, the dog turned and gave her a beseeching look. She made a hand signal releasing him, and Rasty shot off to catch up to Isaac. Isaac could send him back if he didn't want him along. As usual, her other dog, Misty, came to sit quietly by her feet.

When Isaac reached the surrounding trees, Amanda stepped away from Luke—he seemed awfully close—and set Nellie down in the yard. "I'd better go inside and unpack my things."

Luke turned red. "I guess you'll notice me and Isaac aren't much on housekeeping. Mary always made keeping the house and minding the kids look easy, but it isn't. The twins aren't bad, but I've considered hog-tying Nellie so I can get some work done."

"That little thing." Amanda laughed, looking at the toddler, who had again made it to the corral and was once more trying to climb the fence. "I bet she's no trouble at all."

"You'll see."

Amanda quickly covered the distance to the fence, scooped up a surprised Nellie, and started for the cabin. "Don't worry about the house now that I'm here. If you want to take care of things outside, I'll see what I can do inside."

"If I'd known you were coming, I'd have cleaned up some." Having made his apology, Luke grabbed a stack of slats from the goats' cages and disappeared into the barn.

The minute Amanda opened the screen door, she fully understood Luke's hasty retreat. *Heavens above!* The house was a pigsty. To think that Isaac had hesitated back there in town

when she'd offered to come and help! Acting as if he didn'
need a woman around!

She'd never seen such a mule-headed man. If Isaac Wrigh
didn't need a woman's help, she'd like to see someone who
did.

CHAPTER FOUR

Amanda set Nellie down and stood with both hands on her hips surveying the chaos created by two bachelors and three young children over a six-week period. Shaking her head, she asked the toddler, "Have you ever seen such a mess?"

"Kitty?" Nellie responded.

Absently Amanda nodded, then walked through the Wright family's main ranch house. The house consisted of two large one-room log cabins, set side by side and hooked together in the back by a rustic hallway. A combined kitchen and living area made up the older cabin with the front outside door opening to a long, covered porch. The back door of this main cabin opened into the hallway, which led into the bedroom cabin.

Inside the second cabin, she found one room partitioned off as a small master bedroom. The rest of the family's beds were arranged barracks-style in the L-shaped area left after the bedroom had been walled off. The connecting porch opened to the backyard. It would be thirty steps to the fast-flowing spring and double that to the privy. Easy access to all the amenities.

Trailed by the cat, which in turn was trailed by a little red-haired ragamuffin, Amanda returned to the master bedroom where Isaac had deposited her trunk. "No sense in ruining my good clothes cleaning up this mess,'' she said to Nellie as she changed into her oldest work dress.

"Kitty?" Nellie crouched down and peered under the bed.

"Kitty," Amanda agreed. "Come on, darling. This house needs the attention of some hot water, strong lye soap, and good old-fashioned elbow grease."

"Kitty?"

"Quite an extensive conversationalist, aren't you?" Amanda smiled at the toddler.

Nellie grinned back. "Kitty?"

Laughing, Amanda hugged her. She went to work with Nellie playing contentedly inside, chasing the wary cat.

Later, the twins came in and stood close together. "You want us to do something?" Willie asked. "Uncle Luke told us to stay the hell out of his way and see if you needed any help."

Amanda winced. Willie used Luke's curse word so casually. She intended to have a serious discussion with the men about the language they used in front of the children.

In response to Will's offer to help, she answered, "You could show me where you keep the food supplies."

Willie pulled up a dusty rug and pointed to a trap door in the floor. "We keep most everything in the root cellar here."

What wonderful planning went into this place. She made note of the staples. Her touch lingered on each of the four remaining jars of jelly. Mary probably had put them up last fall. Tears threatened. Drat! She couldn't cry; she'd upset the children. They needed an adult, not a bawl-baby. Forcing a smile, she sent the twins outside. "Run along and play, but don't pester your Uncle Luke."

Amanda looked up from the floor she was scrubbing and found Luke standing in the doorway, staring at her.

"Luke, I was just about to look for you. What were you planning for supper?"

"Well, probably I was going to cook mush." He shifted

uneasily. "It's the only thing I know how to cook except tinned stuff. Isaac did the cooking before Mary came. After that, she kept us fed. Until lately, I haven't had to cook much."

"The children look like you've done all right. But I'll be glad to do the cooking while I'm here."

Obviously relieved, he returned her smile. "There's venison in the smokehouse. Would you like me to get a hunk of it for supper?"

"That would be fine. Before you go, will you carry the flour Isaac bought this morning over to the bin?"

Luke hefted the sack of flour and carried it to the bin in the corner of the kitchen. If she didn't know better, she'd think he was showing off. Her younger sister, Anne, would love his show of strength. Truth to tell, Amanda could see a lot to admire in Luke. He lacked the physical maturity of Isaac, of course. Luke still had the puppy look to him. That would fade as he got older. In time, he would develop into a powerful male like Isaac. Exciting in some inexplicable way. And challenging.

While Luke dumped the flour into the bin, Amanda called the children and fetched the candy she'd bought at the store. "Here, Joe Pete. Would you divide this among you children?" She turned to Luke. "The tobacco is for you and Isaac."

"Isaac and me never got the habit. Thank you anyway."

"Let's put it in Pa's tobacco pouch and save it for when Hawk gets here," suggested Susie, winding her long blond braid around her finger, first one way, then the other. "Hawk likes tobacco for his pipe. Pa always kept some for him."

Luke shot her a quelling look, and Susie's eyes immediately filled with tears. "Aunt Mandy is family," she insisted. "Uncle Isaac said I can talk about Hawk in front of family."

"You need to check before you ever say *anything* about Hawk to *anybody*. A careless word could cause Hawk's band trouble."

Susie looked down at the floor. "I'm sorry." She glanced toward Amanda, then back to Luke. "What we gonna do now?"

"I'll talk to your Aunt Mandy. You kids get outside."

After putting the tobacco away, Luke cleared his throat. "Susie shouldn't have mentioned Hawk."

"Who is this Hawk that I'm not supposed to know about?"

"He's a friend of Isaac's."

"And . . . ?"

"The fact of the matter is . . . well, he's a Sioux brave. Before all the trouble about the gold in the Black Hills, when he and Isaac were kids, his tribe lived and hunted in this area. Afterward, the Sioux were supposed to turn themselves in at the agencies or be classified as hostiles. Hawk's people simply disappeared. A couple of years back, his band showed up in the mountains behind us. Only Hawk comes in as close as our place."

"Why only Hawk?"

"One man can move quiet. If the cavalry got wind of Hawk's band, they'd try to move them to the reservation. Hawk's people aren't causing trouble, but many folks hereabout have hard feelings about Indians. Ain't no point in anyone getting hurt."

"What did Mary think about all this?"

"She never said much, but she always cooked up a storm when Hawk came around. She sent jellies and such to his wife."

"My sister had a good feeling for the heart of people. If Mary liked Hawk, then I'll like Hawk. No one outside this family will ever hear a word about Hawk or his people from me."

"Isaac will be pleased to hear that."

The twins stuck their darling freckled noses inside the door for the fourth time in perhaps an hour. Willie smiled. "Do you need any help, Aunt Mandy?"

"Thank you for offering, dear. But I'm doing fine." They were so sweet, checking on her like that.

She walked to the door, just to look at them, and overheard Willie comment to his sister, "She still ain't cooking."

Good heavens. Where had the time gone? The sun had started to go down. No wonder the children had been checking on her. The poor things must be starved.

* * *

Luke sighed as he sat down to supper on the bench between the twins, leaving the head of the table unoccupied. "This food smells great, Amanda. I'm not much good at this being a ma and a pa and cooking and ranching all at once. I'm glad you're here."

She put the pan of biscuits in front of him and laid her hand on his shoulder. "I'm happy to be here, Luke. I already think of you as the brother I never had."

"I don't think I want you to think of me as a brother." He looked at her with a flirtatious grin.

"Behave yourself." She gave him a friendly thump to the back of the head, then moved to her chair. It had been on the tip of her tongue to tell him that she had a fiancé, but what a fool she'd look if she told everyone in Lariat she had a fine doctor fiancé, and then Tom never showed.

In all honesty, she'd never talked with Tom about coming to Wyoming before Mary's death, though homesteading had long been her dream. Of course, Tom wasn't interested in her dreams. She'd almost accepted being merely a building block in Tom's life until fate dealt her this new hand. Still, given time, surely Tom would see that she had responsibilities here, and he would come join her and the children. Wyoming needed doctors desperately. Here, he could continue to practice medicine, and she could raise Mary's children and homestead at the same time.

Coming out of her reverie, Amanda marveled as the heaping platter of meat and a huge pan of biscuits disappeared. Who would have thought four children and one man could eat so much, so fast? Maybe she should have cooked more.

"This here is real good grub, Aunt Mandy." Willie sopped up his gravy with a biscuit. "You cook almost as good as Ma."

Almost as good as Ma. Well now, from a five-year-old boy, that must be the ultimate compliment.

As bellies got full, and the eating slowed, Luke picked up the biscuit pan with its four remaining biscuits, stabbed the last

three venison steaks and laid them in the empty end of the pan.
He handed it to Amanda. "Set this in the warmer oven. If Isaac
gets home tonight, this will be a real treat."

Thank goodness. She'd been thinking there'd be nothing left
for Isaac. He'd said he might get home, if he found the cows.

After supper, Luke and Joe Pete returned to work out in the
barn. Will hauled in wood while Susie and Amanda did dishes.

Without looking directly at Amanda, Susie dried a cup and
asked, "Are you mad at Nellie because she wet her drawers
at supper?"

"Of course not. She's not much more than a baby."

"Before Ma died, Nellie used the chamber pot a lot."

If Nellie had been trained before her mother's death, she'd
catch on again with a woman around to remind her from time
to time. Men had the most lackadaisical attitude about some
things.

Amanda put on water to heat for baths. She knew Mary
wouldn't have tolerated her children being dirty, and she felt
a compulsion to put her dead sister's house in proper order.

While the water heated, she called Joe Pete to the house.
"Are you afraid to sleep alone in the loft above the kitchen?"

"You want me to sleep in the house?"

"Of course. Where did you think you would sleep?"

"I don't know. I didn't think on it."

"Where did you sleep in Cheyenne?"

"Before Pa was killed in that hunting accident, my family
lived on the edge of town in my mother's tepee. After she died,
someone burned the tepee. This winter, if I did a good day's
work, a few of the white folks gave me food and let me sleep
in their woodsheds or barns. I ain't never slept in a house."

It took Amanda a moment to realize what Joe Pete meant.
A few *white* folks let him sleep in the outbuildings. The bigoted,
self-righteous, intolerant . . . !

Luke had joined them mid-conversation. He spoke to
Amanda. "Isaac wouldn't have a kid sleeping anywhere but
in here with us where it's safe. Mary and Josh always had plans
for their boys to sleep up in the loft. Until now, Will was the
only boy and not old enough to sleep up there alone." Looking

at Will, he asked, "Are you ready to sleep over the kitchen now that you've got some company?"

Will danced about with excitement. "I'm ready, all right! You bet I am."

While the boys explored their new bedroom, Amanda returned to the sleeping cabin. When she entered the room, her stomach tightened into a knot. Susie stood scrunched into a corner, with her back to the room, sobbing.

Laying down the clean bedding, Amanda went to her. "What's the matter, honey?"

"Willie doesn't love me anymore," Susie gulped between sobs.

"Of course he loves you."

"He moved into the dumb old loft with Joe Pete."

"That doesn't mean he doesn't love you. That means you're growing up and need separate beds."

"I always sleep with Willie. Always! Always! Always!"

Tears filled Amanda's eyes as she took Susie in her arms. "Perhaps Nellie will sleep with you now. Would you like that?"

Susie sniffed and glanced at Nellie before nodding.

Amanda kissed the top of Susie's head. "Enough tears. Help me make up your bed."

Susie smiled tentatively.

As they made the bed, Amanda talked to Nellie about how big girls did not wet their drawers. The attentive way Nellie listened made her think that the child understood a great deal.

On the way to the kitchen, Amanda passed Isaac's bed. She straightened it, wishing he'd been here for supper and for her talk with Susie. He'd have seen how she could handle things.

"Why are you smelling Uncle Isaac's pillow?" Susie asked.

Why *was* she smelling Isaac's pillow? She quickly plumped the pillow and placed it back on his bed.

She had the girls in the washtub when Luke stuck his head inside the door. "I'm going after the sheep."

Open-mouthed, Amanda stared at him. "Sheep? On His Majesty Isaac Wright's cattle ranch?"

Luke grinned. "It's a long story. I'll be back soon."

After he closed the door, Amanda called, "Luke!"

The door opened again. "Yeah?"

"Why don't you take Misty with you. I think she'd like to help with sheep. She's always trying to herd the chickens."

"I'll do that. Our old dog got to the age where he wasn't good for much, but he didn't miss bringing in the sheep."

Amanda returned to her work. Susie's thick blond hair needed washing, but it would never dry before bedtime. Nellie still had an infant's wispy hair, so Amanda washed and towel-dried it. "Your hair is the exact same red as your ma's."

Nellie grinned, then spotted her new playmate curled up on the rocking chair. "Kitty?"

Amanda turned her loose with a pat on the backside, then called Willie. As late as it had gotten, she decided Joe Pete's afternoon bath in the river would suffice for him.

Luke came in soon after, bragging about Misty. "It only took her a few minutes to catch on to herding sheep. She's smart."

Amanda agreed. "In many ways, she's a better dog than that Rasty who chased off after Isaac. Rasty's a roamer. Misty sticks close and will do whatever she can to please."

She laid the cleanest of the dirty towels on the kitchen bench by the washtub. "Your bathwater is on the stove, Luke. If you'd like, I'll put the girls to bed while you bathe."

"A bath sounds great, but I'll take it later. Right now, I think I'll make a pot of coffee to get me through the evening."

Through the evening? Judging from the way her legs were shaking with exhaustion, it was time for bed. All she had left to do tonight was put beans on to soak and get a pan of sourdough biscuits set for breakfast. "Are you always such a night owl?"

"Not me. Isaac now, he likes the nights. When he's here, he settles everything for the night, and I get up first in the morning and start the chores." Luke grabbed the coffee pot and started toward the spring out back. "I'll make coffee; then

I need to haul in what's left of that deer, cut it up, and get it to soaking in salt water so we can jerk it tomorrow. It's two days old now. I don't want it to spoil.''

Amanda forced a smile. He was right. Even the way they ate tonight, they couldn't eat a whole deer before the fresh meat rotted. ''I'll get the girls settled, then come and help you.''

''You go on to bed. I know you must be tired, and Isaac would strangle me if I let you stay up late doing extra work.''

''He probably thinks an *old maid* needs lots of rest, huh?'' She watched with amusement as the color climbed up Luke's neck.

''What gave you that idea?'' he asked after a long pause.

''Never mind. I'll be back in a while to help.''

In the bedroom, with Amanda's encouragement, Nellie used the chamber pot. ''You're such a big girl.''

''Big girl,'' Nellie agreed, beaming at Amanda.

The girls said their prayers, then snuggled in bed together and listened while Amanda told them a story. ''Once upon a time there were three little bunnies who had an aunt and two uncles who loved them very much.'' She ended the story with, ''And they all lived happily ever after.''

When she came out from the bedroom, she found that Luke had sent the boys to bed. She checked on them, thinking they might want a story, but Joe Pete had already fallen asleep. She kissed a drowsy Will good night, and he rewarded her with a tentative, one-armed hug. Sitting in the loft, Amanda held his hand and watched him slip into dreamland. Will had the white-blond hair characteristic of all the Wright men, but his was curly like Joshua's and Luke's, instead of wavy like Isaac's. The only sure thing Will inherited from his mother was her freckles. All Mary's children had freckles. Amanda rather liked freckles. But she didn't expect any child of hers to be freckled, not with Tom as a father. His skin and hair were far too dark.

Of course, if Tom didn't get off his high horse and come to Wyoming, she'd probably die a childless spinster. Tom had told her that she had to be back to Denver in one year or he'd replace her. He said he had no intention of moving anywhere or changing his career plans to suit her whimsy.

Still, she reassured herself for the millionth time, he'd see the error of his thinking when she started writing him about this beautiful country. Where else could a woman get free land just for working it? Amanda smiled to herself just thinking of all the glorious things she'd be able to tell Tom in her letters.

She kissed Willie again before climbing down the ladder. It wouldn't take but another hour or two to cut up the venison.

CHAPTER FIVE

During the night, the rumble of a man's voice woke Amanda. A man's voice? Instant panic. Then she remembered where she was—on the Lazy W, in Josh and Mary's bed.

From the outer room came the unmistakable clinking of a chamber pot. "Big girl?" she heard Nellie ask.

"Yes, you're a big girl," Isaac agreed. "A fine big girl."

"Hold you?"

"Nellie Belle, I'm tired. You need to go back to sleep."

"Hold you!" Nellie insisted with a breaking voice.

"Okay, honey. I'll hold you a little while."

Rhythmic creaks began from the rocking chair next to the potbellied stove. The words to Isaac's soft lullaby sounded suspiciously naughty, like some saloon song. Smiling, Amanda drifted back to sleep. It seemed only minutes later that she awoke to Susie's frantic cries.

"Ma! Ma!"

Flinging back her own blankets, Amanda struggled to her feet. Before she got her bearings, she heard Isaac call softly.

"You're okay, Susie. I'm coming."

Amanda sat on the edge of her bed, shivering from cold, wondering if she should offer to help. When it became apparent that Isaac had the situation under control, she crawled back under her warm blankets and again fell to sleep to the creak of the rocking chair and the strains of a rowdy-worded lullaby.

When Susie cried for her mother the second time, Isaac muttered, "Oh, hell," so low that Amanda would never have heard him if her partially open door hadn't been three feet from his bed.

She pushed back her blankets, intending to rise, but the squeaking floor assured her he was already moving when Luke offered sleepily, "I'll take care of her, Isaac."

"You have a hard ride in the morning. I'll get her."

The soothing words and creak of the rocker began once more.

If this were a typical night, it was no wonder Isaac looked tired and seemed cross. She considered relieving him, then decided maybe it would be better to wait until morning and talk with him.

She listened in the darkness until he returned Susie to her bed. He lay back down on his narrow cot with an exhausted groan.

At daybreak, Amanda lay relishing the warmth of her quilts and listening to the girls talking.

"Nellie, let's get Uncle Isaac." The pitter-patter of little feet was accompanied by intermittent giggling.

"Tickle his ear," coaxed Susie.

There was a roar. Judging from the squealing, the "bear" must have caught someone. Peeking out her bedroom door, Amanda smiled as Isaac nibbled on little ears and tickled the girls.

As the game wound down, Amanda closed her door to dress. By the time she got to the main cabin, Isaac had gone out to help with chores. He'd wrapped the girls in a blanket and left them tucked cozily on the couch in front of the fireplace.

After kissing them, she put on coffee, cautioned the girls not to get close to the fire, and went to milk Nanny. The boys were up when she returned. Willie had crawled in with the girls. Joe Pete nodded to Amanda, then silently left to join the men.

During breakfast, Joe Pete and Nellie sat on the bench opposite Luke and the twins. Isaac sat at the head of the table. Amanda took the remaining seat at its foot.

The second Isaac finished saying grace, Willie reached for his cup of goat's milk. The other children watched anxiously. After the second sip, Willie grinned. "It tastes good!"

Chattering happily, the younger children drank their milk immediately. Joe Pete savored his, sharing it with Nellie.

At breakfast, Isaac assigned morning chores to the kids. Susie would do dishes after she gathered eggs. Willie should haul wood, both for the kitchen and the fire outside, where Amanda had declared her intent to wash clothes. Joe Pete could help Luke.

Isaac helped Amanda stack the dirty dishes on the end of the table. "The house looks real nice, Amanda."

A compliment from Isaac? She didn't imagine he gave many.

"I'm mighty grateful for the biscuits and meat and the bath water you left me last night."

"To tell the truth, I was too tired to empty my bath. I didn't mean for you to have to use secondhand water."

"It was fresh enough. Of course, I never had a bath that smelled like lady's lilac water, but I'm not complaining."

Amanda couldn't believe it. He was grinning. She smiled back. "I heard you up several times last night. Is that usual?"

"Susie's nightmares have been bad since Mary and Josh died."

"Then I didn't upset things? I feared letting Willie move to the loft might have caused Susie to have bad dreams."

"You did what needed to be done. Will needs to start standing on his own two feet; he depends on that smart little Susie too much."

Amanda noted the dark rings under Isaac's smoky gray eyes. In an effort to help, she offered, "I'll start getting up with the girls at night so you can sleep."

His tone lost its easy familiarity and picked up a curt, defensive edge. "When I'm here, I'll take care of them."

"Yes, Your Majesty." Amanda made a little curtsey.

He looked at her in exasperation. "Amanda, I don't have the time or inclination to put up with sass in my own house."

Now here was the Isaac she'd come to know and anticipate.

"Who died and made you God?" she retorted.

Isaac looked as if someone had slammed him in the chest with a bullet. He stormed across the room and had almost reached the door before she recovered enough to stop him. "Isaac."

With his back to her, he stopped and waited.

"I didn't mean for that to come out the way it did."

Without turning around, he said, "You and the kids will be here alone today. Luke needs to check the water holes, so he'll stay out a few days. I won't be back until late afternoon." He let the screen door slam.

As Amanda watched him cross the yard, she scolded herself. *I must watch what I say. But he asks for it, the way he whips out orders and expects everyone to hop to it.*

Hurrying, she spread gravy in the middle of leftover biscuits for the men's lunches, then gathered some canned goods to see Luke through a few days.

Luke thanked her profusely when she handed him his grub sack, making her wish she'd had time to bake something special.

Isaac's perfunctory thank you made her wish she'd had something special to put in his lunch, too. *Like dried flies.*

Isaac gave each little girl a good-bye kiss. When he got to Willie, the boy eyed the extra horse hopefully.

"You think you can handle a day's ride?" Isaac asked.

"I can ride for a whole year without getting one bit tired."

"You promise not to talk my leg off?"

Willie nodded his head emphatically. "I'll only talk if I see something. Or hear something. Or think of something."

Smiling, Luke and Isaac glanced at each other.

Isaac gave Willie a hand up, then turned to Amanda. "Do you know how to use the shotgun we keep on the mantel?"

She nodded, not mentioning that she needed some target practice. Isaac was so high and mighty about everything, she'd practice when he wasn't around.

"Have Susie show you where the ammunition is before you

go to work out here.'' In his authoritative tone, he continued giving Amanda orders. ''When both of us men are away from the house, I expect that shotgun to be within twenty feet of you at all times.''

Yes, Master, Amanda answered in her mind.

''I've got some horses in the corral that aren't completely broken, so keep the kids out of there.''

She nodded, biting back the retort that she probably had enough sense to do that without being told.

She made it without comment until he said, ''Watch out for rattlesnakes!''

''If I see one,'' she drawled coquettishly, ''shall I kill it all by my little helpless self, or shall I stand on the porch and wait for you to come home and take care of the big, bad snake?''

Luke snorted, then roared with laughter.

Isaac stood there, speechless for a moment. He turned to Luke and snarled, ''I thought you had work to do.''

''I do, big brother. Indeed I do.'' Still chuckling, Luke mounted and left.

Completely ignoring Amanda, Isaac turned to Joe Pete. ''Did Luke talk to you about those ewes he left in the lower pasture?''

Joe Pete nodded.

''If I don't get back before dark, take a horse and fetch the rest of the flock.''

''Yes, sir.''

''Don't go getting lost when you go after the sheep. I don't see any point in providing mutton for the coyotes if we can help it, but I damn sure don't want to have to come looking for you.'' He turned back to Amanda and asked curtly, ''Can you think of anything else you might need to know today?''

She counted things off on her fingers. ''Shotgun, corral, rattlesnakes.'' Acting as if she'd just remembered, she touched a fourth finger. ''And make sure no one gets lost because *you* damn sure don't want to look for them. I believe I've got it.''

Shaking his head, Isaac turned his horse and left in a cloud of dust. Willie looked startled, but he caught up quickly.

Isaac had gotten fifty yards or so before he spun his horse

around and returned. "I don't want that cat in the house when I get back. I hate cats in the house."

"I hate mice in the house. The cat stays." Amanda turned her back to him and began to sort the laundry.

After a long moment, he jerked his horse around and left.

She watched covertly as he rode away, thinking Will had better hold on tight and keep quiet for a while. Isaac had to be the bossiest man she'd ever laid eyes on. She hated to be told what to do. That was one of the reasons she wanted a homestead. No man would have the right to dictate what she should or should not do on her own place, not even Tom. But at least Tom usually phrased his commands as requests. Isaac just plain gave orders.

As soon as Isaac was out of sight, Amanda called Joe Pete to her. "Why did Luke leave some sheep up here close?"

"He thinks they're about ready to lamb."

"Lamb?" Oh, well, she could handle that. She'd taken care of pregnant milk goats as long as she could remember.

Amanda had Susie show her where they kept the ammunition. While she examined the gun, Susie sat beside her on the porch.

"Aunt Mandy, why does Willie always get to do the fun stuff like ride with Uncle Isaac or Uncle Luke and look for cows?"

Amanda pushed a strand of fine blond hair back from her niece's forehead. "Don't you ever get to go?"

"No. When I grow up, I get part of Pa's share of the ranch. Now I just get to help cook, do dishes, and watch the baby."

"Cooking and watching babies isn't so bad. Look at me. I get to spend all day with my two precious little girls." She pulled both girls in for a hug.

"But you're not always going to be here."

An opportunity like this might never arise again, so Amanda asked, "Would you like to move away? Like to a nearby homestead?"

Susie looked at her in total amazement. " 'Course not. I belong here. I just wish I was a boy, like Willie."

She sympathized with Susie's longing for something more than a housewife's boring day-to-day routine. She, too, wanted to do something more, to be something more. Tom didn't understand. All he wanted was a woman who looked good on his arm and someone to keep his house in order. And a son, of course—though he was obviously in no hurry for an heir or he wouldn't have tolerated all the marriage-delaying tactics on her part this last year.

Looking at the longing in Susie's face, Amanda added to the list of things she wanted to discuss with Isaac. *Susie's rights.* She had a feeling that Isaac was going to love that conversation.

Joe Pete stood at the corral fence watching the horses. She called him over to explain what she knew about the shotgun. At his age, he could be a big help if there were trouble.

As she examined the gun, Amanda had gotten up three times and hauled Nellie away from the corral fence. *No wonder Isaac had been concerned about the child's safety.*

Back inside, she poured water into dishpans and set them on the table. Susie worked on dishes while Amanda gave the house a kiss and a promise. Nellie occupied herself chasing the cat.

By lunch time, the clotheslines and the corral fence held wet clothes from one end to the other. More laundry lay on the porch.

Amanda groaned when she entered the kitchen to fix lunch and spotted the big kettle of salt water and venison strips. The jerky had slipped her mind. While the children ate mush and canned peaches, she sorted the beans and started soup for supper.

After lunch, she sent Susie outside to play, put Nellie down for a nap, located Mary's big darning needle, and started threading thin strips of jerky onto some black thread. As she finished each string, Joe Pete carried it out to the smokehouse to dry.

The pan of venison to be jerked still had layers of meat left when Susie showed up at the cabin door. "Aunt Mandy, there's sheep down in the lower pasture."

"Your uncles left them there because they're ready to lamb."

"That's what I mean. There's two down. I've been watching, and that one's been down a long time."

Shoot! As if she didn't already have enough to do! "It's good you noticed. I'd better check. Stay here with Nellie. When she wakes, give her a drink and bring her down to me."

On her way past the smokehouse, Amanda called to Joe Pete, "After you hang up that string of jerky, come down to the lower pasture. I may need your help."

As best Amanda could tell, one ewe just needed to be left alone to tend to her natural business. But the black-faced one seemed to be working awfully hard with no visible results. Poor thing. Down at the business end of the sheep, Amanda peered at the proceedings. On the next contraction, she saw the lamb. Then it was swallowed up again. A glance at all the blood under the ewe told her that she'd better do something soon.

Glancing toward the cabin, Amanda saw Joe Pete and the girls start her way. Joe Pete had the shotgun in one hand. *Good heavens!* She'd forgotten about the gun. It was such a nuisance.

During the time it took the children to walk the quarter mile, one ewe delivered, struggled to her feet, and began nudging her lamb to its feet. The ewe having problems still lay panting.

Cautioning the girls to stay back, Amanda asked Joe Pete to help her. "If she tries to get up, hold her down." Pushing up her sleeves, she reached into the birthing canal with one hand. *The lamb was right there!* She got a hold on it. When the ewe followed the dictates of nature and pushed, Amanda gave a mighty pull. She landed smack-dab on her backside, empty-handed.

Nellie stomped with excitement and giggled. "Do it again!"

On the third try, Amanda pulled out a huge lamb. The ewe looked at Amanda with soft brown eyes, bleated piteously, and died. A pool of blood spread out around the animal.

"What we gonna do with the lamb?" asked Joe Pete.

"There's not much we can do. Let's get it to its feet, dry it with grass, and go back to the cabin. Maybe one of the other ewes will let it nurse if we're not around."

"Sheep nighty-night?" Nellie asked repeatedly on the way to the cabin. Susie had a grim set to her mouth and didn't say a word. Amanda took her hand. There'd be nightmares again tonight.

From time to time, Amanda looked toward the meadow. Poor little orphan lamb stood alone, head hanging.

Shadows were long before Isaac and Will returned.

When Amanda looked up from where she was struggling with the heavy laundry tub, she splashed the front of her dress.

Without a word, Isaac dismounted, picked up the tub, and poured it into the flower bed. "I should've told you to wait for me to do the heavy lifting. Where do you want this tub?"

Standing in her sopping dress, Amanda knew she must look for all the world like an incompetent, frumpy fool. She could feel tendrils of hair drooping around her face. Her bodice stuck to her like a second skin, wet from the sloshed laundry water. But Isaac looked exactly as he had when he left that morning. Not a bit dirty or sloppy. His pants hadn't gotten any looser, either. They molded to the muscles in his legs. She could even see a bulge up front where a lady would never admit knowing there should be a bulge. A generous bulge. Sometimes, when Isaac got too close to her, she felt so nervous.

"Where do you want me to put the washtub?" Isaac repeated.

She felt herself flush. "Please put it by the fire. I didn't finish with the laundry. I'll work on it tomorrow."

On his way to the wash area, he stopped to wipe the baby's mouth. "No, Nellie Belle. We don't eat dirt."

Oh, drat. Nellie must have gotten into the dirt in the last ten minutes. She'd had a clean face when Amanda took her to the privy earlier.

"How did things go around here today?" Isaac asked.

Amanda hated to tell him that not only had she not gotten the laundry done, but she'd left an ugly job in the pasture for him. "I had to give one of the ewes a hand with delivering. She died and left a lamb. It's in a bad way." She didn't look Isaac in the eye. "I know I should have put it out of his misery. I just couldn't. The dead ewe is still lying in the pasture."

"I'll go take care of things. Why don't you milk the goat and check for eggs before dark?"

She heard none of the hated bossiness in his voice. Thankful to him for giving her something else besides dead sheep to think about, Amanda nodded. She slipped inside to stir and taste the soup. *Delicious, but too thin,* she decided. After adding a couple of chunks of wood to the stove to hasten the simmering down, she grabbed the milk bucket and returned to the yard.

"I gave the twins permission to play," Isaac said. "You can see their hideout up in that big cottonwood." He pointed it out.

By the time she finished her chores and locked up the chickens, Amanda could see a fire flickering in the pasture. *He's burning the carcasses.* Her stomach rolled over dangerously. *At least I don't have to take care of it this time. I'll be stronger next time.* She and Nellie walked in the opposite direction from the fire toward the twins' hideout. She called to them.

No answer.

They're probably going to pop out and try to scare me. She prepared herself to be appropriately terrified, but a quick check assured her the twins weren't hiding in the little grove of cottonwoods. It was getting dark. Frightened for their safety, Amanda scooped up the baby and ran. Isaac came around the barn leading his horse just as she reached the house. The twins sat perched atop his big gray, as proud as peacocks.

Putting the heavy toddler down, Amanda scolded. "William and Susan Wright, you two scared me to death! I thought you were going to play in your hideout."

Clouds moved into Isaac's eyes, but Amanda stood firm. She didn't care if he didn't like her scolding *his* children.

To her surprise, instead of tearing into her, he turned to the children. "You didn't stop and tell Amanda you were coming down to the pasture to see what I was doing?"

Their guilty looks told the whole story.

"You know better than that! If you change your mind about where you're playing, you let your Aunt Mandy know. You hear me?"

"Yes, sir," they answered in unison.

"Will, I'll see you in the woodshed if this happens again."

"It won't, Uncle Isaac."

"It better not. Now help Aunt Mandy carry in those clothes before it gets pitch black out here."

Arms loaded with clean clothes, Amanda and the children neared the door to the cabin. A horrible stench from inside greeted them. Burned beans.

"Damn," was all Amanda could think to say as she stared at the smoke curling out from under the lid of the stew pot. She must have put too much wood under the pot when she tasted its contents earlier.

CHAPTER SIX

Later that night, as she closed the girls' window, Amanda listened to their chatter. "I want you to go straight to sleep," she said. "We have a big day tomorrow."

"Are you going to tell us a story?" asked Susie.

"Not tonight, dear. It's well past bedtime."

As Amanda left the room, Susie spoke to Nellie. "Ma used to tell us one story and sing one song every night. You remember?"

" 'Member?" parroted Nellie.

Another job she didn't do right. Wearily, Amanda climbed to the loft. She smiled when she found Willie asleep. She kissed his forehead and fought the urge to do the same to Joe Pete. He wouldn't appreciate it. She tweaked his nose instead.

She'd better make some sourdough biscuits and leave them to rise for morning baking. While she was at it, she might as well mix up some mush and tuck it in the oven. Thank goodness, she didn't have to mess with venison tonight. She'd had to use all she hadn't jerked for their supper after she'd burnt the bean-and-venison soup she'd been cooking all day. The very thought of the ruined supper and wasted work made her angry with herself again.

After finishing breakfast preparations, Amanda poured a bucket of steaming water into the washtub, added cool water and a generous sprinkle of her lilac scent, hung a dish towel over the kitchen window, and latched the door. Groaning with fatigue, she lowered herself into the comforting, scented water. Afterward, she removed the towel covering the window and straightened the kitchen. A gentle tapping reminded her to unlock the door.

Isaac smiled when she opened the door. "You don't need to lock the door. Mary had us all trained to stay away when the window's covered."

"I should have realized Mary would have used the covered window signal. Sometimes Pa complained that he might as well take up residence in the barn for all the time he spent out there while his seven daughters bathed and dressed."

"Seven girls. That must have been some frilly household."

"I suppose. I guess I'm the least frilly of my sisters."

Noting Amanda's gorgeous green eyes surrounded by heavy black lashes and the way tendrils of her deep-brown hair flirted with the collar of her nightgown, Isaac decided he'd never sleep tonight if she were any more female. Even with her robe closed, he could see swells and curves that made his pants feel decidedly tight. "You're frilly enough," he commented dryly.

She tried not to look flustered. *Was that a snide comment or a compliment?* He wasn't smiling. Nervously, she returned to moving the tub toward the front door so she could dump her water.

"Leave it," said Isaac. "I'll use your water. Go on to bed." Isaac unbuttoned his shirt and pulled the shirttail free before sitting to take off his boots.

Amanda couldn't resist peeking at Isaac's bare chest as she left the room. Long, lean muscles, with a masculine smattering of chest hair.

She shouldn't be noticing such things.

What would Isaac think if he knew Mary's old-maid sister had been observing his handsome body? *Well, it didn't hurt to look!* Besides, even if she weren't engaged to Tom, she'd never make overtures to a man who already had a woman.

Thinking about the scrawny Widow Brown, Amanda briefly wondered what the older woman had that kept a man like Isaac interested. *Probably skills I've never had the chance to learn.* She began to give her hair its nightly hundred strokes. Of course, as her fiancé, Tom might have taught her some things about physical loving over this past year. She studied her reflection in the mirror. Maybe something was wrong with her.

Of course, Tom wouldn't do anything improper. He laid great store by what society deemed acceptable. When he'd proposed, he'd said he needed a suitable wife to keep his house in order. And she'd been honest with him. She'd told him right out that she'd accepted his proposal so she wouldn't end up without a husband and childless.

A tapping interrupted her thoughts.

Isaac stood outside her door, shirtless, with his long blond hair slicked back. He'd left his tight trousers unbuttoned at the waist. In one hand he held a tin of salve. "At supper, I noticed how raw your hands are." He eased into her bedroom.

Amanda looked down at her rough, red hands. The echo of Teresa Brown saying, "Isaac does admire my hands," sounded loudly in her mind.

Scooping out a generous portion of the salve, Isaac took one of Amanda's hands and worked it in. He apologized when she winced. "It burns, but it heals a cow's udder in no time."

"A cow?" She jerked her hand away.

When he laughed, Amanda scolded, "You'll wake the girls."

He put his fingers to his lips and reached for the door. After closing it, he spread the salve on her other hand. In a low tone, he explained, "Everyone knows a cattleman takes better care of his cows than he does of his woman. Besides, I don't have anything else, and your hands are a mess. Maybe you shouldn't wash the rest of the clothes tomorrow."

"The children don't have anything clean to wear."

"There's no one around but us."

"You never know who might drop by."

"We haven't had anyone drop by in years. Our nearest neighbors are fifteen miles away in Lariat. So don't be trying to get everything done in one day. This work has been building up since we all felt so poorly before Josh and Mary died."

Isaac's eyes filled with sorrow when he mentioned his brother and Mary. Amanda suddenly realized she was going to cry again. *Drat!* She'd managed not to cry all day. Now, right in front of Isaac, she was going to start blubbering.

Without a word, he gathered her into his arms.

She returned his embrace as she leaned against his wide, bare chest and sobbed. "I don't want Mary to be dead."

"I don't want her to be dead either." His voice sounded husky. "And I don't want Joshua in a grave next to her. But they're gone. I've told myself a million times. They're gone."

Gradually Amanda stopped crying, but they stood for a while, wrapped in the comfort of each other's arms. At last, she stepped back and brushed the tears from her cheeks.

"Now you've got salve all over." Isaac dug out his handkerchief and wiped at the greasy smears on her face. "I want to thank you for all you did today."

"All *I* did? There's laundry on the porch, the house needs cleaning, Susie's hair needs to be washed, and supper burned." Tears threatened again. "Worse, I let a ewe and her lamb die."

"Hold on now. Don't be so hard on yourself. Everyone has clean sheets and underthings. Susie's hair is no dirtier today than yesterday. That supper of tomato gravy and venison over cornbread tasted mighty fine." Isaac reached over and pulled down the covers of her bed. "You're plain beat or you'd remember you jerked half a deer, fixed meals for a bunch of us, and kept Nellie out of the corral." He guided Amanda to sit on the edge of the bed. "As for the sheep, there's no accounting for sheep. Sometimes I think they like to die. Besides, I'm real hopeful of having a surprise for you in the morning."

Amanda pulled her slippers off and scooted back, sitting on the bed with her legs tucked under her robe. "I don't know if I can handle any more surprises. This month's been full of them."

"That's the gosh-awful truth. You could've pushed me over with a feather when you got off the train yesterday."

"I'm not so bad. You'll get used to me."

Isaac gazed at her, thinking how beautiful she looked now, and remembering how her damp dress clung to her that afternoon. *I'm afraid I could get used to you, Miss Amanda Erikson. But I'm not going to let that happen.* Aloud he said, "I don't know if I can get accustomed to pots of bean soup sailing past my head."

"You were clear over by the barn, not even close to the front door when I threw that burned mess out." She smiled a bit sheepishly. "I guess I might have acted a tad temperamental."

"If I knew you better, I'd say you had a temper tantrum."

"I don't have temper tantrums."

"If you say so, but there's still a pot of bean soup lying out in the yard." He pulled a blanket from the trunk in a corner and hung it over the foot of her bed. "You've got to quit doing so much. All you really need to do is keep an eye on the kids. You don't even have to cook for Luke and me. Although I'd appreciate your cooking for the kids when we're not around."

"I've no intention of leaving the house unattended. Nor do I want a couple of men cluttering up the kitchen. I'll do what I can to help, and gladly."

"That's mighty decent of you, especially considering how things are between us."

"All I want is what's best for the children."

They'd have to talk about the kids, but not tonight. They were both tired. "We better get some rest," he said. "I'll take Willie with me again tomorrow so you'll only have the girls to watch." He'd almost reached the door when she stopped him.

"Isaac?"

He turned.

"You took Willie today. That would make it Susie's turn to go with you tomorrow."

"Willie needs to learn the ranching business, so I take him along and teach him what I can."

"It's my understanding that you never take Susie. She's part owner of the ranch. Doesn't she need to know all about the workings of the ranch, too?"

"Don't worry about Susie. We'll take care of her until she marries, then we'll buy her out. She'll have a nice nest egg."

"What if she doesn't want to marry or sell out? What if she wants to stay and work this ranch as a full partner?"

"Hell, Amanda. You don't know what you're talking about. A woman has a different role from a man on a ranch."

"You mean, she knows her place."

"Her place?"

"Her place! Right smack dab in front of a cookstove, with a well-worn path between a man's bed, a laundry tub, and a cradle."

"Some women don't think that's so bad!"

"And some women are probably bored to death. If you love Susie, surely you want her to at least have the option of not marrying unless she wants to."

Isaac looked at Amanda with sudden understanding. *This was the old maid in her talking.* Maybe he'd better hear her out, make her feel like she was saying something worth listening to.

"What if, God forbid, something happens to Willie?" Amanda continued. "Susie will need to know how to ranch. Susie and Nellie, when she gets old enough, need to be out riding with you, learning the ways of the land and animals."

"What makes you think being out on a horse in the hot sun or bone-chilling cold is barrels of fun?"

"It's got to be better than washing clothes and cooking."

"So that's the problem. You're unhappy with your lot in life and you're trying to make it sound like I'm not treating Susie right." He shook his head. "I already told you, if you don't want to do things around here, don't do them!"

"We aren't talking about me. We're talking about Susie."

"Susie's never complained."

"Not to you. She probably suspects you'd get a little hostile—like you are now."

"I am not hostile."

"You're gritting your teeth and your neck muscles are bunched up."

"They're my damn muscles. They can bunch up if they want."

"While you're already tense, there's something else."

"And I bet I get to hear it."

"I appreciate your backing me up when the twins didn't tell me they changed their playing area. But if Willie's going to get a licking, so should Susie. They were in on it together."

"Hell, Amanda, I can't go whipping a girl."

"It's only fair. She needs to learn her actions cause consequences."

"You don't have to beat on a girl. You can talk to her and she'll behave."

"Are you saying Willie's too stupid to talk to? He needs a licking to learn things? And Susie, who needs to know nothing about ranching, is so smart that talking teaches her?"

"For Pete's sake, I didn't say anything of the kind. Women are easier to explain things to." He added pointedly, "Most women."

"Too many women get through life batting their eyelashes, pretending ignorance or innocence."

"Hell! I came in here to thank you and all you've done is find fault. Anything else you want me to change?"

"Stop swearing in front of the children."

Isaac groaned. "You don't quit, do you?" He stepped out and pulled her door closed.

"Isaac?"

What now? He stuck his head back in the door in time to see her stand and drop her robe on the end of the bed. *Damn.* He could see shadows through the nightgown. And what he saw looked good! How could anyone so lovely be such a pain in the patootie?

"Please leave my door open a crack so I can hear the children. I'll want to help with them during the night."

"We already talked about that." He enunciated the next sentence slowly and carefully so she couldn't mistake his meaning. "When I'm home, I'll tend the children at night." He paused, looking into Amanda's challenging green eyes. "If you don't like my decisions, you can go to he—" He saw those clear green eyes begin to sparkle with anger. "Heck." He closed the door very firmly.

He'd hardly reached his bed when Amanda reopened the door.

"Isaac?"

He looked up.

"Has anyone ever mentioned that you're a pain in the posterior?" She blew out her lamp, leaving the door wide open.

CHAPTER SEVEN

When the roosters woke Amanda with an exuberant crowing contest, she dressed quietly. The day before had been a fiasco. Today she'd get the laundry finished, put the house in order, and cook a decent supper.

Tiptoeing out of her room, she glanced at Isaac's empty bed. Surprised, she hesitated, then remembered Isaac would be doing the morning chores while Luke was riding the range.

She peeked at the sleeping girls. Such darlings. Susie had cried out twice during the night, but Isaac had responded so quickly that she hadn't had a chance to help. Oh, well. Susie was used to him anyway. She'd settled right down.

Outside, her dogs gave her a royal welcome. She threw a stick for Misty, then scratched Rasty's ears. "What do you mean by pretending you're so glad to see me? I've seen you sneaking off with Isaac." The dog grinned happily at her. "Mrs. Teresa Brown is liable to have to speak with you about claim jumping."

When Amanda walked inside the barn to milk Nanny, Isaac laid aside the shovel he'd been mucking out a stall with. "Good morning. I thought you'd never get out of bed."

Such a tyrant! Thinking he could even dictate when she

rested. Maybe this day *wouldn't* go any better than yesterday. "I didn't realize I had a sleeping schedule, Mr. Wright."

His smile faded. "I didn't mean it like that. I want to show you that surprise I told you about at bedtime."

"Oh." She felt herself flush. "I'm sorry. I guess I got up on the wrong side of the bed."

"You're probably still tired from all you did yesterday. How about it? Do you feel up to a little walk down to the pasture with me?" His gaze followed Amanda's glance toward the cabin. "We can see the house from the pasture. Besides, the kids usually sleep until full sunup. I want to show you something."

When he offered his hand, her stomach did a flip before settling into a nervous knot. She suddenly discovered that she wanted very much to walk with this long, lean, hard-headed, cussing rancher. But, as she had just reminded Rasty, Mrs. Teresa Brown had already staked her claim on Isaac.

Then there was Tom. She had to remember Tom.

Still, who would know if she held Isaac's hand and walked only as far as the pasture with him? In a few weeks, she'd be on her homestead and there would have been no harm done.

She hung the milk bucket on a fence post, took his calloused hand, and strolled silently beside him through the dewy grass.

In the lower pasture, Isaac pointed to a fat ewe nursing a large lamb with a pathetic-looking coat. "Do you recognize that fellow?"

Amanda moved a little closer. The ewe immediately got between her lamb and them, but not before Amanda realized the lamb had a jacket made from the skin of another lamb.

"That old ewe was standing guard over a dead lamb when I went to bring in the sheep last night," Isaac explained. "I did like I've seen Josh do. I slipped the dead lamb's hide on that fine, big lamb you helped deliver yesterday. It looks like this ewe was either tricked into thinking he was her own or wanted to believe. At any rate, the lamb has a ma, and the ewe has a baby."

"You did a good job."

"No. *You* did a good job. That lamb would've died with its mother if you hadn't helped it be born."

Amanda returned his smile, noting that his gray eyes had a way of changing colors with the light. Right now, they matched the soft gray of the morning sky. But they looked tired.

She'd underestimated his dedication to the children, and she owed him an apology. "I'm sorry if I came across too critical, Isaac. I heard you up in the night with Susie. Though you and I don't agree on every little thing, I still appreciate what you've done for the children."

"Susie's in a bad way, still having nightmares," he said as he leaned against a fence post and stared into the distance. "Maybe it's good you're going to be here a while. Do you think she needs a woman's touch?"

"I honestly don't know. Perhaps she needs more time. We'll see what we can do working together."

He raised a skeptical eyebrow. "You think we can do that?"

"We can try."

Isaac smiled slightly and took her hand again. They walked back in silence. When they reached the yard, he examined her rough, chapped hands. "Your hands look awful. Forget the laundry for now. I'll do some each evening when I come in for supper."

"I'll do the laundry. My hands aren't *that* bad."

"I disagree. I expect you to keep them out of the water today and put some salve on them when they get to hurting."

"Yes, Master."

Isaac grimaced. "You're sure a sassy thing."

"I can't help it. Things pop out of my mouth before I think about them." *Much like your cuss words.*

"You take it easy. I don't want you so tired you get sick."

"A little work isn't going to make me sick."

"Ranch work is hard."

"You forget. My father is a farmer, and I've been his chief helper since I could walk."

"I'll bet you haven't been trying to take care of four kids and feed two extra men as well." Isaac gently smoothed the top of her hands with his thumbs before he let them go. She could hardly believe they'd spent almost half an hour together and hadn't seriously irritated one another. Maybe this would be a good time to tell him about her homestead. The words were on the tip of her tongue when the little girls came out onto the porch.

At breakfast, Isaac ate his mush salted, without the goat's milk in the pitcher in the center of the table. When he finished, he spoke to Amanda. "As much as I hate the idea, I guess I'd better go spend some time with those sheep. I counted at least ten new lambs this morning, so I'll keep the herd in close today. It seems like Josh spent most of his time with them during lambing. I'm not sure what I'm looking for or what I'll do when I find it, but I can't bring myself to leave dumb animals without care. And believe me, sheep are dumb, in every sense of the word." He drained his coffee cup and stood up.

"How does it happen that you have sheep, Isaac?"

"Joshua insisted on having some sheep. He had some fool idea that cows and sheep can graze together, that they even like different greens." Isaac warmed to the subject. "Another thing I hate about sheep is that they need a lot of tending. Now, an old cow, you can put her out on the range where there's food and water, and she pretty much takes care of herself and her calf. These damn sheep, you have to move them around every day." As he walked around the table, Isaac took Nellie's spoon and helped get a few bites of her mush inside her mouth instead of on her chin. "Personally, I wish Joshua had got rid of every da—" He paused, glanced at the children, who were listening attentively, then finished, "I wish he'd got rid of all the sheep last year."

"Why didn't he?"

"There's a cash market for wool. Josh felt it best not to have all our eggs in one basket. I don't disagree with that, but I prefer to invest any extra money in more land. Joshua kept every ewe born last year. I'm telling you, he got plumb loco about those sheep. He even ate mutton. Claimed it tasted good."

"Mutton *is* good, Uncle Isaac," Susie interrupted. "Ma said you're being contrary about it."

"Your ma said that?"

Susie and Willie nodded.

"Then it seems your Aunt Mandy isn't the only sassy woman in the family." On the way out, he grabbed his cowboy hat from the hook by the door.

Midmorning, Luke came home. He skinned the rabbits he'd brought for supper, and played with the children for a few minutes before he came over to where Amanda had her sore hands deep in the laundry water.

"How's everything?" he asked.

"Okay, I think. I watched you with the children just now. You have a nice way with them."

Luke beamed. "I'd like to have ten or twelve of my own."

She laughed. "Your poor wife! Look at all this laundry, and there's only seven of us. I shudder to think how much work it would be to have a dozen to keep clean and fed."

"Now you sound like Isaac. He's always spouting off about how too many children and too much work can drive a woman to an early grave." Luke grinned and looked toward the lower meadow. "And speaking of an early grave, if I don't get down there and help with the sheep, Isaac's liable to wring my neck."

When Isaac entered the yard later, he stomped to the corral where Joe Pete was walking a big bay mare in wide circles. Amanda could see from the set of his back that he relaxed as he watched.

After a few minutes, he called to Joe Pete, "If you can get a saddle on her, I'd like you to ride with me today."

Joe Pete looked her way and smiled when she nodded.

While he saddled, Isaac came to where she stood wringing out his shirt, stretching this way and that to relieve the soreness in her lower back.

"Not that I'm surprised," he said, "but I see you decided not to wait for me to finish the laundry." Without asking, he rubbed the small of her back, then her shoulders. "That any better?"

"Much." *Of course my stomach did a cartwheel when you touched me, and I'm having trouble taking a deep breath, but my back is much better.*

He nodded toward the corral. "Did you see Joe Pete saddle that horse by himself? The boy's small, but he's got spunk."

"I've been worrying about him in there with those half-broken horses."

"I've watched him. He can take care of himself. Some people are like that with horses. They have a gift or something. In this country, being a good horseman is a sure way to get respect. In the years to come, Joe Pete will have to work hard to get the respect other men get by walking into a room."

"What makes you say that?"

"You know how folks are. Some won't be able to let go of the fact that he's half Indian."

"He's also half white."

"And that may keep him from being accepted by the Indians."

"Poor Joe Pete." Amanda felt her eyes moisten. She hadn't realized that Indians might be prejudiced against him. But remembering how she'd come to have him with her, she couldn't deny the truth of Isaac's statement about white folks. "I don't understand how anyone can be so cruel to an innocent child. You've been around him. He's a dear boy, grateful for the least favor and always ready to do more than his share."

"What you and I know, and how the world works, are two different things. I've been thinking, Amanda. For his sake, you may want to leave him here with me when you return to Denver. He fits in fine with the kids. Another mouth to feed isn't a problem around here."

That Denver thing again. *Now!* her mind insisted. *Tell him you aren't going back to Denver. Tell him Joe Pete will continue to fit in just fine with the children—on a homestead at the edge of the Lazy W.*

But before she could decide how to phrase things, Isaac started toward the barn.

Just as well. She wasn't a coward, but one had to choose

the right moment to discuss some things. Perhaps tonight, after a good supper, they could have a chat.

While Isaac and Joe Pete prepared to leave, she got two hard-boiled eggs out of the teapot that sat on the back of the stove.

"Thanks, Amanda," Isaac said when she handed him the eggs and some leftover biscuits. "I know it must sound selfish, but it's good to have someone taking care of me for a change."

Her stomach cartwheeled at his kind words. "I suppose we all feel that way at times. Last night when you put salve on my hands, I felt pampered. I hope I remembered to thank you."

"My pleasure." Isaac mounted and began a review of the previous day's instructions. "Keep the kids out of the corral."

"I will."

"Keep an eye out for snakes."

"Yes, Isaac."

Isaac looked toward the laundry area. "Where the hell's the shotgun?"

Amanda could feel her face growing hot, and this time it wasn't with embarrassment. The man and his orders were infuriating. "In the house," she snapped.

"Damn it, Amanda! You should've gotten that gun out the minute I left the yard this morning!"

That did it! She must've been insane to have held his hand and taken a walk with him at dawn! What right did he have to tell her what to do? Especially when he used that tone of voice!

"Yes, oh Great Master." She held her exaggerated, humble curtsey until Isaac, Joe Pete, and Rasty were clear of the yard.

When they were out of sight, she stormed into the house to get the damn shotgun.

CHAPTER EIGHT

In spite of Isaac's offer to help, Amanda had insisted on finishing the laundry herself. At supper, he set the rabbit stew on the table, then took the serving ladle from her. Her hands were beet-red from all that hot water and lye soap. They had to be hurting. "I'll be glad to dish out the stew. You sit and enjoy it."

For once she didn't argue. Except for the scrape of spoons against tin bowls, all was quiet at the table for a few minutes; then Willie broke the silence.

"You cook way gooder than Uncle Luke, Aunt Mandy."

Luke agreed, laughing at his ineptness in the kitchen.

The twins gleefully took turns telling Amanda about the mishaps that occurred when Uncle Luke cooked for them.

"His biscuits looked like sugar cookies once," said Susie. "But they were so hard we couldn't eat them."

"He let me chuck them at tin cans. They was good rocks," offered Willie.

Isaac joined in the laughter. It felt right to have Amanda in the house. He couldn't keep from looking at her. He liked the easy way she laughed, the sound of her voice, the brisk way she moved. He even liked her sassy mouth—if she just wouldn't undermine him in front of Luke and the kids. Tonight, however, she didn't seem the same bustling woman he'd been watching the last couple of days. "You aren't eating, Amanda."

"I'm a little tired. If you'll excuse me, I think I'll fold the clothes." She started to rise.

"Sit!"

"Yes, Master." She threw herself down on her chair.

Every eye at the table turned to Isaac.

He put his hands in the air in a sign of surrender. "I'm sorry. That didn't come out the way I intended. I meant sit and rest. I'll fold the laundry after the chores are done."

For a moment, he had the crazy thought that she'd accept his apology without comment. He should have known better.

"You are the *bossiest* man! I bet you give orders in your dreams!"

Luke grinned. "I'd say Amanda knows you real well, Isaac." He chuckled and, after Amanda smiled, the kids laughed with him.

Looking around the table, Isaac welcomed even this uneasy laughter. Mealtimes had been grim around here since Mary and Joshua died. It gave the family a wholeness to sit down to supper and talk and laugh together. Amanda was good for all of them.

By supper's end, every bite of the food had disappeared. Concerned, Amanda looked at the empty plates. "Did I make enough? Are you full?"

"My guess is that there are more full bellies tonight than we've seen in a while." Isaac smiled and reached over to gently prod Susie's tummy. "This one feels full. Luke, check Willie."

After tickling the boy's belly, Luke declared it full.

Nellie stood on the bench and offered her protruding baby tummy for Joe Pete's assurance that she'd also eaten her fill.

Amanda laughed at the shenanigans. *Isaac could be a dear with the children. If only he'd quit ordering her to do things.*

As Isaac stood up and started to clear the table, he said to Susie, "Get on out and play. I'll do the dishes."

The startled little girl didn't take time to question her good fortune. She grabbed Willie's hand and cleared the room.

Luke gave a satisfied stretch. "Supper was extra good, Amanda. If you'll excuse me, I want to work on those rabbit hides I skinned out today. You coming, Joe Pete?"

Joe Pete nodded toward Nellie, who was standing on her tiptoes trying to lift the latch on the screen door. "Nellie wants to go out. I'll watch her close, if it's okay." He shifted his gaze between Isaac and Amanda, seeking permission.

"That's very sweet of you, Joe Pete," answered Amanda.

Isaac started to stack the dishes. "It didn't take Susie long to skedaddle when I told her I'd do the dishes."

"It's no fun for her to be working in the house all day, then have to do more work inside after supper," Amanda said, scraping the bottom of the stew pot into a dish for the cat and dogs.

While Amanda fed her small animals, Isaac stared out the window at the kids playing chase. He had to watch what he assigned Susie to do. Amanda was right. She was just a kid.

He poured steaming water into the dishpans and shooed Amanda away when she reached for the dishcloth. "Why don't you get a start on those clothes you want to fold?"

The sight of her swollen, red hands at supper had upset him, but he hadn't wanted to comment in front of the kids. They might worry if they thought anything was wrong with Aunt Mandy.

He began washing the cups. "Joe Pete and I had a talk today. Did he tell you his mother was Sioux?"

"He only told me his parents were both dead and he had no one." Amanda rapidly folded a clean towel, laid it on a pile with one hand, and reached for another item with the other.

Isaac took his time, trying to phrase things right. Amanda was so damned touchy. He didn't want her to go flying off like a mad hen. "Keeping Joe Pete around might be trouble. After talking to him, I agree it's not likely he'll have any white kin looking for him. He told me about his pa. I know the mountain-man type. When they get woman-hungry, they court or buy an Indian bride. If he bought her, her family might have been glad to let her go. But if he courted her, she may have run away with him, and the Indian family could want Joe Pete."

"I thought he wouldn't be welcomed by the Indians."

"Not all of them are prejudiced, just like not all of us are. They love their family the same way we do. They have a different upbringing, is all."

"I suppose Joe Pete's Indian family have the right to make decisions about him, but how would we find them?"

"With your permission, I think I have a way to locate Joe Pete's family."

With her permission? She bet that was an expression Isaac didn't often use. "Would your plan involve Hawk?"

Isaac washed a plate slowly. "Sounds like someone has been talking when they should have been keeping their mouth shut."

"Perhaps other members of this family have more faith in me than you do."

"It's not a matter of faith, Amanda. I don't think you're deliberately trying to hurt any of us."

"Of course I'm not trying to hurt any of you!" She slammed another dish towel onto the pile.

"Don't go getting your dander up. I know you've got good intentions. What do you know about Hawk?"

"He's the leader of a little renegade band. They don't want to live on a reservation so they camp back in these mountains."

"That's about it, except Hawk's my close friend, and it might happen that I'll see him this summer. I'll talk with him about Joe Pete. Maybe he'll have an idea of what to do."

"Isaac, please make sure Hawk knows that Joe Pete is safe, and that I want him to stay with me."

Amanda looked at him with those big green eyes, and Isaac darn near dropped a plate.

"I couldn't bear to send him to his Indian family if there's any danger they'll mistreat him. When I picked up Joe Pete in Cheyenne, some bully had chased him under the depot platform. I think he might have shot Joe Pete if a couple of fancy-dressed women hadn't happened along and persuaded the brute to come with them." Looking perplexed, Amanda stopped folding clothes. "Why would any woman want someone like that to come with her?"

He shrugged.

"Anyhow," continued Amanda. "The train wasn't ready to leave so I tried to get Joe Pete from under the platform. He was so terrified, he scrunched himself as far back as he could get."

"Poor kid."

"The really odd thing is this. About ten minutes after the women left, one of them came back, and he came right out for her. She told me that the man who was tormenting him earlier had taken to beating Joe Pete every time their paths crossed."

"I saw his bruises when we bathed at the river and wondered about them. I'm surprised someone didn't put a stop to it."

Amanda's eyes filled with tears. "That's what I said to the woman. She said no one besides herself seemed to care whether a half-breed kid lived or died. She offered me twenty dollars and the price of a ticket if I'd take him as far as I was going." Amanda folded the last piece of laundry. "I decided he'd be better off with me than where he was, so I bought his ticket myself and put her money away to save for Joe Pete."

Isaac studied Amanda while he scrubbed the stew pot. Contrary as she was, she had a good heart. Unfortunately, she had some mistaken ideas, too.

While they had a civil conversation going, this might be a good time to talk to her about something else. After giving it some thought, he had a plan of sorts about the kids. Maybe they could work things out, compromise. "We need to talk about your taking the kids away."

Shoot! She got that obstinate set to her chin right off. He decided to try anyway. Perhaps if he said things right, she'd think on his ideas at least. "I don't know about you and Mary's agreements when you were young, but my brother—*and* your sister—wanted their children raised here. Luke and I love those kids. If it makes you feel better, I could hire a housekeeper, and I'll send you money so you can visit anytime you want. When the kids get older, they have to go to school. I can send them to you for the winters instead of boarding them in Lariat."

Amanda seemed to be studying on his words. She smoothed a towel before looking him in the eyes. "I've been meaning to talk to you about the children, and to more fully explain my intentions. I suppose this is as good a time as any.'' She cleared her throat. ''This isn't easy.''

''Then maybe you'd better say it right out.''

''I've heard you aren't a big supporter of homesteading.''

''Of course I am. I told you that's how we got our start here.''

She smiled. ''That's such a relief. From what I'd heard, I gathered you'd be upset when I told you that I filed on the homestead next to your ranch. I'm going to farm it.''

Isaac dropped a pan to the floor.

''That way,'' she continued, ''the children will be close to you. Why, I imagine you can see them every day if you want to ride over and check on them.''

''Whoa! Back up there. What the hell do you mean, you filed on a homestead next to the Lazy W?''

''I wrote to the land office in Buffalo and filed on the homestead bordering the Lazy W on the east. Mary provided me with an affidavit saying Mr. Anderson left three summers ago.''

''Mary wrote you?'' Mary knew that he liked to use the meadows surrounding old Anderson's homestead for grazing.

Amanda shifted in her seat. ''Well, we wrote back and forth about it occasionally.''

Remembering all the letters he carried to town from Mary for Amanda and all the returns, it suddenly dawned on him that Mary always read only the first part of Amanda's letters aloud. Then she'd make some blithe remark about the rest being girl-talk and put the letter away. Sounded to him now like he should have been more concerned about the content of the remainder. This country was getting to where there were more fenced-in places than not. Ranchers were having trouble finding water and places to graze. He didn't want any homesteader farming close to his ranch.

Not only that, he wondered if Mary had told Amanda about why Eric Anderson up and left his homestead. Judging from the way Amanda acted at the river about one little water snake, he had the idea that Mary hadn't revealed all. There wasn't any point to bringing all that up—unless Amanda forced him.

Rather than cause any more hard feelings, Isaac decided to

try reasoning, even if pointing things out logically didn't seem to affect Amanda's decisions. "Homesteading's too hard for a woman alone. It's da . . ." He rephrased. "It's darn near more than one strong man can do with a woman's help. That's why Luke, Joshua, and I were in this ranch together, to help one another."

"I can see where you need help on a place as big as this, but I'm going to have a hundred-and-sixty-acre homestead."

"In this country, you can't make a living on one-hundred-sixty acres. You've got to get your additional one-hundred-sixty under the Timber Land Act and buy the six-hundred-forty acres of desert land allowed. Then, if you can find enough open grazing, you *might* have a chance."

"I don't need all that. I'll have a few goats, maybe a milk cow, chickens, pigs, a team of horses, those kinds of things."

"You aren't listening to me. Most years we don't get enough natural moisture to grow much grass. One-hundred-sixty acres isn't enough land to feed the animals you're planning."

Amanda laughed as if he were joking. "My father is a farmer. I know how much land it takes to feed animals, and I'll do fine."

"Damn it, Amanda! What you're wanting to do can't be done on a hundred-sixty-acre homestead!"

"You're impossible. Here I am, telling you the children will be nearby, and you're still fussing." Stomping around him, she jerked open a kitchen drawer and threw in the clean dish towels. "I'll simply do what I have to do, and you'll have to learn to deal with it." She started back by him, then stopped. "By the way, I'd appreciate it if you'd learn to discuss things without raising your voice and cursing at me."

Isaac took hold of her arm. "If you don't want me yelling, then try listening to what I'm saying when I *talk* to you." He realized that he'd made a tactical error when he saw the angry glint in her sea-green eyes.

She glared down at his soapy hand where it gripped her upper arm. "Let go of me!"

He dropped his hand, but stepped in her way so he had her sandwiched between the table and the still-hot stove.

"I didn't mean to grab you like that."

"But you *did* grab me! And now you're blocking my way!"

"I took hold of you because you're like trying to keep up with a damn tornado. You move around so fast, I can't hardly keep track of you, let alone talk to you."

"You won't have to worry about the way I move much longer. I intend to go to my homestead—with the children—as soon as possible. Now get out of my way!"

In an effort to relieve the tension, Isaac threw his hands straight up in the air and moved aside. Amanda didn't smile.

"Don't ever try physically to stop me from anything again!" She stormed across the living area. On her way to the sleeping cabin, she scooped up the girls' clean clothes.

Isaac called after her as she left the room. "I don't suppose an old maid with a temperament like yours has to worry much about men handling you in any way!"

Instantly, Amanda returned to the room, laid down the clothes she still carried, and walked toward him threateningly.

What the hell? Holding silverware in one hand and a dish towel in the other, Isaac backed up until she had him wedged between her slim body and the cupboard. His knees grew weak as he watched her expression change from one of hostility to one of soft promise.

She moved in close, almost touching him with the length of her body. He could feel her breath on his neck, smell her lilac scent. Sliding her hand up his sleeve, she brushed an imaginary something from his shoulder.

"Excuse me," she purred into his ear. "I meant to move the salt and pepper over here." As she reached into the open cupboard behind his head, her wonderful full breasts, the very ones he'd been trying not to look at for three days, pressed into his chest. She leaned back, surveyed the new placement of the spices, and shook her head. "No, I believe they were in a better spot before." Again, she leaned into him to move the shakers. It took her a few seconds to position them to her satisfaction. "That's better."

Immobilized, he watched the sway of her dress as she moved back across the room and picked up her armload of clothes.

When she reached the doorway leading to the sleeping cabin again, she turned and said sweetly, ''Isaac, when you finish there, be a dear and call in the children. It's almost time for bed.''

Able at last to take a deep breath, Isaac looked at the doorway she'd gone through, then down at the bulge in the front of his pants. *Damn!* After pouring himself a half cup of coffee, he sat at the kitchen table. Maybe he'd better rest a minute or two before he called in the kids.

CHAPTER NINE

Amanda leaned against the closed door to her bedroom and took deep breaths, trying to settle the butterflies in her stomach. *Honestly! Sometimes I do the most impulsive things. How am I going to face Isaac after almost climbing all over him?* Things hadn't turned out exactly the way she'd planned. She'd thought to show him that she wasn't exactly unattractive to men. She'd ended up enjoying the feel of Isaac's lean body next to hers. Very much enjoying it, in fact. Her cheeks burned.

Even with Tom, she'd maintained a chaste relationship. Not that it had been hard to do. Nothing in Tom's actions or words led her to believe he wanted it any other way. She'd been engaged to him for a year and had not been as close to him physically as she had to Isaac this third day of their acquaintance. Tom kissed her hello and good-bye on the cheek. *Tom* was a gentleman. *He* would never have made disparaging remarks about her being single.

Amanda hated remarks about her being unmarried, although no one had been as rude as Isaac, calling her an old maid to her face. Her family and friends generally phrased it carefully, or told her inspiring stories of single women they knew who *seemed* to have almost normal lives. *As if being twenty-five years old and not married makes me a defective person!*

Staring into the mirror, she wondered if she were abnormal in some way. A humiliating thought occurred to Amanda, darkening the blush already in her cheeks. What if Isaac hadn't been moved in the way she intended by her performance? He had a woman friend in town already. The last thing he probably wanted was some old maid acting a fool, rubbing up against him so . . . so . . . boldly.

At any rate, she'd be darned if she let on to Isaac that she'd embarrassed herself! She stood tall, tucked a few wisps of hair back into the bun at the nape of her neck, and marched back into the living area to get another load of folded clothes.

Isaac glanced her way, then drained his coffee mug. By the time she returned for more clothes, he'd called in the children and left to do the last of the evening chores.

Alone in her room that night, Amanda tried five times to get her waist-length hair braided, but her hands were so raw and rough that they kept getting snagged in her hair. She finally had a braid of sorts started when she heard a small tap at her bedroom door. The door swung open, revealing a surprised Isaac.

"I guess the latch didn't catch," he said.

Suddenly he smiled, and she knew how a mouse felt when there was a cat in the room. After pushing the door closed with his hip, he silently moved toward her, not stopping until she was trapped between the chest of drawers and his body.

"What do you think you're doing?" she hissed in a whisper. The last thing she wanted to do was wake Luke or the girls.

"I brought some salve for your hands. I thought I'd put it on the dresser here." He actually touched her breasts with his chest as he leaned around her and laid down the salve. He studied the salve's placement. "No, that's not right." He leaned around to her other side and nuzzled her hair as he moved the salve. "I think it would be more convenient for you over here."

"Out!"

Isaac bent and whispered in her ear. "But I'm not sure I've got that salve in just the right place yet."

"You are a rat!" she snarled into the hollow of his neck when he reached around her again.

He backed away and just plain grinned.

Reluctantly, she smiled back.

"Now, turn that lovely old-maid body around and let me see if I can fix your hair."

"Old maid" didn't sound so bad when he put it like that.

It took Isaac several minutes to get some semblance of a braid. "That's not too good."

"It'll keep my hair from tangling while I sleep. Thank you."

"You sure you don't want anything on this dresser behind me? I'd be glad to stand here while you lean around me to look."

Amanda felt the red creeping up to her face.

After he had left the room, she turned down the lantern and climbed into bed. *Too bad I'm such a coward. I think he might have liked me to get something off the dresser.* She again reminded herself that Isaac had a woman friend. And she had a fiancé in Denver.

Lying awake for a long while, Amanda replayed the moments when he had her backed up against the dresser. She'd liked the feel of his masculine body so close to hers. Too much.

The next morning she awakened to the sound of Willie's excited voice, "Susie! We get to go to town with Uncle Isaac."

"Who said?" Susie demanded.

"Uncle Isaac said. I've got to wake up Aunt Mandy."

Amanda feigned sleep.

"Aunt Mandy?" Willie whispered. He gave the bed a shake.

Doing an imitation of Isaac's bear roar, Amanda grabbed him. He wiggled, squealing, but not really trying to get away.

The girls joined him on her bed. After tickles all around, Willie begged Amanda to get up. "Me and Susie get to go to town. Uncle Isaac said to tell you he used the goat's milk for some lambs whose mothers died, so you'll have to make flapjacks for breakfast. And he said you're supposed to make a list.''

"A list?''

"Like Ma used to. Of things you want from town.''

"Is Isaac ready to go?''

"Nope. He has some stuff to do before he can hitch the team. He says for you to get up.''

"All right. You three run along while I dress.''

A few minutes later, a forlorn Susie appeared in the bedroom doorway, wrinkled dress in hand. "My dress isn't ironed. I don't think Ma would like me to go to town with my dress wrinkled.''

"Don't worry, sweetheart. I'll have that pretty dress ironed before Uncle Isaac is ready to go.''

Less than thirty minutes later, Amanda had Nellie tended to, Willie's and Susie's clothes sprinkled and rolled into balls to dampen evenly for ironing, and a batch of flapjacks mixed. While she cooked, she occasionally added to the supply list.

As the men washed up for breakfast, one or the other of them would call in and have her put such-and-such on the list.

She considered adding a few things she'd need for her homestead, then discarded the idea. Given his opinion of her homesteading, she suspected Isaac wouldn't be over-pleased to pick up supplies for her. Besides, it would be best to purchase the necessities first and see how far her money went. Perhaps one day when Isaac didn't need the wagon, she'd ask to borrow it. That way she could get her trunks from Jim Callahan's livery and do some careful shopping at the same time.

"Be sure to get all the staples we'll need for a while on that list,'' said Isaac as he sat down to breakfast. "The snow up high will be melting and running off soon, making the creek flow over its banks. We won't be able to get the wagon to town for a month or so when that happens.''

"Do I need to be careful how much we spend?'' Good excuse to ask something she'd been wondering about anyway.

"Put everything on the list.'' Isaac helped himself to more flapjacks. "If it looks like too much to haul, you and I will go through the list and decide what we can do without this trip.''

We'll decide? Surprised, Amanda looked toward Isaac. She thought he singlehandedly made all the decisions on the Lazy W. But if they could buy all the supplies they wanted, it sounded as if money wasn't a problem to the Wright family. That was pretty much what she'd gathered from Mary's letters.

"I'm sorry we all can't go into town today," Isaac told the family at breakfast, "but we need room in the wagon for supplies. With this late start, we'll have to stay in town tonight."

Poor man, Amanda thought. How will he ever cope with a night in the Widow Brown's boarding house? Her appetite suddenly failed her and she excused herself from the table. "I want to iron the children's clothes." As she started pressing Willie's shirt, she said, "I don't know what you want to wear, Isaac. If you'll get a shirt, I'll iron it for you."

"Don't you worry about ironing Uncle Isaac's shirt, Aunt Mandy," Willie bubbled, " 'cause we're in a hurry. Widow Brown will do his shirt for him."

"From what I've heard," Amanda said, wetting her finger and testing an iron, "the Widow Brown will do most anything for your Uncle Isaac."

Isaac dropped the food from his fork. Luke choked, trying not to laugh.

"Yeah," Willie continued, "I don't think she likes me and Susie much, but she likes Uncle Isaac real good. When we used to stay at the boarding house, her and Uncle Isaac would wrestle all night. That's why Pa told Uncle Isaac to let us kids stay with the Callahans when we go to town with him."

Amanda looked at Isaac and raised her eyebrows. "Oh, really?" she drawled. "How interesting."

Willie started to add something, but Isaac stopped him. "Quit flapping your jaw and eat, or I'm damn well going to leave you here."

They finished breakfast in silence.

Glancing at Isaac, Amanda noted that he didn't look her way. Of course not, she thought. Why would he want to look at an old maid? He was headed to Lariat and a more *experienced* woman.

Less than an hour later, Isaac stripped off his work shirt and reviewed the supply list with Amanda as he washed. "Put canned milk on the list in case we have some more bum lambs."

Amanda tried not to watch the play of Isaac's back muscles as he vigorously soaped his chest and underarms.

"We had three lambs born during the night whose mothers died or wouldn't claim them. I'm taking them to town." Isaac filled his cupped hands with water from the basin and rinsed his face. "Jim and Martha have milk cows. They'll be glad to hand-feed the lambs and use the mutton this winter. That way, I don't have to mess with the orphans, and I don't have to put them down. I hate to put an animal down, but if we hadn't had your Nanny's milk, I would've had to put those bums out of their misery."

Isaac took the supply list from Amanda. Reading and nodding his head in agreement, he lathered his shaving brush.

Fascinated, Amanda caught herself looking up from the note she was writing to her family. It reassured her that Isaac, who sometimes seemed so forbidding, made the same silly faces Pa made shaving. Smiling to herself, she half wished Isaac would ask her to check to see if his cheeks were smooth enough the same way Pa asked her mother to check his. Her mother always cheerfully protested, but Pa sneaked a few kisses after every shave.

Amanda considered writing to Tom, but she hated to keep Isaac waiting. She asked her mother to send a message to Tom saying things were going smoothly in Wyoming and that she'd write soon.

Outside, she helped Susie and Willie climb into the back of the wagon with the orphan lambs. Isaac looked devastatingly handsome, all cleaned up with his wavy blond hair slicked back. Amanda almost envied Teresa Brown. Her stomach knotted. She shouldn't think of what might be happening at the boarding house this coming night. It was none of her business. None.

Isaac scanned the area carefully, as Amanda had seen him do each time he prepared to leave the ranch yard.

She saved him the trouble of giving her orders by reciting,

"I'll keep Nellie out of the corral, watch for snakes, and the shotgun will be my constant companion."

He shook his head in mock frustration, but smiled slightly.

Amanda handed up the lunch she'd prepared for them. "Have a . . ." She paused. "A pleasurable trip." Pointedly, she added, "And be sure to tell the Callahans how much I appreciate their having the children stay the night with them so you and Mrs. Brown don't disturb their sleep with your wrestling."

Enjoying the flush on Isaac's cheeks, she picked Nellie up and showed her how to blow kisses toward the departing wagon.

Nellie didn't realize she'd missed the trip until the wagon cleared the yard. "I go!"

"Not this time, honey." Amanda strode back into the house with her skirts whipping around her ankles. She set Nellie down and handed her a rag doll.

Nellie flung the doll away, then ran to the screen door. When she found it locked, she threw herself to the floor.

Ignoring the child's tantrum, Amanda began her work. She tried not to picture Isaac's lips and the way he wet them with the tip of his tongue before he spoke. She'd watched his lips for three days now and wanted so much to feel his mouth on hers. But tonight, while Amanda slept in his house, Isaac would be "wrestling" in Teresa Brown's bed.

If she ever had to stay in Lariat, she'd rot before she slept in the boarding house and chanced overhearing Isaac and Mrs. Brown together. Not that what Isaac Wright did was of any concern to her. She'd simply be more comfortable somewhere else. Anywhere else.

Staring at the howling toddler, Amanda dried the same mug repeatedly. She wondered what it felt like to lie with a man. Until now, she hadn't thought about actually being with a man in the physical way—at least, not very often. But when she thought about Isaac's long, muscular thighs and how they strained at the seams of his pants when he mounted his horse, Amanda ached in the most secret of places.

Heavens above!

Hastily, she put the dry cup on a shelf. She shouldn't be thinking about Isaac's legs this way. The way her mind acted, a body would think Tom lacked muscles or good looks. He most assuredly had both. Tom was considered a catch, a fine man, an excellent doctor, prosperous—and ever a gentleman.

Deep inside she felt an uncomfortable, niggling suspicion that most engaged men were a lot more ardent with their fiancées, and a lot less polite. She never had to worry about Tom backing her against a dresser and leaning in to "accidentally" rub his chest against her breasts. As near as Amanda knew, Tom hadn't even noticed she had breasts.

But Isaac had noticed, and leaned. She gave a shake of her head. This obsession with Isaac was unseemly. What if Tom were to suspect how . . . lustfully she felt about Isaac? Worse yet, what if Isaac found out? Even standing alone in the kitchen, Amanda could feel her cheeks burning with humiliation. *I've got to move to my own place. I simply must get off Isaac's ranch.*

She scrubbed the last of the breakfast pans with a vengeance, then walked out to the barn to speak to Luke. "I believe I'll take the children and go check out my homestead."

Luke obviously chose his words very carefully. "Isaac doesn't want you going over there."

"There are some things in the world that even the great Isaac Wright doesn't control. Now if you'd kindly point me in the right direction, I'll leave you to your work."

He offhandedly gestured toward faint wagon tracks leading into the trees. "That trail ends on the Anderson homestead."

"You mean *my* homestead."

Luke stood as if undecided what to do, then ventured, "I thought I'd ride up to check on Joshua and Mary's homestead. No one's been on the place since before they fell sick. Maybe you and the kids would like to ride with me instead of going off on your own today."

"Thank you for asking, Luke. But to tell you the truth, I'm sure seeing Mary's homestead would just make me cry again. And I'm so tired of crying."

"I know what you mean. Me and Isaac cried a lot at first. Especially Isaac. He blames himself, you know. Isaac figures if he hadn't gone to town, he wouldn't have got sick. Then none of us would have got sick the way we did. Mary and Joshua wouldn't have died. It eats at him. But he didn't do it on purpose."

"Of course he didn't." As overbearing as Isaac could be, he was a family man. His gruff love showed in every move he made with the children. "I'll have you take me to Joshua and Mary's place someday, Luke, but not today. I want to see my homestead. It's time to start looking forward instead of back." Preparing to walk, she called to Joe Pete and lifted Nellie to her hip.

"Isaac isn't going to like your going over there, Amanda."

"Nevertheless, I'm going."

"Then I'll saddle some horses and we'll ride over together."

"Aren't you afraid of what *Isaac* will do when he finds out you took a day off without his permission?"

His response was curt. "It happens I often agree with Isaac because what he says is good for the Lazy W. And it also happens I agree with him about you going to that rattlesnake-infested homestead." He started toward the barn. "I'll have the horses saddled in about a quarter hour. Just wait for me!"

When Luke got riled, he had the sound of Isaac. She decided to wait. It would be easier to ride than carry Nellie anyway.

While she waited, she might as well pull the weeds in Mary's little flower bed. After reaching for a handful of weeds, Amanda hesitated.

Rattlesnake-infested.

The words hit her. Luke had referred to her homestead as rattlesnake-infested. She looked down at the overgrown flower patch in front of her. A snake could hide in there easily. Or right under the porch. Or anywhere really. She hated snakes. Amanda pulled back her hand. *Don't be silly,* she told herself. Five minutes ago, she'd have had no trouble reaching into the flower bed to weed it; now she shook like a complete coward. She'd just run the broom handle through the undergrowth before she pulled the weeds.

She started for the broom on the porch, then realized Luke could see her from the barn. He'd likely tell Isaac that she was so frightened of snakes, she had to poke around in the front flower bed with a broom handle. She'd have to pull the weeds as though she hadn't a fear in the world about snakes.

Taking a deep breath, Amanda grabbed a handful of weeds. Luke chose that moment to walk over to her. "I don't want any hard feelings between us. I had no call to use that tone of voice with you earlier. You have a right to your homestead."

"Forget it. I shouldn't have made that remark about you needing Isaac's permission."

Luke smiled. "What say we make a day of the trip to your homestead? Can you fix us up with a little picnic?"

"I'll need a few minutes, but a picnic would be fun."

As Luke walked away, Amanda gave the weeds still clutched in her hand a good pull. Nothing wriggled. Of course nothing wriggled! This fear of snakes was plain childish. She pulled three more handfuls of weeds before she went inside to put together a lunch.

During the ride to her homestead, Amanda studied the area carefully. They passed through an evergreen forest, moving down into an area dominated by quaking aspen, and at last came out into an open river bottom. At the homestead's fence, the barbed wire gate had been thrown off to the side.

Brimming with excitement, Amanda dismounted in the yard and took Nellie from Luke. She started to put the toddler down, but Luke stopped her. "I'll carry her."

"She probably wants to get down and run."

"Not here. I told you this place has an extra-bad reputation for rattlesnakes. No one's been around, so likely the sons-of-guns have taken over."

Good heavens, sometimes Luke sounded *exactly* like Isaac! Amanda refused to let either of them spoil this day. "Since you're that worried, would you hold her while I look around?"

"Be careful. I'm not exaggerating about the snakes."

Snakes, snakes, snakes. That's all she heard from him. In spite of her firm intentions not to be afraid, she felt goosebumps rise on her arms and neck.

Joe Pete moved to her side. "I'll look around with you."

Inside the barn door, he picked up an old pitchfork. Now and again as they walked around, he'd stab at a pile of hay and they'd both listen, but they heard no spine-chilling rattle.

The barn had withstood time remarkably well. Of course, things needed to be cleaned and repaired, and cobwebs and dust dominated. She'd expected that. What she hadn't expected were the multitude of things the Swedish family had left behind. She wondered what made a family up and leave everything like that.

She knew from the land office records that Eric Anderson had never filed a legal claim on this land. Earlier, she'd had little compunction about filing. Now she wondered if she'd done the right thing. What if the Anderson family came back one day?

The damp-smelling dugout hadn't survived as well as the barn. But here again, the house had many necessities to make life comfortable—a serviceable cookstove, a big bed with a trundle bed beneath it, a table and benches, even a few cooking pots and some dishes. Everything was covered with cobwebs and dirt. She'd have to make new mattresses.

She would've liked to roll up her sleeves and start to work immediately, but Luke was waiting out in the yard. Reluctantly, she returned to his side. "I suppose we'd better find a place to feed these children," she said. "I'll come back tomorrow."

Luke shifted uneasily. "This place is no good, Amanda."

"No good? It's exactly like Mary described in her letters. The barn is big and solid. The well is dug. I have a shelter over my head. And Wild Horse Creek is on my border, so there's a never-fail source of water for irrigation."

"If you're dead determined to homestead, I'll show you other places. I'll even help you dig a well and put up a cabin whether Isaac likes it or not. The west side of the Lazy W— where I've staked out my homestead—is prettier than over here."

She spun slowly. "Look at these mountains sheltering three sides of us. Here in front of the dugout, I can see forever. No place could be more beautiful, or more perfect for what I need."

"Damn it, Amanda! Isaac's right. You never listen! This place is crawling with snakes!"

"*Crawling?*" She laughed. "I might not like snakes, but I see no reason to let a snake or two scare me off my land."

"Isaac will fight you on this one. He doesn't want the kids over here. And this time I'll back him all the way."

Squaring her shoulders, Amanda stared at him. The amiable young man she'd known for three days had been replaced by a determined, protective uncle. "No one but the government has the right to tell me where I can or cannot homestead. You and Isaac better get used to having me as a neighbor." She took Nellie from his arms. "Now, do you want to go back to the Lazy W, or are you going to take me on that picnic you promised?"

"Ah, hell, Amanda. I'm going to take you on a picnic." He helped her mount, then got on his horse, muttering, "Someone should have warned me that women were so all-fired stubborn."

CHAPTER TEN

Amanda spent a restless night, partly because of homestead plans spinning in her mind, and partly because she missed Isaac's gentle snores. Her stomach felt a little sick, thinking about Isaac with the Widow Brown. At first light, she rose, anxious to put her mind and body to work.

She felt cowardly relief when Luke announced at breakfast that he'd be gone for the day, moving cows to a high mountain pasture. When she left for her homestead, she wouldn't have an unpleasant argument tainting the first real workday on her land.

After Luke left, she rushed through her chores. Joe Pete caught a horse and rode bareback with Nellie in front of him while Amanda walked. Even on foot, she made good time. Isaac couldn't possibly object to the children being less than an hour's walk away from the Lazy W's main ranch house. When he and Luke got over their unwarranted nervousness about snakes, they'd have to admit this location was perfect.

The gate in the fence had a broken pole. She'd fix it on her way out. Then she could drive the goats over here, out of Isaac's way. The sooner she moved to the homestead, the better.

Amanda left Joe Pete and Nellie waiting outside the dugout

while she fetched a shovel and went inside to check for snakes. After a search for slithering things, she batted down the overhead cobwebs, placed Nellie on her hip in a makeshift sling, and spoke to Joe Pete. "I want to clean out the area where the back wall collapsed. You can play outside. Watch for snakes."

The boy left, but soon returned to the dugout with an empty can. In spite of her assurance that she could clean the dugout alone, he used the can as a scoop and went to work alongside her.

Well past midday, Amanda gave a sigh of satisfaction. "Doesn't it look nice in here with all that dirt gone?"

Seeing the skepticism in Joe Pete's glance around the room, Amanda laughed, then picked up their burlap grub sack from the table. "Well, it looks much better. Let's go eat lunch."

She settled upon a picnic spot about thirty yards from the dugout in a small grove of quakies. Nonchalantly, she called Misty to her. If there *were* any snakes, Misty would warn her.

The toddler had gotten increasingly heavy after the first hour or so, and Amanda gladly put her down. She started to untie the lunch sack before she realized how filthy her hands had gotten. She looked at Nellie and Joe Pete, then groaned. They couldn't possibly eat this dirty. "Joe Pete, keep Nellie right beside you while I draw some water so we can wash up."

Leaving the children and the dog in the shade, Amanda strode to the well. Just as she bent to lift the first of the boards covering it, she heard an ominous rattle.

She froze, her eyes frantically searching the area around her. She saw a movement, then watched a thick, gray body slither completely under the board she would have lifted first.

Not wanting to alarm Nellie, Amanda called casually to Joe Pete, "Pick up Nellie, then bring me the shovel." She kept her gaze glued to the area where she'd seen the snake.

With Nellie riding on one hip, the boy loped to the dugout. "Thanks." Amanda didn't look up when he handed her the shovel. "Now I'd like you to take Nellie into the dugout and play with her for a few minutes."

Joe Pete was no fool. She could tell that he'd caught on to the problem by the way he'd hurried to get the shovel.

"You want me to take care of things out here while you go inside?" he asked.

"This is my problem."

"I thought you were scared of snakes."

"I am. But I'm going to get over that, starting now. Take Nellie inside so she won't be frightened."

Cautiously, Amanda lifted the board with the scoop of the shovel. The rattler moved quickly, trying to escape. Keeping well back, Amanda took a mighty stab with the shovel. She cursed when she realized she had the snake pinned but hadn't decapitated it. The shovel was ten inches back from its ugly triangular head. *What should she do now?* She couldn't use her foot to press the shovel down. That would put her foot within striking distance. She darn sure couldn't let go. Misty wasn't helping matters by standing back six feet and barking.

The snake thrashed under the shovel. Summoning her courage, she gritted her teeth and stabbed repeatedly. After what seemed like hours, the snake quit moving.

Shaking, Amanda walked out of sight of the dugout door and vomited. When she returned to the yard, she found Joe Pete standing outside the dugout with Nellie playing at his feet.

He said, "I watched from inside. You want me to bury it?"

"Deep!" she answered.

"Can I have the rattles?"

"What in the world do you want the rattles for?"

"A collection. I think I'll start a collection."

Amanda shivered in disgust. *The things boys came up with!* "You can keep the rattles, but bury the rest of that thing far away from the house."

"Yes, ma'am."

When Joe Pete returned from disposing of the snake, Amanda was still trying to work up the courage to lift the remaining boards from the well.

"You don't look so good," he said.

"I'm still a little frightened, I guess. I keep wondering what might be under the rest of these boards."

"Give me the shovel. I ain't scared of them."

Amanda looked at the boy, then around the beautiful valley. She glanced back toward the roomy barn and the sturdy dugout. *Her homestead. Her home.*

No lousy, good-for-nothing snakes would keep her from having what was lawfully hers. This land might have belonged to the crawling things once, but she was serving them notice. They'd better clear out! This was her land now!

From this day on, Joe Pete could keep the rattles of the snakes *he* killed. She was making a rattle collection of her own. If a gunfighter could count his battles by making notches on his gun, she could count hers by hanging rattles over the barn door. "Please go watch over Nellie a while. I have to do this."

Praying she didn't end up with the largest collection of rattles in the country, Amanda braced herself, then cautiously lifted a board with the shovel.

CHAPTER ELEVEN

As Isaac approached the ranch yard, he scanned the area carefully. Fifteen years ago, he'd been riding the range when Indians raided the ranch. He'd been working his own homestead the day his father had been struck by lightning as he rode into the Lazy W's yard. And he'd been in town the day Mary fell on the icy porch and lost her second set of twins. Over the years, he'd become almost superstitious about his homecomings.

Since Mary and Josh died, he'd worried more than before about something happening to the kids while he was gone. Thank God he had Amanda to help with them now.

This evening, he smiled in relief. Amanda was on the front porch cutting Luke's hair, and Nellie was hanging on the corral fence watching Joe Pete work the big sorrel stallion. With the twins bouncing around on the wagon seat beside him, Isaac could account for all the people who were important to him.

"Hello, strangers," Amanda said when they reached the porch. "I'm almost finished here. Then I'll lay out your supper."

"We ain't too hungry," Susie explained. "Mrs. Callahan fixed us a big noon meal."

"And it made the Widow Brown real mad, too," added Willie. " 'Cause Uncle Isaac ate with Callahans. Show how she did when Uncle Isaac told her that he was eating with Callahans, Susie."

The little girl sniffed and dabbed at the corner of her eyes with an imaginary handkerchief before swishing down the steps in a perfect imitation of Mrs. Teresa Brown.

Luke roared, and Isaac took a half-hearted kick at Susie's behind with the side of his foot. Giggling, Susie and Willie disappeared around the house with Nellie hot on their trail.

Isaac shook his head. "It's bad enough the way those two act around here, but I live in fear of what they're going to say or do in town."

Amanda smiled and snipped off a lock of Luke's hair. "Children have a way of being disconcertingly honest."

Don't I know it, thought Isaac, remembering Willie's remark in front of Amanda about he and Tess wrestling all night. It hadn't rightly mattered so much before Amanda came if anyone knew a little wrestling might be going on over at Tessie's. But for some reason, he didn't want Amanda to know anything about him that might make him less in her eyes.

He watched Amanda run her hands through Luke's hair. He didn't like the relaxed, contented expression on Luke's face one bit. Or the friendly way she and Luke bantered back and forth.

"Watch it," Luke complained. "I don't want to be bald."

"I like bald men," Amanda teased.

"Then hand me a razor."

She laughed as she dusted the loose hair off Luke's shoulders and pushed him out of the chair. "Get on down there and start unloading the wagon while I dish up Isaac's supper."

Though he wasn't hungry, Isaac followed her inside, just wanting to be with her. "The house looks nice."

Amanda smiled. "Thank you. I didn't do too much around here. After you left yesterday, Luke took me to my homestead. I went over and worked on my place most of today. The children and I should be able to move over there in about a week."

With a bite halfway to his mouth, Isaac stopped and stared

at her. Pleasantries forgotten, he threw down his fork and stood up. "I told you before, but I guess you weren't listening. Those kids aren't going anywhere with anyone."

"As you said the other night, we can cooperate on this."

"You're absolutely right. We'll cooperate. I'll go out every day and keep this ranch running so they have a roof over their heads and food in their bellies. You can stay here with them if you want, and make sure they're safe and cared for until I return. If you don't like that plan, you can *cooperate* by getting your cute little fanny off my land."

Amanda stepped up to him and tilted her head to look him in the eye. "Don't give me orders! I'm just as much blood relation to those children as you are. Now, since it appears you're finished eating, why don't you take *your* cute little fanny outside and unload the wagon."

Isaac glared at Amanda. He was going to strangle Luke. What the devil did the fool mean by showing Amanda the way to Anderson's homestead?

"You kids, get inside!" Isaac commanded as he let the screen slam. He snarled at Luke. "I'll see *you* in the barn! Now!"

Luke rose to his full height, maybe three or four inches over Isaac's own six feet. "You better have a damn good reason for talking to me in that tone of voice."

Isaac stomped toward the barn. Luke followed him, rolling up his shirt sleeves as he walked.

From the kitchen window, Amanda watched the barn door. As she filled plates for the subdued twins, Nellie climbed up to the table to eat another supper.

"Do you want to eat again, too, Joe Pete?"

"Naw. I ain't hungry."

The frightened look on his face as he stared out the screened door reminded Amanda of how he'd looked when she first picked him up. "Everything will be fine. The men have some things to talk about. Come and cut up Nellie's meat, please."

Once the children were settled at the table, Amanda took off her apron. "If I'm not back from the barn when you finish eating, wash your dishes. Stay in the house until I return."

* * *

She pushed the barn door open just as Isaac said, "Maybe we *will* be all right without the kids until Amanda comes to her senses. But will the kids be okay without us?" The anger in his voice had been replaced by sadness. "Damn it all, Luke, have you forgotten what happened to the last child on that place?"

Luke shook his head. "I ain't forgot."

Isaac was leaning up against a horse stall, with his hands draped over the top rung, his head leaning against his forearms. He didn't acknowledge Amanda's approach.

"What happened to the last child on my homestead?"

When neither man answered, she asked again, "What happened?"

"Juliana Anderson was tiny, not yet four years old," said Isaac, with a rasp in his voice. "Cutest little thing you ever saw. She ran right into a rattler. When she fell on it, it struck her in the chest. I heard Eric fire his rifle signaling for help, but she was dead before I got there. Poor baby, all bloated up and sick-looking. You could tell she died hurting."

Isaac straightened up and brushed at his eyes with the back of his hand before turning to Amanda and finishing his story. "Gerta lay down on the bed and never got up again. She refused to talk, eat, or drink. With his woman and his child gone, Eric up and left one day. Now you're wanting to take the kids away from me and onto that godforsaken, snake-infested homestead."

"There are snakes everywhere! I suppose you're going to tell me you have never had a rattler on this place."

"We've had a few over the years."

"And any of them could have bitten one of you. You're being ridiculous! I refuse to let snakes run me off a homestead!"

Isaac glared at her. "Ridiculous or not, I want those kids in their beds on the Lazy W come nightfall. If you cross me on that, Amanda, I'll put you in that wagon, haul your butt to town, and buy you a one-way train ticket home."

"Sending me home on the train will be mighty hard to do,

since my home is three miles east of here on the banks of Wild Horse Creek.'' She started toward the door, then turned around suddenly. ''By the way, you frightened the children half to death,'' she told Isaac. ''You better go speak to them.''

''You're the one responsible for this house being in an uproar. You go speak to them!''

''If this house is in turmoil it's because you aren't willing to make a simple change in your life.''

''Moving the kids away from the Lazy W is not a simple change!'' His voice had grown loud again.

''Poppycock! They were gone from the ranch many times. The children lived on their parents' homestead every summer.''

''But they had both Mary and Josh to watch over them.''

''Then I'll have to watch hard enough for two people.''

''It's impossible to get the outside work done and watch over the kids at the same time, Amanda! Luke and I have been trying.''

''I'll have one-hundred-and-sixty acres. If I climb up on a high rock, I can see all four corners of my homestead. I bet you can't ride the perimeter of your ranch in a day.''

The men glanced at each other.

''Not only that, I have three goats, some chickens, a cat, and two dogs. You, on the other hand, probably only have a vague notion of how many cattle you really have. I don't have the same land or animal responsibilities you have.''

''When you talk about my responsibilities, you forget to include the kids,'' said Isaac. ''I want them here at the end of every day, or I'll put you on that train to Denver.''

''I've done everything I can to make you understand that I share your concern for the welfare of the children,'' she said. ''Right now we need to put this aside and get inside with them. The way you've acted has upset them enough for one day!''

Isaac slapped his hat against his thigh, clicked his heels, and bowed to Amanda. With a mock-gallant wave of his arm, he gestured for her to lead the way. Once in the yard, Isaac called to the children in his normal bossy roar. ''You kids get on out here and help unload this wagon.''

All four children came out to the wagon slowly, giving Isaac a wide berth at first, but they were their bouncing selves before the supplies were unloaded.

That night, after she finally got the children to bed, Amanda followed a now-familiar routine. She made a huge batch of sourdough biscuits to bake first thing in the morning, then put the mush into the still-warm oven so it would be ready for breakfast.

Exhausted, she carried a basin of warm water to her bedroom. She put an extra drop of lilac scent in the water before she washed up and slipped into her best nightgown.

The light knock on her bedroom door didn't surprise her. She half suspected Isaac wouldn't be able to sleep with things as unresolved as they'd left them that afternoon. But she'd be darned if she'd open the door!

"Come on, Amanda," Isaac said in a loud whisper. "I made you some tea and the cup's hot."

She reached for her robe, then changed her mind. God forgive her, but she wanted Isaac to see what little her modest night-gown revealed. And she wanted him to approve of what he saw.

Opening the door, she silently appraised Isaac. Barefoot and shirtless, the dark blond hair on his chest still had a damp look from his bath. His wet, slicked-backed hair revealed a white strip of forehead where the sun never hit, a dead giveaway of a man who works outside all day and wears a hat.

He handed her one of the two steaming mugs he held. "You didn't eat much supper. I thought maybe you'd like some tea."

"Thank you." She reached out and took the cup, determined not to invite him into her bedroom.

They heard a snort as Luke's rhythmic snores broke.

With a glance toward Luke's cot, Isaac whispered, "Maybe I should come in so the light doesn't bother him."

Maybe so, thought Amanda. She had absolutely no control of her mind when Isaac was around! How could she be so absolutely furious with him and yet still want him near? It made no sense. She quietly closed her bedroom door behind him.

"What with the way things went when I got home, I forgot

to ask how your hands are.'' He took her hands in his. ''They still look mighty sore. Turn around and I'll braid your hair.''

Feeling self-conscious, Amanda stood in front of the mirror and let Isaac pull out the pins holding her hair in a bun at the base of her neck. He brushed through her waist-length locks in smooth, steady strokes. It felt wonderful, partly because it was so relaxing, but mostly because Isaac was touching her. His touch had become far too important to her. Her legs grew weak when he gathered a handful of her hair and smoothed it across his cheek. ''Your hair's so soft, and it smells just like flowers.''

After he finished the braid, he glanced at her bare feet. ''I bet your feet are cold. Why don't you climb into bed?''

Amanda scooted her legs under the covers and propped up her pillows so she could sit.

Reaching into his pocket, Isaac pulled out a packet. ''I brought you something from Martha and forgot to give it to you.''

''Assorted flower seeds. How thoughtful of Martha.''

''She picked out the pink yard goods for the girls' bedspread, but I chose the stuff for the boys. Do you think I picked out the right things for Joe Pete?''

''He's delighted. I'll bet he's never had a new pair of boots or a warm coat. And he's smitten with the pocket knife.''

''He's a good kid.''

Amanda tried to stifle a yawn and failed.

''I guess I better let you get some sleep.'' Isaac stood beside the bed for a moment before sitting down next to her. He smoothed back a lock of hair and leaned toward her. When his lips almost touched hers, he paused, an unspoken question in his eyes. She knew what was coming. She could have stopped him, but she'd sooner have cut off her right arm.

Gently he kissed her, then opened his lips a little and moved back and forth over her mouth with a touch as light as a butterfly. The second kiss was firmer and, fool that she was, she kissed him in return. He rubbed his cheek across hers and she heard him sigh. Three more quick kisses, placed here and there on her lips. ''I'd better go,'' he said at last.

Every feminine instinct Amanda possessed told her it would be sheer folly to stop him. Still, she felt a deep sense of loss as she watched him pick up their empty tea mugs.

At her bedroom door, he raked through his hair with one hand before speaking. "Amanda, don't misinterpret what I just did. You might tempt me, but your kisses don't change what I expect. Those kids better be in their beds at night or you're gone."

He might as well have thrown a bucket of cold water on her. He knew she'd deliberately tempted him. She should have put on her robe before she let him in her bedroom. No, she should never have let him in her bedroom. And she should never, never have kissed him. She kept her disturbed thoughts to herself, meeting the challenge in his eyes. "I'm not so naive that I think you're especially picky about who you kiss."

"What?"

"As you say, casual kisses change nothing between us." *But I won't be stupid enough to let the kisses happen again.* Still holding eye contact with Isaac, she reassured him. "For now, it will be as you command, Your Majesty. The children will be here each night."

When Isaac's eyebrows drew together and he looked as if he were going to say something more, Amanda slid under her covers and turned her back on him. She didn't want him to even suspect how badly he'd hurt her—not that an insensitive lout like Isaac would care whose feelings he hurt.

Before he opened the door, Isaac said, "I know you had your mind set on that crazy plan of having a homestead, but I'll make it up to you."

Impossible! Nothing can make up for trying to kill my dreams. Not that it mattered. Her dreams weren't dead. But the budding feelings she had for Isaac had just suffered a killing frost. She didn't want Isaac Wright ever to touch her again as long as she lived.

CHAPTER TWELVE

When Isaac woke the next morning, Amanda's mattress lay bare, the quilts folded in a neat pile on the trunk.

The sleeping girls looked like little angels with their heads together on the pillow they shared. Isaac watched them for a minute before he went out to help Luke with the chores.

Amanda already had towels and white things strung over the clotheslines. She was bent over the tub, busy stirring another load. He walked over, intending to put his arms around her waist from behind, give her a little hug. It seemed to him that anyone who'd returned his good-night kisses would welcome a morning hug. She might have been upset when he left her room last night, but likely she'd be over it now. Unless he missed his guess, she hadn't minded his kisses. He'd surely liked hers.

He'd hardly gotten his arms around her when she grabbed a wet towel and walked out of his loose embrace, slick as a whistle. Red-faced, he followed her to the clotheslines. "You mad?"

"I'm busy."

He'd give her some space. Let her think about how right he was to want the kids safe on the Lazy W. She could pout all she wanted. He still intended to have those kids safe at home. Right now, he might as well help Luke with the chores.

Amanda had the sheets from the adults' beds hanging on the corral fence when he and Luke finished. Susie was sitting on the porch looking lonely, so Isaac gathered her up and cuddled her while Amanda filled the washtub with more clothes. After blowing Susie a kiss, Amanda hurried into the barn with the milk bucket.

Ten minutes later, Isaac had two little girls in his arms, a towheaded boy leaning against his side, and one ornery billy goat with stubby horns attacking the soles of his boots. From inside the house came the enticing aroma of biscuits and fresh coffee.

When Amanda came by them on her way to the kitchen, she shooed Billy Boy off and bent to kiss the children. Isaac blatantly stuck out his jaw for a kiss. She ignored him.

Yes, sir! He was in big trouble. But he'd see how long she'd hold out when he took a cup of tea to her room tonight. She might be all business the rest of the day, but Amanda turned into a woman through and through when she pulled on her nightgown and let down her hair. The thought of Amanda's nightgown made Isaac long for the day to pass. She'd be fit to be tied if she knew how much he could see through that white cotton.

He sent the kids inside. In the barn, he adjusted his pants. Having Amanda around had become downright painful.

At breakfast, Isaac announced that they would have a family meeting as soon as they cleared the table.

"A family meeting?" asked Amanda.

In his usual fast-talking way, Willie explained. "We have family meetings when something big needs to be decided about the ranch, or someone isn't doing their chores. But I been doing my chores, so this must be something else."

Susie spoke up, "I like family meetings. Even us kids get to vote, 'cept Nellie. She's too little."

After Amanda and Susie cleared away the dishes, Isaac and Luke poured themselves cups of coffee and sat at the table. The twins took their usual places on either side of Luke. Since this appeared to be the start of the family meeting, and she wasn't family, Amanda excused herself and headed outside.

Isaac called her back. "We'd like you to stay for the meeting. And call in Joe Pete. This decision concerns the kids. We don't want it said that we went behind your back."

When everyone was at the table, Isaac wasted no time. "I want to get rid of Joshua's sheep. They're a blamed nuisance."

Luke argued in favor of keeping the sheep. "They aren't that much trouble except right now while they're lambing."

When Luke finished, Amanda spoke. "I think Luke's right. My family always keeps a few cattle and a small herd of goats, and they do fine together. Lots of small farmers back home have sheep and cows together."

"We aren't small farmers. We aren't farmers of any kind!" Isaac insisted loudly.

"Excuse me! Before you say anything negative, I'll remind you that some of my favorite people are farmers." Amanda added pointedly, *"And* I suggest you're trying to influence the children by raising your voice like that!"

"Like what?" Isaac came to his feet and glared at Amanda.

"Like this!" She stood up and shouted back at him.

Isaac looked stricken. He glanced down at the twins, who had scooted in close to Luke's sides. Joe Pete, eyes cast downward, had moved as far to the end of the bench as he could. Luke grinned, looking from Isaac to Amanda and back.

Amanda sat down.

Isaac ran his hand through his hair and poured another cup of coffee before he sat down. "I didn't mean to get so loud. I want to take the sheep to town and sell them now instead of in the fall. Luke wants to keep them. Are we ready to vote?"

"I've got a suggestion," said Amanda. "Why don't I take the sheep to my homestead? There's ample grazing land around there."

"Your homestead?" Isaac asked through gritted teeth. "I thought we had that settled."

"Your edict was that the children be in their beds on this place at night. That's how it will be."

"A woman alone on a snakey homestead won't have lots of time for sheep!"

For the first time, Joe Pete spoke. "Amanda won't never be alone. I'll always be with her. I can help with the sheep."

When they voted, Isaac's was the only nay.

Obviously resigned, he turned to Luke. "Would you ride to town and leave word for the shearing crew to come out when they get in the area. I led Jim to think we wouldn't be needing them this year. We'll move the sheep to *Amanda's* homestead after they're sheared."

"You want me to go to town?" Luke asked in surprise. "That's an all-fired first."

"I already made the blamed trip once this week. I've got things to do around here. Can you take care of town or not?"

"Brother of mine, I'd love to go to town. The way things are going around here, I could stand some friendly faces."

"Does anyone else have something to discuss?" asked Isaac.

Amanda raised her hand.

Isaac groaned dramatically. "I might have guessed. Go ahead, Amanda. What's your problem now?"

"Your and Luke's cursing. It doesn't set a good example to the children."

"We don't cuss that much," Isaac protested.

Nellie chose that moment to come across the room to the table, sporting a fresh scratch on her arm. She showed the scratch to Isaac and declared, "Damn Kitty!"

Both men looked toward Amanda, and she raised her eyebrows.

"All those in favor of banning cussing from the house, barn, and yard of the Lazy W?" Isaac said.

The vote was unanimous.

Impishly, Willie grinned. "Do Uncle Isaac and Uncle Luke have to go to bed without supper if they cuss?"

Amanda laughed. "I don't think we better make that rule. Your uncles could wither away to nothing. How about they have to do supper dishes if they curse?"

The two dissenting votes came from Isaac and Luke.

Isaac declared the meeting adjourned. Things sure didn't turn out like he planned with Amanda around.

He turned to her. "See if you can find Susie some of Willie's old pants," he commanded. He saw her eyes narrow ever such a little. Shoot! He'd forgotten to *ask* politely. Now she'd be on him about bossing her around. Before she could express her displeasure, he added, "It's Susie's turn to ride. Her legs will get rubbed raw if she rides in a skirt."

Amanda's mouth dropped open. About darn time he'd gotten the last word in.

"My turn? You mean it, Uncle Isaac?" asked Susie. "I get to ride with you?"

"Your Aunt Mandy thinks you need to learn to ranch." He added, "With her setting the example, you'll probably want to take over the whole outfit some day."

Susie ran over and gave his legs a big hug.

"What about me?" Willie demanded.

"It'll be Joe Pete's turn next. I figure you all need to know what to do around here. You can go every third time."

Willie burst into tears and slammed out the door.

In three great strides, Isaac reached the door. "William Wright, you get your butt back in here!"

When Willie returned, he lit into him. "I make the rules around here, and you're going to live by them. You'll let the others take their turn without throwing a tantrum or you won't go when it is your turn. You got that?"

Willie nodded.

"Now close that damn screen door real careful."

Willie did as he was told.

As the men headed toward the door, Amanda said, "I'm glad you reconsidered about taking Susie." She reached for a grub sack. "By the way, Isaac, don't make any plans for the evening."

"What? Why?"

"Butt? Damn screen door? As near as I can judge, you just volunteered to do the supper dishes."

Isaac shook his head in disgust and headed out.

Luke hee-hawed and beat Isaac on the back as they moved out the door.

From the kitchen window, Amanda watched them tussle like a couple of boys on the way to the barn, knocking off each other's hats and each trying to trip the other.

When she took Isaac the lunch, she said, ''Luke told me you know Eric Anderson's address. I'll need it so Luke can mail a letter for me when he goes to town tomorrow.''

''I assume you're planning to take the kids and go to that homestead the minute we're out of sight today?''

''I'm going to finish my work here first.''

''When are you going to admit you can't homestead with three kids to watch?''

She raised her chin and stared at him.

''Remember this. If *anything* happens to those kids over at that homestead, I'll never forgive you.''

Amanda watched him ride away with a burning dread in her stomach. A million things could happen to children. Isaac would never forgive her if any one of them happened while they were on her homestead. She would have to be very, very careful.

The clean clothes were folded and supper was waiting on the stove when the men and Susie returned early that evening. During supper, Susie entertained the family with her day's adventures.

Amanda had the kids tucked in bed before Isaac finished the dishes and his outside chores. Too tired to heat water for herself, she washed in frigid water in her room then crawled into bed. She didn't respond to Isaac's knock.

Before anyone else got up the next morning, she prepared antelope stew and put it on the back of the stove to simmer for supper. Then she scrubbed the floor in the main cabin and planted half the flower seeds Martha had sent.

That day set the pattern for the next couple of weeks. Each morning, Amanda rose before the rest of the family and did her day's work. One child rode with the men. She took whoever stayed with her to her homestead. She returned to the Lazy W in time to get supper on the table. After she closed the door to her bedroom at night, she rubbed the ointment Isaac had given her into her sore hands, then fell into bed, exhausted.

One evening, Isaac came in while she was still preparing supper. She glanced in his direction. "Supper's not ready."

"I didn't come in to see about supper."

At the stove, he tried to put his arms around her from the back, but she found something she needed to do at the table. The farther she kept from him, the better. She and Isaac were like oil and water. They didn't mix. But when he so much as touched her, her body seemed to take over.

"Is this the way it's going to be with us, Amanda?"

"I'm doing as you ordered. Nothing has happened to any of the children. What more do you want?"

"How about a kind word?"

Isaac watched her reaction. He'd had a bellyful of trying to get close to Amanda and being avoided. He'd had to content himself with catching glimpses of her as she moved around like a whirlwind, getting things done so she could go to that snakey homestead and play farmer. Looking at her wasn't enough. He longed to touch her and ached for her touch in return. It wasn't just a man's need for a woman. Dang it all, he needed Amanda.

She looked up from her cooking. "I didn't realize I'd been unkind, Isaac. I'll be more careful."

"Da—" Isaac caught himself. He'd done the supper dishes four times in the past five days. "Darn it, Amanda. We haven't had a minute alone together for over two weeks. I've tried to hurry with my chores at night so we could talk a while, but you're always asleep when I get in the house."

"I'm very tired at night."

"Too tired to talk? Or maybe let me kiss you good night?"

"If you want to kiss someone, I suggest you ride to town. Maybe the Widow Brown has more energy than I do."

Isaac eyed Amanda's dress. He grabbed a handful of material on either side of her waist. "You keep working this way and losing weight, and she'll have more of everything than you do."

Her eyes filled with tears and she jerked away.

He reached for her. "I didn't mean that, Amanda."

She shoved him away with her elbow and put the fried potatoes on the table. "Please call the others for supper."

"Amanda, I didn't come in here to pick a fight."

"No? Then why did you come in?"

"Luke and I need to be gone for a few days. We have some cattle missing and need to track them down. Before we leave, I wanted to remind you that Luke's birthday is the first of May. I thought we could all go fishing or have a picnic. It seems like a fellow should have a celebration of some kind when he reaches twenty-one. Besides, once he moves to his homestead, we won't see much of him, except when he comes in for supplies."

Amanda nodded, mentally planning a big birthday cake.

She stepped out of reach when Isaac tried again to take her in his arms. She didn't need the heartache Isaac Wright offered. If she did what he wanted, how he wanted, he approved of her. But if something happened to the children, he would never forgive her. She needed someone who would help her be strong when things went wrong, not someone who would blame her.

"To hell with it then," Isaac muttered after she stepped away from him. "I don't give a damn if you die a dried-up old maid." He stomped to the door and shouted that supper was ready.

Tears came to Amanda's eyes as she wondered why she put herself through all this. She should just pack up the kids and move back to Denver. At the very least, she should tell everyone that she had a fiancé waiting so Isaac couldn't keep making his old-maid remarks. Since she had no intention of doing either thing, Amanda wiped away the tears with the back of her sleeve and reached into the oven for the pan of biscuits. Dry-eyed, she smiled and welcomed the family to supper.

CHAPTER THIRTEEN

Pulling the team to a halt, Amanda surveyed the swollen stream. In her mind, she let loose with one of Isaac's favorite curse words. This high water looked treacherous.

Yesterday, she'd had some doubts about going to Lariat with the children. But the men were out looking for missing cattle for a few days, so she didn't need to worry about their supper. It had seemed like such a good opportunity to go to town. She'd intended to be home ahead of them.

Now it appeared she might not beat them home after all. The placid, ankle-deep creek she and Isaac had crossed when he first brought her to the Lazy W had disappeared. Twenty-four hours ago, it had been maybe a foot deep when she crossed it on her way to town. Now the roiling water had to be well above her knees.

She'd had no trouble crossing yesterday with the empty wagon and the lower water level. This morning, though, she'd loaded the wagon heavily with things she needed for her homestead. Handling a full wagon had been harder than handling an empty one.

Willie hung over the edge of the wagon. "Oh, boy! This is

almost as high as last year when I came home with Uncle Isaac.''

Amanda stared out at the muddy water. Isaac had mentioned that this creek isolated the Lazy W once the snowmelt made the water rise. The high water would get worse before it got better.

She tried to sound calm when she questioned Willie. ''Did you and Uncle Isaac cross right here when the water was so high?''

''You bet! It takes more than a creek to stop Uncle Isaac!''

Of course, she thought sarcastically. *Uncle Isaac can do everything. It's only old-maid aunts that can't do anything.*

Maybe she should unhitch the team and walk the horses and children through the water. The children and she could ride bareback to the house, leaving the wagon for Isaac to fetch. But the creek would be higher tomorrow. What if Isaac couldn't get the wagon across until after the spring thaw? She needed her supplies now. Besides, she hated to leave Isaac's wagon and harness out in the elements. He took care of his belongings. She had to cross.

Better to carry the children across first so they could walk to the ranch if she got into a bind with the wagon. Not that she'd get into trouble. Still, if she did have problems, it would be better for the kids to be on the Lazy W's side of the creek. Joe Pete had stayed at the ranch to do the daily chores. He could take care of the little children until the men got home.

Leaving the twins to watch Nellie, Amanda waded across the creek with her coat and pistol in a bundle held high over her head. *The current's not too strong. The water comes only halfway up my thighs. I can get everything across, but I'll have to get this dress and petticoat off. They'll trip me for sure.*

She hung her coat, gun belt, and soggy clothes over some willows. Clad in her pantaloons and chemise, she carried Susie across piggyback without incident, then Nellie. Willie thought the whole thing a lark. He waved his hat in the air and bounced so exuberantly on her back that she lost her footing and fell, submerging herself and the boy. The cold dip sobered him, and he clung to Amanda's neck as she struggled toward the far bank.

The minute she lowered the boy to dry ground, she intended to scold him, but Susie clutched his hand. "Willie, I thought you was going to drownded. You shouldn't been bouncing around like that." She kissed his cheek.

"I lost my hat." He swiped at his eyes with his sleeve and pointed to where his beat-up cowboy hat swirled down the stream.

Susie's compassion lasted only so long. "Serves you right for horsing around and almost drowndeding Aunt Mandy!"

Amanda agreed with the little girl. It served him right. Still, he looked so pitiful, standing there shivering. She jerked her old black coat from the willow where she'd hung it earlier, tearing off two buttons that had become entangled in the branches. She stuffed Willie's wet body into it, wrapping it snugly around him. "You children get to the top of the hill and wait for me. Keep hold of Nellie's hand no matter what! If she decides she doesn't like it, too bad. Let her howl."

She aimed the children up the trail. "If I get into trouble, walk to the ranch and stay with Joe Pete. Understand?"

The twins nodded.

"Hurry now. Get on up the hill and out of the way."

After the children were well away from the water, Amanda gritted her teeth and sloshed back out into the icy stream. When she reached the wagon, she was shivering violently.

The horses couldn't be coaxed into the water from the wagon seat, so again she entered the rushing flow, this time leading the four-horse team. In midstream, the lead horse on the upstream side tried to turn back, causing the other three horses to slide about on the slippery rocks at the creek bottom. Amanda lost a rein, then her footing. She went under the water several times fighting frantically to retrieve the elusive strand of leather. By the time she got out in front again, the current had slammed her to the bottom several times. Somehow, she and the horses made it to dry land on the right side of the swollen creek.

Once she had the wagon out of the water, Amanda stopped

and strapped on her gunbelt. She tied the holster down before shoving her wet dress and petticoat under the seat.

At the top of the rise, she held and comforted Susie and Willie, who were on the verge of tears. "Everything's fine. You don't want to scare Nellie by crying." Still too young to understand all the fuss, Nellie simply crowded close for a hug.

The wind began to blow, chilling horses and people. Making a quick transfer, Amanda wrapped Willie in a blanket and put her damp coat on over her soggy underwear. After tucking a second blanket around the girls, she headed for the Lazy W.

It started to sleet before they reached the yard. Joe Pete saw them coming and ran to open the barn door. She drove inside.

"Take care of the horses," Amanda said. "I'll be out to help after I've settled the children."

Inside the warm cabin, she toweled the children's hair. They put on their nightclothes while she heated some water for tea. Leaving them wrapped in quilts in front of the fireplace with the warm drinks, she hurried back to the barn.

When Joe Pete and she had three horses wiped down and put in stalls, Amanda sent Joe Pete inside to check on the children. "Fix some bread and jelly to hold you kids until I can cook supper."

He'd been inside a few minutes when Amanda heard a galloping horse approach. She rushed to the barn door in time to see Isaac ride into the yard. Swinging his powerful body from the saddle before the horse quit moving, he charged for the house.

Amanda ran across the yard, all manner of fears crossing her mind, wondering what could have happened to make Isaac move so fast. He was alone. Maybe something had happened to Luke.

She stopped in the open doorway. Isaac had his back to the door and was hunkered down with all three little children in his arms. The children were chattering about what had happened at the creek as if it had been a big, wonderful adventure.

Knowing Isaac wasn't going to consider it wonderful at all, Amanda decided that her best bet would be to get the last horse dried and settled before Isaac got to the barn to discuss it with her.

She'd almost finished rubbing down the horse when she sensed Isaac behind her. "I'm almost done here," she said. "And I'm very tired. Would you mind yelling at me later?"

He turned her around and smoothed her straggling hair away from her face. "I'm going to yell like hell at you later, but first I'm going to hold you." He pulled her close and kissed her forehead.

She felt so safe in Isaac's arms. How had she reached this point? Engaged to one man, and wanting to be held by another. Right now, the need to be comforted by Isaac far outweighed any duty she felt to Tom. Or her jealousy of Teresa Brown.

"Lord, Amanda. I was scared to death. Luke and I saw Will's hat in the creek down a mile or so. Luke's riding the bank looking for him. I headed home to see what's going on."

"He lost his hat when we crossed the creek. I didn't even think about your seeing it." She started to pull away. "I better go find Luke and tell him Willie is okay."

"Stay." Isaac tightened his embrace. "I put my slicker on Joe Pete and sent him after Luke. He's still kid enough to think riding in this weather is a good time."

Envisioning Joe Pete riding through the sleet, Amanda had to agree. He loved doing anything that involved a horse.

"Susie said your legs are bleeding. Let me see."

Amanda clutched her buttonless coat closed as he knelt and pushed up her pantaloons. A quick survey revealed nothing more serious than a multitude of scrapes and bruises.

"You're going to be hurting tomorrow. The kids said the big black acted up and knocked you around in the water."

"I think he was frightened. I'm fine."

"You look like a drowned rat." He wrapped a strand of her long wet hair around his finger.

"I was worried about your horses. I didn't take time to do anything with my hair."

"I can replace horses. I can't replace those kids or you." He lowered his head so his lips were near hers. "Please don't pull away, Amanda. I want to kiss you. Really kiss you."

She wouldn't have moved away from his lips for all the riches in the world. His slow, gentle kiss ignited a fire that had been smoldering deep within her heart since the night he first came to her bedroom to tell her good night. She fought not to return his kiss. Sliding his arms inside her coat, he encircled her waist, caressing as he coaxed her close.

Though she'd promised herself not to allow this to happen, Amanda put her arms around him, reveling in the emotions invoked by his warm hands. He placed soft little kisses down her neck, across the tops of her breasts. There was no mistaking his reluctance when he groaned and pulled away. He closed her coat and wrapped both arms around her waist again, bringing her body intimately against his.

"Why did you go to town?"

"I needed my trunks and some supplies for my homestead. After you rode out yesterday morning, I got the idea that while you were gone would be a good time to go." She didn't meet his eyes as she added, "I guess it's obvious I used your horses and wagon without permission."

"You don't need *permission* to use anything on the Lazy W," Isaac said. "Why didn't you say you wanted to go to town earlier? I would have taken you in."

Amanda stared at him with raised eyebrows.

He shifted uneasily. "I would have when I got the time."

"I have garden seeds and other things for my homestead in my trunk. You told me the creek soon would be too high to cross and I need to plant now. The water looked fine to cross yesterday, but today it had risen considerably. Willie assured me you crossed when it was even higher, so I decided I could do it, too."

"I've been handling a team since I turned eight years old."

"Don't think I didn't wish you were there!" She didn't want Isaac to think she'd neglected the children. "The children were safely across before I took the wagon into the water."

"The kids told me."

"I got your wagon soaked."

"It's been wet before. You're mighty soggy yourself." Isaac backed up, opened the coat again, and looked at her wet pantaloons, clinging chemise, and the heavy gun belt with its holster tied to her side. "I'll grant you one thing. That's the goshdangdest, river-crossing, horse-grooming outfit I ever laid eyes on. You are one beautiful woman. Are all the men in Denver blind that someone hasn't made you a wife and mother already?''

Her cheeks burned.

He laughed and pulled her back into his arms. ''What am I going to do with you, Amanda Erikson?'' He smoothed the back of his hand over her hot cheeks. ''You better get something on before you catch pneumonia, and I get myself in trouble.''

''I haven't finished with this horse yet.''

''I'll take care of him. Then I'll milk the goat and finish the chores. Scoot.'' He pushed her gently toward the barn door.

Amanda had moved a few feet toward the door when Isaac took three long steps and caught her to him. She allowed herself to be wrapped in his arms one more time.

That expression *one more* seemed to have become her motto with Isaac. One more kiss, one more touch, one more argument, one more anything from Isaac. She should stand right up and say, *no more.* No more touching, no more arguing.

Before she reached the door, he stopped her. ''Amanda?''

She turned to him—one more time.

''I hate it when you freeze me out and won't let me get close, like you've been doing the last few weeks. It's getting physically harder not to kiss you, and even more difficult to kiss you and let you go. You know what I mean, don't you?''

She hesitated, then nodded. She did know. Maybe a single woman shouldn't know, but instinctively she knew. A virile man like Isaac had an intense itch that needed to be scratched regularly.

As she walked across the yard toward the cabin, she didn't try to fool herself about Isaac's cozying up to her in the barn. It obviously didn't bother him who scratched his masculine itch. It could be Amanda, Teresa Brown or maybe even someone else.

He didn't care a whit that the Widow had gotten a little long in the tooth or that he was against everything that Amanda stood for. All he wanted was a woman who'd make herself available from time to time to satisfy his physical needs. When he went to town, Isaac stayed at Teresa Brown's boarding house. When he was trapped on the ranch with work, he made up to Amanda.

A woman was different, though. If she ever let Isaac scratch *his* itch, she'd have to break her engagement. She wouldn't offer Tom spoiled goods. If she didn't watch it, she really would end her days an old maid, living on a homestead next to Isaac Wright's cattle ranch, watching anxiously down the road for him to get back from town and ride over for a little visit.

For the first time, Amanda felt compassion for Teresa Brown, waiting for Isaac to come to town and make an honest woman of her. At least Tom would make Amanda his wife—*if* she "came to her senses" and returned to Denver within the allotted year.

Amanda stood on the porch and stared at the barn through the pouring rain. She fingered the crumpled letter in her coat pocket. Tom had reiterated his original ultimatum. He would consider their engagement at an end if she did not return in one year's time. Tom had signed, *As Always.* His letter contained no mention of love, only duty.

As Always. That's what her life would be like back in Denver. *As Always.* Each day would be like the previous one. She'd live in Tom's house, with his mother, with nothing more taxing to do than give the cook the week's menu on Monday morning.

She should never have agreed to marry Tom despite what a wonderful "catch" he was considered to be. She hadn't minded being single. What a hypocrite she'd proven herself to be, accepting Tom's proposal to avoid the social stigma of being an old maid.

She wished that at least once Tom had kissed her the way Isaac had just kissed her in the barn, tasting her as if she were the most savory of pastries. If only Tom had ever held her close and said he couldn't bear to let her go. Or told her that his physical need for her was strong, too strong to ignore.

But he hadn't. Tom had never guided her with gentle pressure at the small of her back pressing her intimately against him or groaned with the effort needed to pull himself away.

Tom had kissed her on the cheek and warned her. She had one year to get over her "imbecilic" notions about homesteading and return to Denver. Tom, of course, understood her moral obligation to raise her late sister's children. After she returned to Denver and they'd reviewed his schedule for a convenient wedding date, he'd immediately have separate quarters for the children added to his estate. He'd hire a governess himself— a firm one, who knew how to raise respectful children.

Undoubtedly, Tom would take care of Amanda's material needs and those of the children. But could he take care of their other needs? Deeper, unexplainable, more important needs? The needs Isaac seemed to sense. She couldn't picture a bone-weary Tom singing lullabies to a grieving child in the night. Or rushing to the barn to check on a bedraggled woman, making her feel like the most beautiful, most desirable woman in the world.

Maybe she was underestimating Tom. He had a reputation as a fine doctor, so he must be used to demanding situations. Perhaps his station in life and his fine estate didn't mean as much to him as she thought. He might like the daily experiences of working hard, caring for children, loving his wife, and carving something rewarding out of the wilderness.

It was only fair she give him a chance to show the kind of man he could be. She'd write and ask him again to join her in Wyoming.

When she opened the door to the cozy cabin, Amanda shook her head. Both rooms of the homestead cabin would fit into the kitchen of Tom's home. She shuddered to think what Tom would say when he saw her dugout.

Well, she'd cross that bridge when she came to it. Right now, she needed to change out of her fancy river-crossing, horse-grooming outfit. Then she had to prepare supper for seven tired, hungry people, including four children whom Tom assumed she couldn't care for without a governess to help.

A governess, of all things!

She could raise these children without any help, thank you. And she could prove up on her homestead at the same time.

CHAPTER FOURTEEN

Isaac stood on the banks of Wild Horse Creek fishing. Though he hadn't had a fish on his hook for twenty minutes, he didn't care. He had his mind on Amanda, snuggled up with Nellie on the picnic blanket, both of them sleeping soundly. Luke and Joe Pete had taken the twins upstream to look for good holes.

He wished they'd get on back. The day had been beautiful until about an hour ago. Now dark thunderclouds covered the sky. They should start back to the Lazy W soon, or they'd have to ride in the rain. He hadn't thought to line up the kids or Amanda with rain gear. Next time he went to town, he'd be sure to get slickers for them.

Especially Amanda. If she were going to continue with this homesteading, it wouldn't be long until she discovered that carrying an umbrella around in one hand severely cut down on how much work a person could get done.

From where he stood, he could see Amanda's little homestead.

When they first settled in the area, Pa had given this fertile area serious consideration for a homestead, then decided against it. Of course, Pa had to keep in mind the Indian problem that existed twenty years ago. The Lazy W's ranch house backed up to the foot of a steep, rocky ledge, so they had no fear of being attacked from behind.

Water had been another problem. The spring in the back yard on the Lazy W had never faltered, summer or winter. Isaac remembered Eric Anderson hauling water clear from Wild Horse Creek to the dugout. That's why he and his brothers helped Eric dig the well a few years back. They'd seen five rattlesnakes the week they'd worked on the well. Isaac shivered involuntarily. *Lord, he hated snakes!*

Reminded, he pulled in his fishing line and checked the ground around Amanda and Nellie's blanket again. Sitting down next to Amanda, he studied the dark circles under her eyes. He couldn't continue to let her work so hard. She'd been doing the woman's work on the Lazy W, then going over to her homestead to do both a man's and a woman's work.

At first, he figured all the work would get too hard and she'd let go of this homesteading idea. Now that he knew her better, he suspected that would never happen. If he didn't put a stop to it, she d be stubborn enough to continue traveling back and forth between her homestead and the Lazy W every day, trying to take care of things in both places.

She lay on her side, with one arm over Nellie. Isaac's gaze slid down Amanda's curvy body, past the dip in her waist to the rise of her hips. Womanly, inviting hips. Her skirt outlined her long, slim legs. Looking back to her full breasts straining against the buttons on the front of her dress, he feasted his eyes the way he'd never dare do if she were aware of it. He'd like to lie down beside her and run his hand down past her waist and over her hips, just to feel how she was put together.

Isaac found pictures of her popping into his mind all the time. Quick flashes of her working, of her with the children, and of visions so private that he'd be embarrassed for Amanda to know he thought of her that way. Especially since she kept brushing aside his overtures.

Staring at her now, he wished this damn country weren't so hard on women. The work and weather were too demanding. It took the prettiest, hardiest women and worked them to death. What the work didn't do to women, their men did. In the name of love, men lay with their women, leaving their wives' tired, overworked bodies with more to do. The same men who wouldn't consider breeding an overworked animal, didn't take care not to impregnate their women.

Not him. After his mother died bearing Luke, he'd decided he'd not marry and inflict this life upon a wife.

He'd renewed that promise to himself when he dressed Mary for burial. Damned if Joshua hadn't impregnated Mary again! Four times in six years! And she'd borne two sets of twins in that time. Mary had gotten so thin that her best dress buttoned all the way down in spite of her distended stomach. His brother, who acted as though he loved Mary more than life itself, had used damn little self-control.

When it started to thunder and lightning, Amanda opened her beautiful green eyes and smiled at Isaac, sending his guts into a whirl. He bent to kiss her, and she welcomed his kiss as if they were familiar lovers. If Nellie hadn't been lying beside her, if the rest of the family hadn't been running toward them, Isaac would have covered her body with his. No amount of self-talk would make his intense desire for her go away.

But the family *was* near, so he said, "Get up, sleepyhead. We need to head back before it rains." As he spoke, a clap of thunder roared and a lightning bolt shot through the air.

He picked Nellie up, then he and Amanda ran to the horses. Another roar was followed by a lightning strike. Amanda mounted, and Isaac handed the child up to her. "If the next lightning strike is any closer, you get off this horse and walk. You know what happened to my pa."

Nodding, Amanda kicked her horse into action. She heard thunder behind her and looked back in time to see a tree burst into flame about a half mile up the ridge. Leaning over Nellie, she rode for her homestead.

Safe inside the dugout, she watched a wall of rain moving in behind the rest of the family. The children were laughing and running ahead of the men while Luke and Isaac led the horses.

She had time to light the lantern before the twins hit the door, dripping wet and bouncing with excitement. Stripping their wet things off, Amanda wrapped them in blankets and toweled their hair, all the while keeping an anxious watch out the small window. Coffee had come to a boil before the men and Joe Pete came in from the barn.

Misty tried to look invisible as she slunk in and found herself a dry spot under the bed. Amanda decided to let her stay. On the Lazy W, Misty slept on the porch, right by the door. Here, there was no protective porch. The little dog had become accustomed to staying close to the children, and Amanda wanted it that way. If a snake made its way inside the dugout, Misty would alert her.

Isaac put the picnic leftovers on the table, then looked around as he removed his wet slicker. "You covered the walls with yard goods. I never saw that done before."

"I splurged at Callahan's store. It's supposed to help keep things a little cleaner and keep the bugs down."

"Does it keep the snakes out?"

"It must," Amanda quipped. "We haven't had any inside."

Obviously, Isaac wasn't amused. "And outside?"

"A few."

"Didn't you see Aunt Mandy's rattle collection above the barn door?" asked Willie. "She killed six rattlesnakes, not counting the first one. After she kills a hundred, she's going to let me have the rest of the rattles."

Amanda sent Willie a quelling look, then met Isaac's hostile gaze.

"How many were close to the dugout?" he demanded.

"A couple. Now let's quit talking about snakes and start talking about what we have left from lunch."

While the men hung their wet things around the room to dry, she laid out the leftovers and poured coffee into her only three cups. The children passed one cup between them, Luke had one to himself, and Isaac insisted on sharing his with her. He shared his chair with her as well since they hadn't enough seats at the table. At first they sat like a couple of kids, perched side-by-side on the edge of the chair, then Isaac pulled her into his lap. Being in his lap made it hard to concentrate on her food.

Luke sat at the head of the table in honor of his birthday. They laughed and sang to him for the second time that day.

Later, while the children played on the big bed, Luke eased down on the rickety trundle bed for a nap. She played poker with Joe Pete and Isaac, losing all her matchsticks early and having to borrow from Isaac so she could keep playing.

After his nap, Luke walked to the window. "It's still pouring, but the thunder and lightning have stopped. I guess I'll ride on to the Lazy W and get the chores done." He turned to Isaac. In a challenging tone, Luke said, "I suppose you intend to stay here with Amanda."

Isaac raised an eyebrow. "I'll be along in the morning. There's no point in taking these kids out in the rain."

"I figured." Luke jerked his coat off a hook and slammed out the door.

She looked at Isaac. "I've never seen Luke act like that."

"This has been coming. I'll go talk to him."

In the barn, Isaac watched as Luke stomped around, saddling his horse. "You planning to start for your homestead early tomorrow?"

"Since you'll evidently not be home, I'll do the chores, then leave at sunup," answered Luke.

Ignoring the sarcasm in his voice, Isaac rubbed the nose of Luke's horse. "Take good care of this fellow."

"I always take good care of my horse."

"I hate to see you go off for so long by yourself. With the kids and Amanda to look after, I won't be able to come to see you much. You'll have to check that whole side of the ranch. Don't go taking any chances. Even if we haven't seen any sign, you and I both know there's something damn suspicious about all the cattle we're missing. If you see any strangers, make yourself scarce. Get on home. We'll deal with them together."

Luke nodded.

"If you see Hawk, warn him about the new homesteaders east of Lariat, and mention our missing cows. Tell him to come to the Lazy W through Amanda's homestead. It'll be safest that way.''

Tightening his saddle's cinch, Luke gave another curt nod.

"Being spiteful won't change the way things are, Luke."

"What the hell do you mean?"

"You know what I mean. I've noticed the way you freeze up when Amanda or I pay attention to one another."

"It's your imagination!"

"I don't think so. But you'll get to Amanda over my dead body. She's going to play her little homesteading game for awhile. Then I intend to see that she goes back to her old life. A life where a woman doesn't get worked to death."

"Meanwhile, you're leading her on. Right? Trying to do her like you do the Widow Brown?"

"What I do or don't do with Tess—or with Amanda—is none of your business."

"I intend to make what you do with Amanda my business. Maybe you don't want a wife and family, but I do. It doesn't take much imagination to know Amanda would be right nice to snuggle up to on a long winter's night."

Isaac gripped the edge of a stall. "I've never laid a hand to you, but you're lucky I didn't flatten you over that remark."

Luke squared off in front of Isaac. "I'm not a kid anymore. I'm ready to take you on. And I'm ready to take on a woman."

"You wouldn't know what to do with a woman if you got her."

Luke loomed closer. "It can't be that hard to learn. Why don't you ask Amanda next year about this time?"

Clenching his fists, Isaac tried to control his jealousy. Then good sense overtook him and he relaxed his hands. Luke was more than a younger brother. Joshua and Luke had always been his closest friends. "There's no point in having bad blood between us. Amanda is my woman until she leaves! That's the way it is."

"You don't want a permanent woman. You've told me so a hundred times. You don't love Amanda."

"I suppose you do?"

"Maybe not the forever kind of love, but it'll come. As far

as I'm concerned, Amanda is anyone's woman until *she* tells me otherwise." Luke went back around his horse and mounted. "I'll tell you something else. If she were my woman, I'd take care of her, not cause her to work herself to the bone trying to take care of four kids *and* two places." He mounted and rode off.

Isaac watched until he lost sight of him in the rain. *Fool kid! Thinks he's a man. Thinks he can take care of Amanda better than I can. It's not like I make Amanda get up early and work like hell all day.* Still, Luke's words hit a sore spot.

Back inside the dugout, he stared out at the rain, listening to Amanda tell the children a story. She had all four kids in the big bed, the three little ones across the top, Joe Pete tucked in crossways at the bottom.

After she pulled a curtain separating the big bed from the rest of the room, Amanda came to stand at the window with him. He wrapped his arms around her waist and held her tight. When he kissed her neck, she sighed and leaned back into him. Lord, he loved it when she didn't fight his every move.

"Is everything all right with Luke?" she asked.

"It will be. A summer on his own will do him good."

"I didn't get a chance to say good-bye."

"Did you want to say a special good-bye?" His heart rose to his throat when Amanda paused a moment.

She turned to look into his eyes. "I just hate to have him go away for the summer if I've done something to upset him."

"You haven't done anything. Besides, he'll be down to the Lazy W from time to time to get supplies. We'll see him some. Don't forget, we all go to town together for the Fourth of July."

Her lips were so close. Just a few inches away. Fearing she would pull out of his arms, Isaac moved slowly, bending slightly to kiss her. When she leaned against him and put her arms around his neck, he made the kiss last a long time. Damned if he hadn't been needing this for weeks. Sometimes it seemed as if he couldn't get through another hour without feeling her touch.

Poor Luke. The kid didn't realize how it was between a man and a woman. Somehow Isaac knew that Amanda would never

have allowed Luke to hold her in his lap at supper, or put her
arms around him and return a kiss.

Too soon she pushed his head and shoulders away. Looking
at her flushed cheeks, he wondered if she had enough experience
with men to know the need she aroused in him. Lowering his
hands to her hips, he held her tightly against him.

"Remember the children," she reminded him quietly.

He nodded, but rocked gently against her, coaxing while she
stood staring into his eyes, pulling the pins from her hair. After
her hair fell to her waist, she slipped her hands into his rear
pockets and stopped the motion of his hips. "I don't think you
ought to be doing that."

"Why?" He nibbled on her neck.

"Isaac! Behave yourself."

She looked worried, but she playfully pushed him away and
began to put her hair into its single nighttime braid.

"Let me." After braiding Amanda's beautiful hair, he turned
his back while she undressed and climbed into the small trundle
bed. He bedded down on the pallet she'd fixed in the narrow
space between the beds. In the silent darkness, he reached up
to her. "Let me hold your hand." After kissing the palm, he
smoothed his lips down her slim, calloused fingers. He wanted
her bad. He'd wanted a woman many times, any woman. This
was different. He wanted Amanda with a pressing urgency,
and no other woman would do.

When her breathing told him she'd fallen asleep, he got off
the cold floor and picked up his bedding. Cowardly as it was,
he knew he'd never sleep thinking about the things that might
crawl on the dirt floor of a dugout. He headed for the barn.
Amanda had fixed up the loft so the kids could play safely out
of the reach of rattlesnakes. Though the loft was bare, Isaac
checked the corners carefully before he lay down to wait for
first light.

He wished Amanda were stretched out alongside him. Somehow, he knew she didn't know about physical loving. He could
teach her. Then teach her again and again. And again.

A sudden and unwelcome thought came to Isaac. He'd never
get his fill of Amanda. He wanted her beneath him in love

and beside him in life. Pushing the life-altering idea aside, he concentrated on tomorrow's work. His mind searched for a topic, any topic but Amanda and her long mahogany hair, her enticing walk, her generous breasts, and her hungry responses to his kisses.

Desperately, he tried to remember that she wanted to take the kids away from him. He reminded himself that she had a sassy streak, and that she was for most everything he was against. Damned woman had a stubborn streak a mile wide. She'd likely work herself sick if he didn't do something.

Daylight was a long time coming.

CHAPTER FIFTEEN

Isaac woke Amanda before dawn. "I'm going to help Luke with the chores. It's still raining. You might as well sleep awhile. I'll see you this afternoon."

She watched him slip out of the dugout. He hadn't kissed her good-bye. Not that he was in the habit of kissing her hello or good-bye, but he had kissed her last night—very thoroughly. She wondered if her longing for Isaac's touch showed. She prayed not; she'd be embarrassed if Isaac knew she wanted him so badly.

A worrisome thought entered her mind. What if Tom found out that Isaac had kissed her? Ridiculous! No one knew about the kisses except Isaac and her. Isaac didn't know about Tom. And she certainly had no intention of writing, "Oh, by the way, Tom, Isaac Wright's kisses are nothing like your polite, proper ones. Isaac's aren't the least proper. They make me tremble."

Her conscience urged her to put an immediate halt to Isaac's caresses and kisses. It seemed immoral to want a man the way she wanted Isaac. She thought back to the way she'd responded to Isaac's rhythmic movements last night. She'd wanted to press against him. If she felt like that, it should be for Tom, for her fiancé. What if Tom were to arrive in Wyoming unexpectedly? The thought was so ludicrous, she almost laughed. It was as likely to snow in August as it was for Tom to do something spontaneous. He planned every aspect of his life with meticulous care.

Annoyed with herself for worrying about such nonsense, she rose and did her morning chores. After all, this was the first morning she had awakened on her homestead instead of the Lazy W.

The rain clouds gave way to blue sky. Amanda strapped on her pistol, then carried her new shovel and Nellie to the garden at the top of the rise. The twins and Joe Pete followed, hauling the old shovel and lunch. Joe Pete saw to the children while Amanda dug steadily. Twenty-five more feet and she'd have an irrigation ditch from Wild Horse Creek to the garden.

In mid-afternoon, Misty gave a welcoming bark. From their vantage point on the rise, Amanda and the children watched Isaac drive up to the dugout's door with a heavily laden supply wagon. He had his saddle horse and her goats tied to the back. *What in the world?* She started toward him, but he signaled for her to continue with her work. Though she was curious, she did want to dig a little farther before she took the children back to the Lazy W and did her chores there.

"Joe Pete, Willie, Susie, go on down and see if Isaac needs some help." When the twins began to run, Amanda called and shook her head. "You know you can't run through the brush and watch for snakes at the same time. Slow down and be careful."

Thank goodness for their canine guardian angel. Misty stayed with the twins, and the minute they got ten feet or so apart, she herded one of them back to the other. Twice today, Misty had gone into a point. Once it had been a rabbit. The second time, it had been a bull snake. Joe Pete explained that bull snakes were good medicine against rattlesnakes and insisted on not killing it.

Amanda had helped him get the hissing, writhing thing into a tow sack; then they carried it away from the garden to release it. She hoped it wouldn't slither by while she was down on her knees in the garden. Dealing with a snake from an upright position was one thing. Looking one in the eye was something else.

She hadn't been working long when Joe Pete returned. "Isaac said for me to fetch Nellie so you can work in peace."

"What's going on down there?"

Joe Pete's dimples flashed. "Isaac said to tell you to mind your own business if you asked."

So Isaac had a surprise. Funny, he didn't come across as a man who liked to plan surprises.

Rain clouds began to build up in the west. When the first clap of thunder reverberated across the valley, Amanda began gathering her tools. Her curiosity about the pounding coming from the dugout had gotten the best of her anyway. She reached the barn just as Isaac hung the harness over a stall rail. "You unhitched?" she asked. "I thought you intended to take the children and me back to the Lazy W. What's going on?"

"*If* I get an invitation to supper, I think I might ride to the Lazy W to do the chores, then come back."

"You never need an invitation here, Isaac. For the children's sake, there's always a plate for you at my table."

"For the children's sake?"

Amanda felt herself flush.

He laughed and kissed the tip of her nose as he passed. "I brought the goats over because it makes sense for the milk goats to be where the children are staying."

Where the children are staying? Did that mean he'd let her keep the children over here some nights? That would be such a relief. Afternoons when she was especially tired, the chores on the Lazy W seemed endless. However, she couldn't bring herself to question Isaac for fear it would erase his obvious good mood.

"Come on inside. I've got something to show you." He took her hand, and they ran through the pelting rain to the dugout.

Isaac had built three beds and balanced them one on top of another so they wouldn't take up any more floor space than one bed. "The top one is for Joe Pete. Willie can have the middle and the girls can share the bigger bottom one. You can have the big bed, and I—er, company can use the trundle. No one will have to be crowded or sleep on the dirt floor.''

Amanda gazed at the sturdy beds. Surely he wouldn't have gone to so much trouble if he hadn't intended for the children to sleep in them. She had to ask. ''Does this mean it's all right for the children to stay on my homestead?''

''I wouldn't go as far as to say all right. But I'm afraid you're going to work yourself to death keeping up the cabin on the Lazy W *and* your homestead. Maybe we can work something out until you go back to Denver.''

''Denver again. Honestly, Isaac. Why do you persist in this assumption that I'm going to fail at homesteading and return to Denver?'' She could hear her voice getting steadily louder and more defensive with each sentence. ''You need to get it through your thick skull that I intend to be a successful homesteader. To prove up, I'll need to live on this homestead for the next five years, and I'm going to do it.''

''Don't get your feathers in an uproar.''

''Since my feathers are already in an uproar, I'll thank you to remember I'm raising these children. You can help or you can get in my way, but I *am* raising my sister's children.''

''All I did was try to make things easier around here.'' Isaac directed her gaze to the children. All three were staring, eyes big and tears threatening. ''Look who's carrying on and upsetting children now instead of thanking me for trying to do you a favor.''

Abashed, she knelt to gather the children in her arms. Nellie and Will came to her, but Susie backed up and wrapped a protective arm around Isaac's thigh. Amanda couldn't tell who the girl was trying to protect, her Uncle Isaac or herself. ''Susie, bring that ornery bed-building uncle of yours over here.''

Isaac smiled and nudged Susie forward.

Amanda hadn't expected that. She'd set herself up for another one of his ''what's mine is mine and you can go to heck if you don't like it'' scenes. But Isaac and Susie joined the three-some on the floor. Isaac reached out an arm, inviting Joe Pete into the family hug of togetherness, then gave him a friendly cuff on the back of the head as he joined them.

The arm Isaac wrapped around her waist filled her soul with contentment. If the children, who told all, hadn't been in the room, she might have given him a thank-you kiss—on the cheek, of course. When she glanced at Isaac, he winked. Her cheeks grew warm. If she hadn't seen it with her own eyes, she wouldn't have believed it. Isaac Wright was flirting, just plain flirting.

"I'm sorry for being so prickly," she said. "The beds are perfect. Thank you."

Accepting both apology and thank-you, Isaac mentioned the need for mattresses. "After shearing, I'll help you clean some wool and you can make mattresses." He guided Amanda to the door and gave her a squeeze as he left. "I'll be back for supper."

At bedtime, when she started to pull the curtain that divided the tiny dugout into two areas, Joe Pete leaned out from his bed. "I ain't never had a bed all to my own. It feels real good."

"You need to thank Isaac. The beds were his idea."

"Thanks, Isaac." Joe Pete lay back and cradled his head with his clasped hands. "This is real cozy. I can reach up my hand and touch the roof."

The minute the curtain was in place, Isaac pulled Amanda to him for a hug. She had no intention of moving away. At least not until she heard a chorus of giggles. Only then did she realize the children could see their silhouettes through the curtain.

"Get to sleep," Isaac growled good-naturedly. "A fellow can't get away with anything with those kids around." He eyed the buckets of water on the stove. "I'll pull out the trundle bed, then go check the barn while you bathe."

Several minutes and many muttered curses later, he admitted the trundle bed would no longer fit anywhere in the room. "Never mind," he said. "I've slept in barns often enough."

"You shouldn't have to sleep out there. You've worked hard all day trying to make us comfortable for the night."

"It's all right. But I'd like to come in after I finish in the barn and take a quick bath. Just leave your water for me."

Before he walked out into the rain, Amanda hesitated. She hated to say anything. Still, better safe than sorry. "Take a lantern and watch your step."

"I don't know what you see in a place where you have to watch your every damn step for fear of snakes." Isaac shuddered.

Children or no, Amanda thought, he looked like a man who needed attention. She kept her voice low. "Poor Isaac. Has to go out in the rain and face rattlesnakes."

He pulled her to him. "They're probably huge rattlesnakes, too. I better have a few kisses, just to get up my nerve."

The children couldn't see their silhouettes from here, so she met his lips and relaxed against him as he trailed kisses across her cheek and nibbled his way down her neck. His day's beard prickled her skin and felt reassuringly male. "You better get on to the barn. Next thing we know, the children will be going to town with stories about you and I hugging and kissing."

"What would that hurt?"

"Honestly! You know what the people in Lariat will think!"

"Would that be so bad? Neither of us is married to someone else. We have the right to do a little kissing."

Perhaps he had a right, but she didn't. No right at all. Amanda pulled out of his arms. She turned her back to him and poured hot water into the tub.

When he came in later, she pretended to be asleep on the floor. It was only right that Isaac have a bed. He shouldn't have to go to the barn as he'd done last night. Obviously, he didn't like sleeping on the dirt floor of the dugout, but it didn't bother her too much.

Now, from her pallet on the floor, she listened to Isaac as he bathed in her leftover water. She even peeked when he stood up to get out of the tub. He had a beautiful backside, tight and muscular. She'd never seen a completely naked man. He knotted the towel around himself before turning toward the bed. *Drat!*

After blowing out the lantern, he came to the pallet and nudged her foot. "Get out of my bed, Amanda."

She ignored him, pretending to be asleep.

"Come on, Amanda. I'll sleep on the floor instead of in the barn. Get up on the bed where you belong."

She made no response.

"Stubborn woman," he muttered. The bed creaked when he crawled up from the foot to the head.

She waited to sleep until she heard his soft snores.

In the middle of the night, Amanda awoke with a cramp in her calf. She sat up to try to rub it away.

From the bed, Isaac whispered, "What's wrong?"

"Just a leg cramp." She arched her back in pain.

"It's probably from sleeping on the cold floor. Get up here so I can work it out. There isn't room for me down there."

She gripped Isaac's shoulder as he kneaded the muscle in her calf. It took a few minutes for the cramp to abate. "Thanks."

"Does this happen often?"

"Just the last week or so. I'll be fine once I toughen up."

"Probably. How's the other leg?"

"It's a little tight."

Isaac massaged her other calf and both feet. When the muscles relaxed, she started to return to the floor.

"Stay here." Leaning across her, he grabbed her pillow and laid it beside his. "This bed is big enough for both of us."

"I can't sleep with you. What will people think?"

"If appearances bother you so bad, I'll get on the floor in the morning before the kids wake up, and no one will ever know."

"I'll know!"

"So? Don't tell anyone. I promise I won't touch you during the night if that's what's bothering you." Isaac shifted to the far side of the bed, lay down, and turned his back.

Amanda hesitated. It had been uncomfortable on the hard floor, and chilly. The big bed beckoned, warm and inviting. Conceding that she must be out of her mind even to consider something so utterly improper, she crawled under the covers, staying near the outside edge. The bed felt good. And Isaac lay right there, inches from her. He was right. No one would know.

When she woke at first light, Isaac had rolled over and put his arm across her. They were spooned together, his hand cupped beneath her breast. Enjoying the closeness, she lay quietly until she sensed his awakening.

Isaac nuzzled her neck, and shivers ran down her arms and back. His touch felt so good. Amanda scooted a little closer to him and smiled when she heard his sudden intake of breath.

Slowly he fit his body more intimately to hers. She held her breath as he worked his hand upward, caressing the underside of her breasts through her nightgown, making her feel so . . . so itchy.

"You said you wouldn't touch me during the night."

"It's morning now." He rolled her until he could reach her mouth, then kissed her long and deeply, boldly teasing a sensitive nipple with his fingertip. His tongue traced her lips, gently seeking entrance.

In response to his caressing hands, knowing that she was playing with fire, Amanda shifted to allow him free access. She'd never lain beside a man, never savored the sweet torment of masculine hands awakening the smoldering female inside her body. It took all her courage to stop him as he slowly smoothed his hand across her stomach and downward. She couldn't let this happen. Covering his hand with her own, she held it motionless. "The children will wake up anytime. I need to get into my bed."

"Not yet." He tried to continue his hand's downward journey.

She couldn't let him. "Isaac, I really couldn't bear it if the children told people we slept together."

"I told you before, I don't care what people think."

"Of course not. Having two women is all right for a man. But being one of two women used by a man would be so humiliating."

"Used?" Isaac loomed over her in the thin morning light. "You have some of the damnedest ideas."

"Do I? I suppose you weren't planning to use my body to satisfy your physical needs."

"As I remember it, you seemed to like my loving a minute ago." He sounded defensive and hurt. "Don't worry. Since I offend your sensibilities, I'll not inflict myself on you any further." He flipped over and faced the wall.

I need to tell him about Tom. But she couldn't. Isaac would never understand. She'd better start using her head instead of letting her body and heart control her actions. She slipped onto the cold pallet on the floor, fighting tears of frustration and disappointment. *Don't think about this. Just go back to sleep.*

The children were still asleep when she next woke. Isaac was reading from her Bible as he sipped his coffee.

She crawled out of bed and stretched. Barefoot, she padded past Isaac and poured herself a cup of coffee. As she came back past the table, he wrapped one muscular arm around her waist. After closing the book and taking her coffee from her hands, he pulled her into his lap and queried her with a gentle kiss. Her heart gave her no choice. She returned his soft kisses. Cuddled in a cocoon of togetherness, they reached an unspoken peace.

When Amanda raised her head, she saw no anger lingering in his face. "You have a wonderful way of saying good morning."

"If you'd let me, I could show you an even better way."

I bet you could. Never had she felt so like a woman.

One of the children stirred.

"Damn!" Isaac muttered as she moved out of his lap.

"Another word like that and you do supper dishes," Amanda warned. "Now go check on the horses or something so I can dress."

Isaac grinned and lolled back in his chair. "Don't mind me."

She pointed toward the door.

"Shoot! You won't let me have any fun." He rose from the chair and grabbed his hat.

* * *

When Amanda had a tall stack of flapjacks ready, she said to Willie, "Go call your Uncle Isaac and Joe Pete to breakfast. Take Misty and watch where you walk."

Joe Pete came in alone. "Isaac's digging a ditch up at the garden. Will went to get him."

Amanda stared at Joe Pete. She couldn't have been more surprised if the boy had said Isaac was dancing nude in the middle of Lariat. Isaac digging a ditch? On her homestead? This she wanted to see! She almost collided with Willie outside the door.

"Uncle Isaac said he wants to work, and for us to go ahead and eat."

After breakfast, Amanda let Joe Pete return to the outside chores, then set Susie and Willie to doing the dishes. She tucked Nellie into the sling so she could carry her more easily. Lugging flapjacks and coffee, she climbed the hill to the garden.

Isaac thanked her and wiped his forehead with his bandanna before sitting down on the side of the ditch to eat.

When he rose to return to work, Amanda stopped him. "You're behind on the Lazy W. You need to get back to your own chores."

"The digging's going fast, what with the dirt so wet from the rain. I'll get a little farther for you. I hate like hell for you to be doing this hard work."

"Hard work never hurt anyone." In her mind, she noted that already this morning he'd gotten as far as she had all day yesterday. Still, he did have the Lazy W to look after. She took the shovel from him, saying, "Until I go over to the Lazy W this afternoon, I have nothing more important to do than dig a ditch."

"I've been giving this homestead thing some thought. Sit a minute and let's talk this through."

In fifteen minutes, they had a tentative summer schedule worked out. Joe Pete would ride to the Lazy W with one of the twins every other morning. Isaac would keep Susie on Mondays and Tuesdays, Willie on Wednesdays and Thursdays, and Joe Pete Fridays and Saturdays. They decided Nellie would only be confused by moving back and forth, so Sundays they'd try to be together as a family at the Lazy W or Amanda's homestead.

Amanda couldn't believe he'd given in so easily. She hadn't expected him to agree to her having the kids on her homestead for even one night. After they explained things to the children, she walked him to the barn, leaving the children in the yard to play.

Knowing that she wouldn't see Isaac for a week made her lonesome already. Amanda let him back her up against the wall, enjoying his kisses while she could. He gave her orders between kisses. "Don't leave the dugout without a gun. Don't let the kids play by the creek alone. Watch for snakes."

Interspersed with his kisses, she didn't mind being told what to do. Besides, she had a little trouble concentrating on his words with his hands cupped around her breasts and his thumbs caressing her nipples.

When he bent, kissing his way toward her breasts, she stopped him. This thing was getting out of control again. The way she felt right now, she almost wished he'd take her to the loft and make love to her. But the children were in the yard, Isaac had Mrs. Brown waiting in town, and she had Tom. Why couldn't Isaac and she have met years ago, before they had other obligations?

Isaac groaned when Amanda gently guided his head up and away from her breasts. "I want you so bad."

Shivers of delight crept down her back. "We can't keep kissing and touching like this every time we're alone."

"I think it's more like we can't keep *from* kissing and touching like this when we're alone." Isaac nibbled at her neck, but playfully now. "What am I going to do with you, Amanda?"

"Probably as much as I let you do with me."

He grinned. "You're absolutely right."

She kissed him and pushed him to arm's length. "Animal!"

"You bet I am. Don't you ever forget that."

She started for the barn door. Glancing back at his long, lean body, she smiled, remembering the wonderful feel of him next to her in bed that morning. *He's right,* she thought, *I better not forget he's an animal—a big, virile male animal.*

A nagging ache deep inside reminded her that she, too, was an animal—and the animal in her very much wanted Isaac as a mate.

The last week of May, Amanda and Nellie rode the dun mare to the Lazy W. A loaded packhorse and Nanny trailed behind. The shearing crew had set up business in the lower meadow. Isaac, Joe Pete, and the twins were already hard at work, sorting sheep.

Isaac must have been watching for them because he started up from the field when they came out of the trees. Smiling, he reached for Nellie. He held the toddler tightly to his chest and, wonder of wonders, the child allowed it. In fact, Nellie burrowed her head into his neck and her little hands clutched his shirt.

She's missed Isaac this month, Amanda thought, remembering how often Nellie had demanded, "Unk Isk!"

From the look of Isaac's welcome, he'd missed the toddler, too. Why then, had he not come to her homestead to see the child? The other children had ridden with Isaac the agreed two days each week, with Joe Pete ferrying the twins between the Lazy W and her homestead. Not once since he built the children's beds had Isaac been back to her homestead. Part of his plan to allow the children to stay on Amanda's homestead had been that they all spend Sundays together as a family. But Joe Pete had returned to the dugout each of the last three Saturday afternoons with the message that Isaac had things to do and wouldn't be over Sunday.

Early this morning, Isaac had sent Joe Pete back to the dugout with a message. The shearing crew had arrived, and Isaac would like Amanda to come over for a couple of days and cook. She'd sent Joe Pete and the twins to help him while she battened down the hatches on her homestead.

Watching Isaac and Nellie together, she wondered why Isaac hadn't ridden to her place, to see the toddler if nothing else.

Amanda turned Nanny loose, then moved to unload the pack-horse.

Isaac set Nellie on the porch. Beaming, he came to help Amanda. "Nellie Belle has grown a lot in three weeks."

"Three-and-a-half weeks," corrected Amanda. "She asks for you repeatedly each day. Where have you been keeping yourself?"

The smile disappeared from his face. "I've had lots to do. Why didn't you send word that Nellie wanted me?"

"As you said, I assumed you had a lot to do." She filled her arms with supplies and went inside. On the table, she found two letters, packets of garden seeds, and a new jar of hand cream.

He smiled when she picked up the hand cream and looked at him. "I bought it on one of my Sunday trips to town."

Amanda knew exactly how it must feel to be kicked in the stomach by a mule. Each Sunday, she'd told herself that Isaac had cattle to check on, that he had laundry to do, that he had a cabin to clean, that he went to see Luke. She'd assured herself that Isaac liked to be with her; he wouldn't miss being with her if he could. Surely, their shared kisses and caresses had meant as much to him as they did to her. She'd refused to think he might be going to town to see the Widow Brown on Sundays. Or had she read something into Isaac's kisses that simply wasn't there?

I don't care what he does, she lied to herself. "Thank you for the seeds and the hand cream," she said, congratulating herself on making her voice sound so normal.

"You're welcome. I picked the letters up yesterday. Jim said they came the middle of the week." Isaac settled himself in his kitchen chair, obviously waiting for her to open the envelopes.

Amanda tucked the letters from her mother and Tom into her pocket. She didn't want to share anything with Isaac ever again, including news from the people who cared about her.

He stared in amazement. "Aren't you going to read them?"

"Later." She tied her apron. "Do you have any fresh meat?"

"I butchered a steer this morning. It's hanging in the smokehouse. I'll cut off whatever you want in a minute.'' He tried to take her in his arms. ''Right now, I need a kiss.''

Amanda stiffened and turned her head to the side. ''I'd better get started or dinner won't be ready at a decent time.''

Color suffused his face, and he backed away from her.

Later, as Isaac strode down to the pasture, anger continued to build in him. *What in the hell was the matter with Amanda now? She was the hardest damn woman to please. One day she wanted him to kiss her; the next day she didn't. One minute she'd lie soft and yielding beside him; then she'd be fretting that someone might find out.*

He'd been working on a surprise for her for three weeks, and now she wouldn't give him the time of day. He'd sure misread her, thinking she wanted him and was just going through a case of the jitters, her being inexperienced and all. Well, Isaac Wright wasn't one to knock on doors where he wasn't welcome. Amanda Erikson could die an old maid for all he cared.

As she cooked, Amanda reminded herself that she had no right to be angry with Isaac for going to visit the Widow Brown. He'd made no promises when she'd let him get so familiar. After all, it had been she who climbed into his bed, not the other way around. She could have gotten back down on her pallet after Isaac rubbed the cramps from her legs. Instead she'd lain down beside him. Self-honesty forced her to admit that she'd wanted his touches that morning, that she'd deliberately moved to entice him.

She cringed inside to think what might have happened if the children hadn't been sleeping in the same room. Her eyes burned with unshed tears of embarrassment and disappointment.

At noontime, Amanda fetched the last jars of Mary's pickles, noting that she'd better put up lots of pickles this summer, what with the way they disappeared with Isaac around. Then she reminded herself that she was an engaged woman and didn't have to worry about Isaac's wants. She'd leave that to *dear* Tessie Brown!

Her appetite disappeared with the thought of Isaac with Mrs. Brown, but when she realized Isaac was watching her at dinner, she ate as if she hadn't a care in the world.

After dinner, she watched the children follow Isaac to the meadow. She put Nellie down for a nap, then sat at the table. What a mess she had gotten herself into. She had put off romantic entanglements years longer than any of her friends, and now she was engaged to an affluent doctor, well respected and honorable. She touched Tom's unopened letter hidden deep in her skirt pocket. With Tom waiting for her return, how had she let herself fall in love with Isaac? She should walk away from the Lazy W, give up her dream of homesteading, and just marry Tom.

But she couldn't leave the children; she loved them too much. And she couldn't take them away with her. They loved and needed Isaac. The poor babies had lost so much this last year. She wouldn't be responsible for hurting them again.

Things never would have reached this point if she'd let Isaac know right away that she wasn't the type of woman to trifle with. But no! Instead of making herself unavailable, she'd given in to the longings of her body—and heart.

Fortunately she'd found out what kind of man Isaac was. She wanted no part of his roving ways. The minute the shearing crew moved on, she'd pack up and get back to her homestead. *If* Isaac came to visit the children there, he'd find himself sleeping in the barn with the other animals.

She laid her head on the kitchen table and sobbed, crying until she had no tears left. Then she got up and started supper.

CHAPTER SIXTEEN

In her bed on the Lazy W, Amanda waited for Isaac to come in from the shearers' campfire. When he came in, she'd tell him that she felt uncomfortable with their intimate physical relationship of the past. It was time to put a stop to this insanity, especially in view of his involvement with Mrs. Brown.

And she'd tell him about Tom.

Tom's letter had reiterated his demand that she return to Denver by early spring. He'd even threatened to come and get her if she were not in Denver in time to begin wedding plans. As if Tom would leave his precious career to come for her! Heavens, he'd hardly made time for her when she'd been in Denver. Of course, if he did come to Wyoming, perhaps she could coax him to stay. That way she could keep her promise to marry him and have her homestead, too.

Her homestead. The very word spoke of adventure and accomplishment. Amanda pictured the garden she'd been working on so diligently, then thought about the cozy dugout.

Cozy to her at least. Tom would be horrified. If only she had enough money to build a proper cabin. Unfortunately, she had no money left except train fare to Denver for herself and the three younger children. Before she left Denver, Tom had given her the money along with his original ultimatum about her return.

Amanda did some long-overdue soul-searching. She'd been lying to herself. Tom wasn't coming to join her. And she wouldn't return to the life he offered her in Denver. She should send his money back and end the engagement now. No. She really should have ended the engagement the day Tom gave her his ultimatum about returning to Denver. Deep inside, she'd already known she wouldn't return. Owning land, making a success of her life while answering to no one, had been her dream for too long.

But some cautious, nagging part of her had warned her not to make a mistake by acting hastily. It'd said no real harm was being done by not ending the engagement.

And the same nagging part had reminded her that the train fare gave her a bit of security, a nest egg upon which to rely.

Her choices had been clear that day.

She could end her engagement and follow her dreams to Wyoming. She'd be known as a broke, foolish old maid with nothing better to do than raise her sister's children and try her hand at homesteading. If she failed at homesteading, she'd have to borrow money from Isaac and go home to her parents. Isaac would call the shots. Whether she took the children with her would be his decision. She'd have no way to support them.

Choice number two. She could come to Wyoming a *betrothed* woman, temporarily leaving behind a wealthy, attractive man whom she admired. If she failed in her homesteading attempt, she could use her nest egg to return to a good man ready to make her a bride. Mary's children would come with her because she could give them a home, mother, father, and financial security.

She hated to admit it, but she'd been too much of a coward to make the right decision then. And she was too proud to make it now. She'd hang on to Tom's security just a little longer.

When her homestead started to support itself, she would end the engagement and return Tom's money. A man like Tom could find a wife anytime. She didn't need to set him free right now.

It wasn't as if she were being totally dishonest with Tom. She *would* marry him if he decided to join her. And she'd spend the rest of her life being his faithful wife.

But would she ever ache for his touch the way she ached for Isaac's?

At breakfast, Isaac politely assured her that he could handle the rest of the morning's work. He suggested she return to her homestead whenever she wished. He and Joe Pete would bring the sheared sheep close to her place before night.

Feeling dismissed, Amanda took the younger children home.

At sunset, Isaac and Joe Pete drove the sheep into the fenced meadow below the dugout. Isaac stopped long enough to say hello to the children. Amanda heard no rancor in his voice when he spoke to her, nor any warmth. She hated it. At the same time, she admitted it was for the best. She and Isaac had no future, except as neighbors and co-custodians of three children.

The week crept by. She got her garden planted. The children continued their rotation of riding with Isaac, coming back to the homestead with tales of their adventures. Sunday came and went without Isaac coming to see little Nellie.

Monday morning early, she heard the creak of a wagon. Throwing back her covers, she grabbed the rifle, and flew to the window, then outside with the gun still clutched in her hand.

After pulling the team to a halt, Isaac jumped from the wagon. He smiled broadly. "Look what I picked up in Lariat yesterday. What do you think of her?"

Amanda surveyed the big milk cow. "She's beautiful." She tried to push aside her jealousy. Isaac had gone to town to see Teresa Brown again, but how Isaac spent his time was no business of hers. She should just concentrate on the milk cow.

"After you brought the nanny goat, I saw how hungry the kids were for fresh milk. A month or so back, I sent word to a dairy man in Cheyenne and had him put a milk cow on the train. I've been going into town every Sunday to see if she'd arrived.''

Her heart gave a lurch. *Was this cow the only reason Isaac had been to town?* She chided herself for being so naive. Still, Isaac's voice held a note of cordiality, not just politeness as it had when she last saw him. She ran her hand along the cow's back.

Isaac smiled as Amanda checked out the cow, talking to it in the same way that she talked to those silly goats of hers. Lord, how he wished he could pull her to him for a kiss. He wanted more, much more. Still, a kiss would be better than nothing.

Amanda didn't suspect, but in the sunlight, he could see through her nightgown. Not clearly. But well enough. Her high, firm breasts pushed against the white cotton material. The hint of shadow at the junction of her slim legs took his breath away.

He cursed himself for a fool. She didn't want him. He had no business thinking about how he'd like her long legs wrapped tightly around him. Isaac forced himself to look away lest she realize how much the nightgown revealed. If he let on, she'd never wear it in front of him again.

''I've brought something else that came on the Wednesday train.'' He lifted the tarpaulin covering the wagon bed.

''Apple trees,'' she said when she saw the scrawny saplings. ''Pa said he'd send some after I had time to get settled.''

''I'm not sure apple trees will grow in this climate.''

''Perhaps no one has tried to grow them here.''

Speaking his mind now might save Amanda a lot of trouble later. ''Maybe you'd better plant these trees on the Lazy W.''

''This sheltered valley is perfect for trees.''

''Time has a way of healing wounds. If Eric comes back, will you be able to deny his right, legal or not, to this land?''

''I don't think he'll come back, but if he does, I'll move across Wild Horse Creek. Right there.'' Amanda pointed to the area almost directly across the creek. ''I checked the map. That land is available. I've staked it out, just in case.''

''Starting over is hard.''

"I'm willing to pay my dues. I feel almost guilty about having a barn, a well, and a dugout. It takes many people years to get this much done. When I wrote Mr. Anderson, I offered to pay him for his things. I only hope he agrees to take his money for what he left here a little at a time."

"If he wants it all at once, I'll give you the money." Isaac could hardly believe his words. The other cattle ranchers would run him out of the country if they knew he was sponsoring a homesteader. Of course, if they knew how Amanda looked in that nightgown, any one of them would be happy to take his place.

"That's kind of you, Isaac. I'll figure out a way to pay for it on my own."

Two months ago, he might have doubted her. Now, he suspected she could do most anything. That was one of the problems with homesteaders like Amanda. They were capable people, even likable. Still, there was no way to make a living on one-hundred-and-sixty acres in Wyoming.

Amanda had never mentioned her money situation before. "Do you have money enough to get what you need now?" he asked.

Her answer sounded evasive to him. "The children and I have a shelter over our heads and food to eat."

"If you need something, I want you to charge it to my account at Callahan's store."

"Thanks. If I need things for the *children*, I'll do that."

Isaac didn't miss her emphasis on the word children. He decided Amanda probably needed money. But knowing her, she wasn't about to take anything from him. He'd have to keep an eye open to make sure she had the necessities.

He stayed the day, helping Amanda and the kids put in an apple orchard. Grinning, he helped dampen the soil around the two trees she was sending back to the Lazy W. *She has a lot of nerve accusing me of being bossy. She's been giving me planting instructions for ten minutes.*

"Whoa, there," he said, interrupting her at last. "I helped you put twelve trees in the ground. I can manage two more."

"I guess I'm just anxious for them to do well for you. I'll personally make the first pies from your apples."

"That might not be for years and years, Amanda." Isaac smiled. Her face had the cutest smudges of dirt.

"I know."

Although no man would wish this hard life on a woman he cared for, he fought the urge to pull Amanda close and show her how much he wanted her to stay for years and years. He should want her to go. A homestead in Wyoming was no place for a woman.

In the late afternoon, Amanda left Isaac and the children playing in the creek and went to get clean clothes and a picnic. She changed into a dress, first pulling on the old pantaloons and chemise she wore when she and the children swam in the creek.

When she returned to the creek, she watched the children play with Isaac in the water for a while, then gathered her nerve and went into the willows and stripped to her pantaloons and chemise. She asked Isaac to look away and dashed into the water for a swim. She wouldn't have been so bold had Luke been along. But after all, Isaac had seen her in her nightgown many times. *And lain beside her.* It wasn't as if they were strangers. It was ridiculous to stand on the shore when she could be in the midst of the fun.

Using a massive dose of self-control, Isaac had averted his eyes when Amanda got into the water. But he darn near dropped Nellie when she emerged from the swimming hole.

Joe Pete's gaze flicked toward Amanda; then the boy quickly looked away. Nonchalantly, Isaac shielded Amanda's body from Joe Pete's view while she hustled behind the bushes to dress. He'd have to talk with Amanda before he went back to the Lazy W. *Damn!* He hated to annoy her after the day had gone so well.

* * *

That evening, after Amanda and Isaac put the children to bed, they watched the sun set. Isaac sighed. "The view on this place almost makes it worth putting up with the snakes."

"I think we're getting the snakes under control. We didn't see any today. I killed one last week and one yesterday."

"Where did you find them?"

Drat! She should've kept her mouth shut. "Misty found one by the well. The other had coiled up outside the dugout door."

Isaac shuddered. "You keeping Misty with the kids?"

"All the time they're outside. I praise her to high heavens when she spots a snake. She stays away from them, but she goes into a point or barks, depending on her mood, I guess."

"Keep telling her how great she is. I've heard of a place where I can order another dog if you want me to send for one. But I hadn't thought to go into town until the Fourth of July. I hate to waste any Sundays now that I've got the milk cow."

Isaac *had* been going to town to get the milk cow. Again, Amanda let herself hope that maybe he hadn't gone in to see the Widow Brown. If he simply rode in to check on a cow, he wouldn't have had to stay the night at Teresa Brown's boarding house.

She detested people who asked one question when they wanted the answer to something different. But she had to know and couldn't bring herself to ask straight out. "Does the Widow Brown make a living with her boarding house?"

"I don't rightly know."

"Well, what did you pay her Saturday for a night's lodging?"

"We have an arrangement. I don't pay her by the night."

"Oh." Amanda gave thanks for descending darkness. It hid the tears in her eyes. She didn't want to know about Isaac and Teresa Brown, their "arrangement," or the boarding house. If it were the only shelter in the country, she'd never stay there.

It was a relief when Isaac mentioned Misty again. "Misty's so good about the snakes. Maybe Rasty should be staying here instead of following me around. He could watch for snakes, too."

Amanda laughed. ''If I made him stay when you left, he'd disappear the first time I looked away. You've been adopted.''

''I like Rasty.''

''Obviously the feeling is mutual.'' Amanda glanced down to where Rasty had his chin propped up on the toe of Isaac's boot.

''If Misty had a litter, could you train her pups to stay with the children like Misty does?'' Isaac asked.

''If they take after Misty, I can. However, the only male dog around is Rasty. What if they take after him?''

They looked down at the sleeping animal and laughed.

Amanda's laughter was one of the best things about her, Isaac thought. But then, he liked so many things about her.

She had a head on her shoulders. And put together! Today, when she'd come out dressed in a pair of tight denim pants, he'd almost had a heart attack. Wild horses couldn't have dragged him off once she sashayed by with that glorious backside of hers in full motion.

He had to remember, though, that Amanda didn't want his attentions. The sooner he got used to that idea, the better off he'd be. He'd managed to keep his hands off her today and they'd had a fine day. Unfortunately, he needed to talk to her about her swimming outfit, and he feared it might spoil this time together. Still, it had to be said. ''I need to talk to you about something. I don't want you getting all huffy.''

''Huffy?''

''Maybe not huffy, exactly. I guess what I mean is that I don't want you to get mad at me.''

''What makes you think I'm going to get angry?''

He thought back on what he knew about her, and of one thing he was certain. He didn't have a clue to what made her angry. ''I swear, Amanda. I never know what's going to make you mad.''

Amanda looked at him in confusion. If she lived to be a hundred, she'd never understand men. They were so insensitive. One day they caressed you, making you feel like the most desirable woman in the world. The next day they spent the night with another woman. Men had some nerve complaining

Take 4 FREE Books!

Zebra created its convenient Home Subscription Service so
you'll be sure to get the hottest new romances delivered
each month right to your doorstep — usually before they
are available in book stores. Just to show you how
convenient Zebra Home Subscription Service is, we would
like to send you 4 Zebra Historical Romances as a FREE
gift. You receive a gift worth up to $24.96 — absolutely
FREE. There's no extra charge for shipping and handling.
There's no obligation to buy anything - ever!

Save Even More with Free Home Delivery!

Accept your FREE gift and each month we'll deliver 4 brand
new titles as soon as they are published. They'll be yours
to examine FREE for 10 days. Then if you decide to keep
the books, you'll pay the preferred subscriber's price of just
$4.20 per title. That's $16.80 for all 4 books for a savings
of up to 32% off the publisher's price! Just add $1.50 to
offset the cost of shipping and handling. Remember, you
are under no obligation to buy any of these books at any
time! If you are not delighted with them, simply return
them and owe nothing. But if you enjoy Zebra Historical
Romances as much as we think you will, pay the special
preferred subscriber rate of only $16.80 each month and
save over $8.00 off the bookstore price!

Check out our website at www.kensingtonbooks.com.

Take 4 Zebra Historical Romances FREE!

MAIL TO: ZEBRA HOME SUBSCRIPTION SERVICE, INC.
120 BRIGHTON ROAD, P.O. BOX 5214,
CLIFTON, NEW JERSEY 07015-5214

YES! Please send me my 4 FREE ZEBRA HISTORICAL ROMANCES (without obligation to purchase other books). Unless you hear from me after I receive my 4 FREE BOOKS, you may send me 4 new novels – as soon as they are published – to preview each month FREE for 10 days. If I am not satisfied, I may return them and owe nothing. Otherwise, I will pay the money-saving preferred subscriber's price of just $4.20 each... a total of $16.80 plus $1.50 for shipping and handling. That's a savings of over $8.00 each month. I may return any shipment within 10 days and owe nothing, and I may cancel any time I wish. In any case the 4 FREE books will be mine to keep.

Name _____

Address _____ Apt No _____

City _____ State _____ Zip _____

Telephone ( ) _____ Signature _____

(If under 18, parent or guardian must sign)

Terms, offer, and price subject to change. Orders subject to acceptance.
Offer valid in the U.S. only.

KN020A

4 FREE
Zebra
Historical
Romances
are waiting
for you to
claim them!

*(worth up
to $24.96)*

*See details
inside....*

KENSINGTON CHOICE
Zebra Home Subscription Service, Inc.
120 Brighton Road
P.O.Box 5214
Clifton, NJ 07015-5214

that women were hard to understand. Well, she'd show Isaac. She could talk about anything with him and stay reasonable. "What's on your mind?" she asked in her most matter-of-fact tone.

"Could find yourself a different swimming outfit?"

"I didn't think you'd mind about my swimming outfit not being proper, and there's no one else around."

"I didn't mind." Isaac chuckled. "Believe me, I didn't mind at all. Any time you and I go swimming together or with the little kids, I insist that you wear that getup."

"Then what are you concerned about?"

"Joe Pete."

"Joe Pete?" she repeated.

"Joe Pete's old enough to notice a woman. Especially if the water makes her swimming outfit transparent."

With a sinking feeling, Amanda whispered, "Transparent?"

"Dang-near clear as glass."

She felt the color rising to her cheeks. "Oh." She stared straight ahead, imagining in horror what Isaac must think of her. "Do you think Joe Pete noticed?"

"Naw," Isaac lied, silently apologizing to the boy for spoiling his summer swims. Nevertheless, the kid would have to wait until he had a woman of his own to check out the physical details. Isaac didn't intend to share the vision of Amanda's body with anyone, even a half-grown boy.

He decided the time had come to make a hasty exit. He rose, carried his chair inside the dugout, and returned with a lantern. "I'm beat. I noticed you put the trundle bed from the dugout up in the hay loft. I'll see you in the morning."

Amanda felt a little guilty about not being more congenial and inviting Isaac into the dugout with her and the children. A little guilty and a lot lonely. "You don't have to sleep out there," she said. "I know the idea of snakes bothers you."

"I doubt any rattlesnake can climb the ladder to the loft." Besides, he'd be more likely to sleep in a barn full of rattlesnakes than in a room with Amanda just an arm's length away, and him not allowed to touch her. He went a few steps, then turned to her again. "Don't sit there fretting about this afternoon. You didn't know.'' He gambled that she'd not take exception and receive his compliment as he intended. ''Amanda.''

She looked his way.

''You have a beautiful body.''

His low, sultry tone made Amanda wish he'd take her in his arms and kiss her the way he used to do. But he walked on to the barn without her.

Before he pulled the heavy door shut, he called in a loud stage whisper, ''Amanda?''

''What?'' *Please, God, let him make up some excuse for me to come into the barn with him!*

''I especially like that cute little dimple on your right cheek.''

''What are you talking about?'' Automatically, she lifted a hand to her face. ''I don't have a dimple.''

''Want to bet?''

CHAPTER SEVENTEEN

Until today, Amanda had been pleased that Isaac came to her homestead each evening. He got to see the children, and she got to see him. He slept in the barn and kept his hands to himself. But when she stormed into her homestead's yard late one afternoon and found him playing with the children, she was furious. *Exactly what she had suspected!* Isaac had arrived early.

"Welcome home, stranger," he said with a smile.

As if she were a stranger! He must have seen every inch of her body! Her cheeks burned with anger and embarrassment. Her bath at a secluded swimming hole was the one time each day she managed to have time alone. Now Isaac had gone and spoiled it! She'd never speak to him again as long as she lived!

Without speaking, she swept past him and into the dugout. She stuffed her dirty clothes into the laundry bag and braided her still-damp hair, muttering to herself all the while. *The very idea of a grown man sneaking around and watching a woman bathe!* And moving her clothes so she'd know he'd been there. About the time she decided Isaac had some consideration for her feelings, he had to go and do something so . . . so immature and thoughtless! Well, she'd just tell him what she thought about his watching her bathe right now! She burst out the dugout door intending to demand that Isaac step inside. No need for the children to hear what she had to say to their precious Uncle Isaac.

Out in the yard, the younger children had piled into the free-standing swing Isaac had built several evenings back. Joe Pete was pushing it while the twins chanted a rhyme.

Isaac and his horse were gone.

"Where's Isaac?" Amanda demanded of Joe Pete.

"He said he felt like taking a bath. He went up to your swimming hole."

"Yeah," piped in Willie. "He said he didn't know what the devil was bothering you, but he'd better make himself scarce."

"Uncle Isaac almost said *hell,*" Susie offered. "He didn't, though, so I guess he doesn't have to do supper dishes, huh?"

Amanda shook her head in reply and smoothed Nellie's wispy red hair. She stared up the hill and had a sudden inspiration. She'd sneak up on Isaac and give him a dose of his own medicine.

"I must have dropped my gardening scissors this afternoon, and I want to find them before they're ruined." She fingered the scissors still deep in the pocket of her overalls. "Joe Pete, can you watch the little children while I look?"

"Sure."

"You need to keep all three of them right with you."

"Yes, ma'am."

As she tucked her braid up into her hat, Amanda said, "It may take a while to find my scissors. If you get hungry, you can eat the leftover biscuits with some rhubarb jelly."

The lights fairly danced in the children's eyes. There wouldn't be a biscuit left when she returned.

At the top of the hill, she turned to wave, but the children already had gone inside the dugout. In spite of her anger at Isaac, she smiled. No matter how much she cooked, the kids claimed to be on starvation's doorstep before the next meal.

Thinking of the next meal, which she should really be cooking right now, caused her to hurry. At the edge of the woods surrounding the pool, Isaac had tied old Gray to a tree.

Knowing the little waterfall above the swimming hole would cover any slight noise she might make, Amanda walked Gray far enough away that Isaac would realize someone had messed with his horse. Down on her belly, she slithered toward the swimming hole, trying to guess where Isaac might have laid his clothes.

When she finally could see Isaac, Amanda couldn't decide whether she was disappointed or relieved. Water covered the lower half of his body. Eyes closed, he had braced himself with his elbows on some rocks and leaned back, letting the fast-moving stream entering the pool massage his back.

She looked around, then groaned. Isaac hadn't put his clothes where she'd expected. But if she circled around, she could pull his clothing toward her with a stick. She'd leave his pants down the trail. He'd have to beg for the rest.

She scooted back about ten feet before a sudden pressure in the middle of her back pinned her tightly to the ground. She tried to turn over. The next instant, the barrel of a rifle pressed against the back of her neck.

Oh, dear God! She needed to warn Isaac! He couldn't hear small sounds over the noisy waterfall. "Isaac, run!"

The pressure nailing her to the ground didn't let up, but the gun barrel left her neck and her attacker knocked off her hat. Her braid tumbled down, and Amanda heard a laughing comment. She fought to get to her pistol, but her captor quickly disarmed her. Before she knew what had happened, she'd been hoisted up under the man's arm, and a male voice hailed Isaac.

Struggling to free herself, she saw Isaac hunkered down behind a large river boulder. He had his pistol aimed in their direction, so she stopped wiggling. She didn't want Isaac to hit her when he shot.

A surprised, pleased look replaced the animal wariness on his face. He uncocked his pistol and laid it on top of the boulder. Dripping water, he walked through the shallows toward Amanda and her captor. "Hawk, my friend. I've been worried about you. What are you doing with my woman under your arm?"

From her ignominious position, Amanda craned her head

around to view the most handsome man she'd ever laid eyes on. The muscular Indian looked down at her with a wry smile.

"Are you sure this is your woman?" he asked in English. "I saw her move your horse and sneak into the trees to ambush you."

"Ambush me?" Isaac laughed. "And you stopped her?"

Hawk joined in the laughter and set Amanda on her feet. "Had I known your woman dressed as a man and played games, I wouldn't have interfered."

Isaac reached out to shake Hawk's hand. Without any indication that he was standing stark naked, knee deep in water, Isaac introduced Amanda. "Hawk is an old friend of the family, Amanda. Joshua, Hawk, and I played together when we were kids."

Isaac had nothing on, and little more covered Hawk's lower body. Keeping her gaze carefully on the men's faces, Amanda could feel the rush of blood in her cheeks as she said the polite things. Isaac was stark naked! This didn't seem the opportune time to point out that she wasn't *his* woman.

"Hawk and I have some catching up to do, Amanda. Run along and fix us some supper."

She grabbed her hat from the ground and took off. From behind her, even over the sound of the little waterfall and the blood pounding in her ears, she heard the men roar with laughter.

CHAPTER EIGHTEEN

Amanda glanced in the mirror and smoothed back her hair before calling Isaac, Hawk, and the children to supper. Hawk entered first carrying Nellie. He handed the toddler to Isaac; then he took the chair Amanda offered at the foot of the table.

After a few minutes, she forgot Hawk's lack of clothing. Almost. She tried to concentrate on the conversation instead of his dark, muscular chest. It was a good thing Isaac had on a shirt. If his chest were bare, she'd probably forget how to make polite conversation altogether.

As Isaac dished out the sweetened rhubarb sauce for dessert, he spoke to Amanda. "After supper, please put the kids to bed, then come outside to talk. Just leave the dishes on the table; we can wash them later." He sent the children a stern look. "There'll be no story tonight. I don't want to hear a word after Amanda tucks you in. Do you understand?"

The twins nodded, and Nellie followed their lead.

When the men rose, Isaac spoke to Joe Pete. "Come on out with us. I'd like you to show Hawk the horses you've been working. I'm thinking you and Hawk might want to talk."

Amanda's heart began to thud. She'd deliberately kept Joe Pete busy before supper, trying to keep him away from Hawk.

As selfish as it was, she didn't want Hawk to locate Joe Pete's relatives. Isaac must have sensed something because he gave her a reassuring touch on the shoulder on his way to the door. She settled the younger children, then joined the men at the corral.

Isaac slid an arm loosely around her waist. "When Hawk caught you sneaking . . ." He glanced at Joe Pete, then rephrased his sentence. "When you and I ran into Hawk, he was on his way to the Lazy W."

The barely concealed amusement on the men's faces caused her cheeks to burn. She tried to ignore their teasing. "I assumed that he might have been coming to see you."

"He's got a problem in his camp."

Hawk took over. "One of our women had a baby boy two days ago. The woman died yesterday. I've come to see if Isaac would trade some milk for a horse. But he tells me his milk cows died, and you're the only one with milking animals. Would you consider making a trade? We need milk until my wife has our baby in about two moons. Then she will be able to feed both babies."

"There'll be no talk of trading. If the baby needs the milk, you're welcome to what milk I have, as long as you need it. I'll keep the cow for our three children. You can take my nanny goat. She gives more than enough milk for one baby."

Isaac gave her waist an almost imperceptible squeeze. "I told Hawk you'd feel that way."

A warm sense of pride at pleasing Isaac flooded Amanda. She seldom did anything he liked. She turned to Hawk. "Have you ever milked a goat?"

The look of horror in Hawk's eyes made her laugh aloud. "It's not *that* bad," she teased. "Come along. I'll teach you."

When Hawk didn't move, Isaac took mercy on him. "Amanda, what if you leave a jar of milk somewhere every evening? Hawk's near enough that he can ride over after dark and collect it. That way the baby will have milk, our kids won't accidentally carry tales to town, *and* you can keep your goat right here."

"Would that suit you?" she asked Hawk.

He nodded. ''I see that you can use a horse. One day you will find one in the corral to repay your kindness.''

''That isn't necessary, Hawk. We're neighbors. I'm happy I have the milk to give you for the baby. Besides, Isaac has lent me horses. I need nothing.''

''Then perhaps you'll take the horse for Fights The Wind.''

''Fights The Wind?''

''Joe Pete,'' Isaac explained.

She turned to the boy. ''Joe Pete, you never told me your name was Fights The Wind.''

''Only my mother called me by my Indian name. My father called me by my white name. He said white folks would make fun of my Indian name.''

''I would never make fun of your Indian name. It's beautiful. Why did your mother call you Fights The Wind?''

''Because I'm half white and half Indian. She said that I would have to be strong, that I would have to stand up for myself with the whites and the Indian, and that it would be like fighting the wind.''

Poor child. Her eyes burned, and she fought the urge to hug him. But the way he was standing so straight and tall warned her off. ''There is no wind to fight here.''

''I know. So here I am Joe Pete.''

''Please get the leftover milk from the well for Hawk. We'll hide more in there tomorrow evening.''

After Hawk said good-bye, Isaac caught Amanda's eye. ''Once Joe Pete's in bed, I want to talk to you.''

She had rather expected he would. *Well, she wanted to talk to him, too!* First, she'd tell him what she thought about his sneaking up on her at the swimming hole. Second, she'd let him know that she didn't much appreciate his telling Hawk that she was his woman. While she was at it, she might as well give him her opinion of the way he'd sent her down to cook supper without so much as a please. Ready to do battle, she approached the swing where Isaac sat watching the stars.

Before she could say a word, Isaac drawled, ''Amanda, honey, if you want to see me naked, I'll strip for you anytime, any place. You don't have to come crawling through the brush.''

Amanda almost choked. "I do not wish to see you naked!"

"Then why were you sneaking up on me at the swimming hole?"

"Why was I sneaking up on you?" Amanda's voice got higher as she got angrier. "Why was *I* sneaking up on *you?*" She noticed that her pointing finger seemed to have developed a will of its own as she waved it in front of Isaac's nose. "I have little enough privacy without putting up with you leering at me while I bathe!"

To her chagrin, she burst into the tears of embarrassment she'd held at bay all evening. Appalled by her lack of composure, and seeking a place of refuge, she ran into the barn, climbed the ladder, and flung herself on Isaac's trundle bed.

When her tears were spent, she heard Isaac call up the ladder, "Amanda, come down here."

She threw herself on her back and chose not to answer.

"Amanda?"

She could hear Isaac muttering under his breath as he struck a match. The lantern's light cast long shadows into the loft.

"If you don't come down, I'm coming up."

She stared up into the beams of the roof and crossed her arms over her chest. She'd not give him the satisfaction of answering.

"You are one hardheaded woman," Isaac said as he hung the lantern on a nearby nail. With his back to her, he sat down on the cot's edge and sighed. "Honest to God, Amanda, I try and I try, but I can't please you."

"You call sneaking up on me at the swimming hole and moving my clothes trying to please me?"

Isaac turned to her. "Run that by me again."

"You heard me perfectly well!" Tears threatened again, and Amanda flipped over onto her side, so Isaac couldn't see her cry. *Why did she have to go and bawl every time he upset her?*

"When did all this sneaking up on you happen?"

Something in Isaac's tone made Amanda turn toward him. "This afternoon." She searched his face, then her stomach knotted into a ball of fear. "It *wasn't* you, was it? You didn't come past the bathing pool on the way over this afternoon?"

He shook his head. "I used the wagon road. I hadn't been here five minutes when you came barreling off the hill looking mad enough to take on a grizzly bear."

"It must have been Hawk."

"Hawk wouldn't do something like that. I didn't sneak up on you today, and I'd bet my firstborn it wasn't Hawk."

The hair on Amanda's neck stood up, and chills ran down her back and arms. "Isaac, several times this last couple of weeks, when I was at the bathing hole, I got this creepy feeling, like I was being watched. I told myself I was being ridiculous and wrote it off to nerves or something. But today someone moved my clothes while I bathed."

"Maybe you didn't leave them where you thought."

"I always use the same tree branch. They'd been moved."

"Damn!" Taking her hand, Isaac rubbed his thumb gently across her knuckles. "I hadn't wanted to worry you, but we've got rustlers working the Lazy W. Luke and I thought they were only on the east side of the ranch, but maybe they're working this side, too. Your clothes didn't move themselves."

It seemed natural to move into the comforting circle of his arms. After the first rush of fear faded, it seemed just as natural to lie back, a willing captive beneath the length of Isaac's body. Pushing her conscience aside, Amanda returned his famished kisses.

Isaac shifted and took off his gun belt, letting the gun and holster drop to the loft floor. He covered her again. Gently, he coaxed her to let him lie intimately against her.

Amanda thought back to how beautiful his body had looked as he stood naked in front of her at the river. She had only glanced at him, but she needed no basis for comparison to know that Isaac was a perfect specimen of the male of the human species.

As they kissed, she simply enjoyed the sensations created by the tiny rhythmic movements of Isaac's hips. Then he slipped his hands beneath her buttocks, tilting her body to fit against him. Intuitively, she started meeting his movements.

A soft moan from Isaac let her know she'd pleased him, but

it also reminded her that she was losing control. *I've got to stop this,* she thought repeatedly.

Each time Isaac reached for a button on her blouse, she stayed his hand. But desire for something more blossomed with every taste of his lips, every touch of his tongue, every slow, tantalizing thrust of his hips. She pulled his shirt from his waistband and slid her hands inside and upward, exploring the contours of his muscular back.

The dogs started wildly barking.

Isaac vaulted from the cot and gathered up his gunbelt. Before Amanda could rise to a sitting position, he'd blown out the lantern and pushed the loft's wide window open a crack.

Her thoughts flew to the sleeping children, alone in the dugout. She headed for the ladder. Ignoring Isaac's command to stop, she flung herself down and dashed across the yard.

The dugout plunged into darkness as she extinguished the lantern. After securing the door, she grabbed her new rifle and the old shotgun Isaac had lent her and placed them on the table within her easy reach. At the window, she buckled on her holster while her eyes searched the area in front of the baying dogs.

"Hello, the dugout!" came a familiar voice.

Amanda sagged against the wall as Isaac called off the dogs. Hawk entered the yard and spoke to Isaac.

By the time Amanda controlled her shaking hands, lit the lantern, and unbarred the door, Hawk had gone. "What's going on?" she asked when she reached the barn.

Isaac threw the saddle blanket on his horse. "Hawk spotted some sheepherders moving across my range about three miles north. I need to remind them whose property they're on."

Amanda did some quick figuring. "Isaac, three miles north of here is public grazing land. I remember Luke telling me that."

"Did he also tell you that we run about four hundred head of cattle in that general area?"

She nodded.

"Then figure it out for yourself. There isn't grass enough for our cattle and someone else's sheep, and we were here first.'' Isaac adjusted the cinch on his saddle. ''Maybe this answers the question of who was hanging around your swimming hole this afternoon. At any rate, Hawk said it's the same outfit that came through here last year. I talked to them real nice the first time. Too nice, I guess. Obviously, I didn't make my point.''

She watched in horror as Isaac checked his rifle and the ammunition in his saddlebags. ''You aren't planning to use that gun, are you?''

''I'll do what I have to do.''

''You can't just shoot people who don't do what you want.''

''Who said anything about shooting people?'' With a creak of leather, he hoisted himself into the saddle. ''If I'm not back by noon tomorrow, get those kids to the Lazy W and send Joe Pete after Luke.''

Immediately after he left, she'd heard Rasty's barks and the protesting bleats of the sheep. Why was Isaac moving the sheep now? Sick with worry, Amanda held vigil at the dugout's window most of the night. Once she thought she heard gunshots.

At daylight, she could wait no longer. She fed the children, then sent Joe Pete to saddle the three horses Isaac insisted she keep in her pasture.

The twins rode double, and she put Nellie in the saddle with her. As she expected, it didn't take much to follow the trail of a herd of sheep. In less than an hour, she came upon a disaster area.

Hidden in the trees, Amanda looked down into a lush valley. Bleating sheep milled about, held in a flock by two dogs. An old herder was rebuilding a wrecked camp while three younger men worked to separate the Lazy W's sheep from their own. Off toward one end of the valley, Amanda could see a small group of Lazy W ewes, some grazing peacefully with their lambs, others trying to get back into the main herd, probably seeking their offspring.

She surveyed the area closely, guessing that Isaac had created the chaos and wondering how in the world one man had managed to make such a mess. And why?

Repeatedly she scanned the area looking for Isaac, but she

couldn't spot him. Surmising that he must be all right, she decided she'd better help the herders sort sheep. If she calculated right, some Lazy W ewes and lambs might have been apart for ten or more hours by now. The poor lambs must be starved, and the ewes in pain from engorged udders.

She moved Nellie to Joe Pete's horse. "I'm going down. If anything goes wrong, take the children to the Lazy W and wait for Isaac." She handed her rifle to him. "Use this if you need to."

She was out about ten feet from the edge of the trees when the sheepherders saw her coming. The four rifles trained on her made her realize she might have made a tactical error.

From his hidden position on the far side of the valley, Isaac cursed and came to his feet. Opposite and slightly below, he watched Amanda dismount and take off her gunbelt. Then she removed her hat and shook her hair loose. With her hands in the air, she continued her approach to the sheep camp on foot. Isaac didn't exhale until the herders lowered their guns and walked to meet her. After some talk, Amanda sent Misty to the far end of the valley where the men had been driving the Lazy W sheep.

Isaac cursed again when Amanda signaled and the children rode out of the trees and started down the hill. Just what he needed. *His whole family at the mercy of strange men!*

Wondering how to rescue them from the valley without getting anyone hurt, he watched helplessly as Amanda hung her gunbelt on a wagon. She braided her hair, anchored Nellie to a tree with a rope, and set the twins to helping the camptender. With Joe Pete on horseback driving the Lazy W sheep down the valley, Amanda began sorting sheep.

Hidden in the trees, Isaac worked his way around the valley where he would be in range if he had to use his rifle. As he rode, he could hear the men whistle to their dogs or call to one another. Occasionally, the sound of the children's voices or Amanda's would sail to him on the wind. Dag-blasted woman!

At midday, the camp-tender dished out food to Susie and

Willie, then carried some to Nellie. Isaac watched as the man hand-fed her. The little minx ate as though she was used to such babying.

He was going to strangle Amanda when he got his hands on her. Not only had she put herself and the kids in danger, but with her help, the sorting of the herds moved quickly.

His point in driving the Lazy W sheep into the strange herd had been to cause the herders to lose grazing days. If sheep lost enough grazing days, the weight of marketing lambs would be low in the fall; then perhaps these and other sheepmen would stay out of his territory. Unfortunately, with Amanda and Joe Pete's help, instead of losing four or five grazing days, these herders would have the Lazy W sheep cleared out by tomorrow and their own herd calmed down and eating again. Dag-blast it!

Isaac still hadn't made a plan other than to keep watch over his family when Amanda glanced up the hill and caught sight of Rasty. She loaded the younger children on a horse and led it up the hill. His relief turned to irritation when she wordlessly handed him the reins and stomped right back down the hill.

With three rowdy children clamoring for attention, Isaac headed for the Lazy W. Amanda could dang well take care of herself. *She got herself in the middle of that mess; she could get herself out!*

An hour later, he stormed into the sheepherders' camp with the children in tow. He eyed the rifles pointed at him and swung down from his horse. "Put your guns away. I've been on the ridge for hours and could have shot all of you if I'd wanted."

He enjoyed the looks of confusion on the herders' faces as he tethered Nellie to the tree and helped himself to a dipper of camp water. After a word of caution to the twins about their behavior, he remounted and rode to help Joe Pete move the Lazy W sheep on down the canyon toward Amanda's place. If he had to work with sheep, he'd damn sure do it from horseback.

Along toward suppertime, it appeared the lambs and ewes had been matched, although some Lazy W pairs still grazed in the main herd. Isaac went to pick up the kids and Amanda. If he didn't get them home soon, they'd be riding in the dark.

When he dismounted, Amanda walked past him without a word. He reached out and grabbed her arm, but her pointed look at his hand reminded him that she had strong feelings about being physically restrained. He dropped her arm. "We need to say our good-byes and get our outfit headed toward home."

"You can do whatever you want. I'm staying here to clean up this mess you made."

"These men are our enemies."

Amanda looked at Nellie, who was again being hand-fed by the camptender, then toward the twins, who had coaxed one herder into a game of hide-and-seek. "They may be *your* enemies. All I see are decent men trying to make a living. Besides, some of the children's sheep are still mixed up in this herd."

"The herders will get them sorted out. They wouldn't dare move with a cattle rancher's stock mixed in with their own. In this country, we hang rustlers first and ask questions later."

"In that case, I'd better stay, since these men don't speak English very well. They might need someone to explain that some idiot rancher drove his band of sheep through their camp and into their herd."

By now it must have been apparent that Amanda and Isaac were arguing because everyone in camp had quit working and playing. All eyes were turned in their direction. In an undertone, Isaac tried again. "Come on, Amanda. You're causing a scene."

"On the contrary. *You* are causing a scene. I'm on my way to help fix supper."

Isaac stood a moment in the middle of the camp, conscious of the sheepherders' nervous stares. Then he gestured toward Amanda, rolled his eyes heavenward, and shrugged as if to say, "Women!"

The herders laughed and visibly relaxed.

Full dark fell as they ate mutton stew and laid out their blankets. Isaac took his long rope and laid it out, encircling his family's makeshift beds.

Amanda rose on one elbow. "What in the world are you doing?"

"Old timers say a snake won't crawl over a horsehair rope. I always circle my bed on the ground with rope."

He threw his blanket over Amanda and Nellie, but Amanda refused to make room for him in their bed. He warned her in a quiet whisper, "As far as these men know, you're my woman, and we're going to keep them thinking like that. Now scoot over!"

For a second, she looked as if she might be going to argue. Then she turned her back and made a little room for him.

As the last of the stars blinked out, Amanda stifled a small yawn. Somehow during the night, she and Isaac had found the same spooned position that they'd awakened in that morning in the dugout. His hand again cupped her breast. Cautiously, so as not to awaken him, she tried to slip out of his embrace, but he pulled her closer.

"No one's up."

"I thought I'd take a quick ride to my homestead to milk. I could be back before anyone missed me."

"We'll have the rest of those sheep cut out in an hour or two this morning. A few more hours aren't going to make a big difference in the milking." He kissed the back of her neck.

She squirmed, trying to get away from the exquisite agony of his lips nibbling at her ear.

He growled playfully. "If you don't want your ears kissed, you better roll over so I can kiss you properly."

"There are people around!"

"They're sleeping."

Being careful not to disturb Nellie, she turned to face him. His lips covered hers and she returned the kiss.

"I need more than one little measly kiss to get through a day tending sheep," he said.

"You call that kiss measly?"

"I do for a fact."

Wrapping her arms around his neck, Amanda did her level

best to see that he had more than one measly kiss. The love
play turned serious when he slid his hand under her shirt and
caressed her breast. She had no desire to stop his explorations,
but this was not the time or place. "Not now."

Raising himself on one elbow, he looked down at her.
"Tonight?"

Amanda marveled at the casual, flirty way he asked, as if
he were requesting a small favor instead of the pledge of her
life. Isaac didn't realize it, but the physical love act would bind
her to him, body and soul. If she let her heart and body dictate
her actions now, she'd never be able to look Tom in the eye.

The clang of a pot caused her to push Isaac away in a panic.
It seemed that he deliberately took his time, keeping her pinned
beneath his chest and shoulders. When he did rise, he stretched
and made a great show of checking the buttons on his pants
before beating the dust from his hat and ambling toward the
camptender.

Mortified by what the other man might be thinking, Amanda
surreptitiously adjusted her clothing under the blanket. Like
Isaac, she only had to button the waistband of her denim trousers, the one concession to comfort they'd made when they lay
down fully clothed the night before.

The camptender and Amanda visited as she stirred the mush.
He owned the sheep. The younger men were his hired herders.

It didn't take long to cut out the remaining Lazy W sheep.
As Isaac prepared to help Joe Pete move their flock back to
Amanda's homestead, he called over to where she stood washing the breakfast dishes. "I'll drop the sheep at your place,
then go on home. I'll be late tonight, so don't wait up for me."

Amanda lowered her head, tending to the dishes so the herders wouldn't notice her burning cheeks. Did Isaac realize he'd
embarrassed her? *Perhaps he didn't even care!*

A few minutes after Isaac left, the camptender bluntly asked,
"You and Isaac Wright are not married?"

What could she say? It seemed a little stupid to pretend any longer. Though she'd openly lain with Isaac the night before, he'd just announced to the herders that they weren't married by mentioning their separate homes. "No, we're not married."

As she rolled up the blankets, the old man talked with his herders; then he came to help her tie the bedding on behind the saddles. His unease made her wary. Somehow, he didn't look so old right now. Nor did he sound old when he spoke. "Would twenty dollars keep you in our camp another hour?"

"Twenty dollars! What for?" Intense heat rose to her cheeks when a possible implication hit her. She glanced toward the twins and Nellie playing in the shade of a tree.

The man followed her eyes. "We will take turns watching over the children. There's room in the tent to be private. We are simple men, with simple needs, and our women are far away."

Amanda could hardly breathe, overcome with humiliation.

The man must have seen her hesitation. "Thirty dollars."

Humiliation gave way to anger. "Get out of my way!" She gripped the horses' reins and tried to push past him.

After looking into her face, he put the money back into his pocket. "I think we misunderstood. Let me help you with the children."

"Don't you touch them!" Silently, she loaded the children onto the horses. At the top, Amanda glanced back. The old man waved to her, but she turned her head away.

The rest of the day she agonized. She'd been forced to face a situation that would surely arise again if she continued to play this dangerous game with Isaac. She knew what people would say if they found out. No, not if, but *when* they found out.

Heavens, she hadn't been in town two hours before she knew about Isaac and the Widow Brown. She didn't want to be another Teresa Brown. And as always, there was Tom.

Tom was a proud man. It was time Amanda remembered her obligations and started using her head instead of letting her traitorous body dictate to her.

* * *

After Isaac dropped off the sheep and Joe Pete, he circled back and had a talk with the sheepherders. He drew them a map, indicating a route around his grazing area, and they shook hands.

Still, he had a feeling deep in his bones. These men or more like them would be coming through next year, and the year after. *Sheepmen and homesteaders. All crowding him, looking for a piece of the promised land.* It had gotten to the point where a cattleman couldn't find enough grazing land.

It was good to have Amanda here to help. Not only did she take good, loving care of the kids, but she'd given him ideas about irrigating and growing feed for the cattle instead of relying solely on the whims of nature to provide grass. He'd have to think about some of her suggestions.

Right now, though, he could think of nothing but the coming night and his throbbing desire for Amanda. She'd gotten under his skin, and it was past time to get this matter settled. She would have to get over her squeamishness about the kids or Luke seeing them touch or kiss. He couldn't keep his hands off her.

One day soon, she'd get tired of the work and worry and go back to Denver where she belonged. Before she left, he'd better make memories enough to last him a long, lonely lifetime.

He spent the rest of the day futilely searching for some cows from a herd that had come up short on the count earlier in the week. Tired and upset at losing the cattle, but more worried that someone was sneaking around his lands, he rode to Amanda's late that night. He needed to hold her.

In the dugout, Amanda pulled the curtain so they wouldn't disturb the sleeping children. She sat with Isaac while he ate his supper. When he finished, he leaned back in his chair and sighed. ''Your good cooking was just what I needed. I'm almost getting to like all that green garden stuff.''

She tried to smile. But knowing what she had to do this evening took the enjoyment out of his compliment.

"You look extra pretty tonight, Amanda. Don't get me wrong, I like your pants, but it's nice to see you in a dress sometimes." He glanced toward the children's beds. "I'm beat. Come tuck me in my bed."

Isaac's slow, sensuous smile told her what he expected as he took her hand and led the way to the dugout door. Outside, he pulled her close.

The only man in whose arms I've ever wanted to be, and now it's got to end. Her heart literally felt as if it were breaking. But she'd made the only reasonable, moral decision. Lowering her head, she denied his kiss.

Isaac froze. "Amanda, I've had a hell of a day! I'm not in the mood for this. What's wrong now?"

She hated it when he talked to her in that irritated tone. It made her next words easier to say. "This thing between us is over. I can't go on like this."

Isaac kissed her shoulder. His voice softened. "This thing, as you call it, is healthy passion. You're a little scared about the first time, is all. That's natural. You'll get over it."

"Isaac, you're not listening to me. There isn't going to be a first time between us. Not tonight, not any night."

He crossed his arms and glared at her. "Something seems to have happened that I missed. Would you care to explain?"

"After you left this morning, I got a heavy dose of reality. The herders offered me money to do for them what they assumed I do for you. Lots of money."

"I'll kill them!" Isaac started for his horse.

She stopped him. "At least they offered me money for my services. What are you offering? The same thing you've given Teresa Brown? A community full of people who snicker behind her back because she's such a fool?"

"Only women have that attitude about Tess."

"And you still leave her to their mercy?"

"Tess isn't unhappy with our arrangement."

Isaac might as well have thrown cold water in her face. "But I would be, Isaac. Very unhappy."

"What do you want, Amanda? A declaration of undying love? A marriage proposal? What?"

Tears blurred her eyes. She fought to keep her voice calm. "I suppose either one of those would have done."

She turned and walked back to the dugout, closing the door behind her.

CHAPTER NINETEEN

As Amanda walked, she thought over the past month. Her days had gone by in a blur of steady work. Every evening Isaac rode to the dugout. Usually, he came late, looking tense and worried. If he arrived early enough, he'd do a few chores, then play with the children or chat politely with her. He was always gone in the morning before she woke at sunrise.

Isaac had come earlier than usual today. He was at the dugout, and Amanda was on her way to bathe, *at his suggestion*. She hadn't bathed in the river since her clothes had been moved that day, but Isaac had assured her he hadn't seen a sign of the rustlers. He'd insisted she take an hour or two for herself.

She'd just as soon have bathed in the dugout. Sometimes, around the dugout yard, she got prickly feelings, as though she was being watched. More than once lately, she'd caught herself studying the trees surrounding her homestead, wondering if anyone could be up there. She didn't want Isaac to know how uneasy she'd been feeling. He might use her discomfort as an excuse to get her to move the children back to the Lazy W.

She'd maybe have talked to him about her unease last month, but she couldn't now. Not with him using the remote, polite manner he'd shown toward her since she'd called an end to their physical relationship. These days, Isaac and she sat far apart to watch the sunset. When darkness fell, he said good night and went to his bed in the loft of her barn. She went to her lonesome bed, thankful that her day's work exhausted her so she slept in spite of her aching heart.

This was how it had to be. However physically attractive she found Isaac, she couldn't reconcile herself to his arrangement with Teresa Brown, or with what people might say if they found out Isaac and she were carrying on together. Or, more important, of the impropriety of being intimate with Isaac when she was engaged to Tom.

She didn't blame Isaac. She hated to admit it, but she'd encouraged him—a lot. The trouble was that men viewed this man-woman thing differently from the way a woman did. When a woman gave a man her body, she gave him her heart and soul. A man, on the other hand, could make love and obviously not be any more emotionally involved than if he were enjoying a meal. If only Isaac were ugly and mean instead of handsome and nurturing. She must be a complete fool to love such a downright ornery, hardheaded, opinionated, and demanding man.

After reaching the secluded pool, Amanda hung her clean clothes on a tree limb. This spot once had been her place of refuge and mental rejuvenation. Now she checked the area before disrobing. Even then, she couldn't bring herself to remove her chemise and short drawers. When she finally entered the water, she still was thinking about Isaac. Of course, it seemed she thought about Isaac all day, every day.

She should be relieved that he didn't ask for intimacies. It made it easier for her to maintain distance between them. If she gave in to her aching desire for Isaac, he'd never respect her again—not that he had much respect for her anyway.

Besides, there was Tom. Always Tom. Her engagement of convenience had become a gray pallor covering her Wyoming sky.

Though Tom and she weren't in love when they agreed to marry, he'd assured her that their respect for each other was foundation enough for a fine marriage. He'd reached the time in life when he needed a wife to tend to his household and bear his children. He'd offered her social acceptance, a lovely home, and, most important, the children she so desperately wanted. Amanda had decided she would be content as his wife.

But now, it was plain dishonest to let him continue to believe she'd return to Denver. She had children. Surrogate, admittedly. Still, Joe Pete, her sister's children, and her homestead filled her life with love and a reason for being.

Being realistic, she knew she'd never convince Tom to leave his prestigious career, his fine home, and his doting mother to live in Lariat, Wyoming.

Floating in the cool mountain pool, Amanda mentally composed the letter to Tom. The letter that would set Tom free—and cut her lifeline to her old, more secure, socially acceptable life.

At the dugout, Isaac gave Joe Pete his orders, then rode quickly toward Amanda's bathing spot. Silently guiding his horse off the trail and onto the thick grass to muffle the sound of his approach, he inspected the shrubbery surrounding the hidden pool. The pinto horse was there, concealed in the trees.

This was the first time he'd seen the animal, but he'd noticed the tracks five days ago. Everywhere he looked, he found many more tracks, all the same unshod horse. Whoever rode that horse had been watching Amanda's homestead for a while.

Isaac hadn't said anything to her, but he'd spent the last five days searching the area and guarding her homestead, leaving to do his chores on the Lazy W only when Hawk relieved him.

A sense of urgency overcame Isaac now, and beads of fear covered his forehead and neck. He spurred his horse up the trail the two hundred feet to an arranged hidden spot, where Hawk, Hawk's young wife, and a middle-aged squaw waited. Isaac nodded at Hawk's unspoken question.

Hawk nudged his mount forward. Isaac spun his horse around and followed the Indians.

They'd almost reached the swimming hole when the older squaw spotted the horse in the bushes. She stopped, looked first at Amanda's clothing hanging in plain view, then at Hawk. Hawk played his part well, shrugging innocently. Without a word, the woman slipped off her horse and entered the trees surrounding the pond. After signaling his wife to wait, Hawk followed her.

Sweat dripped down Isaac's back as he pulled his gun and moved in behind them. He listened for sounds from the swimming hole, praying Hawk was right in his surmising.

The squaw spotted the brave crouched behind some bushes. Eyes on the swimming hole, he had his loincloth pushed to the side, granting his hand free access to his game of self-pleasure.

Hissing in outrage, the woman launched herself at the unsuspecting brave, knocking him to the ground, pounding on his hunched back with furious fists, shouting at him.

In seconds, Amanda hit the tiny clearing, her gun poised. Isaac yelled at her not to shoot, and Hawk threw himself behind a tree. Meanwhile the outraged squaw and the peeper continued to argue loudly, seemingly oblivious to the rest of the group.

It took Amanda a second to realize she was in no danger; then she realized she had on nothing but her wet drawers and chemise. She quickly moved behind a bush. Hunkering down, she demanded, ''Isaac Wright, you'd better start talking fast!''

Hawk came out from behind his tree, raised an eyebrow, and said something in his language that made Isaac chuckle.

Seething, Amanda watched Hawk usher his tribesmen from the clearing. *How dare Hawk make a joke at her expense! To think she'd begun to think of him as a friend.*

When he and his people were out of sight, Isaac started toward her.

''Don't you move another step in this direction!'' She raised her gun and aimed it at him.

''Put that away before it goes off. I want to explain.''

This she wanted to hear, but not until she was dressed. ''Turn around. If you so much as look back here, I'm going to shoot you right through your sneaky heart.'' As he turned his back, his ill-concealed grin further infuriated her.

''I can wait out on the trail for you, if you want,'' he offered.

''Don't you dare leave me alone with these strangers wandering around.'' Tucking her shirt into her pants, she joined him. ''Okay, I'm ready. Let's hear your *complete* explanation.''

Instead of explaining, he took her arm and propelled her toward the trail. ''I'll tell you everything later. Right now, let's go to the dugout. I want you to meet Hawk's wife.''

Amanda plopped herself on the first sizable rock she saw and crossed her arms. ''I'll move *after* I hear why there were four people, including you, within sight of my bath.''

He sat beside her. ''That incident of someone watching you bathe has been bothering me. At first, I thought it might be those herders, but they had no way of knowing you were here.''

Amanda felt her face flush just thinking about being stared at by the herders while she was in a state of undress.

''I happened on some fresh hoofprints this past week,'' Isaac continued. ''Someone has been watching your homestead. When I went to Hawk for help, he got to thinking. One of his braves has been involved in this kind of thing since he was a kid. Hawk checked the fellow's horse. The prints matched. I'm sorry, Amanda, but we set this up today. Hawk sent this brave out hunting alone, figuring he'd detour this way. Then he invited the man's wife to ride along to meet you.''

''How could you let that man watch me bathe? What if he had . . . had . . ?'' She couldn't even finish the sentence.

''When I passed here and rode on to meet Hawk knowing that brave was in the trees, I could hardly breathe. But Hawk assured me the man has never hurt anyone. He just likes to look. Around the camp, the fellow's wife keeps a tight rein on him. Hawk swears that letting the wife take care of matters will be darn near as effective as me shooting him outright.''

''I feel so dirty. Like I need another bath.''

''Later. Hawk brought his wife for you to meet. They're waiting at the dugout.'' Isaac mounted, then reached down to give her a hand up behind him. After the horse started moving, he reached back and caressed her thigh. ''You all right?''

''Ashamed of being seen undressed like that.''

''You don't need to feel ashamed. You've done nothing.''

''I know. I just can't help it.''

She'd been balancing herself on the back of the horse by

hanging on to Isaac's sides. He pulled her arms tightly around him and covered her hands with one of his. Leaning back, he rested against her. She laid her head on his back and felt the beat of his heart. For these few minutes, she'd allow herself the comfort of his closeness.

When the dugout came into view, she moved her hands to his sides, and Isaac sat up in his saddle.

Hawk apologized to Amanda and Isaac for the behavior of his brave. Then he introduced Shining Sky, who was big with child.

Amanda liked Hawk's wife immediately and sensed that the feeling was mutual. As they cooked supper, Shining Sky thanked her for the orphan baby's milk. "He's growing fat. In another moon my baby will be born. Then I will feed both babies."

She tried to explain about the brave at the swimming hole. "We tell our men and his wife when we are going to bathe. No one likes this part of him, but he's a good hunter, better even than my husband. We need him." Shining Sky smiled, and her eyes sparkled wickedly. "We tease and say he can hunt so well because he can sneak up on anything."

They laughed.

"You remind me a little of my youngest sister," Amanda told Shining Sky. "Anne's always ready to laugh, just like you. I miss her."

"I, too, miss my sister."

"Where's your sister?"

"The soldiers took her family to the reservation. Sometimes I talk to Hawk about going to visit her. Others in our band also want to see their families. But if we get caught, we fear we'll get punished for not turning ourselves in to the agency earlier."

"So you don't know if your sister is all right?"

"Sometimes word comes and goes on the wind. I have heard she is well and has another child."

So Hawk's band had communication links with the agency Indians. Was the same wind carrying the news that Joe Pete was with her? Amanda didn't ask. She might not like the answer.

Willie interrupted their talk when he burst through the door. "I got a big sliver from the loft ladder. I didn't even whine." Proudly he exhibited a hand.

Amanda fetched her sewing and got a needle to dig it out.

Reverently, Shining Sky touched Amanda's extra needle with the tip of a finger. "I've seen these. They're very strong."

"You don't have a needle?"

"I use those I make from sharp bone or plants."

"Take this." Amanda thrust it toward her.

Smiling, Shining Sky pushed Amanda's offering back to her. "Thank you. I couldn't take such a valuable gift!"

"Of course you can. I can buy another in Lariat."

"You can buy one? Just like that?"

"If I have money, I can buy almost anything at the store."

"Anything?" She pointed to Amanda's big iron pot. "This?"

"Do you need pots?" Amanda asked.

The young Indian woman laughed and said, "No. I only want them. My husband says I want too many things."

Amanda thought a moment, then asked, "Did you know Hawk brought Joe Pete a horse?"

Shining Sky nodded.

"If he has another horse, Joe Pete could gentle it. Then I could sell it in Lariat and buy many things you want."

"The soldiers would find out and come for us."

The look of fear in Shining Sky's eyes made goosebumps rise on Amanda's arms. "I wouldn't tell anyone where I got the horse. I'd act as if Isaac had brought it to Joe Pete to train. I'd buy a few things for you at a time. No one in town knows what things I need. They'll just think I have lots of money to spend."

"Do you have lots of money?"

A personal question, but Amanda was honest. "No. I have what I need. Like you, I *want* too many things."

Again they laughed. Then Shining Sky spoke seriously. "I will speak to my husband. But he will not want you or Isaac to be in trouble for helping us. Your government calls us enemies."

"You're not my enemy."

Shining Sky smiled. "No. We are friends without sisters."

At supper, Amanda asked where Shining Sky and Hawk had learned English. Hawk explained that a white man who'd lived with their tribe for many years had taught those children whose parents did not object. Hawk's and Shining Sky's fathers had encouraged them to learn.

Occasionally, Isaac talked to Hawk in Sioux. *Probably so I can't understand,* Amanda thought. She wondered what Hawk had said back at the bathing pool that had made Isaac laugh. *Undoubtedly, some remark only a man would think funny!*

After Hawk and Shining Sky left with a jar of milk and a gunnysack full of fresh vegetables, Isaac turned to Amanda. "Thanks for sharing your garden stuff with my friends. You and Shining Sky seemed to get along fine. What did you talk about?"

She enjoyed the confused look in his eyes when she answered. "Her English isn't as good as Hawk's. Sometimes I wasn't exactly sure what we were discussing, but we had a lovely visit."

"Females!" Smiling, Isaac turned to the barn. "I'll finish the chores. Will you come out and watch the sunset after you get the kids to bed?"

Amanda's heart flipped, and she nodded. Before she went outside, she brushed her hair and put on a drop of her dwindling supply of lilac scent.

Isaac rose from the swing and tried to gather her into his arms, but she slid by. She wanted to be held, but he owed her an explanation about this afternoon first. "Why did you send me to bathe when you knew full well it wasn't safe?"

"You were safe enough, according to Hawk."

"Isaac, I was *bathing*. It's a wonder I wasn't stark naked."

"Try to understand. We had to catch that brave in the act, or I could never breathe easy, worrying and wondering who was hanging around watching you."

"I still don't like it."

"Is that why you're standing there with that don't-you-dare touch-my-person attitude written all over you?"

"What did Hawk say about me at the bathing pool that made you laugh?"

"I didn't laugh."

"You most certainly did."

"It was men talk. Just a joke."

"What did he say?"

"He said something about me being crazy enough to sleep in the barn when I could be using your . . . your body to rest my head. Or something like that."

"You *laughed* when he talked about me that way?"

"What did you expect me to do? Challenge him to a duel for your honor? Hell, Amanda. He could see for himself the way you're put together."

"You could have told me what was going on today. I could have worn something heavier into the water."

"Just tell yourself you probably don't have anything the brave hasn't seen before."

She stared at him long enough to see him start to squirm. Then she drawled, "I declare, Mr. Isaac Wright, you do know how to sweet-talk a lady." She stormed toward the dugout.

In long strides, he passed her and stood blocking the doorway. "Come on, Amanda. I want to hold you a minute."

"Get out of my way!"

Isaac stormed toward the barn, muttering about ungrateful women under his breath. He turned and jabbed a finger at her, practically shouting, "Just forget what I said about wanting to hold you. I must have had rocks in my head."

Later, sitting in the dark at the kitchen table, Amanda stared at Isaac's light in the barn's loft until it went out. Then she crawled into her lonely bed, with only the memories of his loving touches to keep her company.

Being close to Isaac had been easy from the first. She couldn't deny how much she'd enjoyed their shared passion. Perhaps this was best, though. If Isaac were angry with her, she wouldn't have to fight the physical attraction she felt for him as well as the emotional battle raging inside her mind.

Amanda buried her nose in the pillow that Isaac had once lain on, but his scent was long gone. She wrapped her arms around the pillow, but felt no comfort. She tried flinging her leg over it, but there was no answering nudge of a muscular thigh, urging her closer. She threw the pillow across the room, hitting the dugout door, then covered her head with her own pillow and cried.

CHAPTER TWENTY

Early the next morning, Amanda woke to find Isaac standing next to her bed, holding the pillow she'd thrown in frustration.

He squatted by the bed and whispered so he wouldn't wake the children. "I didn't want to leave until I told you I'm sorry for what I said last night. I guess I wanted you so badly that I convinced myself you wanted me, too. I thought you were serious when you let me . . ." His voice trailed away. "Oh, well, it doesn't matter anymore. I want you to know I'm glad you're here for the kids. I didn't mean to make you uncomfortable with my attentions. I'll treat you like a sister from now on."

Don't move, her mind cautioned. Don't reach for him. Don't tell him you lie awake at night aching for his body to be pressed against yours—and yearning deep inside for whatever comes next between a man and woman. Wanting doesn't make things right. His treating you as his sister is how it should be.

Isaac paused, then shrugged. "Will you still come over to the Lazy W for the week before we go to town for the Fourth?"

"Of course. The twins are looking forward to celebrating their birthday with you and Luke. You said Luke's lost weight cooking for himself. I'll fatten him back up."

Isaac smiled with obvious relief. "I have cows to check on, so I won't be at the Lazy W or here for a couple of days. Don't let the kids out of your sight. Tell Joe Pete I don't want him off hunting. Keep Misty inside at night and bar the door."

For some reason, his orders didn't seem so routine as they usually did. "Why all the sudden caution?"

"I suppose that brave reminded me how easy it would be for someone to bother you with you here alone with the kids. I don't expect the rustlers to be rash enough to work this close to the Lazy W's ranch house, but if you feel uneasy, don't put the milk in the well in the evening. No milk is Hawk's signal to check on you. Keep a gun handy and make your shots count. I'll come over to help you move the kids to the Lazy W."

"What about the milk for the baby while we're in town?"

"The baby will do all right on that tinned stuff you have stored in the cellar for emergencies, won't he?"

"He should."

"Then explain to Hawk, but tell him to come to the Lazy W for fresh milk if the canned milk doesn't agree with the baby. Why don't you give him all the canned milk so he'll have something extra if it ever looks dangerous to come in close?"

That night she left the lantern burning when she lay down fully clothed. Misty woke her with a low, threatening growl. Amanda opened the door enough to let Misty slip out. The dog's growls changed to a yip of recognition. In the moonlight, Amanda admired the two horses Hawk drove into her corral.

"My wife told me of your offer. I made sure the horses I picked are from the wild herds in these hills so they'll look like Isaac and Luke caught them for you."

"Do you have a list of things you want me to get when I sell the horses?"

"You've been a friend to my people, and you'd be punished if you got caught buying supplies for us. Shining Sky says there are things you want. I think there are some things you also need. Sell the horses and get those things."

Amanda thought to argue with him, but she held her tongue. She'd had to dip into the traveling money Tom had given her.

If she got a good price for the horses, she could replace it *and* buy some things Shining Sky wanted.

After thanking Hawk for the horses, Amanda explained about the canned milk in the root cellar and her plans to be gone for a while. "The night there's no fresh milk in the well, take all the canned milk from the cellar. I'll leave Shining Sky a gunnysack of fresh vegetables at the foot of the dirt steps."

"It was a good day for Fights The Wind when his path crossed yours."

"It was a good day for me, too."

"We hear there is an old woman of our tribe grieving for her daughter, who was Joe Pete's mother. She longs to see her grandson before she dies."

Amanda's heart froze. "Hawk, are you very, very sure she's Joe Pete's grandmother?"

Hawk nodded. "There is no mistake. I'm sorry." He took the jar of fresh milk and became part of the forest.

Later, Amanda stood by the children's beds and watched Joe Pete sleep. He'd grown and filled out some since he started eating regularly. She'd have to tell him what Hawk had said about his grandmother. Her eyes burned.

Several days later, in the thin light before the sun rose, Isaac and Luke arrived to help move the children to the Lazy W. They noticed the new horses immediately.

"Handsome horses, Amanda," Luke said, after giving her a big hug. He turned to Isaac. "Where did you find these mares?"

Isaac glared at Amanda. "I'm right interested in hearing about these horses myself. Especially since I told Amanda to keep everyone close while I was gone."

There he went! The day not even started and he found it necessary to call her to task for something she hadn't done and wasn't his business if she had. "For your information, no one has moved an inch off this place. Hawk left the mares for Joe Pete to work with until I can take them to town and sell them."

"Why did he do that?"

"He said he wanted to repay me for the baby's milk. I didn't think about explaining I got the cow and the canned milk from you. To be fair, I'll split the profit with you, since I wouldn't have had anything but Nanny's milk if it weren't for your generosity."

"You don't owe me for what I've done. Keeping the kids' bellies full and a roof over their heads is my responsibility."

"And mine!" Isaac wasn't going to get away with claiming the children were any more his responsibility than hers.

"Gosh dang, you two!" Luke whipped his horse's reins around the fence and jerked the knot tight. "I mention a couple of horses and you start bickering. Makes a fellow afraid to talk."

Amanda glanced at Isaac. The dark circles under his eyes told her how little he'd been sleeping. And if she weren't mistaken, his belt had been tightened a notch. He had enough problems; this was no time to start fussing over the children. He'd made a big concession when he let her move them to the dugout. Heavens, he'd even helped by building the beds and doing some heavier chores. It wouldn't kill her to be a little more supportive now that he had other worries.

But since he was already irritated, she might as well tell him the rest. "When I sell them, I'd like to let people assume that you and Luke rounded them up for me. I won't lie, of course. I just won't tell the whole truth."

"Why don't you just keep these horses? I don't mind you using mine, but you always like having your own things."

"But . . . well, if you're sure you don't mind my borrowing your horses, I'll use them a while longer. I need a little cash money." She grew uncomfortable under Isaac's searching gaze.

"If you need anything for the kids or yourself, charge it to me at Callahan's."

"And if I need it to homestead?"

His stony silence stood as his answer.

This time anger made her cheeks hot. Anger at herself for asking such a stupid question. She knew his opinion about her homesteading, and she'd given him the opportunity to express it again. Well, she wouldn't give him the satisfaction of a reply to his rudeness. "It won't take me long to get the children awake and moving. They can wait for breakfast until we're on the Lazy W." She turned and started for the dugout.

"Amanda."

She looked at Isaac. The fight seemed to be out of him.

"Outright lie if you have to. Luke and I don't care if people think we can capture wild horses with ease. If the soldiers at the fort ever get suspicious that Hawk's people are out here, they'll come looking."

"I'll be very careful. Only Joe Pete knows where I got the horses, and you know him. He's not telling anything to anybody."

"Keep it that way. My guess is that the rustlers aren't confining themselves to the Lazy W. Some rancher's bound to ask for help from the army. If the cavalry starts checking this area, Hawk's band will have to move out, and move fast."

"Hawk refuses to take any money for the horses, but I intend to give Shining Sky needles and scissors and such as a gift. Hawk surely won't make her give back a gift."

"Don't buy too much. It won't look right."

"I won't. Besides, everyone probably knows I'm working on both the Lazy W and my homestead. I need things in both places. Or I can claim I'm buying my sisters' Christmas gifts early. People will believe I need lots of pins and needles and such since I have six sisters." She thought of Mary, and unexpected tears filled her eyes. "Five sisters."

Before she could brush them away, Isaac had her cradled against his chest, rocking to and fro. "If you start crying, we'll all be bawling. This may be our first Fourth of July without Josh and Mary, but we're going to take their kids to town, and we're going to have a ripsnorting time."

Allowing herself the comfort of his arms, Amanda didn't pull away for a few moments. She took his offered handkerchief and wiped her eyes. "I'll go get the children ready."

While she prepared for a week's absence, Amanda wondered what Isaac would have thought if she had told him she needed some cash because she'd spent the return ticket money Tom had sent with her. Certainly, he'd be surprised to find out the "old-maid aunt" had a fiancé. But he'd probably be so relieved, he'd offer to be best man and escort her to Tom's doorstep.

Well, Isaac would never know she'd had a fiancé. As far as she was concerned, the engagement was ended. The letter she needed to write Tom would be a formality. It pricked a bit to know he likely would replace her in no time. His pride might be hurt a little, but his heart wouldn't be. Theirs would have been a marriage of convenience. They'd never claimed otherwise.

Before she left the dugout, she closed the curtains at her little window. While Joe Pete turned the new horses out in the pasture where they could get to water, Isaac checked her rifle and slipped it into the scabbard on her saddle. He asked to see her pistol, then checked to see that it was loaded, too. As if she'd bother to wear the heavy thing if it were unloaded! He put each twin on a horse alone and placed Nellie with her.

With the dogs driving the milk cow and the goats, Luke led, and Isaac trailed the group. Their vigilance seemed contagious. Amanda found herself feeling edgy. The Lazy W must be having more trouble with the rustlers than Isaac had led her to believe.

The men relaxed when they reached the Lazy W, horsing around with the children while Amanda fixed an enormous breakfast.

"Damn, it's good to be home!" Luke said when he sat to eat.

"You have to do supper dishes," chortled Susie. "You said damn. Didn't he, Uncle Isaac? Didn't he say damn?"

When the men laughed, Amanda scolded, "I warned you about this. Children repeat what they hear." Then she turned to Susie. "A lady does *not* use that sort of language."

Susie looked properly chastised, but Nellie smiled winningly at her uncles and tried out the word herself. "Damn!" She waited expectantly for the laughter. "Damn," she announced again.

Isaac cast a stern look at the others. "The first one of you who snickers will do the dishes the rest of the week."

Amanda ducked her head to hide her smile, but not before she saw him wipe his hand across his mouth in an effort to control his mirth. *Luke's right,* she thought. *It feels good to be home.*

After breakfast, Isaac said, "You kids get on outside."

Joe Pete rose to leave, but Isaac stopped him. "Not you." Isaac turned toward the stove and said to Amanda, "Come over here and sit a minute. Luke and I need to talk to you."

She had barely sat when Isaac announced, "We're missing more cows from the north and west sides of our range. This isn't just a hungry homesteader. Too many cows are missing. Someone's trying to make a profit at our expense."

"What are you going to do?"

"They'll make a mistake eventually," he said. "Meanwhile, Luke and I are extra concerned about you and Joe Pete. Sometimes this wide-open country draws men who have no code of honor like decent folks. I wouldn't want a woman or half-breed boy to get in their clutches. Do you two know what I mean?"

Nodding, Amanda rose and went to stand behind Joe Pete, putting her hands on his shoulders protectively.

"I know you've been riding and hunting every day, Joe Pete," continued Isaac. "But I found strange tracks less than six miles from here two days ago. I want you to stay close to the house unless you're with Luke or me. You can ride with us today. We're going to bring in the extra horses, the ones we use for roundup. Losing cows is one thing. Losing horses is another. If you're careful, you can work with the horses we bring in."

Joe Pete's face broke into a rare, dimple-showing smile.

Isaac turned to Amanda. "If it bothers you to be alone here today, Luke can stay with you. Joe Pete and I probably can handle the horses without him, especially if we take both dogs."

The very idea that Isaac thought she needed a protector irritated Amanda. "I can take care of things!"

"Don't be so quick to take offense! I didn't say you couldn't take care of yourself or the kids."

She instantly regretted her snappish tone. While the men saddled horses, she wrapped boiled eggs and the leftover biscuits in a clean dish towel. Walking to Isaac's horse, she opened his saddlebag and tucked the food inside. "Be careful," she said.

"I always am," he replied. "Keep a close eye on the kids."

That evening as they finished supper, Amanda mentioned work needing to be done on her homestead. "I've been too busy to irrigate the last couple of days. Would you men keep an eye on the children tomorrow? I can finish irrigating over there by early afternoon and be back to help here the rest of the day."

Isaac stopped eating. "I don't want you going anywhere alone. I explained that this morning."

That presumptuous tone again. "I didn't ask for your permission. I asked if you would watch the children."

"I don't like your being alone."

"I'll take Misty with me."

He glared at her. "If you can't be talked out of this, I'll be tickled pink to leave my work undone *again* and help you."

She returned his stare. "You're too kind."

Abruptly, he pushed back his chair. "Since it appears I'll be farming instead of ranching tomorrow, I need to get some work done now." He stormed out the door.

Luke rolled his eyes at Amanda.

She tried to return his nonchalant grin. The effort was futile. She simply shook her head and brushed quickly at her eyes. Turning to the wide-eyed children, she said, "When you finish supper, you can go outside and play until dark."

"Until dark?" Willie asked with disbelief.

"It's too hot in here to sleep."

It would be heavenly to go outside in the cooling breeze with them, but she had ironing to do.

* * *

By the time Isaac climbed out of bed the next morning, Amanda had left for her homestead.

She'd set the table for breakfast and left biscuits to be baked. Mush simmered on the back of the stove. A note addressed to him said she'd be back in time to cook supper. And yes, Master, she had her gun and Misty with her.

Damn woman was going to work herself to death if he didn't figure out some way to slow her down!

The day crawled by. Though his physical desire for Amanda was a continual, pressing problem, his emotional need for her had steadily increased. Damned if it didn't feel like part of him was missing when he didn't have her in sight.

After his mother's death in childbirth with Luke, he'd promised himself that he'd never ask a woman to share this hard life. Sure, he had enough money to move a woman into town where she wouldn't have to work day and night just to help keep body and soul together. But then, he couldn't live in a town; he belonged on his ranch. And what point was there to having a woman and kids if you weren't together?

A dozen times, he thought about leaving the kids with Luke and riding over to Amanda's homestead to check on her. A dozen times, he fought the urge. She wouldn't appreciate his concern. In fact, she'd probably get upset. Amanda had the most disconcerting way of mistaking his motives.

He watched the shortcut trail to her homestead until the middle of the afternoon. When she walked into view, he called Nellie's attention to Aunt Mandy, then followed the toddler to meet her. Amanda had those damn dark circles under her eyes again. "I worried about you this whole blessed day."

"You worry too much about me."

"Maybe. That's something you need to get used to because I suspect there will never be a time when I won't worry about you."

"That's plain ridiculous." Her heart leapt. One sweet or kind word from him and, like a lovesick fool, she forgot how unreasonable he could be.

"Don't you worry about me?" he asked.

"You're a capable man. I think about you sometimes, but I

don't worry unless you're much later than I think you should be.''

Isaac grinned and scooped up the toddler. "Did you hear that, Nellie Belle? At least your Aunt Mandy thinks about me sometimes. I believe I'm making progress.''

Nellie giggled, happily struggling to get away from Isaac's playful kisses and tickles.

Amanda couldn't believe how jealous she felt of Nellie. She would give her right arm for one of Isaac's teasing nuzzles.

When he turned the child loose, Nellie ran ahead of them. Isaac took Amanda's hand and held it for the walk to the cabin.

Before supper, Amanda called the family one at a time to the porch to get their hair trimmed. Joe Pete refused the haircut.

"I wish you'd reconsider," she said after she'd washed his hair and was combing out the tangles. "The other boys will have shorter hair.''

"My mother said the men in her tribe wear their hair long.''

"What about your father's hair?''

"He wore it long to please my mother.''

Isaac caught her by surprise when he said, "A man should wear his hair how he wants, Amanda. Joe Pete's hair suits him.''

Thoughtfully, she combed through the boy's shiny, raven-black hair. "It is beautiful.''

Isaac disappeared and returned with a new red bandanna. He twirled it into a headband and tied it around the boy's head.

Joe Pete smiled into the mirror. "Thanks, Isaac.'' He carefully slipped it off. "I'll save it until I go into town.''

After Joe Pete left for the corral, Amanda motioned Isaac to the wash basin. "Joe Pete looks very much the handsome young brave with that bandanna. What made you think of it?''

"He looked like he needed some encouragement.''

"I've been worried we weren't going to be able to get him to town at all from the way he talked the last few days.''

"Town holds no fond memories for him. You told me yourself how he was treated in Cheyenne. He's got two worlds to learn to fit into, ours and his mother's. Fortunately, he has more talent with horses than I've ever seen. That may be his ticket into both worlds.'' Isaac nodded toward the corral where Joe Pete was walking a horse. ''We've got to start working on this going-to-town thing, though. He needs to go to school this winter.''

''I don't think Joe Pete is going to like that.''

''We all have to do things we don't like. While we're in town this week, I intend to talk to Jim Callahan to see if Joe Pete can room and board with them.''

Amanda bristled. ''You can't make arrangements about Joe Pete without my consent. He's my responsibility.''

''Save your breath, Amanda. I know Hawk told you about the boy's grandmother. We don't know how long he'll stay with us, so we've got to get him some education while we can.''

Joe Pete had taken the news about his grandmother stoically, and Amanda had hoped he wouldn't feel obliged to go to her. Now tears clouded her eyes at the thought of his leaving.

Reaching up, Isaac wiped them away with the side of his thumb and spoke gently. ''We have to do what's best for him. The boy needs to go to school. My brothers and I only went to school for a couple of years, and reading and writing doesn't come easy to us. I don't wish that problem on any man.''

''I can teach Joe Pete.'' Amanda wiped her nose.

''You'll have all you can do to teach the twins this winter. Mary always intended to work with them, but I don't think she ever had the time. In a few years they'll have to stay in town in the winter, too. We can't just keep the kids out here on the range, uneducated.''

''Isaac, I really can read and do arithmetic as well as many schoolteachers. I can teach them myself.'' Amanda stood over Isaac with the scissors poised to cut his hair. ''I don't want them to go to town.''

Isaac reached out and took her hand. ''Now you are beginning to sound like me. Worrying over things that haven't even happened yet. We'll cross those bridges when we come to them.''

She held tightly to his hand and almost fancied she felt love flowing from Isaac's body into hers. *Mercy, I can make myself believe anything.*

She let go and trimmed his wavy blond hair, careful not to take off too much. Like Joe Pete's mother, she preferred longish hair on a man.

CHAPTER
TWENTY-ONE

Near noon on the third of July, Amanda, Joe Pete, and Luke rode into Lariat. They were only halfway down the street when Isaac came out of the livery and walked to meet them.

He spoke to Luke first. "Everything okay on the Lazy W?"

"Fine. I'll get up early tomorrow, ride out and do the chores, and be back to town for the race and dance."

Amanda interrupted. "I wish you two would let me go back to the ranch. After all, they're my animals that need milking."

"We settled that." Isaac took her horse's bridle. "Until we catch the rustlers, I don't want you far from Luke or me."

"They could shoot Luke as easily as they could shoot me."

"Let's not get into all this again. Luke's going to ride out to do chores." Isaac continued, "Let's not spoil this time in town by having a family disagreement in front of everyone."

It dawned on her that Luke, Joe Pete, and Isaac were watching her nervously. "Oh, all right." It seemed they all exhaled at once. She really must be acting like a shrew.

Isaac smiled. "You three look mighty spiffy."

"We stopped and bathed at the river," Amanda said.

"The kids and I cleaned up there yesterday, too," Isaac said. "It's a good thing you sent their good clothes with me instead of dressing them before we left. Willie managed to drag Susie into the only mud puddle between here and the ranch.''

''I hope you didn't scold him too much.''

''You'd be proud of me. I didn't say a word.''

Amanda looked at him skeptically.

''Well, I didn't say too many words.''

From in front of the general store, a girl waved to Luke.

''She's been asking for you ever since I got to town,'' Isaac told him, grinning.

''Shoot! Melanie Dawson ain't but fifteen years old.''

''And don't forget it. Still, it wouldn't hurt to be nice to her. She'll be seventeen in two years, and old enough to court.''

''Two years!'' Luke groaned as he turned toward the porch.

Isaac helped Amanda from her horse. After throwing her saddlebags over his shoulder, he handed the reins to Joe Pete. ''Take the horses to the livery. I saved places for you and Luke to bunk near me in the loft.''

Joe Pete had gone only a few steps when Isaac added, ''I'd be grateful if you'd take Nellie off Jim's hands. Amanda or I will come and relieve you in a little while. And . . . uh, stay where Jim, Luke, or I can see you.''

Nodding, the boy continued stoically toward the stable.

''What was that staying in your eyesight all about?''

''Folks are riled up about the rustling. It seems we aren't the only ones missing cattle. Some people don't have a sense of fairness. First thing you know, they might get to blaming Indians in general, then Joe Pete in particular.''

''Ridiculous. He's a child.''

''To us. To some others, he's a half-breed and not to be trusted.'' Isaac started toward Teresa Brown's boarding house.

When Amanda realized where he was headed, she stopped. ''I asked you to see if Martha could put the children and me up.''

''I couldn't ask. Martha's house is bulging with all her grown children and grandchildren. I always have a room at the boarding house. Tonight, I'll sleep in the livery with the other men and boys. You and the girls can use my room.'' He put his hand on Amanda's waist and gave her a gentle nudge. "Come on."

As he propelled her along the dusty street, her mind screamed in protest. Though she'd never confronted Isaac about his relationship with Mrs. Brown, surely he couldn't think she would sleep in that woman's house! Obviously he did, though, because he swung open the screen door to the big two-story house.

"Tess is with the other women," he explained. "Your room is upstairs next to hers." He led the way.

"I can't stay here!"

"Why the hell not?"

"Because . . ." Amanda searched for words. She could hardly tell him she refused to stay in his paramour's house. He might think it bothered her, that she was jealous.

"Because why?" Isaac demanded. "There's not a thing wrong with this bed. I must've slept in it a hundred times."

Amanda stared at the bed in horror. *What if he and that woman had "wrestled" in this very bed?*

"What's wrong with you? You look like you've seen a ghost."

A ghost? More like a nightmare. Amanda tried to compose herself. "I suppose I'm just tired. Where are the children?"

"The twins are out looking for mischief. Martha brought Nellie to me up at the livery about two hours ago. She said that she and five other women couldn't keep up with our little red-haired bundle of joy. Can you believe that?"

Amanda and Isaac looked at each other. Suddenly she laughed. "Has she been terribly naughty?"

"She's been awful. When you're not around, she doesn't mind anyone. Last night, I slept in here with the girls. Nellie wouldn't use the outhouse, then she wet the bed. I moved the girls to the dry area of the bed, and I slept on the floor."

"She's just testing you, Isaac. You need to be firm with her. Nellie adores you. Her feelings for you won't change if you let her know what's acceptable and not acceptable."

"It's so hard to do."

Amanda looked at Isaac. He was so sensitive sometimes. She'd grown weary of his being distant with her. She wanted—

no, needed—to be held in his arms. She would tell him how she liked that morning in his arms when he had made her feel so much like a woman. He was incredibly dense sometimes. She'd didn't care what people said. She wanted to be more than a friend to him. "Isaac?" She had his full attention. "I want—" She stopped talking when Teresa Brown called up the stairs.

"Isaac, dear. Are you up there?"

Brows furrowed, he kept his gaze on Amanda as he moved back a step into the hall. "I'll be right down, Tess."

He returned to Amanda. "You were saying?"

With Mrs. Brown in the house, she no longer felt the urge to unburden her soul. "I don't recall what I meant to say," she lied. "It probably wasn't important."

Turning her back, she opened the closet. Her two dresses looked crisp hanging beside the girls' slightly crumpled dresses.

Isaac beamed. "After we got to town yesterday, I went to hang up your duds and noticed they got wrinkled in the trunk. I had Tess iron them for you."

Amanda cringed. She didn't sew well. And she hated for Mrs. Brown to know about her weaknesses. But Isaac had tried to please her by having her clothes pressed, just as he had seen that she had a comfortable place to sleep. "That was very thoughtful of you."

"I knew you'd like them all pretty."

A light knock on the wooden door frame announced Mrs. Brown's arrival. "Isaac, dear. I hate to bother you and Alicia, but we need you to come and help with the barbecue pit."

"Her name is Amanda, Tess."

Mrs. Brown tittered as she clung to one of Isaac's muscled upper arms. "It must be that she reminds me of an old maid named Alicia who lived near me during my growing-up years. I don't know what it is about never-married women that makes them look so . . ." The widow let her sentence trail away. "Oh, dear. I do let my mouth get away from me. For a spinster, Alicia looks perfectly presentable, don't you think, Isaac? Perhaps she'll meet some desperate man here in Lariat. After all, a man alone in Wyoming can't be too choosy."

Obviously, thought Amanda. She almost felt sorry for Isaac as he glanced back and forth between her and the Widow. Clearly, he didn't have a clue what Teresa Brown was doing. But she had six sisters, and she'd seen cat fights. No way would she let Isaac's woman friend sucker her into a verbal battle.

Mrs. Brown practically dragged Isaac to the door. He stopped and turned to Amanda. "I'll fetch Nellie so Joe Pete can play. Come along to Callahan's when you're ready."

Tessie laughed. "Oh, Isaac. Do give the poor woman time to clean up. She ought to rest and see if it lightens the circles under her eyes before she meets the local bachelors."

Tessie let go of Isaac's arm long enough to pat the bed lovingly. "Do take a little nap. This bed is very comfortable, isn't it, Isaac dear?" The good Widow smiled knowingly at him.

He turned beet-red and hustled Mrs. Brown out into the hall.

Amanda watched from the window as Isaac stomped down the street with Tessie clutching his arm. Once, Teresa Brown looked back up at the window and gave a gay little flutter of her hand as if to say to Amanda, "You see how it is."

Yes, Mrs. Brown, Amanda thought, *I see how it is.*

She jerked the pins from her long, wavy hair and shook it. Back when they were on better terms, Isaac used to love handling and braiding her hair. Maybe he liked to look at it, too. She figured she could get by with wearing it tied back with a ribbon the next couple of days. It wasn't as if she were a married woman, or even a scrawny widow woman.

In a flash of daring, Amanda unbuttoned two buttons at the neck of her dress. After all, who could blame her if she felt a little warm—what with the heat of the day.

She dug into her saddlebags and found her lilac scent, then she pinched her cheeks and bit her lips to add a little color.

Amanda left the boarding house and swished down the street to do battle for physical possession of one stubborn, long-legged, opinionated cattle rancher.

But for the life of her, she couldn't figure why on earth she wanted him, or what she'd do with him if she got him.

CHAPTER
TWENTY-TWO

Even in the strange bed at the rooming house, the exhausted little girls fell right to sleep. The afternoon had gone nicely, Amanda thought. More than once she'd caught Isaac staring at her. He'd joined her and the children at the Callahans' for supper, then stayed with them until an hour ago, when she'd brought the girls to their room. He mentioned going to play horseshoes.

Yawning, she bent to unlace her shoes. The sound of a knock stopped her. She heard Teresa Brown next door give the command to enter. With horror, Amanda recognized the familiar rumble of Isaac's voice followed by a click as a door closed.

No! Oh, please, God, no. Bile burned the back of her throat as she stood frozen in the middle of the room. Terrified of hearing further noises from the adjoining room—more intimate noises—she rushed out of the room, easing the door shut.

On the back porch, she slid down on the top step and clung to the edge of her sanity. After a bit, she let go of the porch rail, clutched her stomach, and rocked back and forth.

When Joe Pete came creeping around the outside of the house a while later, he asked, "You okay?"

Of course she was okay. No one died of things like this, did they? *Life would go on despite where Isaac slept tonight.*

"I thought you'd gone to bed." She looked pointedly at the rolled blanket under Joe Pete's arm. "What are you doing here?"

The boy studied his boot. "I told Luke I was hot. He said I could come and sleep on the back porch here."

"Are you ill?" She reached out to feel his forehead.

Joe Pete shook his head and sat next to Amanda.

"Did something happen to you?"

Again Joe Pete shook his head. In contradiction to the negative gesture, he added, "Anyway, Isaac told Mr. Dawson he'd beat the hell out of him if he came within ten feet of me again."

"Did Mr. Dawson do something to hurt you?"

"Mostly he just said things. You know, about half-breed nits and stuff. But when he knocked me down on his way to play horseshoes, Isaac talked to him real good." Joe Pete smiled slightly. "Mr. Dawson was awful scared of Isaac!"

"Luke shouldn't have let you come over here alone. What if that Mr. Dawson had caught you out in the dark by yourself?"

"I sneaked real careful. Can I go on back to the Lazy W tonight? Please, Amanda—there's plenty of moonlight."

"Isaac doesn't want you riding alone. You know that."

"Hawk's been teaching me the ways of my people. I know how to stay hidden. If you're worried, I could go on to his camp and stay until you come home. They like me there."

"I'm sure they do. You're a wonderful boy." Amanda wrapped an arm around his shoulder. "But people here like you, too."

"Not very many. I don't want to cause no trouble here in town. I just want to be somewhere else."

Her sentiments exactly. She could leave Isaac a note. If one of the girls woke and called out, he'd hear them from Mrs. Brown's room. Lord knew, the walls were thin enough. Still, Joe Pete had to learn not to run from trouble. "If you leave, you'll miss the horse race. I've heard you, Isaac, and Luke planning to win first, second, and third prizes riding horses from the Lazy W."

"That was just bragging man-talk."

"You don't want to disappoint Luke and Isaac, do you?"

Still staring at his feet, Joe Pete shook his head.

"So you need to get a good night's sleep. Spread your blanket on the porch."

Reluctantly, Joe Pete settled on top of his blanket.

Amanda managed a smile. "Take off your boots. You look like you're ready to run."

"I'm always ready to run," came his terse reply.

"You don't sleep with your boots on at home."

"I'm safe at home."

"You're safe here, too. I'm going to sleep out here with you. My room upstairs is . . . is uncomfortable." Propped against the wall of the porch, Amanda wondered if Mrs. Brown and Isaac were finished yet. How long did such things take anyway?

At the break of dawn, she decided Joe Pete would be safe on the porch in the daylight. In the upstairs hallway, she met Teresa Brown. The look on the woman's face made Amanda realize how wrinkled and disreputable she must appear. But she owed the hussy no explanations. Nodding, she slipped into her room.

The girls were cuddled together, and the empty side of the bed beckoned. Amanda pulled on her nightgown, determined to sleep an hour or two in comfort before the day began.

At mid-morning, Isaac stood outside Amanda and the girls' bedroom in the boarding house. He smiled at the domestic sounds from within, then knocked on the door. Susie threw it wide open.

"Goodness, Susie." Amanda buttoned the back of the girl's dress. "You don't open a door until you have your clothes on."

"It's only Uncle Isaac."

"You didn't know that when you opened the door." Amanda

tied Susie's pinafore. "Isaac, get that baby, will you? The way she's jumping on the bed, she's going to bounce herself off."

He gathered up Nellie, settled himself on the edge of the bed, and watched Amanda tie ribbons to the ends of Susie's braids.

Amanda looked pretty with color in her cheeks that way. The neck of her robe had slipped open just enough to offer a hint of the delights hidden within. Life didn't get much better than this. Healthy kids, a beautiful woman, and twenty-four hours with nothing more demanding to do than race a horse, throw a few horseshoes, watch the fireworks, and dance all night.

Yes, sir! He'd done the right thing last night when he'd knocked on Tess's door. It was time and past that he cleared up any misunderstanding. He didn't want to embarrass Tess in public, but he didn't want Amanda to get the wrong idea—or the right idea, depending on how you looked at it. He and Tess had been friends, good friends, but he'd never promised her anything other than a beef a couple of times a year. Sure, she'd shared the comforts of her female body, but she got as good as she gave. He knew other men visited the boarding house too, and he didn't begrudge Tessie the company.

Last night, she'd even offered him a last fling. But he didn't need or want anything from her. Hadn't since the train pulled in with Amanda. Lord knew how hard these last months would have been without Amanda's help with the kids.

Amanda looked exhausted. Maybe he should take the girls off her hands. "What say I take these ruffians outside?"

"Thanks. Don't let them get dirty before the day starts."

Amanda watched Isaac shoo the girls out into the hall ahead of him. He turned back and gave Amanda a long look, the kind of look she would have killed for yesterday.

"Are you going to leave your hair down?" he asked. "I like it that way."

Instantly, she changed her mind about her hair. What did she care if Isaac liked her hair down? She'd never do anything to make herself pleasing to Isaac again.

Her cheeks burned anew with humiliation and anger. The

very idea of his going to Mrs. Brown while she slept in the next room! He must think she had no pride at all!

After he sauntered off, she jerked her comb through her hair. She had to try three times before she got her hair up. Satisfied at last, she promised herself that no matter what happened the rest of the day, she would not cry. *What Isaac did last night did not concern her. Not at all!* She intended to enjoy this day if it killed her. She repeatedly doused her burning eyes in water from the pitcher on the dresser.

Opening the front door, she came nose-to-nose with a rancher whom Isaac had introduced her to the previous day. Weathered face shiny clean, the middle-aged man stood with his hat in one hand and a small bouquet of wildflowers in the other.

"Good morning, Miss Amanda. I wondered if I might have the pleasure of walking you to church this fine morning."

Looking past the man's shoulder and into the yard, she saw Isaac's surprised expression. Without hesitation, she stepped to Allen McIntosh's side. Taking the bouquet, she tucked several flowers in Susie's and Nellie's braids. She handed Allen the biggest flower. "Can you put this into my hair?"

Flustered, it took the burly man a minute to work the stem of the flower into her hair. All the while, she smiled absently at the playing children, ignoring the rage in Isaac's face.

Starting toward the trees where the outdoor service would be held, she took Allen McIntosh's offered arm. With her other hand she held on to Susie. Isaac carried Nellie and stomped up the street on the far side of Susie.

Down the block a bit, Luke and Willie stepped into the line beside Isaac. Joe Pete straggled behind until Isaac growled at him, "Get up here with the family like you belong."

Walking abreast, their grim entourage stretched halfway across Lariat's dusty street. Amanda suspected they looked like outlaws on their way to watch one of their own hanged instead of an extended family on their way to a church service.

While they waited for the service to begin, Isaac spoke to Luke. "I didn't think you'd be back to town so early."

"The full moon inspired me to ride out to the Lazy W last

night instead of waiting until this morning. I looked around town before I left but couldn't find you.''

In her mind, Amanda retorted sarcastically, *Of course you couldn't find him, Luke. You didn't look in Mrs. Brown's bed!*

"Tell you what," said Isaac. "I've lost my taste for the dancing. Why don't you stay in town and enjoy the festivities? I'll ride out myself later."

"I lost the coin toss," argued Luke.

"I said I'd do it," Isaac snarled. "If it weren't for my being so lily-livered, we wouldn't have a bunch of damn milking animals on the place anyhow."

Amanda felt herself color. If it weren't for *her,* he meant. The milking animals were her responsibility. She should have stayed on her homestead where she belonged. If she'd stayed at the dugout, she wouldn't even know where Isaac spent the night. Somehow, *thinking* he might be with Mrs. Brown hurt less than actually *hearing* him enter the woman's bedroom.

Thankfully, Lariat's preacher finally began his annual Fourth of July service. She tried to focus on his words and not on her mind's picture of Isaac lying naked on Teresa Brown's bed, putting his strong arms around that scrawny old biddy.

Briefly, she wondered if he nibbled on the other woman's lips the wonderful way he used to nibble on hers.

She'd never make it through the day, watching Teresa Brown flutter around Isaac. Even if she had no rights to Isaac, even though she had a fiancé she still hadn't done anything about, a letter she still hadn't written, the fact remained. She loved Isaac. And he'd spent the night in another woman's bed. She had to get away soon, or she'd surely embarrass herself by either screaming or crying the first time Isaac looked at Mrs. Teresa Brown.

CHAPTER
TWENTY-THREE

''Aunt Mandy, you re going to miss the race!'' Susie shouted.

Scooping up Nellie, Amanda ran from the Callahans' back-yard to the main street, where the men and older boys had their horses in an unruly line. Jim Callahan shot his pistol and the race began.

Amanda joined in the wild chorus of encouragement. When the horses made the turn around the old cottonwood, dust boiled up so high she couldn't tell who led. A hush fell when an undersized, half-breed boy riding bareback came out of the brown cloud first. Urging his mount, Joe Pete leaned low over its mane and pounded its sides with his feet. Luke and Mr. Dawson were in close contention for second. Isaac's horse was tight behind them.

A second after Joe Pete's horse crossed the finish line, Mr. Dawson caught up to him. The man backhanded the unsuspecting boy, knocking him from his horse. Before Amanda could react, Isaac jerked his own horse to a stop and dismounted in one smooth movement. Reaching up, he wrenched Dawson out of his saddle.

The fight couldn't have lasted more than five minutes. Though Isaac was bleeding from the corner of his mouth and a cut above his eye, it was Dawson who couldn't rise from the ground.

Amanda started toward Isaac, but Mrs. Brown went into a fainting act that could have won a standing ovation on any stage. Fortunately for good old Tess, Isaac caught her before she fell to the ground.

Looking perplexed, he stood bleeding in the dusty street with a seemingly unconscious woman in his arms. When his glance fell on Amanda, he motioned toward Joe Pete. "See to the boy."

She and one of Martha's girls, Colleen, led Joe Pete to the Callahans' backyard. Subdued, all three Wright children anxiously hovered around Joe Pete while she cleaned him up.

An hour later, an elated Joe Pete, sporting a swollen, split lip claimed the ten-dollar prize for winning Lariat's Fourth of July horse race. Few people clapped when Jim Callahan handed over the first-place prize money.

Amanda fought the urge to move closer to Joe Pete, to shield him somehow from this unkindness. Though Isaac had warned her, she couldn't believe such animosity existed toward a mere child because of the color of his skin.

The clapping intensified considerably as Luke accepted the five-dollar prize for second place.

The preacher announced that the other racers had taken a vote and disqualified Dawson for hitting Joe Pete. The disqualification made Isaac the third-place winner.

Dawson raged at his wife. "Get your lazy butt moving and gather up those good-for-nothing brats of yours. We ain't staying in a town what lets a breed enter a white man's race."

The preacher waited until the Dawson family left before presenting the two-dollar prize money to Isaac. Isaac handed his prize money to the town's schoolteacher. "I'm sure you can find something to do with this."

In spite of Mrs. Brown's clinging to Isaac's arm, Amanda felt proud to be a member of Isaac's household. He was a good man. Teresa Brown was a lucky lady. *And a heck of an actress.*

Luke followed Isaac's example with the second-place money.

Martha Callahan whispered to Amanda. "Traditionally, the winners of the race give their money to the schoolteacher."

Amanda hadn't heard the men mention this tradition. With a sinking heart, she saw the crowd turn to Joe Pete. She hurt for him when he looked at the expectant crowd with obvious confusion.

Pretty Colleen Callahan whispered in his ear, then nudged him, much the same way any woman would nudge a man she loved.

Joe Pete straightened his shoulders. Head held high, he walked to the schoolteacher with his money. "Here, ma'am."

The clapping from the crowd built slowly and precipitated a brief show of Joe Pete's dimples.

Through the mist in her eyes, Amanda watched Isaac put his free hand on Joe Pete's shoulder, then stare at several men who still stood silently with their arms crossed.

During the entire presentation, a faint-looking Teresa Brown, acting as though she needed Isaac's strength to stand, clung like a leech to one of his arms.

Amanda decided that if she didn't get out of town, she'd likely pick out the woman's eyes! She carried Nellie to the boarding house, changed into her pants, and packed her saddlebags. She'd tell Isaac her plans on her way to the livery to get her horse.

When Amanda got outside, Isaac and the other men were talking to a homesteader. She'd saddle up first. Perhaps by then she could speak to him without interrupting.

She made a detour through the Callahans' backyard to thank Martha for her hospitality. "I appreciate your keeping the twins. They've been looking forward to the fireworks."

"They won't be any trouble. At their age, I just see that they get fed and come in at night. You want me to keep Nellie?"

Laughing, Amanda hugged Nellie. "Thanks, but Miss Contrary here is exhausted, which makes her more headstrong than usual. Besides, she's so young, she doesn't know what she'd be missing."

"There'll be a mass protest when the men find out you're gone. A single woman is a rarity around here."

"There's always Mrs. Brown."

Martha rolled her eyes, making Amanda laugh.

Once Martha and she quit chuckling, Amanda asked, "Have you seen Joe Pete? I thought he might want to go home with me."

Martha tilted her head toward the far end of the yard. "I doubt he wants to go anywhere."

Joe Pete and Colleen sat at a table, sharing a bowl of ice cream and grinning at each other. At twelve, Colleen had already grown several inches taller than Joe Pete. Though she wore her hair in pigtails, the bloom of womanhood showed on her slim frame. Joe Pete had the wiry build of a child accustomed to hard work and little food. The dark-skinned boy and the pretty blond girl definitely looked like an unlikely combination.

"A little puppy love, do you suppose?" Amanda asked.

"Maybe. I've never known Colleen to share her ice cream."

Impulsively, Amanda hugged Martha. "I can see why Mary liked you so well. I'm glad you were here for her, Martha."

The older woman brushed away the tears forming in Amanda's eyes. "Now don't start crying or you'll have me bawling, too."

Amanda sniffed and reached for her handkerchief. "I hardly ever cry over Mary anymore." After she composed herself, she looked toward the group of men. "What's going on?"

"That new homesteader, Parks, came in a bit ago. He asked who was moving cows on a hot day like today instead of being in town. In two shakes, every man in town had gathered round him."

"It does seem an odd day to be herding cows. You know everyone around here, don't you Martha? Who's missing?"

"I've been trying to decide. Other than that worthless Dawson family who just left, nobody that I can figure."

Amanda shrugged. "I better ask Joe Pete if he wants to ride home with me or stay in town and eat ice cream with Colleen."

Martha smiled. "My money's on ice cream."

Joe Pete looked up when Amanda approached.

"I'm taking Nellie and going home to do the milking and other chores. Do you want to come with me?"

Colleen pleaded, "Don't go, Joe Pete. We have fireworks and a dance later."

After hesitating, he asked, "Do you need me to help?"

"I'll be fine." She shifted Nellie to her other hip. "When Isaac finishes talking, please tell him where I've gone. Watch out for yourself. And help Martha with Susie and Will."

Joe Pete nodded, then turned back to his pretty companion.

She'd ridden halfway down the street when Isaac hailed her. "Where the devil are you headed?"

Raising her eyebrows at his cursing, she answered, "Not that a question phrased liked that deserves a civil answer, but I'm going home. I left you a message with Joe Pete."

"I don't suppose you care that I intended to hurry the chores and get back to dance with you every chance I got."

"Oh? Did you get written permission from Mrs. Brown to dance with Mary's old-maid sister, Alicia?"

Color crept up his neck. "What makes you think I take my orders from Tess?"

"Oh, my. Isaac, dear!" Amanda gushed, putting the back of her hand to her forehead, batting her eyes, and swaying in the saddle. "I do believe I'm going to faint."

"I can't control what Tess does."

"But you're in perfect control of what you do, aren't you?" Imagining him in Mrs. Brown's room last night caused her eyes to burn. In spite of her best intentions, tears threatened.

Looking perplexed, Isaac asked, "What's wrong now?"

Amanda shook her head. "Nothing."

He studied her a moment, then shook his head. "I just don't understand you. And I don't have time to figure things out now. We have big trouble. Come on over here." He reached for Nellie.

Over the last few months, she'd learned the futility of arguing with Isaac when he used that certain tone of voice.

As they walked toward a gathering crowd, Isaac explained. "Like we figured, the Lazy W isn't the only ranch missing cattle. Most everyone has come up short on their counts. Parks, the new fellow homesteading northwest of the Lazy W, spotted five, maybe six, men driving a sizable herd toward Montana country."

"Did he recognize anyone?"

Isaac shook his head. "We've accounted for everyone from Lariat. It's bound to be the rustlers. They must have figured we'd all be in town and wouldn't notice a herd being moved. Parks didn't get close enough to see brands. Doesn't matter; they've probably altered them with running irons anyway. We're going after them."

Suddenly, Amanda felt like doing a clinging Teresa Brown imitation and begging him not to go. But Isaac wasn't a man to let anyone ride off into the sunset with his cattle.

From the porch of his store, Jim Callahan called, "Isaac, these men have offered to go with us. Do we need them all?"

Still carrying Nellie, Isaac addressed the crowd. "We aren't likely to surprise the rustlers if we go with a bunch of men. On the other hand, maybe if they see so many of us, they'll run instead of fight. I'd like to get my hands on those polecats, but I can do without getting shot."

There were shakes of heads and murmurs of agreement.

"Numbers won't necessarily protect us." Isaac shifted Nellie to his other arm. "We don't know who we're dealing with or how desperate they are. You homesteaders likely don't have many cows in that rustled herd. We won't hold it against you if you don't ride with us. I think we all need to talk this over with our families. Let's meet back here in ten minutes."

As if of one mind, the homesteaders drifted off to one side of the street, while the ranchers moved to the other.

With Nellie in one arm and his other arm wrapped tightly around Amanda's waist, Isaac spoke to Luke. "I'd like to tell you to stay, but I suppose it wouldn't do any good."

"I'm going."

"I figured." Isaac turned to Amanda. "Can you take care of things on the Lazy W until we get back?"

"Of course." She felt she could take care of anything when Isaac had his arm around her. *Why couldn't he tell that? Why did he go to Teresa Brown?*

Jim Callahan and his family joined Isaac's. "Are you and Luke both riding?" Jim asked.

Isaac nodded.

"My boy here wants to ride with us." Jim indicated his grown son. "It'd give us another man, but I need someone to look after the stable and do the heavy lifting for Martha at the store. These women will need wagons hitched and supplies loaded before they go on back to their homes tomorrow."

Joe Pete stepped up. "I can do that for you, Mr. Callahan."

Jim started to smile, but Isaac spoke to Amanda. "Can you get along without Joe Pete for a couple of days?"

"I can manage."

"Wait a minute," said Jim. "I appreciate Joe Pete's offer, but it takes a grown man to get horses into a heavy harness."

"There isn't much Joe Pete can't do with horses," Isaac said. "The preacher's boys are getting some size to them. Maybe one can help Joe Pete and the other two can give Martha a hand."

"You sure about Joe Pete?"

"The boy's stronger than he looks."

"What do you say, Martha?"

"I think you men have your minds all made up and it isn't going to make any difference what a mother thinks."

Jim kissed her on the top of her head. "I knew you'd agree. Would you set us up with some grub?"

The crowd again gathered in front of the general store. A spokesman from the homesteaders' side of the street came up on the porch with Isaac. "All told, we ain't missing but ten head. But we don't cotton to raisin' our families where men of the rustler type are hanging around. Neighbors have to stick together. We drew straws. Ten men will ride with you. The other five will check on our families while we're gone. They'll check on any nearby ranches if you want."

Isaac welcomed the homesteaders with a handshake. "That'll make twenty-nine of us. That ought to put the fear of God into the rustlers."

The preacher stepped forward. "Most of us men need to leave, but my wife figures the kids should have their Fourth of July fireworks all the same. Any adults staying in town tonight, meet my wife and Martha around back. They'll divide the work.''

The town went into motion. Luke and Joe Pete headed to the stable, while Isaac walked Amanda back to her horse. ''I hate to leave you to take care of things alone, but I'm dang near positive the men I've been nervous about are herding some of my cows toward Montana right this minute. Just in case I'm wrong, I want you and Nellie to get moving so you'll be home before dark.''

''Maybe I should take Susie and Willie. Martha has too much to do to watch out for them.''

''It'd break their hearts to miss the fireworks. Joe Pete will be in town. He'll keep them in line.''

Isaac held Amanda's horse while she mounted.

''How long do you think you'll be gone?'' she asked.

''If we don't catch them in four days, we've agreed to turn around. If we do get to the herd, we'll need to push cattle back. Allow maybe eight or ten days before you get worried.''

Before I get worried! I'm frantic now and you're not even on your horse yet! But she managed a smile as she reached to take Nellie from him. ''I don't worry about you, remember?''

''Take care of yourself.'' Isaac turned loose her reins.

Amanda rode about thirty feet, then turned her horse and came back to where he stood. ''Isaac, be careful.''

''I will.''

''Watch out for Luke.''

''I always have.''

''You have three children to help me raise.''

''I'll be home as soon as I can.'' He reached out and patted her denim-covered thigh in a gesture of reassurance.

Last night, with Isaac in another woman's arms, Amanda had felt as if her love for him had shriveled into a knot and died.

She hadn't been that lucky.

CHAPTER
TWENTY-FOUR

With Isaac and Luke chasing rustlers and Joe Pete in town helping Martha, Amanda did the chores on the Lazy W, going to her homestead only to water and harvest the garden.

By the fifth day, she began to worry in earnest. *Why was Isaac gone so long?* He'd told her eight or ten days, but it shouldn't have taken that long. *What was keeping him?*

On the sixth afternoon, she put a load of tomatoes into the canning kettle and left the stifling kitchen to clean the chicken coop. As she crossed the yard, the dogs began barking. Isaac and the homesteader, Parks, rode into view. Parks raised his rifle in a salute when he spotted her, then turned his horse and left. Slumped in his saddle, Isaac rode on into the yard alone.

Isaac never slumped! Never! She ran to meet him.

"You're a sight for sore eyes." He handed her his rifle. "Give me a hand off this horse, would you?"

Amanda hurried to the porch, putting his rifle down beside hers. On her way back to the horse, she had a clear view of Isaac's right leg. His pants had been cut wide open, exposing a bloody bandage from his hip to his knee.

Groaning, he threw the wounded leg over the back of his horse. He balanced in one stirrup with his good leg, then slid into Amanda's waiting arms. Inside, he gritted his teeth as she lowered him to the wooden couch. Once settled, he leaned back and closed his eyes. "It's good to be home."

"How did you get shot? Is the bullet still in your leg?"

He gave a tiny grin. "I almost wish it were a bullet wound. Then the rest of my life I'd be known as the hero who got shot that Fourth of July we all chased down a bunch of rustlers."

It wasn't a bullet wound. She sagged against the couch arm with relief. "What happened?"

"The rustlers hightailed it just like we hoped. We did corner two of them. Jim and a couple of men took them to town to wait for the marshal."

"Where's Luke?"

"The Lazy W had over sixty head in the rustled herd. He's moving our cattle into the high country behind his homestead. Then he's going to backtrack the rustlers and find out where they had a herd that size hidden." Isaac reached for her hand and covered it with his. "Don't look so worried."

"I don't worry about you, remember?" She swiped at the tears in her eyes with the back of her free hand. "If you're not full of bullets, why are you wearing a bloody bandage?"

He looked ruefully at his leg. "We were moving the herd this morning when a couple of cows broke away. I took out after them and managed to skewer my leg on a snag sticking out from a pine tree. Luke pulled out the big chunks of wood, but he's pretty heavy-handed. I told him to leave the rest for you."

Relief washed over her in waves. *Thank you, God.* Splinters she could handle. "You scared me to death. I'm going to lift your legs up on the couch." Gently, she bore the weight of his legs and moved Isaac around. Jerking the seat cushion from the rocking chair, she tucked it behind his head. "Rest a bit while I get some water and bandages."

She tripped over Rasty as she turned. "What are you doing in here?" Pointing toward the door, she commanded, "Out!"

For the first time ever, Rasty disobeyed her direct order. He hunkered down and pressed against the couch where Isaac lay. Even if she'd had the heart to shoo the dog out, she wouldn't have after Isaac spoke. "Leave him, Amanda. If I'd had him with me this morning, none of this would have happened. I'd have sent him into the trees after those mavericks. I wish we had a few more dogs like old Rasty here."

"You may get your wish. He and Misty were getting along quite well the first few days after I got back from town."

Isaac scratched Rasty's ears. "That right, boy? You been lifting Misty's skirts?"

Rasty dog-grinned at Isaac and his tail thumped the floor.

"Believe me, he doesn't need any encouragement!"

She threw some wood into the stove and pushed the canning kettle to the back. During the five minutes or so she'd spent getting Isaac settled, Nellie had beat on the screen door and howled. Still ignoring her, Amanda grabbed a couple of buckets and headed through the living area toward the spring out back.

"You want to let Nellie in before you get water?"

Remembering the guns on the porch, she dropped the buckets and muttered to herself, "I'll get water next." She flew out, picked up the guns, and hustled Nellie inside. She popped the toddler onto a chair. "Don't you move until I get back."

Working as quickly as possible, Amanda removed the bridle from Isaac's horse and jerked off the saddle, then turned the animal into the pasture. The poor tired thing was rolling in the tall grass before Amanda got back to the porch.

When she swooped back through the cabin to grab the water buckets, Nellie had cuddled up with Isaac on the couch. He let that child get away with anything!

By the time she'd gathered what she needed, Isaac had dozed off. His face, bruised from the Fourth of July fight, had a pasty pallor. Blood seeped from under the bandage, staining the couch cushion. Amanda sent Nellie to the far side of the room.

Beads of sweat formed on Isaac's forehead as she helped him get his boots and pants off. Eyeing his bloody bandage, she took a deep breath and reached for the knot holding it closed.

"Wait a minute." Isaac stayed her hand and shifted nervously, wincing as he moved. "Luke and I have a few bottles of whiskey in the hayloft.'' He grinned sheepishly. ''For medicinal purposes. This might be a good time to break one out.''

Five hefty doses of ''medicine'' later, he declared himself ready.

Amanda carefully shuttered her eyes when she saw the yawning, irregular gash in Isaac's thigh. Filled with splinters of wood, the wound's lips oozed blood. Kneeling, she calmed her shaking hand and began to remove splinters, almost crying with frustration when big splinters would fall apart into little ones.

Gripping the edge of the furniture, Isaac continued to sip whiskey and bore the pain in silence. A couple of times, Amanda shooed Nellie off impatiently or pushed Rasty out of her way.

Finally, both dog and toddler moved to a corner of the room. Nellie wrapped her arms around Rasty, and they sat quietly.

After what seemed an eternity, Amanda rocked back on her heels. ''I don't see any more splinters. Can you feel any?''

''At this point, no one place hurts worse than another.''

She had avoided thinking about the inevitable, but it had to be done. ''I have to sew it closed. It's too long and deep to heal properly unless I do.''

''I'm sorry, Amanda. I know it's a nasty job. I had to sew up a three-inch cut on Josh's arm one summer.''

Three inches! She wished the gash in his leg were only three inches long. Isaac's leg lay open from right above the knee almost to his hip. Standing beside the couch, Amanda tried to stop the quivering of her hand long enough to thread a needle. When she knelt at his side, he handed her the whiskey bottle.

''You better take a swig.'' Isaac offered her the whiskey.

Amanda considered the bottle, then tipped it up. Tears clouded her eyes as the fiery liquid burned its way down her throat. She choked and coughed.

After she got her breath back, Isaac commanded, ''Another.''

This swallow didn't burn so badly. Looking at the whiskey bottle in her hand, she recalled something she'd seen her father do with injured animals.

Isaac bellowed and writhed when she poured the whiskey into the gash. Nellie started crying and Rasty whined. Ignoring all of them, Amanda cleaned the wound carefully with the whiskey, saving two generous swallows, one for Isaac—and one for herself.

With a fussy toddler clinging to her back and a dog trying to crowd between her and her patient, Amanda began inflicting intense pain on the man she loved. Not long into the ordeal, she looked up and discovered that Isaac had fainted. *Thank you, God.*

After she finished sewing the cut together, Amanda tucked her needle into the pin cushion, then laid her forehead on the edge of the couch and sobbed.

The following week, Amanda stayed on the Lazy W, returning to her homestead only long enough to irrigate. In spite of her attention, the more jagged tears on Isaac's leg became infected.

More than once the thought occurred to her that a good doctor like Tom would know what to do. Guiltily, she counted the days since she'd decided to write to him. She had to let him know she wasn't returning.

Isaac tossed and turned throughout the hot summer nights. She moved his cot and her mattress to the main cabin, hoping to catch any breeze coming through the screen door.

It seemed like years before she woke to find Isaac smiling down at her. She reached up, felt his forehead, then smiled back. *Completely cool, for the first time in two weeks.*

He put a finger to his lips and motioned to the far side of her mattress. She'd shared her bed with Nellie and two kittens.

When she started to rise, he stopped her. "Rest a while longer," he whispered, smoothing his hand across her cheek.

"I'd best wake Luke. We have things to do."

"The chores will keep. You look tired."

She felt exhausted. She lay back and Isaac took her hand. After kissing the palm, he pressed it to his cheek. Fingers entwined, she stared into his eyes until sleep reclaimed her.

*   *   *

Willie and Susie woke them the second time. Susie held their storybook reverently in both hands, offering it to her.

"We can have a story tonight, darling. I have work to do now."

Isaac intervened. "How about just one?"

Sitting on her mattress, Amanda leaned up against Isaac's cot. He put one hand familiarly on her shoulder. The little children wasted no time cuddling in close. When Joe Pete came down from the loft a few minutes later, he sat on the edge of the mattress, a part of the cozy family group, but too old and too reserved to get in the midst of things. Halfway through the story, Amanda looked up and welcomed Luke with a smile.

After signaling for her to keep reading, Luke put on a pot of coffee, then joined Joe Pete on the edge of the mattress.

"The end!" Amanda announced when she finished the story. "Now scoot, every one of you. We have a ranch to run."

She had clothes hanging all over the yard by mid-afternoon. Joining Isaac at the woodpile, she admired the wide, tanned chest he'd bared to the sun. "You look like you're feeling better."

"I feel good." He leaned on the ax handle.

"Good enough to stay alone while I take the children to my homestead to work for a couple of days? Luke needs to ride the range and won't be around."

"Are you far behind on the chores on your homestead?"

"Not too bad," she lied. "I need to weed the garden."

"What say I go with you to your homestead?"

Amanda hesitated.

"What's the matter?" he demanded. "I may be lame, but I can still do some menial chores around the barn."

"You are not lame. And it's perfectly obvious you can do some chores." She gestured toward the fresh stacks of wood. "The thing is, I don't know where you'll sleep. I won't have you trying to climb into the loft and breaking open your stitches."

"Then I'll bunk on the dugout floor."

"I'd rest easier having you with me than here alone. But

with that leg, *I'm* sleeping on the ground and *you're* in the bed.''

Reaching out, Isaac pushed a stray curl back from her face. ''If you weren't so stubborn, we could share the bed.''

She laughed. ''You must be feeling better! At this rate, maybe you can ride into town and visit Mrs. Brown.'' Having said her piece, she fled, determined not to let Isaac see the tears. Life would be so easy if men loved the right women.

The wagon ride to Amanda's homestead was excruciating for Isaac. Feverish again, he slept most of the first day. She sent Joe Pete to Hawk's camp for help. The boy and Hawk returned with herbs, some to be made into a compress and some to be made into teas. He stayed two days, helping her doctor the leg.

The morning after Isaac's fever finally broke, Amanda mentioned her garden. ''I *have* to weed. If you need anything, yell. I don't want you overdoing. Just sit out here and rest. Maybe fresh air and sunshine will help that cut. We've tried everything else.''

''Quit worrying. You're a regular mother hen these days.''

She raised her eyebrows.

''And I love having you taking care of me,'' he added hastily, throwing his arms up as if to ward off blows.

Laughing, she called the children. ''Let's go up and get those weeds before they get our vegetables.''

Isaac looked to where Nellie was busily digging in the dirt. ''Why don't you leave Nellie Belle down here with me?''

''You wouldn't get a lick of rest.''

''I can handle one little girl and rest at the same time.''

''You'll have to be up and down all morning.''

''That probably would be good for my leg.''

''You make her mind if I leave her here. It's not only bad for her to think she can always have her way, it's not safe to have her doing whatever she wants.''

Isaac agreed, but Amanda knew he was simply appeasing

her. He never made Nellie behave. They'd talked about his
need to be firmer with Nellie more than once.

Amanda was on her knees weeding when she heard a gunshot
from the direction of the dugout. Frantically, she gestured for
Joe Pete and the twins to get into the trees and stay quiet. She
jerked her pistol from its holster. Heart beating wildly, Amanda
peeked through the long grass and down at the dugout.

Hunkered down near the woodpile, Isaac had his good leg
bent, his injured leg out stiffly to the side. *Where was Nellie?*
As quickly as the thought occurred to her, Isaac struggled to
his feet, clutching Nellie to his chest. The toddler had her arms
wrapped around his neck, and her howling traveled up the hill.

By the woodpile, Rasty stood at a point.

When Amanda started running down the hill, Isaac signaled
for her to stop. He gave Nellie another hug. Then he sat the
child down on her feet and proceeded to scold her. "Do as I
say," floated up the hill on the constant Wyoming wind. "Do
you understand, young lady?" sailed up behind it. Isaac gave
Nellie a firm swat on her behind and pointed toward the dugout.

As a squalling Nellie minded, Amanda's heart slowed to a
more normal cadence. She called to the other children. "It's
all right. Joe Pete, keep a close eye on the twins, will you?"

Nellie's dramatic cries still issued from the open dugout
when Amanda reached the yard. Sprawled on the porch swing,
Isaac didn't look so good.

"What happened down here?" Amanda asked as she lifted
his injured leg up onto the stump she'd pulled over earlier.

"I just had a lesson in what happens if you let children get
spoiled. From now on, that little red-haired cyclone minds."

"What did she do?"

"I was sitting here watching the kitten stalk something by
the woodpile. I figured it had spotted a mouse; then I realized
the stupid animal had cornered a big damned rattlesnake."
Isaac shuddered.

"Why the gunshot?"

"Well, all this time, Nellie had a stick and was digging in

the dirt right beside me. Next thing I knew, she headed for the kitten. I called to her, but she didn't even slow down.''

"Oh, dear God," Amanda whispered. The story about Eric and Gerta Anderson's little girl running into the rattler had played through her mind many times since Isaac told it to her.

"I couldn't catch Nellie with this bum leg. I had to shoot right past her to hit that snake. If she'd changed direction, I'd have shot her in the back."

Amanda wrapped her arms around Isaac, held him close, and rocked him, uttering words of comfort as he shook.

After a bit, he leaned back and studied the sky. "I don't know what I'd have done if that snake had got her."

"I don't know what either of us would have done. She wiped the trace of tears from his eyes, then her own.

"We've got to start making her mind," he said.

Amanda swallowed an *I told you so.*

The crying from inside the dugout had subsided. An occasional demand issued forth. "I want my Aunt Mandy." Once Nellie tried, "I love you, Unk Isk."

Amanda turned toward the woodpile. "I'll bury the snake."

"You want me to do it?"

Reluctance almost oozed through his pores. "I'll do it." She grabbed a shovel and headed to where Rasty stood guard over the dead prairie rattler. In spite of her brave talk, Amanda shook while she looked for the fangs. They'd still be full of poison. She didn't relax until she dropped the snake's fangs into a deep hole and covered them with dirt.

It took her a few minutes to coax the frightened kitten from behind the woodpile. Stroking it, she carried it to Isaac.

He talked to it as he smoothed its fur.

"I thought you didn't like cats."

He smiled sheepishly. "I guess Kitty has convinced me differently. I haven't told you thanks for leaving one of her kittens on the Lazy W. I enjoy having it around."

"You'll find a cat keeps down the mice around a place."

"And snakes," Isaac added hopefully.

"I doubt that. This kitten would have been the loser if you hadn't been around."

"You know a lot about kids, animals, and gardens."

She laughed. "I think you must be feverish again."

"I'm trying to give you an honest compliment here."

"Well, thank you, Isaac. I'm very flattered."

Nellie came to the dugout door. "I out?"

"You get back on your bed, young lady," roared Isaac.

Nellie disappeared. Her bawling started anew.

"Is until after lunch long enough for her to stay inside?" he asked.

"I think you will have made your point by then."

That night, after the children were in bed, Amanda noticed a sheen of sweat on Isaac's brow. "I want to look at that leg. Get your pants off."

"For you, anytime." Though obviously in pain, Isaac stood by the big bed and grinned wickedly while he unbuttoned.

Determined not to be scared off by his teasing, she crossed her arms and glared at him. When it became evident that he intended to drop his pants, she whipped around. "Honestly, Isaac."

Behind her, he chuckled. The squeak of the springs didn't drown out his involuntary groan as he lay down. "You can turn around now." He had a blanket pulled across his hips. His ashen face testified to the intensity of the pain he must be feeling.

Some of the stitches pulled at his skin, forming little sores. The time had come to remove the stitches before the cure became worse than the disease. He lay silently enduring the pain. At last, she reapplied the herbs Hawk had brought for the leg and stood. "I think you'll be more comfortable now."

"Thanks, Amanda."

"Nothing I wouldn't do for any dumb animal."

The infuriating man grinned.

"Oh, for heaven's sake!" she muttered. "Let me help you out of your shirt. I'll get you some water and you can wash up."

After she finished the dishes, Amanda blew out the lantern

and slipped on her nightgown. As she moved toward her bed, Isaac reached out and took hold of her gown. "Lie with me."

"Isaac," she protested.

"I won't ask for anything more. I just want to hold you."

Knowing better, but needing and wanting to be held by him, she lay down next to his long, warm body.

He wrapped her in his arms and pulled her close, kissing her forehead. "Lord, but I love to have you sleep next to me."

Lying very still, she memorized the feel of his body—the swell of the arm muscle cradling her head, the spring of his curly chest hair beneath her hands, the touch of his lips still pressed against her forehead. She wanted to belong to Isaac so badly—in every way. Who cared if he had another woman somewhere else? What if she did have a fiancé? All she could think about was the dull ache of her heart.

CHAPTER
TWENTY-FIVE

Each evening for the rest of the summer, Isaac returned to the dugout. The children fell into the routine of having a story from Amanda and prayers with Isaac.

One evening in early fall, Amanda noticed Isaac favoring his leg. "Let me look at that leg." She ran her hand down his thigh. "It's feverish again."

"I moved a herd for marketing in closer today. It's always worse after a hard day. Maybe you need to rub it some more."

Something in his voice made her glance at his face. She caught his wicked smile. "Isaac Wright, you behave yourself." Their laughter gave way to seriousness as she cleaned the raw areas. Sympathetic tears filled her eyes each time he winced, so she kept her head down.

Isaac wasn't fooled. He lifted her head and brushed away the tears with his fingers. "I never want to cause you tears."

"I know the name of a doctor. When you take your cattle to market in Omaha, you'd better go see her."

"Her? I'm not going to any female doctor."

"You've been letting me doctor you for over two months."

"Not because I needed it." He grinned. "I just want your hands on my body every night."

"Quit teasing!" Amanda thumped him on the head as she walked to the stove. "I hear she's excellent. But if you won't see her, I'll give you the name of another doctor."

"How is it that you know doctors from Omaha?"

"I met them at a medical conference in Denver."

Isaac stretched and scratched his back against the bedstead. "What were you doing at a medical conference?"

"I frequently acted as hostess for a friend of mine."

"Is that the man who writes you?"

Now, Amanda. It was the time to tell him about Tom. But the next time she went to town, she intended to mail Tom a good-bye letter. She'd sold Hawk's horses and would send his ticket money back to him. No use admitting to Isaac how flagrantly she'd been disregarding the implied vow of faithfulness she took when she agreed to marry Tom. Instead of answering Isaac, she countered, "I didn't know you kept track of my mail."

"You've only had seven letters. I couldn't help noticing a man's handwriting. So is he your medical friend?"

"I suppose that's one way of putting it." She straightened a dish towel. "I'll step out so you can get ready for bed."

"There's no reason we can't get ready for bed together."

Amanda felt herself blush, and she let herself out of the dugout. She couldn't go on much longer with things the way they were between Isaac and her. His casual touches lasted longer these days, and the good-night kiss between them gradually had become more than routine—much more.

She had to write Tom.

Tom's recent letter to her had been almost identical to his first. He wanted her home so they could make wedding plans. He made sure she knew what an inconvenience and embarrassment all this homesteading nonsense was to him. Her letter breaking the engagement was becoming easier and easier to write.

As usual, when Amanda started for her pallet that night, Isaac reached out and pulled her to lie beside him on the big bed. Normally, he kissed her good night, then rolled over and went to sleep. Tonight, he leaned over her and his mouth lingered. She fought the urge to raise her arms and welcome him. That was all it would take. One returned embrace stood between her and respectability.

Her heart ached. The moment a woman bonded physically with a man should be one of shared love. Knowing only she felt love gave her the courage to turn her back to Isaac's warm kisses. "Good-night, Isaac."

He hesitated, then lay down on the far side of the bed. "I want you bad, Amanda."

He wanted her! She wanted him, too. Only Isaac could ease the ache deep inside her. She couldn't let him. "Go to sleep."

Just as she had for weeks, she woke spooned into Isaac's body, with his hand cradling her breast. Feigning sleep, she enjoyed his warm, masculine fragrance. She sensed when he awoke, but she didn't pull away. Isaac ran his thumb lightly over her nipple, to and fro, then in circles, then began kissing her neck.

He's breaking our unspoken rules, Amanda thought as he turned her so that he could reach her mouth. His tongue begged, and she opened her lips. She was already aching for him when he bent to her breasts. As he suckled slowly, deeply, he undid two buttons of her nightgown.

"No, Isaac!" She stopped his hand and gently tugged his head away from her needful breasts.

"You taste so good." He came to her mouth for another kiss and toyed with the next button on her gown. "I want to see your beautiful body naked, and I need to feel it next to mine."

Shivers of delight ran down her neck. If only she could bring herself to let him continue. But on top of everything else, the children could wake at any minute. "I have to get into my own bed right now!" Shaking, she slipped onto the pallet to wait until it was light enough to work outside. She needed to work.

She shouldn't and wouldn't lie beside Isaac again until she'd dealt with Tom. Her mind and body couldn't handle any more temptation.

* * *

In late September, Isaac sent the children off to play so he could talk to Amanda. "I want to move you and the kids to the Lazy W for the winter before I leave for Omaha with the cattle."

"I can't leave my homestead now. You know I need to live here five years to prove up."

"I told you before. We all stay together in the winter. You can still prove up. No one will know you weren't on your homestead all winter. I've mostly done things your way this summer, but we can't stay in your dugout all winter."

"And why not?"

"The dugout will be too cold. It's too far from the Lazy W. I could give you a hundred reasons. And right up there is my need to move farther away from you at night. I lie on that bed thinking how much I want you and, I swear to God, some nights I'm about ready to roll off the bed and take you by force."

She couldn't quit staring. She just couldn't look away.

"Well, damn it, there's no use looking at me that way. I can't help it. Gol-darn, Amanda, don't you know anything about men?"

"How would an *old maid* know anything about men?"

"Quit with the old-maid stuff. I may have run off at the mouth a little before I met you, but I've kissed you now. You don't have an ounce of old maid in you."

"How do you know that?"

Isaac propelled her into the barn. Hands braced on either side of her head, he pressed her against a wall with the length of his body and kissed her, long and hard. He slid his hands along her body, stopping to caress her breasts, then lower to cup her derriere. Lifting her, he ground his body into hers.

She wrapped her legs around him, pulling him closer.

Many desperate, hungry kisses later, Isaac quit moving, then circled the lobe of her ear with his tongue and whispered, "See? No old maid in you." He nibbled at her neck.

After he lowered her to the ground, she arranged her clothing and tried to regain her composure. "Honestly, Isaac! You'd do anything to make a point."

"Some things are easier to do than others." As they left the barn, he popped her on the backside.

"Isaac!"

"I'm never going to buy you a dress. I'm dressing you in britches forever. Tight britches." He was still smiling when he spotted Misty. "Isn't it about time for her to have those pups?"

"Any day."

"Then that's another reason we need to get back to the Lazy W. Misty will need to stay with her pups instead of watching the kids. And the snakes will be moving soon. When the night temperature drops, they begin searching for a place to hole up for the winter. It'll be easier on my mind if you and the kids are settled on the Lazy W before I leave for Omaha."

"I've got to work my garden. It's coming off by the basketful."

"Then you can come over to do what has to be done. We start roundup day after tomorrow. I want you moved before then." As an obvious afterthought, he added, "Please."

Reluctantly, she nodded. Perhaps he was right. She didn't mention the four rattlers she killed last week. "Do you need me to help with the roundup?"

"It'd be real helpful if you could cook a big noon meal for us. Jim Callahan and a couple of his boys are coming to help." Isaac cleared his throat. "There's something else I need to tell you. Hawk's band has moved deeper into the mountains."

"Oh, Isaac. I wanted to go see Shining Sky's baby girl."

"I know. But there're too many folks around these days. Someone's going to discover them. Hawk sent you a message. He thanks you for the stuff you sent Shining Sky, and he's bringing you another horse. He wants you to keep it for yourself."

"I didn't spend much on those things."

"You'll hurt his pride if you don't accept the horse."

She'd been wondering about what Jim Callahan had said when she sold him the horses Hawk had brought her. He said he could always sell good horses. Joe Pete was riding the stallion Hawk had given him. If Hawk gave her a mare, she and Joe Pete could maybe raise horses to sell. It was something to think about.

Isaac helped get the last bunch of cows headed to Lariat with Luke and the other men; then he swung by the Lazy W. He arrived in time to tuck the children into bed and caution them to mind while he was gone to Omaha. As he shaved, he talked with Amanda. "I'll sell the cattle and be back as soon as I can."

"We'll be fine."

"I suppose." He pulled off his boots while Amanda poured his bathwater. "Why don't you stay and wash my back?"

Tempting. But she threw a towel in his direction and left the room. Later, lying in the darkness, she heard her bedroom door open, and Isaac came to sit on the edge of her bed.

"Amanda, this may be our last night all winter without Luke around. Let me sleep with you tonight."

"We've been through this before."

"You slept with me half the summer."

Amanda could feel the heat in her cheeks as she answered, "But no one knows except you and me." She sat up in bed and touched his shoulder. "You wouldn't tell anyone, would you?"

Isaac took her in his arms. "What would my silence be worth to you?" He gave her a lover's kiss, open and warm.

It didn't come as a surprise when his hands cupped her breasts. Every ounce of good sense told her that letting him in her bed tonight was trouble. Her body didn't care. She didn't even pretend to protest when he climbed under the covers.

His freshly shaved face felt soft as he nuzzled her neck and opened the top of her nightgown. When his warm mouth moistened her breasts, suckling them through the thin gown, she groaned with pleasure. He was working the hem of her gown up when she stopped him. "I have to write a letter."

"Now?" He rose on his elbow and stared at her.

"I'm sorry." She slipped from the bed. "Please wait for me."

"Do I look like I'm fixing to go anywhere? Who the hell do you have to write to this very moment?"

"No one important. But it has to be done now."

She was no silly adolescent. Isaac wasn't offering her a future. He wouldn't know or care that their mating would bind her body and soul to him for all eternity. But it would. She needed to do this one thing correctly. Because after tonight, her life would never be the same.

Sitting at the kitchen table, she composed a long-overdue letter to Tom. Once, she felt Isaac's gaze on her, and she looked up. "Go on to bed. I'll be there soon."

"Honest to God, Amanda. I don't understand you."

After she finished, she folded the letter and put it in her robe pocket. She'd take it to town when she went for supplies.

Isaac's soft snores welcomed her to her bedroom. When she turned down the lamp and slid in beside him, he instantly awoke.

"It's about danged time."

She didn't mind being scolded when his lips were kissing her face and neck. This time she didn't stay his hands, but let him unbutton her gown all the way. His first tastes of her bare breasts held great tenderness. Still, she longed for the demanding pull of his lips that had created such exquisite sensations in her womb earlier. Isaac didn't disappoint her. He feasted until she was squirming with desire. Only then did he work her gown up and over her head.

For one panicky second, she considered stopping. This wasn't right! When Isaac ran his hand across her belly, she quit thinking. He slipped a hand lower.

Isaac caressed her, not daring to believe this was finally happening. He slid his fingers through the thick nest of hair at the junction of her thighs, glorying in the way she opened to his coaxing hand. She felt hot down there. And tight. Her body told him no one had ever touched her like this. *Go slow,* he reminded himself. *Don't hurry.*

He'd never been first with a woman, but he'd heard other

men talking. *Go slow.* Part of him wanted to rush. Another part wanted this time never to end.

She moaned as his hand moved, teaching her the rhythm of mating. He smiled to himself when she shuddered and grew wet. After waiting for her to rest, he guided her hand to his body.

Amanda caressed his aroused manhood with her fingertips. So incredibly silky on the outside and so rock-hard on the inside.

Isaac closed his hand over hers and showed her what he wanted. Even after he stopped her, Amanda instinctively knew that he needed more, just as she needed more. She waited, scared a little, but anxious for him to cover her. Instead he knelt between her legs and lowered his head. Her face burned, and she pulled him up.

Isaac kissed her. "It's all right. Lie back and let me make love to you."

Amanda writhed as he tasted and tantalized.

Later, she wanted to please him as deeply as he'd pleased her. She kissed her way down his body. His groans of pleasure made her feel powerful and bold. As her lips touched his sex, he stiffened and pulled her head up to his mouth.

"Did I do something wrong?"

"You did everything perfectly." He was still shaking when he gathered her in his arms and took a deep breath. "But I've been wanting you since you arrived. I'm afraid I'll lose control if we don't stop for a few minutes."

"I think I want you to lose control."

Chuckling, he pulled her close and slid his hand down to caress her again. "Hush and relax."

Amanda could concentrate on nothing but the longing created by the rhythm of his hand. She didn't realize the dogs had started barking until Isaac leapt from the bed, cursing.

Jerking on his boots and pants, he grabbed his rifle and rushed outside. A screech, sounding for all the world like a wounded woman, followed his shot.

Isaac burst back into the house. "I winged a mountain lion.

I need to go after it.'' He finished dressing and gave Amanda
a peck on the cheek. ''Don't go locking the bedroom door.''
    ''I won't.''

At first light, he rode into the yard empty-handed. ''The cat's
wounded. Luke will have to hunt it down when he gets back.
I've got to hurry or I'll miss the train.'' He pulled her close
for a last kiss. ''I'm sorry the night turned out like this. Will
your bedroom door be open to me when I get home?''
    ''If we're alone with the children. They sleep heavily.''
    ''Amanda, Luke is a big boy. He knows about men and
women.''
    ''I can't help worrying about what he'll think about me. I'm
even more worried about the children telling stories in town.''
    ''Why are you so worried about what other people think?''
Isaac asked such stupid questions sometimes.
    He was gone in his usual flurry of last-minute instructions.

While Isaac was gone to market in Omaha, Amanda and
Luke agreed to make alternate trips to town for supplies.
    Recurring storms complicated the trips to Lariat. The first
time Amanda made a trip in, she hurried. She hated to be away
from the children. She didn't see anyone except the Callahans—
and she discovered Tom's letter still in her robe pocket when
she got ready for bed that night. Drat!
    With the roads muddy, Luke made the rest of the trips. He
handled the wagon much better on the slick trails. She thought
about sending Tom's letter with him, but it seemed something
she should do herself.
    One afternoon, she and the children went to her homestead
to dig potatoes. She'd been working a couple of hours when
the children started shouting, ''Uncle Isaac's coming!''
    Amanda ran with the children, but she slowed when she
realized Isaac had someone with him. In the next instant, she
recognized the tall, darkly handsome visitor and came to an
abrupt halt.

Tom!

His good-bye letter was still in her reticule.

Her gaze flew to Isaac's hard face, and her heart skipped a beat at the disgust she saw in his expression. She wiped her hands on the rear of her britches, took a deep breath, then continued down the hill to the yard of her homestead.

Tom swung down from his horse, gathered her in his arms, and kissed her as he never had before. "I couldn't wait until next summer for you to come back to Denver." When Amanda pushed at his chest, he must have thought her shy because he laughed and kissed her again. "Don't worry. Isaac knows we're engaged."

Isaac said nothing as he dismounted. She could tell his leg was bothering him by the way he rubbed his upper thigh.

With his arm at her waist, Tom guided her to where the children had gathered around for Isaac's hugs.

Amanda tried to step away from Tom, but he kept her clasped tightly to him. "Oh, no, you don't. I've had enough of this being separated from you—although you don't look like the woman who left me alone in Denver six months ago." Tom winked at Isaac. "But she'll probably clean up fine, don't you think? Get her out of these unsightly britches and into a nice dress and we'll be able to forget we ever saw her like this."

"We'll damn sure try." Isaac handed the children a bag of candy and sent them off. "I'll take the kids to the Lazy W with me," he said to Amanda. "I imagine you and your *fiancé* want to be alone to make up for some lost time."

The way Isaac drawled out the word fiancé made Amanda blanch. She should have told Isaac about Tom at the very beginning. And she should have mailed a good-bye letter to Tom the second week after she arrived. Everything was going to be so awkward now. Sending Tom away and explaining to Isaac.

Tom smiled. "I appreciate your giving Amanda and me time alone. Of course, I saw you with Mrs. Brown on the train, so I know you're a man in love and understand these things."

The Widow Brown? On the train? Amanda's eyes darted to Isaac's face, and she didn't like the answer she found there.

She forced her legs to carry her inside to help the children gather their things while Tom took a walk to the creek to "loosen up my muscles."

When Amanda reached Isaac's horse and handed up Nellie, she said, "You didn't mention that Teresa Brown was accompanying you on your business trip."

Isaac raised an eyebrow. "You didn't tell me you were engaged to be married."

CHAPTER TWENTY-SIX

Isaac had taken Teresa Brown to Omaha! Standing by Tom's side in front of the dugout, Amanda watched Isaac ride toward the Lazy W with all four children. Hours after Isaac and she had almost become lovers, he'd taken Mrs. Brown to Omaha!

Thank God for that mountain lion the night before he left. Another undisturbed hour and she might have been standing here pregnant with Isaac's baby. What had Isaac intended to do if she'd become pregnant? She'd acted like a lovesick fool. She'd never put herself into such a vulnerable position again. From now on, her heart and body would not dictate her actions! It didn't surprise her when Tom dropped his hand from her waist.

With tight lips, he evaluated her appearance. "My dear, I wouldn't have believed it possible for you to look so . . ." He searched for a word. "So . . . common. Your elegance, poise, and careful grooming have always made up for your voluptuousness."

Her voluptuousness? Isaac had led her to believe her "voluptuousness" was one of her stronger physical points.

Tom spotted the well. "Perhaps I can draw water for your bath. I have news, but I can't bring myself to discuss my future with you until you clean up and put on suitable woman's clothing.''

No declaration of loneliness at being so long separated. No lingering kisses. No words of love. Simply a demand that she make herself presentable before they discussed *his* future.

Luckily, she'd harbored no romantic illusions about her position in Tom's life. He expected her to keep his household in order and to mother his heir. In return, he'd promised to provide her with a home and sire the children she wanted.

She really should clean up a lot of things, herself included. ''Don't draw water. I'll go up to the river.'' Partway up the hill, she hesitated, then came back to Tom. ''Would you like to come and bathe with me? I could use someone to wash my back.''

It took him most of a full minute to regain his composure. Then he laughed. ''For a moment, I thought you were serious.''

''I am.'' Of course, she didn't know what she would do if he called her bluff and said yes.

Tom gaped at her, then drew himself up haughtily. ''I wouldn't dream of imposing upon a woman's bath.''

Isaac would. If she'd invited him, he'd have been naked and halfway up the hill by now. But then, Isaac might have been naked and halfway up the hill no matter who suggested the bath.

She didn't cry until she could no longer see the dugout. Isaac had intended to make love to her . . . no, love didn't enter into it. At least not for Isaac. He'd planned to have *sex* with her, knowing he was taking Mrs. Brown with him on his trip. There was nothing left between Isaac and her. Nothing!

When her tears of humiliation, disappointment, and despair were spent, she took stock of her situation. If she had only herself to think about, she could continue to live in a dugout on a snakey homestead. But she had Mary's children to consider. Accepting any help from Isaac now was out of the question.

When Amanda returned to the dugout, Tom had the good sense not to mention her denims and tightly fitting blouse.

Fixing supper, she concentrated on small talk. Tom said her family was fine. Anne was more beautiful than ever.

She asked about his mother. Though plagued by headaches, Mother valiantly carried on with her charitable works. Tom was sure Amanda would want to take over her charities immediately so Mother might get more rest.

She asked about his work. That was the big news. He'd been invited to France to lecture. While there, he planned to study some of the latest medical advances. Amanda and he would make the trip a combination business trip and extended honeymoon.

"I can't imagine Isaac approving of my taking the children to Europe. He practically forbade me to bring them to my homestead."

"First, I have no intention of taking the children. Second, you must remember to whom you owe explanations of your actions. That cowboy has nothing to say about what you or the children do." Tom produced a legal document. "I had my solicitor arrange for you and I to be made guardians of your late sister's children."

Holding the paper, Amanda blinked away the tears. This would break Isaac's heart.

Tom pointed out a paragraph. "Of course, there is a clause stating that guardianship is contingent upon our being married. The judge was adamant on that point. Therefore, I have taken the liberty of announcing November sixth as our marriage date."

"November sixth of *this* year?"

"I would have consulted you before setting a date, but you have been noticeably unavailable. I feel a need to deal with trivial personal details so that I can prepare my lectures."

Trivial? That was what this marriage was to Tom. A trivial personal detail that needed resolving.

He was still talking. "Obviously your family is unable to provide you with a suitable trousseau, so I spent one entire afternoon with Mother ordering your trousseau and wedding dress."

"You chose my clothing, including my wedding dress, without asking my preferences?"

"According to Mother, it was imperative that the dressmakers got started. I chose colors to compliment your green eyes, and I kept in mind your . . ." He shifted uneasily. "I ordered styles to hide your overly generous bosom. Mother took care of the more intimate apparel. She also ordered the wedding invitations. They need to go out soon, so she'll be addressing them for you."

"Heavens, I don't know why you need me in Denver at all."

The sarcasm was lost on Tom. "The dressmakers can only do so much before they need to do detailed fittings," he said.

"You gave me until April before I had to return to Denver."

"It is no longer convenient for me to wait until April while you have your little homesteading adventure."

"My little homesteading adventure, as you call it, is extremely important to me. I want to prove up and own this land."

"Is your homestead more important to you than a respectable marriage, more important than the children you wish to have?" He paused. "If you are so determined, I'll buy you a farm and you can play homesteader when we are free of social engagements. I can tolerate your idiosyncrasies as long as you do not embarrass me by talking about them among my friends and colleagues." Tom reached for his hat. "You *will* board the train in Lariat the day after tomorrow. Otherwise, we are no longer engaged. I'll expect your decision after I settle myself in the barn for the night."

"You don't have to sleep in the barn. I can sleep in one of the children's beds and you can have the big bed."

He shook his head. "Amanda, I do *not* understand this flaunting of conventions. Mother would be distraught if she knew we were even staying on the same homestead without a chaperon."

That would be one way of getting rid of Mother. She could tell her about how she'd been sleeping in the same room, in the same bed, with Isaac much of the summer. Amanda smiled slightly.

"If you find something humorous," Tom said, "I wish you would share it. I find this whole situation an irritating nuisance."

"It's nothing. Go make your bed." He'd opened the door before she added, "Be sure to take the shovel propped outside the door. I have a problem with rattlesnakes in the barn. This time of year, it appears they're seeking a warm place to spend the night."

Alone in the dark that night, she replanned her life. She'd return to Denver and make the best of a marriage to Tom. What good was a homestead if you spent your life alone, never having a husband, never having a child? She wanted to escape, to get away from Isaac and the heartache he'd caused her.

Amanda rose early the next morning and carefully wrapped the bedding from each bed into tight packs; then she suspended the packs from the roof support beam so rodents couldn't get to them. In the cupboards, she separated perishables from the other things and made a mental note to tell Isaac to pick them up when he came after the potatoes and the canned goods from the cellar. She left her clothes in the trunk at the foot of the bed. Nothing she'd been wearing would suit in Colorado. She turned her buckets upside down before walking up to the garden.

One last time, she knelt and washed her face and hair in the clear, frigid water of Wild Horse Creek. Shivering, she toweled her hair, rebraiding it as the sun came over the horizon.

The dugout below looked cozy and inviting, although she knew it would be damp and cold without a morning fire. Tom was striding around the yard now. Judging from the set of his shoulders, he was irritated. Had he always been so critical? She didn't remember that about him. Of course, in Denver, things had been going his way. She studied him as she walked down the hill. He turned away, waiting for her to approach him.

Isaac would have walked to meet her. If the children were still asleep, he'd have drawn her into his embrace, maybe have guided her into the privacy of the barn so he could touch her more intimately. Of course, that must be how he treated Mrs. Brown, too. Her eyes burned with unshed tears. She'd cried her last teardrop over Isaac Wright.

Without greeting Tom, Amanda picked up her shovel and turned over a pile of boards near the well, almost hoping for a snake so she could casually dispatch one of the critters in front of him. Drat! There was never a snake on the place when you needed one. She carefully covered the well with the boards, then went into the barn and saddled her horse while Tom saddled his.

They rode to the Lazy W in silence. She would ease into telling Isaac about the legal guardianship arrangements Tom had made. There was no point in hurting him out of hatefulness. To be honest, Isaac hadn't promised her a thing except a pleasant experience in bed. He had a right to take Teresa Brown anywhere he wished.

Regardless of how she felt about him, he was devoted to the children. But the children were young and needed her now. She'd get them to Isaac for visits. When they were old enough, they could make their own decisions about where to live.

When Tom and Amanda arrived on the Lazy W, the children were playing in the yard. Isaac was in the barn. She'd better go talk to him. "I'll unsaddle our horses," she said to Tom.

He closed his eyes, sighed with impatience, and shook his head. "Amanda, how often must I remind you of your position in life? I've been up for over two hours, and you still have not offered me coffee or breakfast. If it's not asking too much," he added curtly, "I would appreciate both. I'd also appreciate it if you'd rest enough today to rid yourself of those circles below your eyes. They are most unflattering."

From time to time, Isaac had mentioned the dark circles, but he'd been concerned that she was working too hard. He hadn't mentioned they were unattractive. She found Tom's bluntness annoying. Still, to keep peace, she'd feed him, then talk to Isaac later.

Later came sooner than she'd anticipated. Isaac stormed through the door, waving the guardianship paper under her nose. "You know what this is?" When she nodded, he flung it across the table. "Like hell you're taking these kids anywhere."

Tom stepped into the room. "I assure you that document is in perfect legal order. And I object to you speaking to my future wife in that manner."

"Until she *is* your wife, I'll talk to Amanda any way I wish."

Shrugging, Tom raised an eyebrow. "Then enjoy your show of power until the sixth of November. After that, I'll see to it that she never has to deal with you personally again. For now, Mr. Wright, we can do this the easy way or I can get in touch with the representative of the law in this godforsaken place. Amanda refuses to leave without the children, and I refuse to leave without Amanda. I've had enough of this bickering. While you two work out the details, I believe I'll take a walk and get to know the children who will be living under my roof."

After Tom left the kitchen, Isaac stared at Amanda until she averted her gaze.

"I love those kids," he said.

"We both love them. But while they're young, I'm the better guardian. You're too busy running a ranch."

"You've been busy on your homestead, too. Between us, we've managed. We both get to see the kids every day. They're happy."

"Life changes. I'm returning to Denver with Tom." This was Isaac's chance to tell her he loved her, to ask her not to go, to give her any reason in the world not to go.

"I can't believe you're going to leave that damn homestead of yours to marry that pretentious, self-righteous bastard!"

"Tom has offered me respectability, a lifetime of financial security, his name in marriage, and my own children. Weigh that against what I have. In your words, I have a snake-infested homestead that I need to live on for over four more years."

"Your homestead's coming along."

"I have exactly four dollars cash."

"I told you to charge anything you need at Callahan's."

"Unless it was for my homestead." She paused and enjoyed

his slow coloring. "And lastly, I have a neighbor who's willing to give me an occasional tumble in the hay, leaving me with the possibility of bearing an illegitimate child."

"I was going to take care not to get you pregnant. If something did go wrong, I'd marry you."

"You're too kind!" Amanda turned her back and set the irons to heat on the stove. "If you'll excuse me, I have to get the children's clothes ready for a train trip to Denver."

Holding Nellie, Isaac stood beside the train watching Amanda. That morning, she'd walked into Martha's house dressed in a calico dress with her hair in a braid. She'd emerged looking like the perfect fiancée for a physician.

Of course, he'd recognized her beauty all along. He just hadn't realized how regally she carried herself. Things like that tended to escape a man when a woman was running around tending children, gardening, and milking goats.

He should have told Amanda he hadn't taken Tess anywhere. Tess had gone to Omaha on her own and happened to be on the same return train as he was. He couldn't help it if she hung on him. Short of being rude, he didn't know how to get shed of her.

Besides, where did Amanda get off putting on a tortured, betrayed act. She had a *fiancé* she'd neglected to mention!

She sure had him fooled with her come-hither, then go-away routines. He'd bought that innocent act of hers!

Instead of standing here feeling like the south end of a northbound mule, he should be happy to be rid of a cheating, teasing woman. Because that was what she'd been doing all summer—teasing him and cheating on her fiancé.

How in the hell had Amanda got lashed up with someone like Tom? She came off fighting mad when Isaac even suggested something, calling him Your Majesty and curtseying. But Tom didn't even give her free rein to breathe—and she put up with it! Still, she must have strong feelings for the man. She was leaving her precious homestead and going back to Denver with him.

Well, that was how it should be. Wyoming was too hard on a woman. He'd always said that.

Slowly, he carried Nellie toward the open door on the pullman car. Letting the kids go was hard. Amanda had assured him she'd send the kids to him while Tom and she went to Europe in the spring. He could make it through one winter without the kids.

He stepped into a little hole, and the resulting jolt made him wince. But the pain in his heart was infinitely more intense than the pain in the newly opened wound on his leg.

At Amanda's insistence, he'd let Tom remove splinters festering deep in his thigh muscle. He hated to do it, but the damn leg hurt all the time. He supposed it would heal now.

His heart wouldn't be so lucky.

After all they'd been to each other, he didn't understand how Amanda could do this. She knew how he felt about these kids. And she was taking them away.

The engineer signaled and Isaac steeled himself for what had to be done. With Nellie in one arm, he kissed Susie and hugged Will, then watched the subdued children disappear into the train car. They reappeared with their noses pressed to the windows.

He took Amanda's offered hand. "You've got your money for that fifty head I marketed in your name?"

She nodded. "But I still don't feel right about taking money for caring for the children."

"You cooked and cleaned for Luke and me, too. I'll keep track of Joe Pete's ten head for him."

Amanda glanced toward where the boy stood, silent and unsmiling. "If he's terribly unhappy, may I send him to you?"

"If anyone's unhappy in Denver, I want them home where they belong." *Did she understand?* He glanced in Tom's direction, then surreptitiously tucked a roll of bills into her hand. "Here's enough for return tickets. Put it away somewhere."

She pushed it back toward him. "Tom's family is wealthy. I'm not going to need money."

"There are no stipulations to using this money, Amanda. When you step off the train in Lariat, you're free. You can homestead, live on the Lazy W with the kids, anything you want.'' After what seemed an eternity, she slipped the money into her pocket. Isaac thanked God. He touched her sleeve. ''I'm still going to fight like hell for custody of these kids, Amanda.''

''I know you will, Isaac. And I will fight to keep them.''

Tom arrived to help Amanda board the train. Then he turned toward Isaac and held out his arms for Nellie.

Isaac fought the urge to bash him in his smug face. Giving Nellie to the bastard would take every bit of self-control he could muster. Kissing her cheek, he nuzzled her sweet baby neck and whispered, ''I love you, Nellie Belle.'' After she rewarded him with a loud smacking kiss, Isaac started to hand her to Tom.

Joe Pete stepped between the men and took the toddler. He gave Tom what could only be described as a challenging look. ''I take care of Nellie.''

Good for you, boy. Isaac gave him a friendly cuff on the ear, then watched him climb onto the train with Nellie.

Standing in the midst of a swirling snow flurry, Isaac waited until the train disappeared, carrying away his reasons for living. When he could no longer see or hear the family-eating metal monster, he climbed into his wagon and headed for the Lazy W.

He had a ranch to run.

CHAPTER TWENTY-SEVEN

Standing in a bedroom of her parents' home, Amanda hardly recognized the sad-eyed woman reflected in her mirror. "Is there anything I can put under my eyes to hide these dark shadows?"

"I'll bring some powder with me tomorrow," answered Madame Silvia from her position on the floor, where she was marking the hem of Amanda's flowing white wedding dress. "Maybe if mademoiselle would get some sleep, the circles would go away before the wedding."

Sleep? She hadn't slept all night in weeks. She'd have liked to blame it on Susie's nightmares. But Susie's dreams weren't to blame for the blue smudges under her eyes. "I haven't slept well lately."

"You still have eight days before your wedding," continued the seamstress. "Perhaps mademoiselle would like me to get some sleeping potion from one of my friends?"

That would be easy. She could just take a sleeping potion every night for the rest of her life. Then she wouldn't lie awake wondering if her animals were all right, wondering if her fruit trees were alive, wondering if another family was staking a claim on her land. And worrying about Isaac. Did he miss the children? Had he ridden to town and stayed the night at the Widow Brown's?

She chided herself. Why was she unhappy when she had a fiancé who treated her with polite affection? After that evening on her homestead, Tom never mentioned the deplorable state in which he'd found her. Instead, he showered her with creams to soften her work-callused hands and insisted on buying her new clothes. He'd given her a proper engagement ring and other jewelry so she'd look nice when he took her places.

But could she live her life as a trinket on Tom's arm when in Lariat there was a chance for her to make something useful out of herself? If she lived here in Denver with Tom, the most pressing thing she'd ever have to do would be supervise a maid.

She wouldn't have to be concerned about any frustrated ''hells'' or ''damns'' escaping Tom's lips. Tom expressed himself clearly. ''Amanda dear,'' he'd said the other day, ''that brown you're wearing isn't the most flattering color for you. I'll have Madame Silvia pick something more appropriate.'' He'd tactfully approached an even more delicate subject. ''The cut of that dress emphasizes your . . . overly generous bosoms. Perhaps Madame Silvia can suggest something to conceal your physical problems.''

She wondered what Tom would say if he knew how greedily Isaac caressed and kissed her ''overly generous bosoms'' at every opportunity. She remembered the times she'd caught Isaac looking at her as if she were the most beautiful woman he'd ever seen, and it hadn't mattered what she had on at the time.

She supposed her marriage with Tom *could* be amicable— if she could get used to keeping her mouth shut. Tom had a penchant for treating her as if she didn't have a single opinion worth hearing.

Without consulting her, he made plans, and he expected her to go along with them. The children would stay with her parents while he had a wing built onto his house. He'd hire a nanny to see to the Wright children. Amanda could visit them when she could spare time from her duties as his wife and mother of his children. Joe Pete would be sent to boarding school next session.

Amanda could only imagine what Isaac would think of Tom's plans. Isaac liked the children close, even took them to ride with him whenever he could. His idea of privacy was a curtain pulled between his bed and theirs. The children, including Joe Pete, were an integral part of his life, not a nuisance to be relegated to some obscure corner of his existence.

Walking to the frosted window, Amanda looked north. North to Wyoming. North to Isaac.

Had his leg healed? It had turned unseasonably cold in Denver. Was he coming in from his chores to a cold house and no supper? Was he sleeping alone every night? Or was he riding to town from time to time?

What about her homestead? Had Isaac finished digging the potatoes? Had he remembered to pick the cabbages and haul the canned things from the cellar over to the Lazy W? She leaned against the window pane. How had she ever left her homestead?

How had she ever left Isaac?

Tom had been directing a medical conference at the hospital. She hadn't seen him for days. Thank heavens. She remembered when his overbearing attitude hadn't bothered her much, when maybe she did have a little affection for him. But she'd grown weary of his constant criticism and demands. She didn't belong here.

She had children to raise and a homestead to prove up on.

Today was Amanda's wedding day. Isaac had gotten up long before daylight and saddled his horse. He'd ridden over to Amanda's homestead intending to dig the potatoes before the ground froze solid. He ended up sitting in the dugout until midday. Just sitting there like a blamed idiot, staring out the window at the barn.

He wondered, did the church bell ring when Amanda came out after the marriage ceremony? He'd seen that once when he passed a church in Omaha. The bride and groom stepped out of

the church door, and someone started ringing the bell. Amanda
would be a beautiful bride. Did she put her hair up, or had she
left it down? He bet it was up for the ceremony. Probably down
tonight when she put on her nightgown for her husband. His
memory of Amanda in her soft cotton nightgown tortured him.
Had she ever been with Tom? Really been with him? Didn't
matter. She would be tonight. Amanda would belong to another
man tonight.

When he rode over the crest of the hill at dusk, Isaac noted
with surprise that someone had moved the sheep into the Lazy
W's lower pasture. Perplexed, he angled down toward the ranch
yard. Suddenly, kids boiled out of the door, shouting their
hellos. Dismounting, he scooped up all three of the little kids
in a bear hug, then carried them back inside out of the cold.
He shoved a grinning Joe Pete with a friendly elbow as he
passed.

Watching Amanda set the table for supper, he listened with
only half an ear to the kids' babble.

"You should have heard all the hollering, Uncle Isaac,"
declared Willie. "Tom said he'd be a laughingstock."

"Yeah," agreed Susie. "He told Aunt Mandy that she'd rue
the day." The little girl sobered and asked, "What's rue?"

Amanda met Isaac's gaze. Next thing he knew, they were
smiling at each other, then laughing. He went to her. Taking
her hands, he caressed their tops with his thumbs. "Thank you
for coming home."

The touch of Isaac's hands, the sound of his voice, were
exactly as she remembered. Amanda fought the urge to lay her
head against his chest and breathe in the scent of man, horses,
and leather that was Isaac. She struggled to remember her
promise to herself. There'd be no repeat of the poor judgment
she'd shown when she allowed Isaac access to her body and
bed.

But there was no point in not being on friendly terms. The
children tied them together as a family.

"I missed you," he said.

She responded with forced gaiety. "Let's see if you feel the
same way after a winter in the cabin with all of us."

"I have never looked forward to a winter as much as this one." Isaac raised an eyebrow playfully.

The sooner she stopped his flirting, the better. Otherwise, he might interpret her return to the Lazy W as an unspoken agreement to a continued physical affair.

Matter-of-factly, she stepped away from him. Steadying her shaking hands, she opened the oven on pretense of checking the biscuits. "It *is* all right if we stay here, isn't it?"

"This is the kids' home. And you and Joe Pete will always be welcome at my table."

She longed to throw herself into his arms, but she had a little pride left. Very little. "If you're sure you don't mind, we'll stay the winter as we planned originally. In the spring, I'll move back permanently to my homestead."

Isaac walked to the window and stared out at the descending darkness. At last he turned to Joe Pete. "I need to get chores done before supper. You coming, boy?"

Joe Pete grabbed his coat and beat him to the door.

Amanda watched from the window as they tussled playfully on the way to the barn. No doubt about it. She'd made the right decision to return. She hoped.

CHAPTER
TWENTY-EIGHT

When she spotted three horsemen through the swirling snow, Amanda pulled the coffee pot forward to heat, then rushed to help Joe Pete take off his frozen coat. "Are you all right?"

"A little cold." His teeth were chattering.

"Sit down and let me pull off those boots." She turned to Susie. "Get me a hot rock from the fireplace and a blanket."

Luke hit the house in the same shape as the boy. Helping him out of his worn coat, Amanda congratulated herself on the coat she'd been making for him. She'd finish it tomorrow and have a day to knit Nellie a muffler before starting the Christmas baking.

Twilight turned into darkness and Isaac hadn't come inside. It was so cold. "What's keeping Isaac out there?" she asked.

Luke winked at her and nodded in the direction of the children. "He had something to finish."

He must be working on a Christmas surprise.

As she rolled out biscuits, her mind returned to last week, when Isaac had tried to kiss her, and she'd moved away. *I had to. If I allow him so much as one kiss, I'll be back in the same mess I let myself get in last fall.* Color rose to her cheeks as she remembered how intimate she'd been with Isaac last fall. She'd promised herself never to let him get close again.

Her promise would be easier to keep if he'd quit staring at her the way he'd been doing lately. It made her heart pound so.

Finally the light in the barn went out, and she hurried to the back porch to open the door for Isaac. The sooner he got out of the bitter cold, the better. The thud of his boots on the wooden step outside was followed by a curse. He'd been cursing a lot lately. And he'd been so short-tempered.

She peeked out to see him disappear around the corner of the cabin. Waiting for his return, she pulled clothes from the makeshift clotheslines in the sleeping cabin. The thump of wood hitting the pile at the back door reverberated through the cabins. Willie hadn't mentioned the wood being low. Sticking her head into the main cabin, she spoke to Luke. "I'm going out to help Isaac."

When she met him at the corner of the house, he stopped. "It's dang cold. What do you think you're doing out here?"

"The same thing you are." She hustled past him. Some thanks she got for trying to make his life a little easier!

Isaac shrugged. Might as well let her freeze her cute little fanny. Once she made up her mind, that was that. He'd been so happy to have the children and Amanda home that he hadn't let her "don't touch" attitude get under his skin until the last couple of weeks, figuring she'd come around in time. Also, he'd been able to stay out of the cabin more before the sub-zero temperatures had driven him inside. Being close to Amanda when she wouldn't let him touch her was torture, pure and simple.

After they piled up enough wood for two or three days, he helped her take off her coat. Her teeth were like to rattle right out of her head, so he grabbed the blanket from his bed, wrapped it around her shoulders, and aimed her toward the heating stove in the sleeping cabin.

Shaking with cold, he got his frozen boots off and carried them to the stove to thaw.

Wordlessly, Amanda opened her blanket and invited him

into its warmth—next to her body. He thought his heart would stop. Wrapping his arms around her, he pulled her close while she tried to get the blanket edges up over his shoulders. He didn't dare to try to kiss her after the way she'd acted the other day. Instead, he buried his face in her hair, breathing in her faint lilac smell. Lord, how he loved the scent of her.

I must be out of my mind. It's dangerous to stand this close to Isaac. But Amanda wouldn't have stepped away if her life depended upon it. She needed to be in Isaac's arms.

His lips brushed her temple and ear. "Please raise your head and kiss me, Amanda."

Not trusting her voice, she shook her head.

"Are you still in love with that doctor of yours?"

"I never loved Tom."

Isaac's arms tightened. "You agreed to marry him."

"One of my biggest mistakes. We knew we didn't love each other, but we suited each other. It seemed sensible at the time."

"Why did you keep your engagement a secret?"

"I suspected Tom didn't care for me enough to move to Wyoming. I feared people would laugh if he didn't show. And . . . I wanted the respectability and the children Tom offered me."

"If you wanted children and respectability, why did you come back to the Lazy W?"

Her heart finished breaking. Why couldn't Isaac have said, *If it's respectability and children you want, marry me?*

She phrased her answer carefully. "My needs and wants have changed."

"Does your new list of needs and wants include me?"

With a light, forced laugh, Amanda answered. "Good heavens, yes. My homestead isn't ready for me to spend the winter. Without you, I would be out in the cold." She tried to pull away.

Isaac held her tightly. "Is that all I am to you? A place out of the winter cold?"

Why did he have to ask? "That's all I'm going to let you be. There are some things in life I don't ever want to share."

"Share? I don't understand."

"It doesn't matter." At least she didn't have to worry about sharing Isaac with Mrs. Brown until the snow melted and he could get to town.

He whispered huskily, "Honey, if you'd let me, I could make this winter one neither of us would ever forget."

No doubt. She recalled the magic in his hands and lips. She should walk away from this. But she wouldn't. His lips reached hers, and she was lost. Closing her eyes, she caressed his neck and returned his long, needful kisses.

He groaned. "I've missed you, Amanda." Like a thirsty man, he again took possession of her mouth. His tongue coaxed, and she opened for him, relearning the taste of his mouth, salty and so warm. Immersed in a world called Isaac, it startled her when the door opened behind them.

"Are you two . . . ?" Luke's question died in the air.

Isaac kept his gaze on Amanda and his arms tight around her. "We'll be right in." After Luke left, Isaac kissed her again. "I want you so much. Can I come to your room tonight?"

Her heart screamed in protest of her necessary answer. "No."

"No?" His eyes narrowed and he cocked his head slightly. She stepped away from him. "I'm not that kind of woman."

"What the hell does that mean?"

"It means I don't intend to let you make love to me because the weather's too bad for you to get to town to Teresa Brown."

"At least I know where I stand with her. She likes a little loving and takes it where and when she can get it."

"And you're willing to be the when and where?"

"*Before* you came, it suited me. Hell, Amanda, it suits about every unattached man coming through Lariat."

The shock she felt must have registered on her face because Isaac added, "Don't go judging. Just because Tess is a woman doesn't make her less lonely or less needful of the opposite sex."

Amanda couldn't believe the self-righteousness in her own voice. "Being needful and lonely doesn't excuse her behavior."

"She's not harming anyone. I could remind you that your body goes off like a firecracker when you let it. You have the same womanly needs. Tess, however, is more honest in admitting hers.''

The nerve! Amanda whirled and left the sleeping cabin.

She was stirring the beans when Isaac came up behind her at the stove. He spoke softly, for her ears only. ''Amanda, I love the way you are. I lie awake remembering every moment of our times together. I got carried away in the other room. But Tess isn't a bad sort.''

''Not a bad sort?'' Amanda hissed. ''Let me tell you something, Mr. Isaac Wright. Teresa Brown is a conniving, lying, malicious hussy intent on getting a man! Any man, but especially you. A woman can tell by watching dear sweet Tess put on one of her performances when there's a male around. Not a bad sort! Ha!''

''Shhh. Luke and the kids will hear you.''

''I couldn't care less!'' She slapped the spoon into Isaac's hand. ''If you're going to stand in my way, you may as well make yourself useful!''

''Come on, Amanda. Be fair. Tess is okay.''

''Oh, really?'' she hissed. ''Well, you better hope she can continue to work you into her busy loving schedule, because the next time you touch me, I assure you I will indeed go off like a firecracker! Now get your hands off me, and keep them off!'' She shrugged her shoulders away from his hands.

Turning to the table with the pan of biscuits, she called sweetly, ''Supper's ready, everyone.'' She moved past him, smoothed the back of her skirt, and sat in her chair. ''Since you're holding the spoon, would you serve the beans, Isaac?''

Christmas morning dawned crisp and white. Isaac got up early and made coffee. He wanted to see the kids' faces when they first saw the sled he'd made them.

He wasn't disappointed. Willie and Susie were ecstatic over it. Luke had fashioned them new hats from his furs. With scarves and mittens from Amanda, they were set to play out-side—if it ever warmed up enough.

Joe Pete gave carved whistles to the little kids and tiny, detailed figurines of horses to the adults. He dimpled when Amanda admired his artistic work. "Hawk taught me," he explained.

While the twins and Nellie were examining their new story-book, Isaac slipped into the sleeping cabin. He returned with Winchester repeating rifles for Joe Pete and Luke.

After watching them sight down the barrels and shine the stocks, Amanda smiled at him for the first time in a week.

He eased down on the couch beside her, considered taking her hand, then discarded the idea. No use ruining a good Christmas morning by getting himself snubbed. He'd just watch the gift-giving and keep his hands off her. If he could.

Luke had picked out two pieces of pretty material for Amanda to make herself a couple of new dresses, and she gave him a sheepskin coat.

She went to her bedroom and came back with several more packages. "I hope you aren't insulted by these, Isaac. But I had the makings, and your old ones are really worn."

Woolly chaps. Well, he might as well be honest. "Don't tell anyone, but I've always wanted a pair of these. My legs get da . . . dang cold riding in the winter." He folded them before opening the second gift she handed him. "A flannel shirt. I like flannel."

She had the same shirt for Luke. "I bought these shirts before I left Denver. My little sister, Anne, picked out yours, Luke." Remembering that shopping trip, she smiled. "I'd told her about your sky-blue eyes. She insisted you needed the blue shirt, and I had to have the gray that matches Isaac's eyes."

Luke ran his hand over the shirt and sighed melodramatically. "Knowing a single woman touched this makes me warm all over."

Isaac, Joe Pete, and she laughed at his joke.

"Don't laugh," Luke said with great seriousness. "I'm sick and tired of being alone. I've been thinking about writing to one of those mail-order bride outfits."

Isaac laughed again. "You're only twenty-one."

"Twenty-one and facing a lot of lonely years. Heck, Isaac, by the time I'm as old as you, I want a houseful of kids."

"Look around. We have a houseful."

"Yeah, and I love them. But I want to make some myself. Preferably with a pretty woman's help."

Laughter again filled the air, then Willie spoke up, loud and clear. "Didn't you get Aunt Mandy a present, Uncle Isaac?"

He had. But he hadn't been real pleased with his choice, and he'd become less so when he saw how delighted Amanda was with the pretty dress goods Luke gave her. He handed her his package. It seemed she hesitated a second after she opened it, but maybe not.

She sounded sincere when she said, "Thank you, Isaac. I don't believe I've ever seen this shade of green."

"I thought you might like to make yourself a new winter coat. Tess happened to be in Callahan's store when I picked out the wool; she thought this color suited you."

Willie voiced his opinion. "It's colored like puke." He made an elaborate gagging noise.

Luke roared, and Isaac felt himself flush.

"Willie, watch your manners," scolded Amanda. "I'm sure it will make a perfectly serviceable coat. Thank you again, Isaac."

He hadn't wanted to give her something serviceable. He'd wanted to give her something nice.

Amanda excused herself. In her room alone, she threw the puke-colored wool on the bed and dressed in a huff. *If she were freezing to death, she'd never wear a coat made out of material picked by that woman!* It figured Mrs. Brown would pick a puke color for her; Amanda would be happy to do the same for her.

The bitter winter continued. The men rarely rode the horses far, declaring it too hard on the animals to work in the cold.

Isaac came in early one afternoon and asked Amanda to sit and talk. "I know how you feel about me, and I wouldn't bring this up if I didn't have to.'' He cleared his throat. ''I can't move the herds far in this snow, but I'm going to lose some cows if I don't find some grass. Could I use the range around your homestead?''

''Of course, Isaac. The area is open grazing.''

''The cattle might walk right over the top of your fence in this deep snow. Cows could play havoc with your new apple trees.''

''Isaac, I *am* living here, eating at your table, taking advantage of your hospitality. I owe you something.''

Isaac shook his head. ''You owe me nothing. This household would be in a mess without you. I guess I forget to tell you how grateful I am.'' He rose. ''I'll be back in time for supper.''

Watching him ride off, Amanda wondered what Isaac would do if he knew how she really felt about him. Sometimes she needed Isaac so badly that she couldn't concentrate on anything else. She wanted him close all the time, especially at night, in her bed, with his warm lips and his magic hands. It seemed positively indecent for a woman to physically want a man so much.

CHAPTER
TWENTY-NINE

Isaac gave up the pretense of reading. He leaned back in his chair facing the fireplace and listened to Amanda towel herself dry. After the rest of the family had bedded down, Amanda had bathed. The temperature outside was cruel. She said she trusted him not to look. She might not have been so confident if she knew the rustle of her nightgown tortured him. Remembering the feel of her full, enticing breasts, he almost groaned aloud.

She stopped by his chair. "That cat is as cross as you've been! Look at what she did to my leg." Amanda pulled the hem of her nightgown up to her knee so he could see the long scratch.

When he saw the way her soft gown clung to her curves, blood rushed to his head. He could hardly breathe. "Put salve on it."

Amanda nodded. "Would you mind helping me empty my water?"

"Go on to bed. I'll warm it up and take a bath myself."

Later, Isaac lowered himself into her bathwater, breathing deep of the lilac smell that wafted up. No need to look down. He knew what would be eagerly poking up through the water.

Soaping up a rag, Isaac said to his swollen manhood, "Get used to it, cowboy. Near as I can tell, I won't get her figured out, so there's never going to be any relief around here."

That was one of Isaac's more philosophical moments.

Mostly, he kept out of Amanda's way, but the cold drove Luke and him into the house more than usual.

The little kids fussed at one another constantly.

He could stand the forced inactivity if only Luke would quit staring at Amanda as she tended to household chores. He wanted to strangle Luke. And do something else to Amanda.

The next day, Isaac spent most of the day in front of the window braiding a lariat. From there, he could catch Amanda's scent as she kneaded bread on the table. Twice he'd stared Luke down when he caught him looking at her. At supper, the twins got to quarreling over the pie, and Willie knocked over his milk.

That was it! Isaac exploded. "Why the heck don't you watch what you're doing instead of worrying if someone gets a piece of pie bigger than yours?" The silence in the room was deafening.

"Calm down," said Luke. "He's just acting like a kid."

"And I suppose you're just acting like a man, staring at Amanda the way you have been? You know damn good and well what I told you about her last summer."

Luke colored, but he didn't back down. "I recall what you said, all right. Do you remember my response?"

Isaac remembered. His kid brother thought he could handle a woman like Amanda. Hell, no one could take care of a female who wouldn't let you get within arm's reach.

With a glare at Amanda, he jerked his hat and coat from the hooks and slammed the door on the way out.

Somehow, Amanda calmly finished her meal, trying to set an example for the children. She didn't have a clue what the men had discussed last summer, but she'd noticed Luke's looks of late. They made her decidedly uncomfortable, and not in the same way Isaac's stares made her nervous. She needed to have a talk with Luke; she didn't want him getting any wrong ideas.

She tucked the children in for the night, put on a fresh pot of coffee, and took a basin of warm water to her bedroom. After washing carefully and putting on a pretty dress, she stared at her reflection in the mirror, then undressed again. Leaving her heavy long underwear on the end of the bed, she pulled on her daintiest chemise and pantaloons and redressed. She twisted her hair up, reconsidered, and let it down.

Luke was reading by the fire when she returned to the living room. He smiled. "You look pretty tonight."

"I hope Isaac agrees with you." She sat in the chair beside Luke. "He's been a little cranky lately."

"A she-bear with cubs is cranky. Isaac's been plain ornery."

Amanda laughed. "I guess you're right. I'm going out to talk to him for a while."

"Oh, I see."

"You're a good man, Luke. I'm proud to think of you as the brother I never had."

Luke frowned and leaned forward, staring into the fire. "What about Isaac? Do you think of him as a brother, too?"

Taking his clasped hands in hers, she said, "I'm sorry, Luke. I wish I did. Life would be so much easier if I felt for him the same kind of love I feel for you and the children."

"You know, he's always spouting off about not marrying. He thinks ranching is too hard on women. I think he's dead wrong."

"He is wrong. When the *right* woman comes along, you're going to make a wonderful husband." The hurt look in Luke's eyes made her feel as bad as she had anticipated it would. "Don't wait up, Luke. And please listen for the children tonight."

In the gloomy barn, she turned up the lantern. "Isaac?"

"I'm up here in the loft. Is something wrong?"

"Everything's fine. I brought fresh coffee." When she got to the top of the ladder, she was surprised to see Isaac in his shirtsleeves and bootless. "Aren't you cold?"

He stepped aside so she could see his makeshift bed in the hay. "I made myself a little nest."

"Go ahead and get back in it before you catch your death. I'll pour us some coffee. I thought we might talk."

Isaac slid his legs under the blankets, propped himself up on some hay, and took the steaming coffee cups.

"How are the kids?" he asked.

"Asleep."

"Luke?"

"He's fine."

"I had no right to carry on like that at the supper table."

"None at all." Amanda removed her boots and untied the ribbon holding her hair back. She slipped under the blankets to sit next to Isaac. They slowly finished their coffee. Out of the corner of her eye, she saw him reach to touch her hair, then pull his hand back. Obviously, she'd said no once too often.

She was tired of lying without Isaac at night. If she had to share him with Teresa Brown, she would. Part of him was better than none. As long as no one knew. Luke would suspect, but he'd never say anything.

However, the way Isaac sat there so upright and tense told her that she'd have to make the first move tonight. She set both coffee cups to the side. Smoothing her hand across his chest, she stretched to kiss him lightly on the underside of his chin.

He closed his eyes. "Please don't pinch me. If I'm dreaming, I don't want to wake up."

She opened the top button of his shirt and slowly traced the curve of his jaw and neck with kisses.

He sighed, then slid his hands into her hair and held her head still while he kissed her lips, wandered away, and returned. When his tongue touched her lips, Amanda opened to him, enjoying the invasion, and invading in return.

Isaac's lips clung to hers as he scooted down into his warm nest of blankets, pulling her on top of him. His hands skimmed down her body, creating warmth wherever they touched. Their exploring kisses became mutually urgent. She felt him hesitate briefly before cupping her aching breasts.

Opening her eyes for the first time, she gloried in the look of rapture on Isaac's face as he caressed her. When he bent toward her breasts, she shifted her body and granted him access.

Almost reverently, he kissed her breasts, first one, then moving to the other, returning to the first to suckle through her clothing.

Fumbling, he struggled with the tiny buttons on the front of her dress. "I'm shaking. Please help me."

She straddled his torso and sat up, watching his soft gray eyes grow stormy as she unbuttoned the dress. Caressing her thighs, he stared as she slid her dress off her shoulders and down to her waist. He slipped her chemise over her head, then smiled as he studied her bared breasts and ran his fingers over her nipples. "Absolutely perfect." He feasted at her breasts until she could bear the torment no longer and pulled away.

With Isaac's hands possessively on her breasts, she again sat up. They studied each other's faces as she unbuttoned his shirt. It became a slow, tantalizing game. After undoing a shirt button, then a long-underwear button, she kissed his newly bared flesh. Her lips and tongue played with his hard, masculine nipple causing him to buck beneath her.

Isaac rolled her over and covered her with his body. Braced on his elbows, he kissed her, then looked into her eyes. "You don't need to go write any letters or anything?"

Amanda shook her head.

"Thank God." Isaac kissed her again, then made his way to her breasts, once more paying sensuous homage to one, then the other. Kneeling between Amanda's thighs, he worked her dress and pantaloons down, stopping to kiss whatever he bared. She could feel her face burn as he rested back on his heels, and leisurely examined her body, running his hand across her stomach and through the curls at the junction of her thighs. She tried to cover herself, but he pushed her hands aside and bent to kiss the spot she'd covered. "You're so very, very beautiful."

She hesitated before laying her hand on him, feeling the hardness through his denims.

He closed his eyes and leaned into her touch. His hard stomach muscles tightened, and he held himself motionless as she struggled with his britches buttons. "Lord, Amanda, hurry."

"I can't get it undone."

"Don't you dare move." After Isaac freed himself of his

clothing and stood towering over her, Amanda admired hi
lean-muscled body. His man parts hung low and heavy, hi
rigid shaft long, thickly swollen, and throbbing. *Magnificen*
She raised her eyes. ''You'll do,'' she told him with a tin
grin.

''I'll *do?* Is that all? I'll do?'' He lowered himself over he
pulling the blankets to cover them. ''We'll see about that!''

His hands and mouth teased her until she begged, ''Please
Isaac, please.'' Only then did he kneel between her thighs an
enter her aching body.

She expected pain, but felt only blessed relief as he brok
the barrier blocking his way. After he first entered, he hesitated
She opened her eyes and met the question in his eyes with
smile. He covered her mouth with his, and she welcomed th
full length of him with a small moan. He felt so good.

Slowly, Isaac began the rhythm of love.

Rational thought left, and nature guided Amanda.

Later, Isaac lay on his back with Amanda stretched alon
the length of his body, their legs entwined.

He'd been without a woman since the night last April befor
Amanda showed up at the train depot. Wanting only her, he'
bided his time. Now he slid his hand down past her waist an
up over the lush curve of her hip. He returned to her fantasti
breasts. He couldn't get enough of the feel of her soft skin an
enticing curves. ''Did I hurt you?''

''No.'' She paused. ''Can we do it again before we go in?'

''It might make you too sore.''

''There's only one way to find out.''

Returning her saucy smile, he rolled on top of her. ''In tha
case, I'm pretty sure we can do it at least *once* more befor
we go in.''

Nibbling at his ear, Amanda's lips moved across his ches
creating fire wherever she touched. ''Prove it,'' she whispere

''Amanda, honey, you better hang on tight this time.''

She slid her hands down to cup his buttocks, shifted he
body, and pulled him tight against her. ''Like this?''

''That'll do,'' Isaac answered after he regained his breath

* * *

Amanda pulled the blankets over Isaac's shoulders and cuddled in close. During the last four nights, he'd proven to be a ravenously greedy lover. He'd admired, explored, and aroused her body. And allowed her to do the same to him.

She knew the length and breadth of him. She could make him groan by tormenting his nipples, and cause him to tremble by kneeling between his hard thighs and caressing him with her lips. Each time she lay with him, she put aside the world and became only a woman. Isaac's woman. Nothing mattered except their shared intimacy, their shared climb to ecstasy. She understood now why women gave their lives to men. *How she loved him.* She drifted to sleep with his heartbeat as her lullaby.

Later she awoke, cold. Her movement to leave their nest disturbed Isaac. "I'm going to put on my clothes."

"Seems like a waste of time. I'll take them off again."

"I'm freezing."

"I think I can do something about building a fire under this blanket." He rolled over on top of her, bracing his upper body on his elbows, trapping her in a very promising position.

"I'm not complaining about your fire-building, but I think this is even beyond your extensive skills." She intentionally placed her icy hands upon his warm backside.

He yelped.

A glittering night sky greeted them, but they didn't stop to admire it. Intense cold caused them to hasten into the cabin.

Isaac helped her spread an extra quilt on her bed. "You wouldn't need this if you'd let me share your bed."

Shivering, she pulled up the blankets. "We've been through all that. I don't want the children going to town with the story that Uncle Isaac sleeps with Aunt Mandy."

"Who cares what people say? You belong with me."

"Isaac, I'd die of mortification if anyone found out what we've been doing."

"A bunch of dang nonsense, if you ask me."

* * *

Amanda lay in the dark and stared through the open doorwa
at Isaac's sleeping area. He was right. She did belong wit
him. Her heart had been Isaac's for a long time. Now her bod
belonged to him as well. Isaac's kisses turned her molten insid
But he was making sure she had no lasting claim on him. Whe
he made love to her, he deliberately spilled his life-giving see
outside her body. Each time, a piece of her heart crumble
away. Carrying Isaac's child in her womb would please h
more than anything in the world. A little Isaac, wavy blon
hair and changing gray eyes. Amanda pictured a small bo
sitting atop a horse, riding in the wake of his father.

But Isaac hadn't mentioned children. Or love. Or marriag
She recalled her mother saying, "We don't always get wha
we want. Sometimes we have to settle for what we get." Moth
would be horrified if she knew what Amanda had settled fo

Since the weather had turned so bitter, she and Isaac hadn
thought it wise to leave the cabin at night to make love in th
barn. They hadn't been out, but it no longer surprised Amand
what an enterprising man could do standing against a door
a woman "forgot" to put on her long underwear.

She'd "forgotten" again this morning, and Isaac had bee
grinning at her all day. Even so, she wished this cold spe
would break.

Almost as if a fairy godmother had heard her plea, the weathe
changed. The men spent long days with the cattle, countin
the winter losses. Waiting for the drifts to melt, Amanda cleane
the Lazy W cabin from top to bottom.

On a beautiful day in the middle of March, she packed u
Nellie and the twins and rode over to check on her homestea
One little chore led to another, and Isaac found her hangin
out the bedding late that afternoon.

"What do you think you're doing?" he demanded in tha
bossy tone of voice she so hated.

Glancing eloquently at the billowing sheets, she replied, "I think it's obvious. I'm airing the bedding."

"That's not what I mean and you dang well know it. Aren't you happy with our relationship?"

She couldn't believe he'd even ask such a thing. As if any woman in her right mind would be happy with a relationship based on a couple of hours in the barn three or four times a week!

"I asked you a question, Amanda. Are we through?"

"Not necessarily. I have no complaints about your prowess as a lover. Anytime you can spare a minute, you're welcome to ride over for a quick relationship, as you call it. However, I recall you have this same *relationship* with Teresa Brown, so now that the road to town is passable, I won't expect you to often."

"What the devil are you talking about?"

"I'm not blind, deaf, or stupid, Isaac. In the winter, I'm obviously easier to get to than Teresa Brown."

Isaac blocked Amanda's way. "Before you came, Tess and I sometimes got together. I've told you I'm not the only rancher she entertains. Frankly, she isn't bad at what she does."

Bile rose to Amanda's throat. She pushed past him and called the children. "Uncle Isaac would like you to ride back to the Lazy W with him. I'll be along in a couple of hours."

That evening, Isaac came close as she cooked supper. "Calling the kids over this afternoon was a dirty trick. Will you come out to the barn tonight after the kids are asleep?"

"Why don't you ride into town? A two-hour ride must be a small price to pay to get someone who's *good* at what she does."

Isaac winced. "Since the day I laid eyes on you, I have not been, nor wanted to be, with Tess."

Amanda glared at him. "You're a liar. I *heard* you enter her bedroom on the third of July, this year!"

"Then I suppose you also heard me tell her I would continue to provide her with a beef every spring and fall like I always have—in return for lodging for my family whenever one of them is in town. And I suppose you heard I made certain she

wasn't under any misconception about my intentions over th
years."

"Exactly what were your intentions over the years?"

"Hell, Amanda! I had no intentions. A man gets lonely.'

"Obviously. You can't even make it to Omaha without her.

"I didn't take Tess to Omaha. She was on the train when
boarded for my trip home. She'd been visiting some friends.

"Now isn't that convenient."

"Tess might have set it up so she had to take the same trai
I did. You've seen her in action. I had nothing to do with it.

"But you and she were lovers?"

"Lovers isn't the right word, Amanda. I don't love Tes
Never have. She saw other men. Lots of them."

Amanda arched an eyebrow and stared until he looked awa

"If you could hear what was going on in that bedroom th
third of July, you know Tess and I only talked."

"Rest assured, I gave you instant privacy. But that's interes
ing. Do you usually go to Mrs. Brown's *bedroom* to talk?"

"I didn't want to embarrass her in public." Isaac touche
Amanda's cheek with the back of his hand. "Tess is an ol
friend, and I feel like I owe her a certain amount of loyalt
nothing more. What I have with you is different."

"How is it different, Isaac?" Now was his chance to sa
the things she longed to hear, that he loved and needed her.

He stumbled over his words. "For one thing, we have stron
ties. We have three kids to raise. And we live together."

"We lived together only for the sake of the children, an
only this winter. From now on, summer *and* winter, I liv
on the neighboring homestead."

"You really intend to move back to this snakey homestead?

"I won't live on your ranch as your kept woman. But I'v
reconciled myself to my station in life. Anytime you want, yo
ride over. After the children are asleep, you can snap yo
fingers, and I'll run up the ladder to the barn loft. Maybe yo
can drop off a beef in the fall and another in the spring."

Isaac stomped to the door. "You know, I don't understan
you one bit. Don't *you* worry about having to hurry up th

adder in the barn. If that's all our relationship means to you,
'm not likely to be snapping my fingers in your direction.''

After he slammed the door, he reopened it and stuck his
ead inside. ''You might as well start making up a supply list.
f you're going to run a separate household again this year,
ve'll need to make some extra trips to town.''

She could hear him muttering as he stomped off the porch.
'Damned horses will be exhausted before the summer even
tarts.''

CHAPTER THIRTY

On the first day of summer, Amanda woke and found Isaac sitting at the table in the dugout, staring at her. She smiled, hoping he'd at least come over and kiss her, but he got up and went outside. Throwing back her covers, she stomped to the barn after him. "Isaac Wright, I demand an explanation."

"About what?" With his back to Amanda he began to milk.

"Forget milking. Turn around and let's talk about this."

He leaned his forehead against the cow's side. "I'm not looking at you dressed in nothing but that nightgown. Now tell me what you want fast and go get dressed."

"Why have you been avoiding me?"

"I haven't been avoiding you. I'm here every night."

"That's not what I mean. Why haven't you asked me to come to your bed? Or kissed me? Or even touched me on the arm?"

He knocked over the milk stool when he stood up, whipped around, and roared, "Because that's the way you told me you wanted it! Now dag-blast it, Amanda. Go . . . get . . . dressed!"

He watched as she stormed toward the dugout. Gol-darn it. Another minute of that nightgown and he'd have been on his knees begging her to marry him. It looked as if he was going to have to ask her anyway, or she'd work herself to death proving up on this rattlesnake-infested homestead.

He'd spent half his life thinking he wouldn't marry because he didn't want any woman to work herself to death on his account. Now he was going to have to marry to keep a woman *from* working herself to death. Dang! He wished he were still a cussing man.

Inside, Amanda jerked off her nightgown and flung it at her bed. Why hadn't she left things alone instead of making snide remarks about Mrs. Brown and about going up the ladder and taking a beef for her services? Why was life without Isaac's loving such a chore? Before she fell in love with the ornery man, nothing had seemed too hard for her to handle. Lately, every little thing seemed a catastrophe—a cold spell killing part of the garden, four apple trees dying, Joe Pete talking about his grandmother, Isaac's light glowing in the barn loft. *Everything* made her cry. Each time she slid her hands across her flat stomach, she wished that Isaac had at least given her his child. Even that made her cry. And it was *incredibly* stupid to cry about not having an illegitimate baby.

At breakfast, Isaac helped himself to four hotcakes. "If you need anything the next few days, I'll be on the Lazy W catching up on some chores."

"Can me and Susie go with you?" asked Willie. "We got a lot of work to do on our fort."

Isaac looked at Amanda. "Do you mind?"

She shook her head. "I think I'll spend the day putting up rhubarb. Besides, a certain birthday is coming up and I have some sewing to do."

The twins giggled and poked at each other's ribs.

"What say I keep Susie and Willie over on the Lazy W a few days instead of us coming over here at night? Maybe we can both get some things done before we go into town for the Fourth."

She'd been looking for a chance to announce her intentions about the Fourth of July. "I'm staying home to do the chores this year so all of you can enjoy the day without worry." No way was she going to chance hearing Isaac in Mrs. Brown's bedroom.

Isaac studied her face. "We'll talk about that."

Joe Pete spoke to Isaac and Amanda. "If there's no big chores, I wonder if I could go to Hawk's camp. They've been talking about moving to the reservation after this summer. I want to see them as much as possible before they go."

Nodding, Isaac answered, "We'll expect you back before dark the day after tomorrow."

Joe Pete went to saddle his horse.

When he was out of earshot, Amanda scolded, "Isaac, I hate when you answer Joe Pete without consulting me. He's my child."

Isaac looked startled. "Sorry. I didn't know you felt that way. I guess I consider him my kid, too."

"Like us," said Willie. "We're all both your kids, huh?"

Isaac smiled and tousled Willie's hair. "You sure are. Now get ready to go to the Lazy W for a few days."

Nellie played as Amanda cooked rhubarb and thought. The children's lessons had come to a halt when she began the spring planting. Willie was getting headstrong. He constantly tested her. Fortunately, he didn't act up when Isaac was around.

Not that Isaac came around much during the day. And that, she admitted, was the long and short of her teary problems. Why had she been so foolish as to begin making love with him? And why had she been so foolish as to stop?

When she had a load of jam ready, Amanda grabbed a shovel. With her arms full of jars and Nellie clinging to her skirt, she fought the wind as she crossed the yard to the cellar.

After sending Nellie away from the cellar door, she lifted it. She detested this dirt cellar. She'd killed three rattlesnakes in it. But it kept things well. The barn got too hot or too cold, depending on the season.

The wind blew out six matches before she finally lit the lantern she kept on the cellar steps. Inside, she checked for snakes. Nothing. What a relief! She had just positioned the last of the rhubarb on a back shelf when a gust of wind blew out the lantern and slammed the cellar door shut.

She rushed up the dirt steps and pushed on the door. It wouldn't open. She pushed, shoved, tried every curse word she'd ever heard Isaac use and some combinations of her own, but nothing worked. Looking through a slit between the boards, she could see that the handle of the shovel had slid into the brace.

Take a deep breath. Calm down. She retrieved the lantern, then realized she'd used her last match trying to light it earlier. Nellie would have to move the shovel. Amanda called, "Nellie, honey. Come over to the cellar door."

Giggling, Nellie peered through a crack. "I see you." She disappeared, only to reappear a moment later. "Peeky-boo." The toddler laughed uproariously and disappeared from Amanda's view.

"Nellie, dear, move the shovel. I want to come out."

"Peeky-boo!" The toddler lay on the cellar door and tried to stick her fingers through her tiny peek hole.

"Move the shovel, Nellie."

Judging from the scuffling and grunting going on, Amanda could tell Nellie was trying.

"Stuck," the child announced.

"I know it's stuck, honey. But you've got to move it. I can't fix your supper until I get out." If supper didn't serve as an inspiration for Nellie, nothing would.

Nellie struggled with the shovel again. Then she sat on the cellar door and cried for Amanda to come out.

Trapped inside, Amanda reviewed the contents of the cellar. Nothing to use as a battering ram. Maybe she could break the shovel handle by hitting the door with her shoulder. After telling Nellie to move away from the door, Amanda backed off, ran up the stairs, and hit the door. It didn't budge. Growing fear for the toddler spurred her to keep trying.

Misty whined and dug at the door. That gave Amanda an idea. Cringing, she felt her way back down into the darkness. Locating a jar on a shelf, she dropped it to the dirt floor. The darn thing didn't shatter. It took her three tries to get it to break. She felt around for a good-sized piece of glass.

Hurrying to the door, she called for Nellie. No answer. Misty was gone, too. Amanda hoped the dog was trailing the girl. She prayed as she dug frantically. "Please, God. Nellie's not even three; she can't take care of herself." Her mind swam with visions of the stove, of rattlesnakes, of the open well, and of the creek. With the broken glass, she hacked at the thick sod wall. From time to time, she'd stop digging and ram the door with her shoulder. After what seemed like an eternity, Nellie reappeared at the peek hole. "I hungry."

"Try to move the shovel again, honey."

It was no use.

The sun would be going down soon. And the nights had been so cold. Nellie should be able to open the dugout door and get inside. "Nellie, listen carefully. I left a crock of jam on the table. The leftover hotcakes are on the shelf. Push a chair up to the shelf and get them. You can make your own supper. You're such a big girl, you can do that."

"I get hotcakes?"

"Yes. Then get a drink from the bucket and go to bed."

"No! Come out. I mean it!"

"I can't, honey. You take Misty and go inside the dugout and close the door. Eat some jam and hotcakes, then go to bed."

Nellie cried, and Amanda had to get firm with her before the child left. Thankfully, Misty left with the little girl.

Throughout the long night, Amanda alternately prayed, dug, and used her body as a battering ram. Morning dawned. The cow lowed. The poor thing needed to be milked. She scratched away another meager handful of dirt. Then she heard the most joyous of sounds. Nellie! Whining about breakfast. "Hotcakes all gone."

"Did you have a good sleep?"

Nellie lay on the cellar door and put her lips to the peek hole. "I cry."

"I'm sorry, darling. Why don't you try to move the shovel handle again? Maybe all those hotcakes made you strong."

Amanda got her hopes up once when she thought she heard the handle scrape against the wood, but eventually the child gave up.

"I hungry."

"I know, dear. But there isn't anything else you can eat. I bet Uncle Isaac will come here tonight. If I'm not out by then, he'll let me out and I'll cook you a wonderful supper."

"Meat and 'tatoes?"

"Potatoes?" Amanda had forgotten about the potatoes in the corner of the dugout. "Nellie, you can get two potatoes and come and sit on the cellar door to eat them. It'll be like a picnic."

"Three 'tatoes," said Nellie.

Amanda smiled. Some things never changed. Nellie had to argue. "Okay. Three. Get your potatoes and come right back."

"Right back," Nellie agreed.

"If you see a snake, go way around it."

"I *way* around."

Nellie didn't return and didn't return. Misty was barking in the distance. Amanda hit the cellar door and called for Nellie and the dog. Finally Nellie showed up at the peek hole.

"Where have you been?" Amanda demanded.

Nellie began to cry. "Necessary house."

Now she'd made Nellie cry. She had to be calm. "I'm sorry, darling. I was so worried about you. Why is Misty barking?"

"Damn snake."

Her blood froze. "Where's the snake, Nellie?"

"Barn."

"You stay right here and call Misty. Don't you take one step away from this cellar door."

The dog came when called. While Nellie ate, Amanda dug. She figured in another four inches or so, she should be able to reach outside and maybe get hold of the shovel handle.

By midday, Nellie had wandered away from the cellar door. Amanda could get two fingers out of her hole. She continued to work, alternately calling to the child and listening for her. Neither Nellie nor Misty responded. The pit of fear building in Amanda had reached the point of terror.

Behind her in the dark, she fancied she'd heard a sound
Each time she backed up a step to bang against the cellar door
she steeled herself. She'd found common bull snakes in this
cellar and a mouse or two. Rattlesnakes weren't the only thing
that might be sharing the cellar. Still, she scrunched up against
the cellar door as she worked at the hole. Another inch or two
and she could get her whole hand out.

CHAPTER THIRTY-ONE

Isaac glanced up from his horseshoeing when Nellie and Misty appeared at the barn door. "Hi, Nellie Belle. Stay outside until I finish." Working carefully, he nailed the horseshoe in place before he came out into the yard.

Odd. Nellie had something sticky on her face and arms. Dirt and grass clung to her skin and clothes. He hadn't seen her so messy since he and Luke were taking care of the kids. He'd never known Amanda to let one of them have a dirty face for any length of time. "You look like you've been in a pigpen."

Nellie smiled angelically and stretched to be picked up.

"Oh, no, you don't. I'm not holding you until you get cleaned up." At the basin on the porch, Isaac went to work with a washcloth. He called into the house, "Amanda, what's this kid been into?" When she didn't answer, he called again, "Amanda?"

Silence.

Carrying a soapy cloth, he walked into the main cabin, then the sleeping cabin. *What the hell?* He hurried back to Nellie and rinsed the soap off her hands. A crawling feeling worked its way up his back. "Where's Aunt Mandy?"

"Shobel's stuck."

"That's all right. Where's Aunt Mandy?"

"Shobel's *stuck!*"

"Did Aunt Mandy bring you over here?"

"Me and Misty comed."

"You and the dog came by yourselves? Without Aunt Mandy?"

A big smile accompanied Nellie's vigorous nod.

There was no point in asking if Amanda knew that Nellie had come three miles by herself. She never let the child get ten feet away from her unsupervised.

"Nellie, listen to me." He held the little girl by the shoulders and looked into her eyes. "Where is Aunt Mandy?"

"Her's stuck." She added, "Damn snake."

Isaac shouted for the twins. He didn't saddle horses, just bridled the first two he caught. He heaved Willie and Susie up on back of one and flung Nellie on the other. "Follow me to Aunt Mandy's homestead," he told the twins. "And be careful!" Without waiting for them, he swung up behind Nellie and rode.

Rasty ran alongside his horse, but Misty shot out ahead. The dog was already digging at the cellar door when Isaac reached the homestead's yard. A bloody hand appeared and Misty nosed it.

"Thank you, God." Isaac slid off the horse. With Nellie tucked under one arm, he galloped for the cellar. "Amanda?"

"Isaac!" she screamed, or tried to scream. She hadn't much voice left. "Let me out!" The hand sticking out the hole waved.

"I'm here, honey." He clasped her hand. "Pull your hand in so I can move this shovel handle."

"Nellie's gone! You've got to find her."

"She found me. Honey, you have to pull your hand inside."

He cringed as she struggled to get her bloody hand back through the hole. That hand must hurt like hell.

The shovel handle was wedged into a hinge. It took him a couple of tries to jerk it loose. He threw the cellar door back and crouched down to lift Amanda.

She clung to him as he knelt in the dirt.

Nellie plopped herself in the middle of the adults. Amid the

ears and kisses, Susie and Will arrived. The five of them sat
n the dust and held each other. After everyone settled down,
Isaac carried Amanda to the dugout.

He built a fire, put on water to heat, and checked her hands.
"You've managed to tear off a fingernail."

Amanda stared out the door at the children. "It caught on
something in the dark while I was digging. Is Nellie all right?"

"She's fine." He came to the table with warm water and
some rags. "Let me see what you've done to yourself."

He tried to chat, but Amanda kept her gaze riveted on the
children outside, answering him only when he insisted. Her
arm hung awkwardly. Rather than chance damaging it further,
he cut off her shirt. "How did your neck and shoulders get
bruised?"

She looked down at her shoulders. "I don't know. Maybe
hitting the door trying to get out."

"You hit so almighty hard, you've dislocated your arm. It's
going to hurt bad when I put it back in place. Hang on to the
table with your other hand."

She screamed when the effort yanked her dislocated shoulder,
then passed out. The children came running, but he sent them
away. He laid her on the bed and slid her shoulder into place
while she was unconscious.

He had only himself to blame, leaving her alone for a whole
day. He thought he'd make a point by letting her get tired
enough to see his way of thinking. Lord, if he ever lost her,
he'd go out of his mind. Almost *had* lost it when she left him
and went to Denver with that Tom character.

He shook when he got to thinking about all the things that
might have happened to Nellie. One parent was not enough to
take care of kids out here!

While Isaac and Willie did the evening chores, Susie watched
Nellie and Amanda. He returned to find Susie weeping. "Aunt
Mandy keeps crying for Nellie in her sleep."

"It's just a nightmare like you have sometimes. She'll be
all right in a few days. We'll let her rest."

At bedtime, Isaac didn't pull the curtain between the beds. If Amanda woke, she'd want to see the kids. He left a lantern burning and climbed in beside her. She might not like the kids knowing he shared her bed, but if he had his way, he was never going to spend another night without her in his arms. Several times during the night, she cried in her sleep. He held her close. The next day, he stayed within earshot.

Joe Pete came back from Hawk's camp about suppertime. He stood by the foot of Amanda's bed. "Is she hurt bad?"

"I don't think so. Just scared and tired. She'll rest easier now that we're all here together."

Amanda regained full consciousness during the night. Over on the table, a lantern burned low. She turned her head to study each child; they looked fine. Isaac had his arm draped over her. She scooted closer to him, and he tightened his embrace. With his gentle snores near her ear, she fell into a restful sleep.

After breakfast, he chased the kids outside and fixed her a warm bath. She was still weak, so he knelt beside her and washed her hair, then scrubbed her arms and back.

"What will the children think?"

"It doesn't matter. From now on, I'll be in the room when you bathe. And I intend to sleep in your bed every night. If that bothers you, I guess you'll have to marry me."

Marry him? Speechless, she stared at him.

He must have thought she was undecided because he started talking fast. "It's the best thing all around. We have three kids to raise, not including Joe Pete. If we were all on one place, someone would have gotten you out of that cellar lots sooner. Also, if we're living together, you'll have time to do the things that make a house a comfortable home. I can keep a roof over our heads and put food on the table."

He was right, of course. If anyone else except little Nellie had been around, they would've moved the shovel.

Clearly, Isaac had prepared his arguments because he hardly took a deep breath before continuing. "I bet you haven't had a moment for weeks to go over the kids' lessons."

She hadn't.

"Will you marry me, Amanda?"

"Can we live here in the dugout so I can prove up?"

"The cabin's more comfortable. Besides, you don't need a little homestead. You'll be my wife, part owner of the Lazy W, one of the biggest cattle ranches in this part of the country."

"I've worked so hard on my homestead."

"I know you have, but what difference would a homestead make if one of the kids got hurt?"

Rocking to and fro in barely perceptible movements, she shook her head. "None, I guess."

"Marry me, Amanda. It's going to take both of us to get these kids safely raised. You and I both want to care for Josh and Mary's kids. We don't need to have kids of our own."

No children of her own. The thought caused her heart to ache. "I'd like to have children someday, Isaac."

"Well, sure, maybe someday in the far future. It's just not the sensible thing to do right now."

Why couldn't Isaac have said he loved her, he wanted her to bear his children, and they could live on her homestead until it belonged to her? She shook her head at the ridiculousness of her questions. He hadn't declared his love because he didn't love her; he hadn't asked her to bear his children because he didn't see a need for their own children; and he hadn't agreed to the homestead because he openly hated the dugout and the snakes.

Be that as it might, he was right about the children being safer with two adults watching over them. Though she hated being sensible sometimes, Amanda agreed to marry Isaac. Her mind accepted the decision, but her heart protested. Marriage wasn't supposed to happen this way. People were supposed to be in love.

While Isaac hitched the wagon to move her and the children back to the Lazy W, Amanda made a pile of clothing on the table.

When he came inside, he looked around. "What else do you want to take?"

"Nothing. I can't bring myself to take anything now. I'll come back sometime and close the place up right."

He started to shut the door to the dugout, but she didn't let him. She'd close the dugout door—and the doors to her other romantic dreams. There would be no loving husband, maybe no babies nursing at her breast. But she still had Isaac, whom she loved. And they had Mary and Josh's children. Life went on.

Amanda married Isaac on the second of July, 1894, in front of the cabin on the Lazy W. The ceremony was attended by the Jim Callahan family, the Isaac Wright household, and Preacher Green. Martha decorated a pretty wedding cake, and Isaac picked her a bouquet of wildflowers. While Isaac beamed at her, she struggled to keep a smile on her face.

By late afternoon, the company was gone. At Martha's invitation, Luke took the younger children into Lariat for an early start on the Fourth of July festivities. Colleen Callahan was openly upset when Joe Pete declined the trip to town.

Isaac helped put away the remainders of the wedding feast. "You look tired, Amanda. Why don't you take a nap?"

"Maybe I will. I don't know what's wrong with me. I'm so tired all the time since I got locked in the cellar."

Dark had already fallen when Joe Pete and Isaac woke her. Joe Pete cleared his throat. "I've got to go, Amanda."

"Go?"

"Hawk's people are leaving for the reservation tonight. Isaac and Hawk say I can't go with them without your permission. I want to go see my grandmother. I need to go."

"Can't you go later, when you're a little older?"

"I don't want to leave you, but something inside says I have to find her now, that I must hurry before it's too late." His eyes glistened with tears.

Please, God, make this another nightmare. But it was no dream. She hugged the boy. "I'll pack you blankets and food."

"I've already loaded his horse, Amanda," Isaac said. "Hawk's waiting on your homestead."

"Be careful, Joe Pete. Very, very careful."

"I am Fights The Wind."

His dimples flashed when Amanda said, "Take good care of yourself, Fights The Wind. Remember you always have a home with me. I love you."

"I love you also. Good-bye, Amanda."

It was very late before Isaac crawled into bed beside her. "Is he gone?"

Nodding, he took her in his arms as she wept again.

Isaac laid his lips against her temple. "We knew this might happen. I rode with him to your homestead and talked with Hawk. He promised to see that Joe Pete gets back if ever he wants to come."

"I forgot to give Joe Pete the twenty-dollar gold piece the woman in Cheyenne gave me for him," Amanda managed between sobs.

"I gave him money and an extra horse. He'll be all right."

Isaac spent his wedding night trying not to disturb his exhausted wife. She looked so sad. He'd have given the world to know how to make things better for her. It had been months since he heard her really laugh, longer since he heard her sing as she worked. Maybe not since winter.

Perhaps he shouldn't have railroaded her into this marriage, but he didn't think she would've agreed to it unless he made a strong case. He could tell she still believed he took Tess on that marketing trip. For sure, she didn't understand how he used to have sex with Tess and not feel anything more than a tolerant friendship for her. Sometimes Tess made it hard to even be tolerant. He'd try to make Amanda understand. And he'd be a good husband to her. She'd never regret marrying him.

He thought about Mary. He used to think that he'd tell

Amanda about Mary's being in the family way when she died, about how he'd sat and cried when he washed Mary for burial and discovered her swollen belly. But he'd decided some things were better never said.

Hell, Joshua should have used some common sense. There was no excuse for Mary to be in the family way again. Even after she got pregnant again, if Joshua had said something, they could have hired some help for Mary. It wasn't like they were destitute.

Isaac would take care of Amanda. She wouldn't be in the family way full-time. He'd find a way to keep her from having to work from dawn to dark every day of her life. He didn't know how, but he'd figure something.

He wrapped his arm around her and kissed her shoulder when she unconsciously scooted into the protective circle of his arm.

This hard life wasn't going to take Amanda from him.

CHAPTER
THIRTY-TWO

Amanda heard the children calling. "Uncle Luke's back from town! Hurry, Aunt Mandy! He has someone with him."

Carrying a cup and a dish towel, she went out onto the porch. Shading her eyes with one hand, she looked off toward the approaching supply wagon. Blinking, she looked again.

"What the . . ." Isaac's voice trailed off as she ran past him.

In another minute, Anne and she were hugging and squealing like a couple of schoolgirls. Holding hands and chattering, they followed the wagon to the yard. "Is everything all right at home?" Amanda asked.

"Everything's fine. The family sends their love."

"When did you get to Lariat? Why are you here? You should have written and we'd have come . . ." Her voice faded away when Luke joined them and Anne slid into the curve of his arm. He pulled her possessively close and beamed at Isaac. "Isaac, I have someone here I'd like you to meet. This here is Amanda's baby sister, my wife, Anne Erikson Wright."

Mouth agape, Isaac stared.

Luke laughed. "Well, aren't you going to say hello or kiss the bride?"

So nudged, Isaac did both.

As Luke introduced Anne to the children, Amanda caugh Isaac's questioning look. She shrugged her shoulders.

He signaled toward the house with a tip of his head. "I'l help you make a pot of coffee." They'd barely made it throug the door when Anne and Luke joined them, full of explanations

"Anne came in on the Wednesday train. She was waiting at the boarding house for one of us to come to town," sai Luke.

"I couldn't believe my eyes when Luke drove the wago into town yesterday. You were right, Amanda. He's fantastic.'

Luke blushed, and the women laughed.

Isaac spoke up. "Let's get to where you two are married.'

After wrapping an arm around Anne, Luke explained. "Well we started for the Lazy W about the middle of the afternoor yesterday. By the time we got to the river, we'd decided to turn back and get married while Preacher Greene was still ir Lariat." He put both arms around Anne and looked into her eyes. "We already knew we wanted to spend our lives with each other."

Amanda couldn't keep from smiling when Isaac looked to the heavens and ran his hand through his hair in frustration Obviously, he didn't know Anne. The Erikson family had long ago learned never to be surprised by anything Anne did. Likely Luke had been a marked man the moment Anne saw him They'd be good together.

"That river is three miles from town. How can you know you want to spend your life together in three miles?" Isaac demanded.

"Brother of mine, I knew in three seconds."

Anne went to Luke's rescue. "Luke told me he'd been think ing about sending for a mail-order bride. Look at it this way My arrival saved him train fare."

Isaac glared at Amanda. "Don't you have something to say?"

"If you'd asked me to marry you three miles out of Lariat it would have saved us a world of trouble."

"Hell, we'd already had four or five arguments by the time we reached the bend in the river."

Luke squeezed Anne. "See. Didn't I tell you they got along like cats and dogs."

"We get along fine." Isaac moved closer to Amanda.

"Sure you do, Isaac. Sure you do."

Amanda changed the subject. "Anne, why *are* you here?"

"Ma sent me. I thought I'd homestead."

They stared at her.

"You're not old enough to homestead," Amanda said finally.

Anne rummaged around in her reticule and brought out a piece of paper. "Pa said he wanted me close to you. He signed this piece of paper saying I would be twenty-one in three years."

"What were you going to do until then?"

"I planned to learn everything I needed to know from you. That way, it would be easy to homestead."

Luke, Isaac, and Amanda all looked at one another.

"Oh, boy!" Isaac groaned melodramatically. He slapped the palm of his hand against his forehead. "Not another one!"

When Isaac and Luke joined in Amanda's laughter, Anne looked from one to the other. "What's so funny?"

Still smiling, Amanda shook her head. "It's a long story. Remind me to tell you sometime. How's Ma?"

"She's fine. Busy like always."

"Pa?"

When Anne's eyes began to twinkle, Amanda knew she'd asked the wrong question. Anne was likely to say most anything.

Looking the picture of sweet innocence with her big blue eyes and silky blond hair, Anne replied, "Oh, Pa's slowing down some. He only took Ma to bed early twice last week."

Isaac choked on his coffee. Luke turned red. The men cleared the kitchen.

When they were out of earshot, Amanda could contain her merriment no longer. "Okay now, Anne, the next time we want to get rid of them, let's start talking about having babies."

Anne grinned and nodded. "Speaking of babies, we have two beautiful, healthy new nephews."

"Who had twins this time?"

"That's the great part. Faith and Charity each had one."

''Thank goodness. Faith looked exhausted when I was home. I feared she might have twins.''

''It's a good thing she *didn't* have twins! As soon as the baby was born, Pa invited Bob to the barn. The way Pa yells, we all heard him clear in the house. He told Bob he didn't want to see Faith expecting any time soon. He said he didn't raise his girls to see them used as brood mares. And if Faith came up pregnant before this baby was three years old, Pa said he'd personally geld Bob.''

''What did Bob do?''

''He didn't say much, just spat, sputtered, and stomped. I hope Pa got through to him. Faith's only twenty-four, but she's had a baby every year for the last three. She needs a rest.''

Amanda thought immediately of Isaac's philosophy about too many babies being too hard on a woman. She wasn't telling him this particular story. No need for him to know how Pa felt.

''Luke told me you got stuck in a root cellar,'' Anne said. ''I'm dying to hear all about it.'' After hearing about Amanda's ordeal in the cellar, Anne offered her congratulations from the family on her marriage. ''We think you made a good decision. Isaac seems like a steady man.''

Amanda gazed out the window at the barn. ''He's good to me. Sometimes he's a little bossy, but he does what he thinks best.''

''Are you happy?''

After a pause, Amanda smiled. ''I'm . . . content.''

''Just content?''

Amanda nodded. ''I'm fine.''

''I'll tell you, Amanda. The way that woman who runs the boarding house talks about Isaac, I think you better keep a close eye on him.''

''Good old Tess?''

Anne rolled her eyes. ''If I catch Luke within a hundred yards of that boarding house without me, he's going to be missing some critical parts of his anatomy.''

Amanda laughed, then decided she might as well get it out in the open. ''I'm sure Luke will tell you about Isaac and Tess eventually. They used to have a relationship of sorts. Isaac assures me it's been over for a long time."

"I should hope so!" Anne poked at the boiling potatoes with a fork. "I didn't tell the whole truth in front of the men, Amanda. Wait until you hear why I'm really here."

Amanda quit rolling biscuits. "Not to homestead?"

"Of course not. Ma sent me because your Dr. Tom Johnson has been coming to see me. Can you believe it? He's so old."

"Tom's thirty-two."

"Exactly. Anyway, we think he was going to ask me to marry him, but Ma didn't give him a chance. She told Pa she didn't want any of her girls marrying the pompous ass."

"Ma? Did she use those words?"

"She did. You know that trousseau that Tom told you to keep, but you didn't want? Well, Ma sold it to a shop. Then she marched over and bought me a train ticket. She told me not to come home until either Tom or I were married—to someone else."

Thinking about her shy, soft-spoken mother selling fancy clothes and buying train tickets made Amanda chuckle. Anne and she laughed until they had tears in their eyes. Each time they'd stop, Anne would describe Ma again as she huffed around getting Anne ready to leave. They'd be off in gales of laughter again.

"Be serious now, Amanda," Anne demanded after a bit.

Amanda acted as if she were wiping the smile off her face.

"That's better," Anne said. "Pa told me to tell you that he tried again to return your engagement ring like you asked. Tom refused to take it, so Pa sold it. He got enough to buy seven Hereford cows and that bull you were admiring for breeding stock. Just say the word and he'll have them shipped. He can get a deal on that Merino ram with what money's left from your trousseau."

Trying to keep cheerful on this special day for Anne, Amanda flippantly commented, "Too bad I won't be needing the Herefords or the ram. Now that I'm married, I've given up my homestead."

"Oh, Amanda. I'm so sorry." Anne hugged her. "No wonder you aren't happy. You wanted that homestead so badly."

"But I want what's best for Mary's children more. Besides, things happen and time moves on." She brushed away a tear. "Now tell me, did my stories about Luke have anything to do with you being here? You'll never convince me that Tom Johnson could run you out of Denver."

Amanda cried when Luke and Anne left that evening.

"They're newlyweds. They want to be alone," Isaac reminded her. "Before you know it, fall will be here and we'll all be crowded together for the winter."

"I know." Amanda wiped her eyes. "But it's so nice to see someone from home. Especially Anne. She always full of fun."

"She is that," Isaac said. "I'd been thinking about adding another bedroom or two to the place. I'd better get on it. The barn could get to be a popular place this winter if I don't."

Amanda noticed his glance at her. He hadn't asked for any husbandly privileges since their marriage. She hoped it was only because of her injuries. Seeing Luke and Anne so eager to touch each other made Amanda long for the days when Isaac couldn't keep his hands to himself.

As they lay next to each other that night, Amanda could tell from his breathing that he wasn't asleep. "Do you suppose Anne and Luke are at their homestead yet?" she asked.

"I don't know. They seem to travel slow. Did you notice that they got married yesterday and didn't get here until today?"

"I noticed."

"The way Luke was looking at Anne, I bet she's naked and he's merrily chasing her through the forest right now."

"Isaac! What a thing to say!"

"What? They're married. Besides, I've always dreamed of chasing a buck-naked woman through the forest—and catching her from time to time."

"Well, don't look at me. I can hardly go running through the forest buck naked. The children would really have stories to tell when they got to town. Besides, if you were chasing me, I probably wouldn't run.'' *Let him make what he wanted of that.*

Isaac rolled over to face her. ''You wouldn't run?''

''Probably not.''

''Why not?''

''Oh, for heaven's sake, Isaac. Use your imagination.''

He trailed kisses along the side of her neck. ''My imagination might get me banished from your bed.''

''This is *our* bed. And as I recall, I rather enjoyed what your imagination came up with in the hayloft. Of course, that was so long ago, I can hardly remember.''

''Maybe I can refresh your memory, Mrs. Wright.''

''Maybe so, Mr. Wright.'' She turned to him.

Isaac covered her face with kisses. She let herself be swept away by his tender loving. In deference to her injured shoulder, he took her gently. With sensuous rhythm, he bound her to him in the way no words spoken could ever match.

By the time Luke and Anne came down for the fall roundup, Isaac had turned back into the man Amanda remembered from the late winter—a happy man, full of passion and plans. And bossy. Good heavens, the man was bossy!

CHAPTER THIRTY-THREE

Isaac helped the men riding roundup bed down the herd right outside Lariat. Saying he'd be back at dawn to help load the cattle onto the train, he put Luke in charge, then headed for the Lazy W and Amanda.

It'd been three weeks since they'd had time to make love, and longer since they'd had time to really enjoy it. He didn't begrudge the kids, but sometimes he wished that he and Amanda had the time to lie in bed together for hours. They could make love, talk, then make love again. He should have taken her on a honeymoon. Still, when you had a ready-made family and a ranch to run, you couldn't just up and do something like that.

He smiled at the welcome of the lantern in the window. Amanda had fallen asleep on the couch. She woke when he kissed her, then made room for him beside her. "I hoped you'd come."

"I hate being away from you." She smelled like lilacs. He trailed kisses along her neck. "Let's go out to the barn."

"What about the children?"

"Anne will hear them. I want you to myself for a while."

In the loft, they made sweet love, then lay and talked.

"I've been wanting to talk to you," he said. "What do you

think about me looking around for breeding stock while I'm at market? Maybe we could get a really fine strain of prime beef going. Concentrate on quality instead of quantity so we don't depend solely on open range. It seems like it's getting harder and harder to find enough open range.''

''It sounds like you've given this some thought.''

''I've been chewing on it a bit. We'll have to take it slow. But we can buy new stock every year and experiment some.''

She thought about the Hereford cattle she'd considered for her homestead, then decided not to say anything. She didn't know much about the Herefords anyway. Just that they could stand cold winters and weren't too picky about their feed. And the Lazy W was Isaac's ranch, not hers. ''What does Luke think about this?''

''I wanted to talk to you first. Luke leaves the business end of things to me; he'll go along with whatever we decide. You have a good head for business. You think we can do this?''

''You always have your land and the other cattle to fall back on if something goes wrong.''

''I'll need to fence hay fields so I can feed in the winter. I can't just let the initial breeding stock roam the range.''

''You mean to tell me that Isaac Wright, the great fence-hater, is going to buy some barbed wire!''

Isaac laughed at the look of mock horror on her face and gave her a friendly swat on her bare backside. ''You're the farmer in this family. What kind of seed should I buy for feed?''

''I don't know. Get something that'll do what you want for the animals. Don't forget to pick something that's fast-growing and doesn't need much water. You know how our weather can be.''

''If I take my time and do this right, I might not be back until almost Thanksgiving. Can you handle things here? Luke's got a lot of range work left to do, and Anne isn't going to be any help to you. Seems like all she does is puke and sleep.''

''She's about past that. She's done better this last couple of weeks while you men were gone.''

''I wish Luke hadn't got her in the family way so soon.''

''Anne loves Luke. She wants to have his baby.''

"I suppose. But don't you do so much you get worn out. We don't need to get all the supplies before the snow flies. I can build runners for the wagon so we can get to town this winter. I probably should've done that years ago."

"We'll be fine." Amanda laughed at his worrying. Then she rolled over on top of him and found her fit. "However, there are some things I just can't seem to do without you, Mr. Wright."

Smiling, he clasped his hands behind his neck. "That so, Mrs. Wright? Tell me about them."

Isaac arrived back in Lariat in a fantastically satisfied state of mind. He helped load the stock cars and paid off the men. Luke took them to the saloon to wash down some of the dust.

The train crew had a hitch disassembled.

"You figure to be a while?" Isaac asked.

"Probably be the better part of an hour."

"I think I'll run up to the boarding house."

"I'll give the whistle a pull about fifteen minutes before we're ready to leave," the engineer said, grinning. "That'll give you time to finish what you're doing and get back here."

That would be about right. Isaac boarded the train, grabbed the box containing his new hat, and got his good clothes out of his valise. Anxious to get to the boarding house, he didn't stop to chat with Martha and the preacher's wife. He just gave them a nod as he passed the store window.

About three-quarters of an hour later, Isaac accompanied a flushed Teresa Brown to the door of Callahan's store. He stuck his head inside, told the ladies good-bye, and made a run for the train.

Stretched out between two seats for a little sleep, he wondered briefly what was bothering Martha back at the store. She hadn't so much as cracked a smile when he said good-bye. Isaac hoped Jim hadn't put her in the family way again. She'd been plenty hard to get along with last time. If you asked him, Callahan's ten children were about five too many.

Isaac had seen to it that he hadn't left Amanda pregnant. For now, at least. He used to think he never wanted kids, but since he married Amanda, he'd started imagining her stomach swelling with his baby. Lord knew, she'd have milk aplenty with all that beautiful equipment.

He could picture a little girl now. With a mother like Amanda and an aunt like that feisty Anne, the girl would surely be a handful. Yep! A pretty green-eyed girl would be a nice addition to their family. Or maybe a boy. Whatever, Isaac decided. Whatever God saw fit to give them. He'd talk to Amanda about having a baby when he got home.

Amanda clucked to the team, then drew in a deep breath of the crisp sage-scented air. Life was wonderful. She, Anne, and the children were on their way to attend church one last Sunday before winter set in. Luke had stayed behind to work on the two new rooms he and Isaac were adding to the cabin. He claimed the weather could change most any time and he wanted the outside work done. But Amanda suspected he just wanted a day to himself. A moment to oneself was a rare commodity on the Lazy W.

The hour she and Isaac had spent in the barn earlier in the week was the first time they'd had any privacy in weeks. It felt so good to make love and talk that he'd almost stayed too long. He must have ridden hard to make the train.

She hitched her team in front of Callahan's. Then she and Anne joined the adults waiting for the service to begin. Most every adult in Lariat was within earshot when Teresa Brown rushed in and handed Amanda a pile of men's clothing and two envelopes.

In a voice that carried across the room, Mrs. Brown said, "Isaac seems so absent-minded these days. Or maybe he was preoccupied the other day." She tittered. "At any rate, after he left, I noticed he left two letters from your sisters addressed to you on the dresser. I didn't think they'd be important, but I'd been wondering what to do. I'll just tell Isaac that you already have them when he comes by on his return. You may as well take these clothes. He keeps another change at my place."

From somewhere, Amanda found a polite response. "Thank you, Mrs. Brown." Casually she glanced at the envelopes, then slipped them inside her purse. She'd rather die than have people in town know how mortified she felt, so she raised her eyes to meet their gazes. But no one looked her in the face.

Though it was a little early, Preacher Greene immediately stepped to the makeshift pulpit and began the service.

Amanda didn't hear a word he said.

After church, Anne watched the children while she sent her father a telegram asking him to ship the Herefords and the Merino ram. She made arrangements for Jim Callahan to drive the animals to her homestead as soon as they arrived; then she loaded the wagon full of winter supplies.

Martha and Jim were unusually silent as they gathered her order.

When she was ready to go, Amanda said, "Charge the supplies to my account." She looked Jim in the eyes. "Not my husband's account. *My* account."

Jim looked at Martha, then he got out his ledger and pen.

Martha put her hand on Amanda's arm. "Don't do anything hasty, Amanda. It might not be what it looks like."

"Just what does it look like to you, Martha?"

Martha's cheeks turned red.

"That's what I think, too."

"Will you be all right?"

Looking at the concern on Martha's face almost made Amanda cry. Almost. Not quite. "Don't worry about me, Martha. I still have my homestead and the children. That's all I dreamed of having when I got off that train a year and a half ago."

Martha silently walked her to the wagon.

It was late evening when Isaac arrived home after a seven-week absence. When he rode in, the dogs made a ruckus. You'd think a man's wife would at least come out to meet him when he'd been gone so long! The kids would be asleep by now.

He'd kind of figured on having a little time alone with Amanda before they went inside the cabin.

Instead of Amanda, Anne came out to the barn. His irritation turned to concern. "Is everything okay?"

"To the best of my knowledge."

"Is Amanda in bed already?"

"I don't know. She's on her homestead with the children."

Isaac looked at the pile of clothes a tight-lipped Anne flung at his feet. "What the hell's going on here?" he demanded.

She shrugged and pointed to the envelope, then crossed her arms, obviously prepared for battle.

Isaac found a golden ring inside the envelope. His mother's wedding band was supposed to be on Amanda's hand. "What's this all about?"

"Why don't you ask Teresa Brown?" Anne swished away, leaving Isaac standing alone in the middle of the barn.

About midnight, Luke came out to fetch him. "Anne's quit crying and calmed down. Come on in. Regardless of what's happened between you and Amanda, you need to talk to Anne. She's my wife, and I don't want hard feelings between the two of you."

Isaac rose and started toward the loft ladder.

"You have more of that whiskey?" Luke asked with a nod toward where the bottle lay.

He nodded.

"Good. Unless you have a hell of an explanation, we're both going to be sleeping out here. Probably permanently."

After Isaac listened to Anne, he told his side of the story. "How could Amanda believe Tess's cock-and-bull tale?"

"Don't blame her, Isaac," replied Luke. "From what I heard when I went to town, I'm pretty sure everyone believes it."

When Anne served his eggs at breakfast, Isaac put a friendly arm around her expanding waist and gave her a gentle squeeze.

She returned his hug. "What are you going to do about Amanda?"

"Can you and Luke watch the kids a couple of weeks?"

''Of course.''

''If Amanda will let me on her place, we need some time to talk and be alone together. Maybe Luke can fetch the kids on some pretense or another without telling her I'm back. I want to surprise her.''

''Shall I bring Joe Pete over here?''

''That would be good. When did he get back?''

''A couple of weeks ago. He got to see his grandmother before she died. Then he wanted to come home to Amanda.''

''It's good he's home, but fetch him over here, too. I want to see the kids before I go to talk to Amanda.''

CHAPTER
THIRTY-FOUR

On the way to Amanda's homestead, Isaac tried to think of the words to convince her to take back his ring. Not that he *ever* knew the right words to say to her. Those dark clouds were blowing in mighty fast. Maybe he should wait to knock on her door until the storm hit. She could hardly make him leave in a blizzard.

Getting off his horse, he stood in his good boots in a half-frozen mud puddle and opened the gate to Amanda's homestead. If he were still a cussing man, he'd be cussing now. Necessary as they'd gotten to be, fences were a blamed nuisance.

He'd just managed to get the dag-blasted thing wired shut when he heard a snort. Not forty feet away, the biggest Hereford bull he'd ever laid eyes on moved out of the trees, pawed the ground, and snorted again. Caught unawares, Gray shied, then jerked the reins from his hand and ran. Rasty tried to move the bull back, but the massive beast had no respect for one puny dog. On his way to the nearest tree, Isaac took up cussing again.

The bull kept him treed a good ten minutes before Amanda

showed up on Gray. She and the dogs drove the ornery critter back toward the dugout.

When she returned, Isaac's rear was leading his dismount from the tree.

"I see you're putting your best foot forward."

"Don't start with me, lady. I've had a bad day or two. It seems my wife has up and left me without a word of good-bye."

"Maybe she heard you have twice as many women as most married men."

Silence overtook them.

At last Isaac spoke. "Amanda, how could you leave me?"

"How could I not?" She looked away for a few moments, then turned back. "For the sake of the children, I suppose I could have learned to live with your keeping company with another woman, but not when it's rammed down my throat in public."

"Anne told me about Tess giving you my clothes at the church service. What I can't believe is that Tess suckered you with that story about me and her. With you at home, why would I go to a woman like Tess?"

"I don't know, Isaac. Why *did* you go to her?"

"With God as my witness, I didn't. After we got the cattle loaded, the train crew had a delay. I hurried over to the only boarding house in town, took a private bath, left my dirty clothes for my wife to pick up when she came in for supplies, and got on the train, as happy as if I had good sense."

"That's not what Teresa Brown said in front of the entire population of Lariat."

"*Implied,* Amanda. Anne repeated her exact words to me. Tess *implied* that she and I had something going on. You've seen Tess in action. I can't understand how you could believe her."

He reached up to help Amanda down from Gray. With his arms around her waist, he lowered her slowly to her feet, then pulled her close. It felt good to have her in his arms where she belonged. Since she ran out of that lilac bath stuff, he'd missed her flowery scent. He'd bought her three big bottles while he was in Omaha. She could smell like a whole danged lilac bush if she wanted.

"I didn't know I'd put my head in a noose until I got home and found my world in shambles." Isaac tipped her head up and looked into her eyes. "I swore to you last spring that I hadn't been to see Tess that way since I set eyes on you. But you left me without even hearing my side of the story. I thought you loved me. You never said so, but that's what I thought."

He's right. All this time I've waited to hear him say he loved me, and I've never told him how much I love him.

"I've tried to show you how much I love you," Isaac continued in a ragged voice. "I've milked goats, put up with cats in the house, learned to plow and irrigate, killed rattlesnakes, and eaten all those damn green things you grow in your garden. I've watched over you and made love to you any time I could get close enough and didn't have an audience. If that's not enough to prove my love to you, I won't hold you to your marriage vows. But I've never cheated on you."

Isaac might be bossy and outspoken, but he wasn't a liar. If he said he hadn't gone to Teresa Brown's house for illicit reasons, he hadn't. And if he said he loved her, he did.

She wrapped her arms around him. Leaning against his broad chest, she held him close. He *had* tried hard, and she'd given little in return. All he ever wanted was to keep his family together and his ranch protected. She'd constantly challenged his right to the children and frequently questioned his ranching ethics. It was a wonder he hadn't gone to Mrs. Brown many times in the last year and a half for the support Amanda had denied him.

Isaac pulled slightly away and began talking earnestly. "If you let me stay here with you and the kids, I'll build a big house right out here in front of the dugout. How's that sound?"

Before she could get a word in, he continued.

"While I was in Omaha, I met a young couple anxious to homestead. I told them about the place across from here on Wild Horse Creek. For a grubstake, they've agreed to hire out to us four days a week. She'll take turns helping you and Anne with the housework. He'll help Luke and me with the outside work. They'll move here in the spring, if it's okay with you."

Isaac was sponsoring some homesteaders! She knew her mouth must be hanging open.

"We'll leave this homestead in your name. In three more years, it'll be all yours. We'll live here forever if you want. I like this location; it's the snakes I hate. Amanda, I'll do anything you want. I love you."

Obviously, his long speech had been rehearsed. Who cared? From the pure joy of having Isaac in her arms declaring his love, she laughed.

Perplexed, Isaac looked in her upturned face. He hadn't expected laughter. Maybe a shotgun, maybe a kiss, but not laughter.

She pulled his head down and kissed him.

He held her tightly and kissed her. He needed her kisses.

Amanda tried to remember what she had planned to say when Isaac showed up. It didn't matter anyway. She didn't want to say it anymore. She only wanted Isaac.

"I'll start the house tomorrow," he promised between kisses. "I'll set it high off the ground so no snake in its right mind will try to get in. It'll have a veranda all the way around so we can let the kids play outside on it without us watching every second."

"The snakes bother you. We don't have to stay here. I'll live anywhere with you."

He smiled. "Here'll be just fine. I want you to have your homestead. I'll help you drive the snakes out. Luke and Anne can have the Lazy W cabin."

"I want a nursery in this new house."

"Lord, yes. I want a nursery, too. Or at least a cradle close by our bed." Framing her face with his hands, he looked into her eyes. "A long time ago, before I fell in love with you, I decided I didn't want the heartache that came with having a family. I was a fool. I want your kids to call me Pa. But I don't think I could stand to lose a baby, or you. Let's take one baby at a time so you can recuperate between them, and we can watch them closely."

"Given my family's reputation for twins, I can't promise only one baby at a time."

"If we have twins, that'll be all right. But I want you to be rested before you get in the family way again. Agreed?"

She nodded.

Great, huge snowflakes began to swirl around them.

He dug in his pocket and held her wedding ring out to her. "Will you put this back on?"

"Are you sure you want me to after the way I've acted?"

"I don't want to live another day without you. I need you as much as I need my next breath."

She slipped her wedding ring onto her left hand, then slid her arms around his waist. "I love you."

"It's going to take a lot of lovemaking to convince me of that." He grinned at her. "Shall we get in out of the storm while I decide how much it's going to take?"

"Maybe so."

Isaac nibbled on her neck and worried her ears with his tongue as she rode in front of him toward the dugout. His caresses abruptly halted when he saw her new cows in the near meadow.

"Gol-dang! The Hereford bull *and* cows?" He stopped Gray and kept his gaze on the cows as he helped Amanda down. Taking a tight hold on her hand, he led the way to the fence. "I saw some Herefords in Cheyenne. They're supposed to be real tough and cold-tolerant."

Smiling, Amanda watched as he hung his arms over a fence post and studied the cows. *Once a cattleman, always a cattleman.* Unless she got demanding, she wasn't likely to get any attention until Isaac finished looking at the cows, so she squeezed in under his arms, between his body and the fence, facing him. "Did you get any breeding stock on your trip?"

"I saw some cattle, but nothing that tickled my fancy. I wanted to talk to you before I got anything." He kissed her on the ear and looked on past her to the meadow. "Gol-dang, those are good-looking cows. Have you put the bull in with them?" They looked down the fence toward the massive animal pawing the ground and squalling. He obviously wanted inside, or he wanted the cows outside.

"I wasn't sure whether to let him in or not."

"You aren't putting them on the range this year. I say put him in and let nature take its course."

Amanda sat on the top rail of the corral and watched Isaac, Gray, and the dogs move the bull inside the fence. When Isaac dismounted beside her, she climbed off the fence. He still had his mind on the darn cows. Enough was enough. Standing on tiptoe, she placed her lips close to his. "Will you *please* forget those cows for a while?"

He startled, then smiled. "What cows?"

Standing in the falling snow, wrapped in Isaac's arms, Amanda drew sustenance from his kisses and tried to give it in return. She whispered her long overdue words of love to him. How could she ever have thought she could live without him?

His hungry hands roamed her body, and he cursed when he couldn't get inside her long winter underthings.

"You'd better put your horse in the barn," Amanda whispered. "I think you're going to be here awhile."

"I'm going to be here all my life." He glanced around the yard and smiled. "Did you notice there isn't a kid needing attention within three miles?"

"Do you think we can figure out anything to do stuck here all by ourselves?"

"We better, because I'm praying for a long blizzard."

As Isaac led his horse into the barn, Amanda hurried to the dugout. When he opened the door later, she carefully stirred the beans before she looked into his bemused gray eyes.

"That is the finest damn cooking outfit I *ever* saw!"

"I hoped you'd like it. I thought I might wear it a few days."

"Don't move. I'll be right back."

In less than two minutes, he came through the door with a limb from the evergreen that grew closest to the dugout. He laid it in the middle of the floor. "That there's a forest."

Keeping his gaze on her, he hung up his coat. He missed the nail, and the coat fell to the ground, which was just as well, Amanda decided. It saved his pistol from hitting too hard when he dropped his gun belt.

She laughed as he hopped around on one foot trying to pull off a boot, then she motioned toward his chair. "Sit down. I'll give you a hand." Straddling his outstretched leg, she tugged on the heel of the boot. When his boot didn't come off, she looked behind her. "Maybe if you'd put your other foot on my backside and push, we could get this off a little quicker."

Isaac leaned back in his chair and clasped his hands behind his neck. He surveyed the shapely curves of her bare derriere and grinned. "I'm in no hurry. Just take your time."

ABOUT THE AUTHOR

Anita Wall grew up in small Wyoming towns. She remembers dirt cellars, wood stoves, washtub baths and outhouses. She prefers cement basements, electric ranges, hot tubs and flushing toilets. Still . . . she loves stories of the old ways and hopes you, the reader, enjoyed *Ties of Love*.

Put a Little Romance in Your Life With
Rosanne Bittner

**LOVE STORIES YOU'LL NEVER FORGET . . .
IN ONE FABULOUSLY ROMANTIC NEW LINE**

BALLAD ROMANCES

Each month, four new historical series by both beloved and brand-new authors will begin or continue. These linked stories will introduce proud families, reveal ancient promises, and take us down the path to true love. In Ballad, the romance doesn't end with just one book . . .

COMING IN JULY
EVERYWHERE BOOKS ARE SOLD

The Wishing Well Trilogy:
CATHERINE'S WISH, by Joy Reed.
When a woman looks into the wishing well at Honeywell House, she sees the face of the man she will marry.

Titled Texans:
NOBILITY RANCH, by Cynthia Sterling
The three sons of an English earl come to Texas in the 1880s to find their fortunes . . . and lose their hearts.

Irish Blessing:
REILLY'S LAW, by Elizabeth Keys
For an Irish family of shipbuilders, an ancient gift allows them to "see" their perfect mate.

The Acadians:
EMILIE, by Cherie Claire
The daughters of an Acadian exile struggle for new lives in 18th-century Louisiana.